Mercury on Guard

Steve Rzasa

Books

Urban Fantasy
Mercury on Guard
Mercury for Hire
Mercury at Risk

Space Opera
The Word Reclaimed: The Face of the Deep 1.0
The Word Unleashed: The Face of the Deep 2.0
Broken Sight: The Face of the Deep 2.5
The Word Endangered: The Face of the Deep 3.0
Quantum Mortis: A Man Disrupted
Severed Signals
Cryptic Commands
Failed Frequencies
Mixed Messages
Empire's Rift: A Takamo Universe Novel
Strife's Cost: A Takamo Universe Novel

Science-Fiction
Man Behind the Wheel
Multiverse
For Us Humans

Superhero
Airfoil: Origins

Fantasy
The Bloodheart
The Lightningfall
Just Dumb Enough (contributor & editor)

Steampunk
Crosswind: The First Sark Brothers Tale
Sandstorm: The Second Sark Brothers Tale

Acknowledgments

Mercury Hale started out as a picture.

The sketch of a young man holding an enchanted staff, fending off an horrific tentacled monster, filled my head a few weeks before I ever wrote the first word. The first sentence of this book popped into my brain as I was driving my oldest son back from an orthodontist appointment. "Ben," I told him, "Quick! Get my notebook. Here. Take this pencil. Write this down."

He thought I was nuts but scribbled the sentence anyway.

So it is that my thanks go to my family—my wife for enduring my fascination with all things geek, and my teen boys for being the best fanboys of my work.

Special thanks go to Mark Bentley and Howard Ohr, as my primary readers, plus Jason Joyner and Josh Hardt for providing valuable insights. The rest of the Masterminds Group—Becky Dean, J.J. Johnson, Liberty Spiedel, Tina Gollings, and Jessi Roberts—deserves kudos along with Jason and Josh for brainstorming ideas for the rest of the Mercury Hale series.

My colleagues at the Johnson County Library, my readers both in the local community and at large—thanks for always asking, "When's your next book coming out?"

I'm thankful as always to God for an imagination that never ceases, and for the chance to pursue this life-long dream. It's been ten years since my first book was published. Ten more years of creating stories will make me a happy camper.

CHAPTER ONE

May

I was eating a pepperoni pizza when a monster crashed through my apartment wall.

Pepperoni's one of mankind's greatest achievements, right up there with nuclear power and the Moon landing. You give me a stick of it, plus a bottle of water, and drop me in the Sierra Nevadas, I'd walk out whistling a cheesy tune from a terrible commercial.

But back to the monster.

It cracked the drywall and splintered studs. A white cloud billowed across the room, scratching at my eyes and making me miss one of the best parts of the giant robot movie on Netflix. Ripped apart my favorite poster, the *Cowboy Bebop* leftover from college.

The monster looked like it could have stepped off Mars before stopping by the lovely city of San Camillo. Gray tentacles swirled around a black core speckled with starry spots, which swirled like a disturbed snow globe. Its "head" was only called that because "big lump of slobbering fangs and three glowing red eyeballs smack in the center of the core" was less concise.

Right. So much for rooting against fictional kaiju. I had the mini version in my living room.

I kicked off my coffee table, spilling the last half of the pizza. It squished face down onto the wood floor. My chair tipped back, greasy cheese smeared on the right arm. Being as the upholstery was powder blue, that was a dandy of a stain. Wasn't going to come out any time soon.

Halfway through I wondered, Should I close the curtains? There's probably a ton of people in the buildings across the way getting a great view of my acrobatics and a nightmare creature. Not my problem, my brain reminded. Good enough for me. I had more pressing concerns.

My tumble carried me clear to the back wall, where a bookshelf teetered on a pair of broken legs. They were reinforced by duct tape. I was going to need to buy more of that. Without turning my gaze from the monster, and remaining crouched in my battle stance, I picked through a lopsided row of Tom Clancy paperback novels.

The pulsar stave was tucked behind them.

Why not? A safe would be impractical. Have you ever tried to unlock one while fending off astral fiends? I wasn't about to start.

The monster slashed through the room. Tentacles lined with shimmering, razor-edged claws disemboweled the chair. White stuffing exploded. The eyes pulsed with fire, and though the beast couldn't speak, it let loose a shrill hiss that dug through my head.

I whipped the stave in front of me and twisted the center with both hands. Stave's an archaic word for staff or rod. Big surprise. The people I worked for loved old-timey stuff. It was a dull brass cylinder, two feet long, riven with dents and inlaid with boxy patterns. Both ends separated into segments. They leapt apart. Brilliant white light tinged with yellow ignited among all five sections and stabbed out from either end.

The whole thing hummed, a subtle vibration barely audible—though with the monster caterwauling in front of me you'd have been hard pressed to hear it. But I felt it. Every molecule of my body trembled in sync.

"You should've knocked," I growled.

Tentacles lashed out. I rolled aside. They snapped the left side of the bookcase, splitting the supports. Edgar Allen Poe took a header, with Jack London plummeting right after.

I brought the stave down on the nearest appendage. The aim was dead on—the blazing energy between the top and second segments seared the glistening skin. Flesh sizzled, and the smell accompanying the smoke made me wish I'd quit eating two slices ago.

The monster was furious. Understandably so, when you consider his primary weapon got turned into a shriveled, blackened stump. Served him right for being a terrible guest.

And the hideous beast broke my favorite chair.

I know, it's petty, and you're thinking, Dude! There's a monster in your living room and you're whaling on it with an enchanted weapon! Forget the chair!

Problem is, you cling to normalcy in my line of work. Overemphasize it even. Otherwise, the nightmares pile up.

And trust me, they suck.

The monster barreled for me as fast as an airliner. His tentacles pounded at the floor which, thankfully, held up way better than the stupid bookshelf. I planted the stave on the floor and vaulted over his back, twisting my body through the air. Always nice not bashing one's head on one's ceiling.

I landed behind him and jabbed the stave deep into the swirling mass of his—well, his rear end, I suppose. Don't ask me about the bodily functions of an astral fiend.

Flashes of light rippled up his hide. The monster flailed about, chipping bricks with those sharpened tentacles. I swore they'd doubled in length. One of them speared the TV.

Bad news for my movie marathon. Good news for my general health and well-being. More flashes poked through its hide, like sun peeking between the blinds on a morning when you just didn't want to get up.

The monster reversed himself—and I do mean reversed, not doubled-back, not flipped over. One second, he was facing away from me, and the next, his whole body inverted so the front replaced the back and vice versa. Nice trick.

The remaining three tentacles slammed down on me with the force of a collapsing building. Only the stave kept me from getting mashed potato-ized. A crack of thunder accompanied their impact on the weapon, and the burst of light left me nauseated. The monster's eyes dimmed a bit, even if that was a product of my imagination.

I gritted my teeth. Sweat slicked my hair to my forehead. I could smell it, too—my fear, present as perspiration and B.O., mingled with the aroma of salty cheesy crust and the sour, tickling the back of your throat gagging nastiness of the fiend. If I kept it up any longer, I was going to hurl.

Good thing I had two weapons.

I slipped down onto both legs, letting the monster's tentacles drive me closer to the floor. A quick yank was enough to pull the center of the stave apart, breaking it into two halves comprised of three segments crackling with their peculiar power. My left arm wielded one in the interest of me not getting pasted. The second I brought around in a sweeping arc, channeling all my determination into one blow.

Sounded like a gunshot in a closet. The monster's hiss mutated into a gut-wrenching scream. A sudden wave of cold washed over me, as tangible as if I'd been dropped into a frigid bath. Tentacles broke free from the stave, and finally found me.

The freezing sensation intensified. My breath came out in feathery gasps. Frost crept up my arms, and my fingertips turned blue. What would it feel like when my heart stopped? The beat was already way too slow.

Not going to happen.

I drew as much power as I dared off the stave, letting golden energy shoot into my arms. Heat tingled through every pore, fighting every square inch against the cold. I didn't dare remove my half a weapon from the monster's gut. It was the only thing keeping it from shattering me into a thousand pieces.

Can't. Let. Him. Win.

It took every ounce of my concentration to shove the upper half of the stave forward, grimacing with each inch gained, until its glowing top edged into the monster's maw. Was the thing glowing? Blue flickers deep in its gullet couldn't be good. It signaled to me, "You're about to get flash-frozen."

Too late for that. I willed the stave to rejoin.

White-gold energies scythed down into the fiend's mouth, and up into its torso. They collided in that blue light. Everything went silent—no hissing, no screaming, no crackling, not even our breathing. Dead air.

Then it exploded. A great blue flash, followed by a sound like snap-boom, and the astral fiend dissipated. And when I say dissipated, I mean popped like a soap bubble. Bits of swirly fiend hide splattered my walls, my floors, my broken chair, my books, and worst of all, my face. It was as if—well, it was just nasty. Gooey gray bits, dripping blue liquid that dimmed from LED bright in the seconds to follow.

The stave's energy faded, too. It went dormant. Got it. I twisted the halves and the segments clanked back together.

"Well, super." My voice sounded as if I was talking through a megaphone. "That was terrible."

I slumped down in what was left of the chair. The final bits of stuffing wheezed out, coating me with man-made snow. My phone was under the crushed pizza box. I stripped a slice of pepperoni off its screen. Tasted fine. Took me a few minutes to order a replacement poster.

The living room was trashed. Plus side, the astral fiend didn't make it into the bedroom, or the kitchen, or the bathroom. Still, it meant I was never getting the security deposit back. And I really, really didn't want to move again.

What was it going to be this time? Fire department? Police? Maybe the super would just stomp up the stairs and tell me to shut up. Someone was bound to notice the hole in the wall. Gave me a great view of the hallway.

My phone rang. The number came across unidentified, a series of numbers I'd never seen before. Could've been a telemarketer.

Sure. One with impeccable timing. I answered. "Mercury Hale."

"It's banished."

"You're not supposed to call me."

"Just answer the question."

"First off, not a question. Second—seriously? How about, 'Oh, Mercury, I'm so glad you're alive!' Right?"

"Oh, Mercury, I am so glad you are alive." The tone of her voice was so sarcastic my apartment should have collapsed under the weight.

I rolled my eyes. "Thanks, Loredana. How's it going? Having a good Friday night?"

"I am monitoring astral incursions."

"Did you happen to monitor the fiend that just ripped

a hole in my wall and crushed my pizza?" I found another slice under the chair. With the fight over, my absent appetite returned with a vengeance. I took a huge bite and kept on talking, mouth half-full. "Yeah, he broke a lot of stuff."

A deep sigh. Normally, I hear a woman's voice on the phone, and I'm a happy camper. This, though, was as much fun as getting a late-night call from my supervisor. Oh, wait. I was getting a late-night call from my supervisor. "We can have you moved in 24 hours."

"Nuh-uh. Not this time. You've got the time. Get someone over here to fix up the place. You've got to do your usual hiding and explanations."

She was quiet so long I thought she'd hung up. "Stay inside. Proceed as if your evening went as planned."

Then she really hung up. Which left me with a blank phone in my right hand, squashed pizza in the left, and a gaping hole where a perfectly good movie was supposed to be playing. "Yeah," I muttered. "Great evening."

CHAPTER
TWO

I lost the entire security deposit and got evicted even with Procyon's intervention.

Loredana sold the landlord a great story about structural failure and electrical shorts. She had a video recording to show the devastating effects, minus the trashing of one angry astral fiend. Don't ask me how she got it whipped up so fast. Bottom line, she threatened to take him to the San Camillo Housing Authority, or worse, tweet it.

He agreed to keep his mouth shut. I agreed to let him keep my six hundred bucks.

"There's a loft on 25th Street of similar size. It should accommodate your belongings." We sat in Granza's coffee shop and breakfast joint down DeLeon Avenue from my former domicile. The late spring sun heated everything to a balmy 70s outside, complete with a breeze off the harbor. Granza's windows were opened, letting in the squawk of seagulls and the chime of the midtown trolley.

Loredana Lark's beauty was unsurpassed by—look, okay, let's not get all mushy. She was hot. Tall, with flaming red hair and piercing blue eyes. She wore a white blouse under a charcoal gray suit jacket, with a matching skirt that showed off her legs. Everything about her was fit, as if she could take off running the hundred-yard dash on a moment's notice.

I could beat her, though.

"Stop that."

"Hmm?" If there'd been a sentence in there besides the one about a new loft, I'd missed it.

"You're staring. I'm not here to be goggled at." She's got the faint whiff of a British accent, which only serves to enhance her professional airs.

"Whatever you say." My egg and sausage sandwich was gone, reduce to a single crumb. I wiped it up. If I was going to move crosstown to 25th, I figured this was the last hurrah for Granza's for a while. "You got anything about my visitor?"

"It was a minor fiend."

"Minor in size only. His giant attitude made up for the rest. Were you standing in the same apartment? Did you see my chair?"

"The pulsar stave made short work of him. I wouldn't be worried."

"I'm not." Not now, because the thing was dead. The waitress came by and took our plates. She was a short, round Latina, smiling the whole way around the diner. What'd she think of the two of us? Loredana in her smart business garb, me nice (read "washed") in gray polo shirt and khakis, with blue and white sneakers. Probably wondered what a scruffy-chinned, buzz cut brunette like yours truly was doing with a gorgeous dinner date. Okay, I admit, I've got good looks, too. It's the five o'clock shadow, olive-green eyes, and my vaguely exotic cheekbones, the latter thanks to some kind of Asian in my blood. Don't ask which kind. I haven't had a DNA test or anything. "Minor or not, it caught you guys unawares."

"We knew activity was high, as did you."

"Yeah, understatement, Loredana. One of them broke into my living room. How many times has that happened? Never."

Whatever was on her phone appeared to hold her interest far better than my critiques. Her eyes never left the screen. Fingers swiped every six seconds. It was either some serious news from the bosses or she was into Tinder in a big way. "It was unusual. Tracking is investigating the matter."

"What does Forecasting say?"

"About what?"

"About whether there's going to be snow in July." I rapped my knuckles on the table. Got her to stab me with those blazing blues, with an arched eyebrow to boot. "Earth to Loredana. Forecasting's supposed to nail where these critters are supposed to show up. As in, far enough in advance I can be waiting for them—or at least, so I'm en route to skewer them with the stave. Instead, I get an astral fiend on Pizza Night."

The corner of her mouth curves. "Pizza Night. Your regular Friday evening involves television, pepperoni, and yourself?"

Heat rushes to my face. "Once in a while. Not *every* weekend."

"Of course not. I'm sure your social life is quite active."

"I wouldn't go that far. Otherwise I'd have no free time to be Procyon Foundation's nighttime hitman."

"Did you bring it?"

I nodded. The stave hung in a custom leather shoulder harness under my polo. The weapon was only a foot long its current configuration, and cool as a refrigerator's crisper against my skin. Talk about private AC.

"Good. Yes, you're right. I'll have a conversation with Forecasting."

I chuckled. "Sounds great."

"Oh? Why is that?"

"Every time you say 'conversation,' I translate it as 'I'm going to verbally tear a new one' for whoever the listener is."

Loredana's expression stayed as stony as ever, but she didn't deny the observation, either. She placed her phone on the table as gingerly as you'd handle a glass vase. "Your next assignment."

"Okay, thanks for the vacation. Nine hours has to be a record." I dug my phone out of my pants pocket. The two devices transferred data, using the handy app Procyon Foundation had installed. Uber-encrypted, highly secretive—something. I don't know anything about apps except how to delete one and reinstall when it gets screwy. Loredana's info treated me to a low-res map of San Camillo, including the city's entire coastline, right out to and including the mile and a half breakwater drawn in a sharp white line across the southwest edge of the harbor. A red diamond pulsed in the industrial district to the south. "Oh. Great."

"It appears we have a potential Icon."

Perfect. Why couldn't it be a straight scoot-and-stab? I liked those. No fuss, no muss. Well, somewhat of a muss. That astral fiend goo faded from existence, over about an hour's span. Still was gross. "Just like the other four."

"No. Forecasting and Tracking concur. The probability is in the 80th percentile. I know the past instances didn't prove fruitful, but we are not exercising our duty unless we investigate every single one."

"Yeah, I got it. Recover the Icon. That is at the top of my job description. I'll put it first on my resumé if we ever find one. Right up there with slaying those monsters—monsters who show up and I've got no idea why they do, or what they are."

"Procyon does its best to manage the threats. It's an historic challenge, one we've never shied from. When you signed on, you agreed to honor that pledge."

Man. Every time she hit me with that spiel, I expected the Stars and Stripes to flap in the breeze behind her. There was no denying the intensity of her words, or the fire behind those eyes. Who was I kidding? If she asked me to jump from rooftop to rooftop, I'd say which ones and how soon. "I remember. You need to remember, I signed up because you guys promised to pay me and keep me safe when the bad guys come looking. Congrats on fulfilling Point One. Point Two? Not the best track record this time."

Loredana reclaimed her phone. "It was … peculiar."

"It sure was—wait. Peculiar?" I frowned. "You paused."

"No, I chose my word carefully."

"Loredana, don't mess with my brain. What's peculiar?"

"We have been tracking the astral fiends for years. They've never acted in this manner before."

"Never's a vague word. You've guys have been at this for what? A century?"

"One hundred seventy years."

"Okay, fine. Somebody must have lost something somewhere. I can't be the only one."

Loredana swiped at her phone. "I can certainly check."

"Sure. In the meantime, I have to get my belongings out of my newly ventilated apartment. Can I expect a crew of movers hired by Procyon?"

"You have to make the arrangements. We can reimburse you for the expense, if you like, but precautionary measures must be taken."

Right. No paper trail. The only thing Procyon wanted to give me with their name on it was a paycheck. All they had written down about me was a W-2 with my annual income and my desk job title. "All right, fine. Do I get to go do that before I'm due in at the office? Or do I have to use personal time?"

Loredana stood. She tucked the phone into her purse and swung it over her shoulder. "Listen. Don't try my patience. Report to Tracking ASAP. When you can find time to relocate, do so, as long as it doesn't interfere with tonight's plans."

"Why? Are we going to a movie? Because unless you bring pizza, I'm not interested."

One more smile flashed on her face. It was gone before I could tease her. "No. I have a prior social engagement. A fundraising gala for the housing initiative branch of the foundation requires my presence. I doubt it is your kind of entertainment."

"I figured as much. I take it Forecasting says the Icon is most likely to be available tonight."

"That's correct. I'll check in with you later."

She headed out for a silver sedan parked opposite Granza's. A Ford. Nothing fancy, but a nice ride. Such was the genius of Procyon Foundation. Benefactor of the community, diligent defender against hideous, interdimensional melting monsters. They did it all while maintaining an inconspicuous appearance.

Too bad that didn't extend to their employees.

I leaned back in the chair and let the rush of air from the passing trolley wash over my face. The breeze carried the smells of San Camillo—sea air, baked goods, car exhaust, and garbage primary among them. Home sweet home. I wouldn't trade it. Most days.

Sometimes, though, it was a pain.

Case in point. My phone. The map of the industrial district was still glowing on it. I zoomed in, triggering the satellite overlay. Hmm. Lots of worn-out warehouses. Lots of empty ones, too.

I shut off the phone and sighed. "Abandoned. And at night.

It figures."

Don't get me wrong. The money was good. Not great, but decent enough for me to live in the city and enjoy my life. But there was a trade-off. I leaned so the cool metal of the stave pressed against my skin again. The bargain meant facing dark things, beings no one else should have to see, or even think about.

The stave was attuned to me.

Just my luck.

CHAPTER THREE

Procyon Foundation operated out of a seven-story building on the waterfront, off Bay Street. Picture a trio of columns, each with bulging sides, joined at the top floor and fourth floor by elevated walkways. Each of the three towers was a couple hundred yards distant from the other, and they were arranged in a triangle formation. Reflective glass bounced San Camillo's harbor and the rocky coastline back, and made the whole thing appear as if it were made of blue sky. A white concrete foundation and supports made an exoskeleton.

The parking lot was a third full, owing to the trolley stop across Bay. I found a spot up front, away from the shade of the *Morus alba*, the fruitless Mayberry Procyon's landscapers favored. Don't get me wrong, I'm all about having a cool car—temperature wise, that is. But I also don't enjoy cleaning bird presents off the hood every afternoon. Hence, leaving my four-year-old Hyundai Veloster out in the sun.

Forecasting and Tracking occupied two offices on the seventh floor of Tower Three, the corner of the triple towers facing the harbor. There wasn't any security up this high. If you made it into Tower Three at all, you had access to everything.

Well, everything but the seventh floor.

Tracking was a dark space, bulging with computers and giant monitors. Maps of San Camillo, the county, California, and the United States sat at the nexus. More maps gave a stunning view of the continent and the world. Some were full of satellite trajectories; others were slathered with coordinates and other data I didn't bother to read. A half dozen men and a couple women were scattered around the terminals, all wearing headsets. They murmured conversations that overlapped. I swore they could have all been playing video games if you ignored the content of their screens.

Winston Yen sat in the middle of it all. He was a short, stocky Asian guy with an athletic build and spiky hair dyed blond. I mean, shock blond. The room's blue and green tint from all the screens made him glow. I thumped the back of his chair.

"Salutations, Mercury. Glad you could join us this lovely day." His cheery British accent could've lit up the room to ballroom dancing standards if you'd plugged him into a socket. "Heard you had a bit of a run-in last night."

"Yeah, it was great. Lost my apartment, and my pizza."

"My sincerest condolences. Gary, route me Case Four Oh Six Oh Nine Eighteen."

One of his tech goons grunted. The guy sounded as communicative as a troll.

Winston had three screens angled at him, like he was sunning himself. One of them cleared all its information and made room for a new data dump that careened down the side. My name and face popped up in the left corner.

"Got your info," I said. "You sure about the location?"

"Mercury, I am wounded. The particle density is spot on.

We have high probability of tachyon emissions."

"Hmm. Quality?"

"Eight point five."

I whistled. "Out of the ten? Nice." I sat on the edge of his desk. Had to shove aside a set of Bluetooth speakers. Classical music—Bach, I think—bled into the air. "Less likelihood of a bust."

"True, true, but keep in mind it also heralds greater danger. Any quality rating of seven or greater means the astral fiend's arrival will be more traumatic, and the beast itself of superior ability, greater endurance."

"Yeah, like my buddy who stopped by for eats."

"Ah, yes." Winston scratched the base of his neck. "About that. Doesn't happen, you know, the fiend seeking you out instead of vice versa."

"Okay, you guys had better quit saying that and give me an explanation why it did happen."

"It isn't as if we get a regular update on where these beasties come from, my boy. What I can tell you is the barrier between our dimensions is fluctuating with greater frequency."

"That's bad, right?"

"Yes. Quite bad." Winston angled his screen, so it was more a tray than a monitor. He swiped aside the map and tapped a folder. Brought up a line graph, with a jagged red slash running across the window. There were a few spikes scattered throughout the years charted. Toward the end, though …

"This represents the past three years," Winston said. "Note the steady increase, with a few plateaus, lacking diminishment."

"Why haven't I noticed anything odd? If the fluctuations keep going up, there should be some major activity out there. I've been on payroll long enough to have seen something."

"True, but a gradual incline in fluctuations doesn't

correspond to astral fiend activity."

"None of that explains how the jerk wound up at my place, instead of me showing up at his."

"If I had a decent explanation, my friend, I'd gladly give it. Marigold did not experience a vision, merely a vague premonition. We had nothing to go on, and not even a proper tachyon pulse to track. We had no idea it was coming until you called our dear Ms. Lark. Rest assured, I'll research the cause. Consider it a glitch."

"Yeah, an expensive one." I sighed. "Okay. Look, about this Icon ..."

"Not my department, Mercury." Winston tapped his panel and spoke into his headset. "Mari, darling, can you spare a moment for the midnight janitor? He's still quite upset about losing his pizza pie."

Cute. "Your latest nickname for me sucks, by the way."

Winston casually flipped me the bird, the double-fingered British version, while nodding to the voice in his ear. "Yes, I will send him. Didn't want to be a bother if you were in the midst of a vision. No, I understand. Yes, I say we go for Moroccan tonight. Well, neither of us fancies cooking so ..."

I took his indifference at my presence as the cue to scram. Forecasting was in the room a third of the way around the tower. Passing through a set of double doors, one noticed the colors were muted versions of their counterparts at Tracking. Even the lights were dimmer, and of a softer yellow hue. There were watercolor paintings of rocky coasts, dense forests, and undulating dunes set every dozen feet, some in clusters, more on their own. The dark-green carpet absorbed all but the loudest sounds. Made it so quiet in there you could hear people dream.

Which was the whole point of Forecasting.

I knocked three times on the wooden door and waited.

Exactly ten seconds later, a female voice answered, "Please enter."

Marigold Yen was curled up on a long couch of gold fabric. She was a foot shorter than me, curvy, with jet black hair that somehow shimmered rainbow streaks under the soft lighting of Forecasting's room. Marigold's eyes were dark as chocolate, the lashes unblinking. She had on a summery white dress with short sleeves, green stripes slashed diagonally in competing lines up the sides. Every step into the office gave the impression she was moving, so much so I had to focus to avoid disorientation.

There was a closed door to the right, with the silver lettering "Forecasting Supervisor" emblazoned on frosted glass. Amber light seeped through. Two chairs were positioned at angles opposite Marigold's couch, one wooden antique with a caned bottom, and the other a thick, plush model upholstered with maroon velvet.

"Hey, Mari." I waved.

"Mercury Hale. It's good to see you again. You're summoned here to confirm my vision of the forecasted encounter. Please, relax yourself and focus your attention." Marigold placed her right palm on a smartphone resting on the end table by her side and gestured with the other hand to the velvet seat.

The chair squashed. I was sitting on a marshmallow. Couldn't find the right way to get comfortable.

"The view is clear," Marigold mused. "An astral fiend, and the Icon."

"Shocker," I muttered.

"Please refrain from comment."

"Just saying. Every one of these we do, the Icon is supposed to be there, and every time I get jack."

Marigold opened one eye. It was a gorgeous chocolate brown. Wasn't going to tell Winston that. "Your attitude does not lend to proper interpretation of the dreams."

I held up both hands in surrender.

"They should be ten minutes apart."

"About par. What's the likelihood of actually getting the Icon this time?"

"You know the dreams are anything but certain where the Icon is concerned, Mercury. Having one such appearance Forecast is rare enough."

"Sure, but a guy can hope. It does bad things for my self-confidence going out on the town in search of treasure and coming up empty."

"The icon is not treasure, and you are not a fortune hunter. It is the key to—"

"Locking the astral fiends out, I know. I read the same memos." I tried tucking my leg under. No dice. Still worse than a metal chair. Crossing a leg over? Even more awkward. Okay, then. The chair's sole purpose must have been to keep me off-balance and irritated.

"Your window between the two arrivals should suffice." Marigold opened both eyes and reached for a mug of steaming tea. I caught a whiff of mint. "Something else troubles you."

"Think so? I had an astral fiend show up at my apartment."

"Sorry. It was a terrible oversight. The dream came only after the breach. I regret I couldn't warn you."

"And that's it? Winston told me how rare that is."

"Rare does not mean unprecedented. Surely, we of Forecasting can't see everything. But don't worry. Together we will take extra care to make sure the misstep isn't repeated, okay?"

Her words had a way of lulling fears. Whatever frustration

I'd been grasping slipped away. "Right. Okay."

"Then, let us return to the vision at hand. With regards to this coming night, do you accept what has been seen?"

"As always, I accept." I'm not much for ceremony, but this ritual gave me the chills. One got the sense of participating in a cause greater than the moment, something bigger and better than walking into an office for the 9 to 5.

"Sign, please."

She didn't move from the couch, but she didn't have to. The form was on her desk, opposite the ring of moisture left by the mug. It was the standard Action Release—I wouldn't sue if I suffered bodily harm, nor would family seek reparations if I were killed.

I snorted. They insisted on keeping that line in there. Like it was any big surprise to them when I filled in "None" under next of kin and didn't check off the box.

My parents dropped me at a restaurant when I was a toddler. Got no recollection of them, not even a hint of a face—just the memory of standing terrified in the middle of a pizza parlor. The smell of marinara sauce. And crying a lot.

Flash forward twenty-some years. I filled out the form and signed my name, twice, right under the part where I swore to maintain the secrecy of Procyon Foundation's true purpose in the world—guarding humanity from the depredations of interdimensional creatures keen on sucking the life from every soul they could get their tentacles in.

Yep, and that was my Saturday morning.

CHAPTER FOUR

A stral fiends dug dark places. From what Mari had told me, they thrived in a gloomy environment. Naturally, when they showed up here, it wasn't gonna be on Stella Beach under a sky blue enough it looked like someone spilled a bucket of squashed Smurf.

Also means I couldn't flip on a light switch and read while I was lying in wait.

And I was literally doing just that—the lying part. Not figuratively. Flat on my back, feet propped on a crushed cardboard box. Protocol dictated I couldn't even turn on my phone. Have you ever been in a dark environment and lit up one of those suckers? I would have been more discreet shooting off a flare gun.

Instead, I opted for Aerosmith bleeding out of my earbuds. If I'd been worried about muggers, I'd have been screwed, because I couldn't hear a thing beyond Steven Tyler's screeching. Fiends had nothing on him. But I was facing right where the probable portal was forecasted to appear.

Which was dead center in an abandoned factory. Right? Where else would a hideous, life-sucking extradimensional monster pick? San Camillo was packed wall to wall with buildings, especially in the industrial district, and a lot of those were empty, courtesy of the decade-old economic slowdown. Plus, the city was fresh out of caves. While the ceiling was stocked up on holes, so much so I got a nice view of hazy urban sky and anemic stars struggling to be seen behind it, it was still black enough inside I couldn't see to the other wall. Scattered piles of garbage, sagging walls, and bold graffiti added a nice, homey feel.

My phone beeped through an impressive guitar riff that had urged me to get up and dance. I declined to indulge. Odds were Procyon had a drone in the air nearby, maybe two, and I was not about to give Winston a set of spastic gyrations he'd be all too tempted to post on YouTube. I tapped my earbud. "Yeah?"

"Mercury, we're showing a jump in tachyon pulses from the forecasted arrival point." Winston yawned halfway through the word *pulses*, as if this were as fun as doing his taxes. I didn't remind the guy I was waiting to gut a monster while he kicked back in a leather office chair. "Do be so kind as to keep this one quick and quiet, unlike, perhaps, your apartment."

"You're a smooth talker, I'll give you that." I sat up and stretched. No point diving into a fight with tight muscles. "Does Mari know you talk to all the operatives like that?"

"Her jealousy knows no bounds, and if you were truly intelligent, you'd not speak of it."

"Tally-ho and Ten Four."

"Stand by. Readings are spiking."

I could have told him that. A spark of purple lightning skittered across the floor, immolating a pair of candy wrappers. Other litter blew out of the way like leaves caught in the wind. I unhooked the stave, let the energy build up, but didn't will it to activate. If a cell phone was as bad as a lighthouse, the pulsar stave in full-on fight mode was a supernova.

The sparks multiplied, their intensity and duration increasing. I could feel the air throbbing, as if a storm were on its way, one of those bad howlers that came roaring up the coast, windows banging at the buildings and dumping a half foot of rain everywhere. This was worse, only more concentrated.

"Come on," I muttered. "Daddy's home."

The faux lightning—and I say faux because according to Winston, it had nothing to do with electricity like I'm familiar with and everything to do with dimensional collisions—rushed together with a roar of air. It slapped, shooting off more sparks, and a great rift traced a jagged line across the warehouse, four feet off the floor. It ripped open, the space between undulating violet light as black as midnight, devoid of even trace illumination. It reminded me of being on a National Parks tour deep in a cave and having the ranger kill the lights. I didn't want to go anywhere near it. Cold bled across the floor, freezing the scummy puddles.

As bad as it sounded, the rip made me feel better. This was how it was supposed to happen. No random monster busting through my apartment wall. Forecasting called the location, and I'm here. Ready.

So was the astral fiend.

It sloughed through the entrance and made a less-than-graceful landing. Upside down. It was a smaller guy, ten feet long, with stunted tentacles coming off at all angles. Didn't make the fangs less intimidating, or the bloodthirsty wail comforting. It staggered out of the rip, which vibrated with every move the fiend made. Soon enough, I'd have a monster just as acclimated to our dimension as the last one I skewered.

I wasn't going to give it the chance.

The stave leapt to life between my hands, giving off a brilliant yellow-white glow. The fiend reacted right on schedule—three seconds and it barreled for me, tentacles extruding sharp prongs. I sliced through the first set without breaking a sweat.

The scream was enough to make me jump, as loud and as close as it was—until I realized it was Steven Tyler again, not the fiend. I grinned. No problem. I'd take Aerosmith over the monster's caterwauling any day. Besides, when I fought like this, there was no point listening for the astral fiend. They could be quiet as a whisper, even though they apparently preferred screaming when they were mad.

Which this guy became, pretty quickly.

He slapped and flailed around, tentacles cutting past me so close the frigid wind in their wake made me pine for a winter coat. Who was I kidding? This was San Camillo. It was still 70 degrees outside, damp and stuffy inside, and besides, I didn't own a winter coat.

I dodged the next strike. Good thing too, because his tentacles bashed a hole the size of my car in the nearest wall. The warehouse didn't like that, if the groans and tremors were any indication. But they settled down, so I stopped worrying about possible structural collapse and focused on the creature trying to kill me.

"The rip is holding steady," Winston said. "Stability is twenty percent greater than norm. This is fascinating! Adele, would you be a lamb and run a comparison on all rip occurrences in the past thirty-six months?"

"That sounds great, Winston, it really does"—I ducked under a tentacle. The prongs tugged at the back of my shirt. Better not be torn. "But I'm kinda busy. So if you want to geek out on pseudo-physics, can we wait until I'm not in mortal danger?"

"Killjoy. I assumed you'd want to know since the rip's increased energy output may put a strain on your environment—and I'm not referring to the weather, in case you were wondering."

Increased strain? I severed another limb. This guy wasn't calming down enough for me to slip in close and end him. In fact, he'd gone from sluggish to dervish far too quickly. His form stretched out to fifteen feet, and I swear his fangs got a half-foot longer. I'd say I was under plenty of strain.

The astral fiend threw itself at me in a twist of sharpened prongs, spinning through the air. No time to dodge. I ran for the back wall, top speed.

As soon as my feet hit the metal, I kept going.

The pulsar stave's energy coursed through my muscles, sending me clean up the vertical surface as if I walked on walls every day. Which I did not. But man, with a rush like that, I'd definitely add it to my calendar.

I backflipped over the fiend, body and mind whirling in slow motion. Made me chuckle to see him squash against the wall, at least until the shock of his impact sent ripples of dust clean up to the roof.

Another groan echoed from the building. Louder, and longer.

Then forty square feet of roof overhead collapsed. Wall sections on either side crumpled in response.

Half the warehouse was falling onto my head.

I hit the ground so hard my shoes left cracked imprints in the crumbling concrete. The stave's power cushioned the blow, but I was betting my teeth would keep rattling for another week.

The fiend reversed himself, same cute trick the other guy

had used at my place, only at twice the speed.

I was ready for it.

The stave struck home, right between the slimy brute's glistening, nightmarish eyes, as I slid under his body. It was a perfect kill—the fiend shuddered and expired within seconds. That was fantastic, as far as I was concerned.

I just hoped his body didn't disassociate before the debris struck.

Ceiling panels, assorted rafters, and a couple of flimsy pre-fab walls heaped atop us. I kept the stave impaled in the fiend's gut, gritting my teeth at the strain. Blue ooze spattered around me. It was *not* going to wash out, but I'm okay with permanently filthy clothes if that means I don't die.

The roar of the collapsing building faded. Fragments jutted through the fiend's body, which was rapidly going translucent. I separated half the pulsar stave and used its energy to blast a cylinder-shaped path out one side. It was enough space for me to shimmy past the rubble.

With the fiend disintegrating, the mess flattened the gooey remnants. I sat on a twisted girder, panting, and stinking like dead monster.

"Ah, Mercury?"

"Yes, Winston, the building collapsed, but only partially. And also, I'm alive, so thanks for asking."

"Drone Six gave me a lovely view of the catastrophe, and seeing as how he's equipped with infrared cameras, I was not concerned about your demise because I could clearly see your body temperature within normal levels and note that you were still ambulatory." Winston sniffed. I mean, he actually sniffed, as if his snooty tone didn't carry enough pretense.

"Whatever." I dusted off my pants. "How's the rip?"

"Still there, still putting out greater tachyon levels."

It sure looked more active. The purple edges writhed with their signature lightning. The black was, well, still black, until a pinprick of white blinked in the middle. Then it was gone.

"What was that?"

"Did you guys see that light?"

"What light?"

I rolled my eyes. Not that he could detect the motion on infrared. "The light at the end of the tunnel. What'd you think I mean? There was a flash of light from the center of the rip!"

"Intriguing. It coincided with a tachyon burst, which while not unusual, was remarkable in its stability. I'd not care to speculate but—"

The pinprick returned, only it wasn't a mere flicker, but a full-on strobe. I looked away, because I was pretty sure the repeated pulsing was going to make me puke. "Uh, Winston …"

" …Full spectral scan! Don't bother me with the details of how, just recalibrate! Gary, you twit, I want both drones overhead, now!"

I winced and downed the volume on my earbud. Since when did Winston yell? "Winston, this thing's acting weird."

"Yes, yes, I know, it's quite clear from our end!" he snapped.

My heart skipped. "Is it an Icon?"

"I don't know. We've never retrieved one, as you well recall. But we've never seen this level of activity before, either. Prepare yourself."

Was he kidding? This was something for which I'd mentally rehearsed every time I cut down an astral fiend at a rip, for three years. I was prepared.

I stepped closer to the rip, ignoring the winds tearing at my clothing, and held out both halves of the pulsar stave.

Purple lightning leapt to my hands, my arms, rolling over

my entire body. It didn't hurt. It didn't feel like anything. If I'd closed my eyes, I'd have told you I was standing in an empty warehouse with absolutely nothing weird going on at all.

So, I closed my eyes. Winston shouted something, but I ignored it. I concentrated on calm.

That's when the afterimage hit.

I blinked.

The rip exploded, waves of violet light and black streaks slamming into every wall, breaking out every remaining window. It knocked me flat on my back.

Then the night returned. Quiet. Only the muffled sounds of a city breathing in the background. No sirens yet, so that was a bonus.

The rip was gone. Closed.

No Icon. Nothing.

I exhaled and sprawled out flat on the floor. Twin drones buzzed high over the tear in the ceiling where roof had collapsed during my fight with the astral fiend.

"Mercury! Answer, please! What happened? Was there an Icon?"

I touched the earbud, my stomach churning. "No, no Icon. Just another false alarm."

Winston sighed. "Very well, then. Report back in. Do avoid law enforcement, if you'd be so kind. Emergency services have been alerted to a building collapse."

"Will do." I unplugged the earbuds and hustled out of there. I'd felt so close—so close to finally getting answers as to why I was doing this. Nothing worse than spending your life to achieve one goal, find one purpose, only to have it time and again be proven a big old steaming pile of nothing.

Nope, no Icon. Super. But I did have to figure out why I saw an afterimage of a person right before the rip fizzled.

CHAPTER FIVE

Debrief time.

First thing I did after every fight was to check in with Marigold. No paperwork, no stern discussions with Loredana—not yet. I went from the warehouse to Procyon's upper floors, via a circuitous route that involved not one but two trolley rides and a quite a bit of walking. It took a while, yes, but Procyon likes it very much when I don't bring my easily-trackable car to the scene of a monster brawl.

Mari was curled up on that gold couch like she'd never moved. She watched me, unblinking, as I sagged into the marshmallow chair. After the battering I'd been through, it was way more soothing than usual.

"Please give me your rendition of the night's events." Mari's voice was soft. The combination of her dulcet tones and the dim, warm lighting put me at ease. Made it simpler to recall what I'd been through—and I had to agree. Semi-formal suited me fine.

I told her about my arrival, the setup, the observation, the astral fiend's arrival, and the subsequent fight. Made sure to emphasize my sick moves. I don't know whether Mari cared;

she smiled at all the appropriate parts, which made me feel better. Of course, she was also recording everything I said on the smartphone propped in its charging cradle next to the couch. Whatever. I enjoyed recounting those tales for an audience.

Then I got to the Icon part of the story. "The stave halves did their trick, but no Icon manifested."

"Yes, the drone cameras confirmed as much," Mari said. "Winston tells me the rip was more powerful than what we've seen."

"It looked bigger. And I could feel the strength behind it, pulling at me. Yeah, it was definitely more powerful. I'd agree with that."

"Why?"

I blinked. "Um, what?"

"Why do you think it was more powerful?"

"Maybe the Icon was close to manifesting, closer than usual?" I shrugged. "Dunno."

Mari's eyes narrowed. "You're leaving something out, Mercury. What's the matter? You should be relaxed."

"I am. Absolutely." Fidgeting in my chair right then didn't help sell the statement. Of course, I knew what she meant. I hadn't said a word about the silhouette. Somehow, she'd pinpointed that omission. Whether or not Mari could read minds was an open-ended question, but for crying out loud, her job was to use *dreams* to nail down the appearance of monsters and a mythical artifact that would help banish them. Wasn't her fault the latter hadn't ever shown up; her dreams about the astral fiends were always right.

"Tell me who you saw."

"Already did. The astral fiend, the rip, and no Icon."

"No, Mercury. *Who.*"

31

I ran my hand through my hair. I really wanted a shower, and a change of clothes. So far Mari hadn't complained about the smell. Like she ever would. But there wasn't any hiding what was banging around in my brain from her. Sitting here in soothing comfort was like having a nice, late-night chat with a friend. A cute friend. Who spoke softly. Focus, Mercury. Not your lady. "Fine. I didn't want to mention it at first because …"

When I didn't finish the sentence, she prodded, "Because?"

"Look, I thought I was imagining things. Right when I thought the stave was going to access the rip and make the Icon manifest, I closed my eyes. You know, to feel the energy off the thing instead of just staring at it."

"I understand."

"When I did that, I saw an afterimage. A shadow. When I opened my eyes, in that split second it might have resembled a person."

"A person."

"A silhouette, I guess."

"You guess?"

I blew out a breath. I shifted my legs, again. The chair's initial cozy feel was wearing off fast, dumping me right back in Unpleasantville. "Fine, okay. It was a silhouette. A fuzzy outline of a person."

"Human?"

"It wasn't an astral fiend, if that's what you mean."

Mari stopped the recording. Her fingers swept dizzying patterns across the screen. Whatever her notes said, they weren't meant for me. After a couple minutes of nothing but the sound of her light taps on Gorilla Glass, I cleared my throat. "Are, uh, we done?"

She stood. I hopped to my feet. Mari was less than a foot away. She smelled like flowers. There was a silver dragonfly clip in her hair, tucked over her right ear. I memorized every line on its body, every pattern on its wings, because I did *not* want to meet her gaze. "You must speak with Winston and Ms. Lark immediately."

"Why? Is it the silhouette? Because that could have been an afterimage. My imagination. Or maybe a bad taco. I ate a couple way too fast before I showed up at the warehouse."

"Mercury, this isn't a joke. Our debrief sessions would better clear your mind of the trauma and cleanse your energy levels of fluctuation if you would treat them with respect."

I scratched the back of my neck. There wasn't any room to back away. Standing this close to a woman, instinct told me I should ask her out. But the way she was staring at me made it clear I was about two seconds from being sent to the principal's office—which is what talking to Loredana felt like. "Okay, all right. I'll get moving."

"Mercury." I was out in the hall, and Mari wouldn't cross the threshold. "I apologize for my stern response but know I would never cut short our time if it was not vital to your survival. What you saw may or may not have been a figment of your imagination. For all the time Procyon has pursued this path, there is still so little we know about these rips in space-time. Dear Winston is quite enamored with his tachyons, yet studies on repeated exposure to the radiation bleeding from the astral fiends' dimension are infrequent and inconclusive."

I nodded. "Thanks, Mari. If I did see something, something that wasn't the Icon—what does that mean? What would your dreams tell us?"

"I don't know. I need sleep."

She shut the door.

❊ ❊ ❊

Winston sipped from a black mug emblazoned with a Star Wars Imperial emblem. Loredana rubbed her forehead, her other arm folded tight across her chest. They couldn't have been more mismatched. Winston was clad in a rumpled white polo shirt emblazoned with blue tropical leaves, and dingy green cargo pants. Loredana must have come straight from her fund-raising soiree, because she wore a red dress that appeared painted on, strapless. The bejeweled necklace had so many diamonds I lost count at twenty. Her hair was pinned up, and everything about her was heavenly.

Tracking was empty. Sure, the screens kept humming. Winston's monitors played back my fight from multiple angles, courtesy of his twin drones. Have to say, it was hard to stand there putting on my best abashed student stance while seeing myself kick slimy tentacled monster hide. Sometimes the job lost its luster when you realized there was no one with whom you could share this side of your life. Couldn't send a video to Mom and Dad to brag.

"Let's recap," Loredana said.

"Nope, I'm all done recapping." I pointed at Winston's monitor. "You got Mari's report. The recording plus her crazy-fast notes. So?"

"So?" Winston snorted. Fortunately, no tea went spurting over the mug's edge, because Loredana raised an eyebrow in the most evident disdain—as in, you could find a photo of that exact moment in the dictionary next to the word. "Mercury, my boy, you've succumbed to the stress of your occupation, or as you opined, stuffed yourself with unhealthy food right before immersing yourself in said stress."

"Don't be too quick to discount what he thinks he saw," Loredana said. "We should be vigilant about all possibilities."

"I don't deny it, Ms. Lark, but I'm not about to recalibrate all my sensing equipment on the hunch of our janitor." Winston smiled at me. "No offense."

"Yeah, none taken." I rolled my eyes. "What are going to do, in any case?"

"Recalibrate the sensing equipment on the drones," Loredana said, with a sidelong glance at Winston, "In order to better assess the rip at your next encounter. It wouldn't hurt to check on the tachyon bleed, as Marigold suggested, and that means fine-tuning our scans of the astral fiends themselves. Winston, do you concur?"

"No, I do not concur, but since I don't share your clearance level, there we are." Winston saluted with his mug, and his smile progressed from normal to super syrupy. "Whatever Ms. Lark desires."

"Ms. Lark desires you do your job and keep our operative safe," she snapped. "Keep in mind Mercury possesses the pulsar stave."

"Fully aware." Winston clanked his mug on the desk. "That all said, I will mull how exactly to re-task our scanners after a good's night rest. The system's alerts will notify us if anything else interesting happens tonight—given this was a potential Icon manifest, I followed the protocols to the T. If you're quite through talking about Mercury's potential hallucinations, I'll take my leave and take my wife home."

Loredana nodded. Had to hand it to Winston—he was braver than me when it came to dealing with her. Stupid, but brave.

He wasn't out the door five seconds before Loredana murmured, "Insufferable."

"You Brits don't mingle well." I slouched into Winston's chair and clasped my hands behind my head. My shoes clumped onto the desk.

"We're not all tea and crumpets. Winston is—more modern in his approach to problems, and quite rigid when it comes to solutions. He's not seen all I have. It's possible he resents my bloodline, as well."

Interesting. "You never talk about your family."

Loredana sat on the edge of the desk, hands folded in her lap. "They're quite proper. My father owns a ten thousand-acre estate in Sussex. It's pleasant enough, if you can stand his condescension long enough to take a breath."

I grinned. "Sounds like a fun place to visit. What's a guy got to do to wrangle an invitation?"

Loredana smirked. "This silhouette incident—do you consider yourself still fit for your tasks?"

Not a yes, but not a no. "Sure. Nothing a good night of sleep can't cure." I checked my watch. "Or five hours' worth, anyway."

"Good. Whenever the next alert comes up, take extra precaution. We can't endanger you."

"I'm touched, Loredana."

"You're something. Don't forget your responsibilities. I took the liberty of unlocking the staff bunks in Tower One. You can spend the night there." She patted the top of my shoe. "Good work."

"Thanks." I shifted in the chair. Muscles ached. Yeah, sleeping this off would feel nice. Of course, so would dancing. When was I last on a date? Okay, so a few weeks prior, and granted, that was Date Three out of Three, but it didn't last. "You done with your party for the evening?"

"I believe so. There's only so many stilted conversations and leering rich old men a woman can stand. I have work to attend to."

"Good night, then."

"Good night."

I leaned my head back in the chair and stared at the ceiling. "Oh, yep, Mercury, you are a smooth one."

The staff bunks were as nondescript as your average college dorm. Cinder block walls, cheap carpet, a few potted plants. Nice harbor painting on the wall, though. No windows. It was meant as a place for complete shut-off from the outside world.

I slept straight through the night.

Next morning, I got a shower in the adjacent bathroom and dug into my stash of clothes. It wasn't my first overnight stay. I'd learned to keep a bag as backup.

Monsters were last night. Daytime meant apartment pickup.

I headed downtown, the Veloster zipping up San Camillo's hills. Traffic was light on De Leon, except for the rush-hour crosstown streams in both lanes of Ridgeview Street. Most of the city's business district lined that road. Nothing for me there, though I mentally mapped a route down to 25th to see about that loft Loredana mentioned.

I wondered what work she had to do so late at night. Beats me. Loredana's business was her own. Maybe that was why she was so intriguing. Plus, well, she was a red-head.

Parking was tight, but what else was new. Taking the trolley would have been my first choice, but I couldn't drag all my stuff out of a ruined apartment and schlep it around the streets. I got out and sucked in a deep breath of ocean breeze. After last night's warehouse stench, body odor, and monster stink, it was like my lungs could take their own shower.

"Hey, Mercury."

The voice killed any sense of relaxation. It belonged to a

Latino guy in mirrored shades.

I winced. Really? First thing in the morning. "Hey, Ramos. Nice to stalk you—I mean, see you."

"You busy? We need to have a chat, Mercury."

"A chat. That sounds awful. Business or pleasure?"

Lieutenant Gabriel Ramos tapped the badge on his belt.

CHAPTER SIX

Ramos, buddy."

My grin was bright enough to be declared a hazard to pilots overhead. Had to lay it on thick for Lieutenant Ramos.

"Save the 'buddy' part. I've been by your apartment. The landlord is very upset." Ramos spoke every word with deliberation, like the guy was taking a millisecond to consider whether not he wants to use each one before allowing a syllable past his lips. "Quite a big mess you made."

"Not my mess."

"Your guest, then."

"Messy eater, what can I say. Next time I'll invite you over. It'd be a blast. You know, literally."

"That isn't funny. You're supposed to keep all this under wraps. The public would panic if they saw what was going on in this city, and I'd rather that not happen on my watch, *comprende?*"

Great, he whipped out the *Español*. As if him glaring at me wasn't enough to let me know he was substantially mad. "Look, that's what I'm doing. Hence the gas leak."

"That's a lousy explanation."

"Best one we could come up with on short notice. If you don't mind, I've got a car to go fetch and the ruins of my domicile to empty before I schlep over to my new digs, so unless there's a pressing need for you to deliver something other than my semi-monthly lecture—"

"There was an attack last night."

I bit back whatever smart aleck quip I had queued up. Another attack? Not possible. Forecasting would have given me the green light. "Ah, yeah, sorry, that's incorrect. I was preoccupied with our guest at a conveniently empty warehouse. No innocent bystanders, unless you count the building itself."

"I'm talking about the corner of Malhorn and Campos, around 11 p.m., under a broken streetlamp in a half block of foreclosed condos."

Malhorn and Campos. Formerly trendy neighborhood built a quarter century ago. "Well, last I checked astral fiends don't do drugs, so they probably wouldn't hang out there."

Ramos glared at me. "Let me understand. You fought one of these things last night?"

"Yep."

"And not in the same neighborhood."

"Nope."

"Then there were two."

I burst out laughing. "That's great. That's the best thing I've heard in forty-eight hours, and believe me, that's saying something. No, Ramos. They don't do coordinated. Your average fiend doesn't the brainpower to finger paint with a chimpanzee."

"So I presumed. And so you've told me. Yet, here I am, and here's what I know." He produced a notebook, hardcover bound in gray fabric, with a slender ribbon serving as a bookmark. It fit. Ramos wore a pair of black slacks, black shoes shined to a mirror finish—I could see double-me smiling up—and pale-green shirt, unbuttoned at the collar. The sleeves were rolled to the elbows with such precision I'd have sworn in court they were identical. His hair was cut short, slicked into place. Aftershave rode on the breeze. "Black female in her seventies. Two witnesses. Both state a creature with multiple tentacles stabbed her and, I quote, 'Tried to suck out her brains.' End quote."

My heart stopped. "She's dead?"

"Thankfully, no. She's in critical condition at SC General."

Relief took over. "Astral fiends don't suck brains. They drain life." A shiver rippled through me. It wasn't easy to forget the feeling when one tries to rip every last ounce of warmth from your body.

"Sounds wonderful. Back to the matter at hand. You weren't there, Mercury. Does that mean I should expect the frequency of these incidents to increase?"

"I don't know. There's—a lot going on." I leaned against the building and watched traffic rumble by. Watched the business people yapping on their cell phones. Listened to the newspaper vendor and sandwich cart guy argue in English and Vietnamese about who had that square of sidewalk. Anything but thinking about two fiend attacks in one night.

I missed one. Impossible. "You're sure about this."

"No, Mercury, my detectives decided to make up a story about unexplained happenings in my city because they were bored, and they know I have a great sense of humor." Ramos scowled. "Don't be an idiot."

"Fair point. Who were the witnesses?"

"Pair of vagrants," Ramos said. "Both were intoxicated. Could've smelled them from a block away. I had them taken to St. Sebastian's shelter, get them dried out. We'll see if their statements improve."

"You're gonna interview them again."

"Obviously. This isn't a mugging where an old lady loses a fifty."

"Anybody else know about it?"

"Only a couple EMTs. They shrugged it off as drunken raving." Ramos slid his glasses down to his nose. Dark brown eyes pinned me to the pavement. "It's getting more difficult to let these things slide. I understand you're in a tricky position—believe me, I want to help. There's a level of trust between us. You kill these *things* and I keep you off the department's radar. But you have to meet me halfway. Someone in the department is going to piece together what's truly taking place. When they do, it's going to be a catastrophe."

I slapped down my imagination's full-color rendering of San Camillo PD engaged in a gun battle with trans-dimensional beings. It was nasty. "I appreciate your willingness to partner up, Ramos, really. Not many people would take what I say seriously."

"I can't deny what I've seen."

"Yeah, but you're not running and screaming. Which is what I'd do if I weren't, uh, appropriately equipped for the job."

Ramos holds up his hands. "Don't want to know, don't care how you do it. Point is, you keep that scum off my streets, and I'll keep sirens from your backside. Assuming you keep people safe."

It's my primary mission—kill astral fiends, seek the Icon. Otherwise, I'm not a cop. In a roundabout way, though, I'm keeping San Camillo safer. Sort of. "Whatever I do isn't going to improve the murder rate."

"Let me worry about crime. You keep these things under wrap."

"Okay, I consider myself duly warned. I'll see if my contacts have any info as to what happened."

"Tell your contacts I'm watching."

Ramos knew way too much. Fortunately, he was a decent enough guy to keep secrets for me—or maybe he was just trying to keep San Camillo from becoming Crazy Town if people knew some of the murders and missing persons cases were actually astral fiends in a feeding frenzy. "Roger that."

"You have my number." Ramos checked his watch, and grimaced. "You will call me if anything pertinent arises, yes? I'm running late for church."

"Yes and *si*, buddy." I gave him a sloppy, two-finger salute. "Hey, we should do lunch some time. You're buying."

Seriously doubted he was going to pick up the tab, but since he didn't stop me from heading into my apartment building, I took it as I was off the hook—for the moment.

What a mess.

The Procyon cleaning crew had been through my living room. They'd scrubbed up any lingering fiend residue. Good for them. I hated that stuff.

That left my remaining personal belongings heaped in a pile where my favorite chair sagged, mostly destroyed, under their weight. Plastic sheeting sealed up the hole in the wall, both sides undulating with the barest whisper of air moving through the corridor.

I grabbed an egg crate from my bedroom and stacked the toppled bookshelf contents. Of course, that got me sidetracked on deciding which books I needed to keep and which ones I was never going to re-read. Obviously, the ones on my Read Again At Least Once A Year shelf were staying. But some were so-so. I'd never gotten around to sorting. Having a handful ripped in half by a monster's tentacles sped up the discarding process.

I soon had the back seat of my car crammed full of clothes, books, and assorted household junk I'd accumulated. I didn't even bother to lock the car. If someone wanted to steal my dirty laundry and my collection of Frank Herbert paperbacks, more power to them.

I'd hoped this depressing version of spring cleaning would give me something else to think about besides my abject failure not only to recover the Icon but prevent an attack on an old lady. How could Forecasting have missed a second astral fiend's appearance? If it'd been a solo incident, I'd have chalked it up to tachyon overlap or some fake-sounding term Winston would have come up with. But coming right smack after a fiend attacked me made the pair of strange incidents too coincidental. I didn't want to ask Winston right away. He was probably still smarting after I got Loredana to pull rank.

So, fine. I filled up garbage bags and packed up the rest of my stuff. It took a handful of trips to the car and back again before the apartment was sufficiently emptied. I frowned, taking in the wrecked surrounding. Not a lot to call home. Well, whatever. When you moved around town every six months or so, you got used to living light. I had my books, and … Okay, that was it.

Guess normal people had family photos to take down. That sinking, empty feeling crept its way into my gut. It was a lot easier to put aside when swiping tentacles off my enemies. Quiet moments meant it blanketed everything.

Okay. Focus. The apartment was the past. New loft. New

questions.

My phone buzzed at me. If that was Loredana, she had good timing. I'd press her with my questions about the very public attack. She'd have some answers—or at least, know where to find them. Plus, the two of us asking Winston and his crew would go better than him snarking at me.

The call wasn't from her number, because her face wasn't on the screen. It was a blank, generic background, with digits I didn't recognize. Sales call? I stabbed the answer button. "Whatever it is, I'm not buying."

"Do you want the truth?"

The voice was soft, gravelly, and wheezy. It could have been someone talking out of the bottom of a garbage can. "The what now?"

"You heard me, son. The truth. Things aren't as they should be, and you better believe it."

"Gotta admit, I wasn't expecting someone to sell me philosophy at 10 in the morning." There was something about the voice, though, that hooked me. I couldn't hang up.

The voice gasped, then coughed. "This would be a lot easier of a revelation if you weren't so sure of yourself. Two attacks in one night? Don't fool yourself. You need to look for answers in the right place."

My eyebrows shot up. "Who is this? What are you talking about?" Deny, deny, deny. It wasn't Ramos on the end of the line. Didn't sound a thing like him, plus, he didn't play games. Pretty sure he didn't back when he was a kid, either.

"Stop yapping and get to work. Start with the Historic Vault in Tower Three. Then we can talk more. Hopefully next time you'll be a better listener."

"Yes, ma'am." Ma'am? It was a woman's voice, I thought. She hung up.

I redialed and got a robot message that the number I was trying to reach was disconnected. "How'd she get my number, genius?" I snapped at the recording.

I tapped the phone against my mouth. This was bad. Very bad. This lady knew about my work. I thought, outside of Procyon, only Ramos was in the know. If he had a leak in his department—or worse, a spy—things would get worse before they got better.

But what triggered me more was the possibility that Procyon itself had a leak. They didn't take kindly to traitors. Loredana would have a fit. After she incinerated me with those icy eyes.

Because nobody outside the organization was supposed to know about the Historic Vault.

CHAPTER SEVEN

Random crazy lady callers and the specter of failure combined to make Mercury one cranky dude. And no, I wasn't falling into the trap of referring to myself in the third person.

But I was irritable. As in, irritable enough that when I stopped by for pizza at Carlito's over on Twenty-Second, I spaced that they're closed on Sundays. San Camillo hadn't had the West Coast equivalent of blue laws since the Forties, however, you couldn't throw a rock without hitting a Catholic or one of the many flavors of Evangelical or even the rare Lutheran, like Ramos. And trust me, you didn't want your rock to actually hit a Catholic.

After spinning around town in search of a decent eatery, I finally wound up grabbing a coffee instead—because I wasn't hungry. That in and of itself meant something was terribly wrong.

I tracked down Loredana twenty minutes later.

She was in her office at Procyon. On a Sunday. It was as surprising as waking up in the morning and discovering Earth had gravity. No elegant evening gown, of course, but a pair of nice slacks and a classy navy-blue blouse. For once, I felt on the same terms fashion wise. I wouldn't catch myself looking like one of those guys you see on the street. You know which ones. The younger fellas of my generation, wearing ball caps and saggy blue jeans, walking with their girlfriends, who are dressed like they're going to a job interview. I shook my head.

"Is there a problem?" Loredana's hands stopped their insane flight across her keyboard. She'd been typing an email, the contents of which were blurred to me. Sunlight drenched the room. Her office was next to the crosswalk on the fourth floor of Tower One, white walls and charcoal carpet. It was a good thing she liked flowers. Daisies and tulips lined three shelves. Splashes of pink and red did the brain good.

"Did my unannounced visit tip you off?" I smiled and leaned against the door frame. The sugary aroma from my cup of coffee put me at such ease I could have inhaled it all day rather than discuss cranky conspiracy phone calls and wayward monsters.

"And you brought me coffee. How considerate."

"Yes. Yes, it is. Because it's for you." I crossed the distance to her glass and steel table, whereupon I set my cup of coffee down with a flourish. Spun it around so she could see The Shattered Mug logo. "Especially for you."

Loredana smiled—just a flicker of the mouth, you realize, but more than adequate to let me know I'd cracked the dour surface. She took a sip. The smile twisted. "That's—a great deal of sugar."

"Don't tell me sugar's not your thing."

"It is, indeed, my thing, but in moderation. This could give a rhinoceros diabetes within the hour."

I snorted. She had an extra chair. "Mind?"

She gestured at the seat. "What is so pressing you couldn't

text or call?"

"First off, I'm not supposed to call you, remember?"

"I do. That was a test. You passed."

"Gold star for me." I rolled my eyes. "I got a weird phone call earlier, right after I had a friendly chat with my buddy Lieutenant Ramos."

"Define 'weird,' Mercury."

"Weird as in, grouchy old lady who tried to give me esoteric advice about seeking the truth surrounding recent events. Oh, and she mentioned she knew about my work at Procyon. My real work, keep in mind, not the 'facilities engineer' it says on the pay stubs."

Loredana froze with the coffee cup halfway to her mouth.

"That's the reaction I was hoping for." I slid my phone across the desk, with the call log visible. "Top number on the list."

She peered at it. "Did you redial?"

"Yep. 'This number is no longer in service.' I'm afraid I ticked off the phone robot with a couple of choice insults."

"As opposed to your usually charming self."

I shrugged.

"It was not Lieutenant Ramos?"

"Nope. Lady's voice, no doubt. Like a grandmother, only less sweet. About as friendly as the clerks at the DMV. I don't think this is something Ramos would go for, anyway. He's no prankster."

"Fair point. He takes a great deal seriously, including his role in our endeavors." Loredana set the cup on the desk, gently. "You'll extend my thanks next time you see him, please."

"Absolutely. But back to the crazy sales call …"

"You said she referred to discovering the truth."

"The exact question was, 'Do you want the truth?' She wasn't clear what that meant, and when I pressed for details, she fudged it. Care to lend insight?"

"I have none. The only truth I am aware of is Procyon's historic mission to recover the Icon and defend this dimension from the predations of the astral fiends."

I scratched the back of my neck. If she was peeved now, she wasn't going to like the next part. "Speaking of historic, she referred to the Historic Vault."

Loredana stood so fast the coffee cup tipped over. I seized it, instantly proud of my reflexes—until hot liquid splashed through the dislodged lid. I righted the cup, reattached its cover, and wiped my hand along the side of my pants.

"She said the Historic Vault."

"Yes."

"By name? This wasn't your inference of a vaguer term?"

"No, Loredana, I'm pretty sure I'm not suffering hearing loss yet."

"With your incessant use of earbuds, I thought it best to bring up the possibility." She scowled. "This is a serious breach of security. No one is supposed to know we have such a vault."

"Did I mention she knew in which tower to look? Because she did."

"That's worse."

"Yep."

"We have to call upstairs. I'll need your mobile. Perhaps Winston and his cave of trolls can trace the call through some other means than the more mundane." She reached for the phone by her computer.

"Hang on." I raised a finger. "There's something else."

Loredana sighed. "I'm not certain a woman can take much more of your 'else' today, Mercury. It's not even lunch."

"Are you hungry? We could get something."

She shook her head. "No, not if Carlito's is closed today."

I opened my mouth for a witty rejoinder but came up empty. "I thought you hated pizza."

"I don't hate any food. Some, however, is best enjoyed in small doses. Now, what's your additional problem?"

"My additional problem is Ramos telling me there was a second attack last night."

Loredana stared at me, then she laughed. It wasn't a full-on chuckle, or a tiny giggle, but a decent, honest laugh. She shook her head, smiling even after it subsided. "Your jokes suffer from ill-timing, but I must say, you do them with such deadpan earnestness I—"

"Loredana." I kept my expression as grave as possible. The return of gut-churning guilt helped. "This isn't a joke."

Her smile faltered. She did her best to recover it, and some of her usual poise, but there was no disguising the confusion. "I'm sorry. A second attack? In the same night? Ridiculous."

"Tell that to the homeless person Ramos says is in the hospital."

"There was a victim?"

I nodded.

"I see. What of official reports?"

"You know Ramos. There won't be anything unless he's backed into a corner. Considering the witnesses were two hammered drunks, I doubt it's gonna be a problem. He'll keep me up to speed."

"Did the victim actually state an astral fiend attacked? Is there an image? Any forensic proof?"

I shook my head. "I don't know. All I know is, if there was a second attack while I was off brawling in the warehouse—and I don't have any reason to doubt Ramos—then I want to know why it got missed. First the fiend shows up at my place, when it's nowhere near a rip, and then two pop up in the same night at different yet simultaneous locations. Both get missed by Tracking and Forecasting."

Loredana drummed her fingers on the phone's receiver but didn't place a call. I couldn't see the inner workings of her mind, but I could imagine the processor of a computer humming along, so I figured that's what that sharp brain of hers was doing. "One moment."

I did my best to relax as she rushed through the rest of her email correspondence. When it felt like she was taking too long, I craned my neck. The light shifted enough I could see the contact info, or at least, the name attached to the address. "Who's Dominic? Friend of yours?"

"Private contractor." She hit send, then put the monitor to sleep. "Let me talk to Winston about this."

"Winston's already surly about the whole recalibration thing. You think he'll like it if I show up with another complaint?"

"If he feels he's being unnecessarily overtaxed, he can file an objection with the manager."

"I know. That's why I need to see him."

"The manager?"

"Make me an appointment."

"No. He doesn't deal with these kinds of disturbances."

"Are you serious? I thought you were willing to help."

"I am. Whatever you need. Except that."

"Well, get me into the Historic Vault."

"Or that."

I threw up my hands. "Come on, Loredana. This crazy lady knows about it! She told me to look in there. At the very least, we should take a peek."

"I will be glad to have the proper personnel conduct a search."

"Not good enough. Operatives have clearance for the vault."

"They do indeed. Have you ever used it?"

"No, but it's not like I don't know where it's at."

Loredana took my phone. "You have no objections to Winston's department tracing your call?"

"Knock yourself out." I folded my arms. "But only if you get me a seat at the manager's office table."

She tapped the phone on the table, a slow, rhythmic *tock-tock-tock*. I wished she'd hurry up. The coffee was getting cold. When she didn't make a move, I reached slowly for the cup and slid it back toward me. I took a noisy slurp. Warmish.

"Fine." If she had shot the word any harder, it would have punctured my lung. "I'll request the appointment. The manager can decide whether or not you're getting into the vault, clearance or not. It's important to realize the vault isn't a room one can simply walk into, as easy as sauntering up to your little café's counter. Operative or not, you must be vetted, your conduct above reproach."

"I've only ever done what Procyon wants," I snapped. "You of all people know that. Doesn't matter what the work's done for my life. This place is my home, and the team is—"

"Family."

"Yeah. I guess so." Nothing like having your family hint that they think you're the weak link.

"I don't doubt your sincerity, Mercury," Loredana said softly. "However, if someone outside Procyon knows of our true purposes—someone unknown to us and unaffiliated with our cause—we have to be careful. With everyone. Our own people included."

"Right. Sorry I bit back."

"Don't be bothered." She smiled. "I'd be disappointed if you didn't."

I shook my head, still sick in my gut, but feeling relief cutting through. "So, we're good?"

"We are." She picked up the phone and dialed an extension. "I need to speak with the manager, please. We have a potential dual emergence. It requires immediate access to the Historic Vault."

Whatever answer came, it made Loredana narrow her eyes, and I was really glad I wasn't the target of her displeasure. "Yes, I will hold, and if it is any longer than thirty seconds you will find me outside your door."

CHAPTER EIGHT

My phone buzzed at me. Ramos.

<Going to talk with victim. Out of critical. Will let you know if anything interesting.>

"Problem?" Loredana kept her gaze ahead as we rounded the corridor on the seventh floor of Tower Three.

"Nope. Ramos is talking with the lady who was attacked." I took a sip of the coffee, then offered it to her again.

She arched an eyebrow.

"Hey, I've been cootie-free since fourth grade. Honest."

"I'll take your word. Please update me if the lieutenant learns anything of interest."

"I think we covered that."

"Indeed. I assumed you could use the reminder."

The manager's office formed a triangle on the curved corridor with Tracking and Forecasting at the other points. Black letters on frosted glass said simply, "Manager of Operations." Never met the guy before. Why would I have needed to? With Loredana as my handler, Winston as my human GPS, and Mari as my counselor, the team worked like a charm. Bureaucracy had a way of fouling the best efforts. I was happy to have the boss stay invisible.

Not anymore.

The office was clean and bright, with a secretary's desk front and center. San Camillo's skyline made for a gorgeous backdrop, with rolling hills and sprawling orchards on the far horizon. There was a wooden door to the left. Bookshelves lined the right side, displaying titles such as *Moby Dick, Frankenstein,* and *The Scarlet Letter.* No plant life. No artwork. The secretary was a tall, slender black man with thick white glasses. He was dressed impeccably in a striped Oxford and a red tie. Slim as he was, muscles bulged against the sleeves.

"I expected you six seconds ago." He didn't look up from his keyboard, or the curved monitor.

"It's nice to see you, too, Calvin," Loredana said.

"The manager is waiting ten seconds longer than I told him he'd have to." Calvin's voice was deep, enough so I swore the glass desk vibrated with every word. He finally deigned to visually acknowledge our presence. I'd gotten a happier expression from a guy whose car I'd backed into. "This the operative?"

"Mercury Hale." I extended the hand that wasn't baby-sitting lukewarm coffee.

He stared at me. This guy—Calvin Hodges was engraved in silver on a black nameplate—didn't seem impressed.

"Operative? Keeper of the pulsar stave?" I lifted the side of my shirt, so he could see the stave in its holster. "Slayer of gross monsters? Fan of *Cowboy Bebop* and other underappreciated sci-fi classics?"

Loredana sighed and walked to the left door. She opened it without preamble.

Calvin gestured in her direction with a simple flick of paired fingers.

"Later, buddy." I banged the stave on the corner of the desk and joined Loredana.

"Always nice to see you making new friends," she murmured as I passed.

"What can I say? My default reaction to 'obnoxious' is 'sarcasm.' Maybe I'll go get recalibrated."

She snorted but didn't offer any further comment.

"Loredana. Come on in!" I don't know what I was expecting of the manager, but it was definitely not a well-tanned guy with silver hair and an equally silvery beard-moustache combo. He had on a white flannel shirt unbuttoned at the collar, and blue jeans. He grabbed her hand and kissed her knuckles. Cute. I hoped I'd get to see a Krav Maga demonstration as a result, but Loredana maintained her poise.

"Sir, thank you for your time. This is Mercury Hale, our prime operative."

"'Course he is. I've read all the reports." The guy wrung my hand like it was sodden laundry and he was a pioneer bound and determined to get it dried out. "Jack Jackson, son. Pleased to make your acquaintance."

Whether it was the attire that tipped me off, or maybe the fact that he was a bit humbler than the rest of my co-workers, I decided this guy was okay. For now. "Good to meet you, sir."

"Aw, don't 'sir' me, son, I can't break Loredana here of the habit!" He slapped me on the back. "Go on, have a seat."

He dropped his linebacker's frame into a huge leather chair behind a sprawling oak desk. It was covered with papers, arranged in stacks of varying neatness. No family photos. There were some awards arranged on a shelf, right above what looked like a minibar. Every award said something about community service, but to be honest, I was way more interested in the crazy guy with the deep Texas accent who was apparently the big boss.

"I've been spending too much time stuck up in here, doing reports for the board of directors, when I'm not soliciting donations from our contributors." He chuckled. "Means I miss out on all the fun stuff. Sounds like you've got some fun."

"Not really." I glanced at Loredana. She gave me a curt nod. "I got a call today from someone telling me to look for what she called 'the truth' in the Historic Vault. Someone outside Procyon."

Jackson's grin stiffened. "Well, now. Ain't that a predicament. What do Winston and his boys think?"

"We haven't been to Tracking yet, sir," Loredana said. "I thought the matter of the utmost importance and wanted to bring it to your attention quickly. There is also the potential of a ... defect."

"Defect?"

"In Tracking. Possibly Forecasting."

"Hmm." Jackson crossed to the minibar. "Whiskey?"

"No thank you."

Jackson poured ice into a tumbler and cracked open a bottle. He poured a fifth for himself, then approached me with the bottle.

I shook my head. "Got enough here with the caffeine, Jack."

He chuckled. "I like this guy." Then he pulled the lid off my coffee cup and gave The Shattered Mug's finest a generous helping of whiskey. "By defect, I assume y'all are referring to the attack on Mercury's apartment."

"Not only that, sir, but there was apparently a second astral fiend incursion at the same time Mercury responded to a possible Icon manifestation last night."

He swigged his drink. "That is mighty peculiar. Best have

a word with Winston and Marigold. We can't have those kind of mistakes go on for long."

"I have already instructed Mr. Yen to better calibrate his equipment."

"Good." Jackson squinted at me. "And this lady? You know her, Mercury?"

"Nope. Don't have any idea who she is."

"What about your contact with San Camillo PD?"

"He's on it." Okay, this guy *was* up to speed on me. Made me feel better knowing the manager was, in fact, managing Procyon. "I've got a promise of more intel once he conducts an interview."

"That a fact. You think you'll get the unvarnished truth?"

"I do. Ramos never lets me down."

"Good man." Jackson polished off his whiskey. "Dang. I'll tell you what. This is disconcerting, but not amazingly so. Request for access to the Historic Vault is denied."

"But sir," Loredana said. "Our operatives have the proper clearance for such access."

"They rightly do, Loredana, however I ain't about to crack that puppy open if we have a potential leak within our organization."

"Yeah, but, me getting into the vault could help us figure out what's wrong," I added. "This lady—"

"Gave you what? A specific file? A case number?"

"I ... No."

"Kinda vague, ain't it?"

"Yeah. It is. Give me some time to figure it out."

Jackson shook his head. "Wish I could help, but it ain't gonna happen. Board will have my head if I let an operative into the vault—an operative who's been targeted not just by a fiend but by an unknown individual with access to our true nature, and who's got a substantial contact on the outside."

"Hey, if you mean Ramos, I told you, we can trust him."

Loredana's hand rested on my leg. When I frowned at her, I was surprised to see she looked worried.

That's when I realized the pulsar stave was crackling with energy.

I'd forgotten I still held it in my hand. The power rippled up my arm, just like when I was preparing for a tussle with a monster.

"Son, I don't doubt you're gifted, else you wouldn't have been anointed for this work." Jackson's words were friendly enough, but there was no mistaking the "Don't cross me" tone behind them. "Truth is a tricky thing. Do I respect you thus far? Absolutely. Do I trust that you're being told the truth by everyone you're in contact with? Not a bit."

I swirled the coffee in my cup. Desecrated coffee was more like it. Nothing left to do but pour it down the sink. I doubted Loredana liked her morning cup spiked, considering she wasn't even a sugar fan. "Look, Jack, we're not gonna get anywhere with you stonewalling me."

"Mercury, I'm gonna stop you right there. 'Cause if you open your trap again and give me more guff, there's gonna be a whole heap of consequences." Jackson clinked his glass on the desk. His smile was sharp and cold. "This problem is officially in-house, so I will handle it in house. Now, you two run along to Tracking and have Winston and his boys trace our mystery caller. I don't want to hear another word about it until we know who this person is, and how she's got herself the inside scoop on Procyon. Loredana, I'm counting on you."

"Understood, sir." Loredana stood.

"So, what, we're dismissed?" I didn't budge from my chair.

"Consequences, son."

I rolled my eyes. "Excuse me if that isn't the scariest thing I've experienced this week, considering I've never seen your face before a couple minutes ago."

Jackson snorted. "You got gall, I'll give you that. True enough, I don't have a need to show my face much around y'all, however you've seen my signature plenty enough. It's on your paycheck. Catch my drift?"

Blackmail? Lovely. I wanted to take back every grudging, charitable thought I had about this guy, which weren't many. But he was the boss. I could tell by the way Loredana was standing there like a good soldier at attention she willing, if not happy, to execute Jackson's orders. "All right. Fine."

"So we're clear," Jackson said. "You stay out of the vault unless you're authorized. Got me?"

"Yes, sir." I snapped off a fake salute with the pulsar stave before I returned it to its holster.

"Son, if you want to help, you'll quit grousing and hit the streets. Talk to your cop buddy, see what he knows."

"That was part of my plan." I smirked. "Glad to know we're on the same page."

"Mighty nice page. You kids run along."

Loredana seethed the entire walk out of the room, through the main office, past the aloof Calvin, and out into the hallway.

"I've heard," I said when I couldn't take the icy silence anymore, "That keeping feelings bottled up is unhealthy. Worse than a lot of sugar."

"If you would, for once, keep that tongue of yours from saying anything stupid," she snapped, "Our chances of solving whatever's going wrong would increase substantially."

"This is on me?" I gestured with the ruined coffee. "Right. I'm not the one blocking us from access to the vault."

"You don't even know what we need from the vault. You're

more willing to follow the promptings of a disembodied voice than the man who provides our leadership."

"Maybe you're right." I dropped the cup into a trash bin. "Maybe my answers aren't in here. Not yet. So, you do what Jackson wants and I'll do what I want."

"And what do you want, Mercury?"

"I want to figure out why my apartment got trashed, and someone innocent got hurt because I wasn't around." I walked around her to Tracking. "And I don't want it to happen again."

CHAPTER NINE

Winston twirled the phone in his hands. "My, isn't this a conundrum."

"You can trace it, right?" I couldn't get the smell of whiskey out of my nose. I was gonna need another coffee. Or better yet, food. Totally forgot I'd skipped lunch because there was no pizza available.

"Certainly. Whether or not your mystery caller still has the phone in her possession once the trace is complete, well ..." Winston shrugged. "That's another matter entirely."

"Will it take you long?"

"Not at all." Winston connected the phone to his computer and tapped in a series of commands. "Cross your fingers that she is like your typical security-blind smartphone consumer, obsessed with apps that constantly update, or one who keeps her Wi-Fi constantly searching for the nearest signal."

Whatever he did took only a few minutes, which passed without him speaking other than the occasional murmur to himself. Loredana tapped her foot, the sound growing more insistent until I swore someone was in the lobby with a jackhammer. When I glared at her, she didn't blink. Figured.

"Good news and bad news, my friend." Winston leaned back in his chair. "Which would you prefer?"

"Door number one, Winston."

"Right, then. Good news: the phone is most likely in an alley between Twenty-Ninth and Thirtieth. I've narrowed the last location to within a block. The bad news? Probably it's been discarded in a Dumpster."

"Okay, but I can still grab the phone. Maybe we can figure out who used it if I bring it back here."

"Perhaps. I doubt, however, that your caller was silly enough to not clean the phone to the best of her ability after taking steps to dispose of it." Winston shrugged. "It is worth a look, I suppose."

"You don't seem bothered by this potential breach of our security," Loredana said.

"Come now, Loredana. Do you honestly think someone's going to run off with our secrets? From here?" Winston waved his hands.

"She already knows about the vault, and our private mission."

"Which we've dealt with before," Winston said. "It must be a disaffected employee—if not from this site, then from one of our others. We've all manner of methods for dealing with such a leak—employee check-in logs, email searches, phone examinations, the list goes on. I have full confidence the manager knows what he's doing."

"The manager's doing a bang-up job," I muttered.

"Don't be so quick to judge, Mercury. He's under a lot of strain from the board of directors. The uptick in astral fiend incursions has not gone unnoticed throughout our wider organization."

"Send out a drone to pinpoint the location," Loredana

said. "Mercury can retrieve the phone once we're certain."

"As if my calculations are off." Winston sniffed.

"With the recent failures to predict not one but two astral fiend appearances, I don't want to take any chances." Loredana pointed at the monitor. "And assuming you have the drones properly recalibrated ..."

Winston nodded. "Yes, ma'am, as ordered."

"Guys, lay off each other." I held up my hands in the "T" shape. "Time out. You're both good at your jobs, and you both have my back. Mistakes happened. Let's fix them and get our work done, okay? Because as fun as it is watching you two play blood sports, I'm really, really hungry and have zero patience for this."

Winston chuckled. Loredana relaxed her stance, and though she didn't join in laughter, did gift me with a nod. "A fair point."

"Yes, the drones will be ready for the trace. I'll task one ASAP." Winston turned to his keyboard.

My phone buzzed on Winston's desk. A familiar number appeared.

"Your mystery oracle?" He prodded the phone, frowning.

"Nope. Ramos." It was a text.

<You're going to want to hear this. Meet me at SC General.>

"See what he has to say." Loredana's voice was startlingly close. When she'd snuck up to within a foot of my neck, I had no idea, but it was as if she were my conscience. Not a bad voice to have in that capacity, don't get me wrong. "Report everything pertinent."

"Don't I always?" I grinned over my shoulder.

She was already on her way out the door.

Winston snickered. "She's in a right snit, isn't she?"

"Loredana likes things orderly. This is anything but." I pocketed the phone. "Thanks, man."

"Cheers. Say, would you like to come by our place for dinner? Marigold and I have rounded up a couple interested parties from Procyon for a shared meal. It's been quite a spell since you've graced our home."

"Sure. That'd be nice." Way nicer than, maybe, spending another night on my own, watching TV, waiting for the inevitable call to slice open a monster. "Want me to bring anything?"

"Salad, if you could."

I made a face. "Rabbit food. Super."

Winston chuckled. "I shall provide the liquid entertainment, so don't put up too much a fuss."

"Why didn't you say so? Salad it is."

San Camillo General Hospital was the oldest and largest of the medical facilities in the city. It was really two hospitals that looked like they'd been slapped together as an afterthought— one a massive, stately stone edifice, and the other a sprawling glass and steel sculpture. Slapped together was an exaggeration, I'll admit. Somehow the architects had made the expansion look like it was growing out of the side of the original, early 20th Century building.

A pair of granite griffins guarded long steps to the old building. The renovation had added a glass and concrete elevator, complete with handicapped access ramp nearby. Ramos leaned against the righthand griffin.

"How was church? Say hi to the Pope for me?"

Ramos frowned. "Lutheran, Mercury. We don't have a pope."

"Whatever. Please tell me you've got some decent intel." I jogged up the steps. "Or at least food."

"There's a cafeteria inside."

"How's the grub?"

Ramos shrugged. "The tacos are disgusting. But you'd like them. Come on. I'll take you up to our guest."

He led my inside, and yes, he was right about the cafeteria. I took one look at the tacos swimming in their grease ponds and walked straight by. The hot dogs, though, appeared passable. I bought two and devoured one on our elevator ride to the right floor.

"She calls herself Wilhelmina." Ramos consulted his vintage notepad. "No date of birth, no address, no ID. Patrol tells me she frequents the waterfront, the parks, but avoids downtown. Doesn't have a criminal record. Pretty good about reporting crimes, actually. A group of younger guys look out for her when things get rough. That's who the two kids were that came to her help when she got attacked."

"Tell me about it. The attack, I mean."

"She got a food kit from St. Sebastien's. The monster attacked her while she was on her way back to the Court Street bridge. One of the young guys said he saw the flashes of light, thought it was gunfire."

"So, he ran toward it? Awfully selfless."

"Like I said, these kids respect her."

"Wait. Weren't they drunk?"

"That's what the responding officers thought. Tox screen is pending."

The nurse admitted Ramos to the room but stopped me at the door. She was a short, wide lady with the palest skin and the darkest brown hair. "You're police, but who's he? Not family."

"Consultant. He's authorized on this investigation." Ramos held the door for me.

I jerked my thumb. "I'm with him."

The nurse's glare tracked me inside, and probably could have zapped me through the door if she had lasers tucked in her head. Which she very well may have.

Wilhelmina was propped up in her bed. She was hooked up to enough monitors for me to realize the nursing staff must be keeping close tabs on her condition. But if I ignored the snaking wires, the beeping instruments, and the glowing lights, it was easy to imagine her relaxing on a couch with the latest issue of Reader's Digest. The fact she held a copy of said magazine helped the illusion.

"Lieutenant." She had a warm, soothing voice. "My, don't I feel blessed to see you twice in a day. And you bring a handsome young man along this time."

"This is Mr. Hale, a consultant I make use of on … odd cases. Yours fits the category." Ramos folded his notebook. "You've already given me your statement. Could you describe what you saw to Mr. Hale?"

Wilhelmina set the Reader's Digest on her lap. Her hair was short, shock white. It stood out like snow against deep, dark brown skin, and when she pursed her lips in thought, wrinkles piled up around her mouth and eyes. Eyes that were a sparkling blue. "What's to say? I saw hell emerge and the Devil at its lead."

"This devil. Was he like an angry, evil octopus on steroids?" I asked.

Ramos scowled.

"What? It's accurate."

"I was hoping you'd ease the witness into her recollection."

Wilhelmina clucked her tongue. "Ease. You boys see a frail

old lady sitting here, do you? Time makes a lot of changes to a body, that's certain, but when the spirit's strong, nothing's going to bow a soul down. Yes, Mr. Hale, I'd say your description's on the money. Cruel beast. I don't mind saying, I was worried for them."

"Them?"

"The two fellas who been watching over me." She shook her head, still smiling. "Don't get me wrong, nice young men, bit rough outside, but hearts as kind as any mother's inside. They was just a tad fearful. Can't blame them, can we? That creature was the stuff of my worst dreams. Lord knows I'm likely to see it again, so I best be brave."

"Wait." I sat on the edge of the bed. "Why do you think you'll see it again? The monster's gone."

She patted my hand. I don't remember my grandparents. Don't even know if I had any. In that moment, though, I wished she was one of them. Her touch banished any worries, even the most trivial fears. Pure comfort. And I was the one with the supernatural weapon strapped to my side. "Child, the monsters are never gone."

Wilhelmina opened her book and adjusted her glasses. "If you boys are done, that's all I've got to say on the matter. Except, maybe, you'd best be on your toes. That critter left in a right hurry after the young men ran up, but it didn't seem too enthusiastic. It'll come back."

"We can give you police protection." I glanced at Ramos. "Right?"

He made a face. "There's the minor matter of how I'd file that request with the department."

Wilhelmina chuckled. "Truth's funny, ain't it?"

She went back to quietly reading her magazine. After a half minute of standing there in awkward silence while Ramos scratched notes, I got the feeling she was done. Crazy, I know. I walked outside, my thoughts colliding. Took me a moment I to realize I hadn't eaten my second hot dog. I chowed down until Ramos exited. He shut the door behind himself.

"So," he said, "What do you think?"

"What do I think? She's either nuts, or suffering some kind of post-traumatic stress that hasn't kicked in. It's going to be a doozy when it does. She's seventy-plus and saw an astral fiend face to face. That's not normal. Neither's her reaction."

"Yes, I gathered, but I meant her conviction the thing is going to return for her. Can you watch for it?"

"I could hang around the hospital, keep an eye out. My people really do have the best methods for predicting and tracking when and where the fiends will appear, even though their record's been spotty as of late."

"Consider it. I can set up something with the hospital, so you can find a corner to operate from."

"Gee, sounds like a blast."

"Don't do that. These things are your responsibility." Ramos backhanded my side. His knuckles grazed the pulsar stave, secure in its sheath under my shirt. "Make up your mind how to handle it."

He left me standing in the middle of the hallway, nurses and family members passing on either side like I was a car stalled in traffic. I shrugged and gulped down the last of the hot dog.

Winston's drone led me to the precise Dumpster. Digging the phone out was an introduction to a new species of terrible smells. Insert Star Wars garbage smasher joke here.

<Got it,> I texted Loredana.

<Excellent. I never should have doubted Winston's tech abilities. Give it to him ASAP.>

<Was hoping to finish moving this afternoon. Dinner?>

<A question, or an observation?>

<I'm at his place tonight. 6. I'll give it to him then.>

<Yes, probably best to keep this outside Procyon for the time. Have a good evening.>

<You should come by.> I didn't know Winston and Mari's rules on uninvited guests, but hey, Loredana seemed to have even less a social life than me. Besides, showing up with a friend was better than flying solo.

Friend? She wasn't that. Handler, yes. Pal, no. Still …

<Thank you, but no. Business.>

Well, it was worth a shot. I climbed into my car.

Phone buzzed again. Loredana.

<I appreciate your efforts, Mercury. Some time, they may pay off.>

I grinned.

Winston and Mari had a townhouse on San Camillo's North Beach waterfront. Newer construction, pastel colors and red tile roofs up and down the whole neighborhood. Freshly planted trees. Theirs was identical to the dozens along the road, but only one had ten cars parked on either side of the door.

Mari met me there, a smile brightening her face. She kissed me on the cheek, rising on her tiptoes to make the connection. "It's nice to see you outside of Forecasting, Mercury."

"Got to do it more often, Mari." I bowed and offered up the salad. "Behold the glory that is spinach and dried cranberries."

"Fresh?"

"Freshest plastic baggies I could find." I winked.

"There's the bloke!" Winston emerged from the hubbub inside, carrying two beers. He pressed one to my chest and took the salad. "I'd call this a fair trade, would you not?"

"Abso-friggin-lutely." I popped the cap and savored the cold drink. For just a while, it'd be nice to not think about killing things or worry about people maybe getting killed by those same things. "Got another present for you, too."

"The phone? Fantastic." Winston grinned. "But let's kick our feet up on the deck, my friend. Tracking and Forecasting concur: It's a night off with companions who deserve a good time."

CHAPTER TEN

Forty-eight hours. That was my reprieve.

The next call came in at 9:55 Tuesday night. I was kicked back on a new-used couch in my new loft. The couch sagged on one end. The view out the single, broad window looked out onto another row of lofts and a jagged line of rooftops. I ignored it for the latest superhero flick. The good guy wasn't going to accept his mission, or so it seemed. I knew better. The movies went the same. He'd come around at the last minute, in time to save the world.

Right. Wonder how the movie would play out if he walked away? Said screw it, took a paycheck, and didn't care.

I felt the pulsar stave humming from its new perch on a bookshelf, tucked back behind novels. Some days, the path's not easy to see.

My phone buzzed.

I paused the movie. "Yello."

"We've got one." It was Winston.

I groaned and pushed myself off the couch. Stretched my arms out, worked kinks from my back, then returned the phone to my face. "Okay, well, once Mari confirms the vision ..."

"Mercury, please, shut up. This isn't a proper Forecast. Mari went to bed early, a half hour ago, and woke screaming. I've just now calmed her down. You have to move."

"Move? Move where? What does Tracking say? Has the Forecast confirmed an Icon?"

"Yes, there's a bloody icon supposed to show, and there's no Tracking other than for you to get to the Promenade with due haste!"

I swept across the room, knocked books aside, and retrieved the stave. I wasn't imagining things. It was humming. Angrily. My wrist ached. "Winston, slow down, man. What's going on?'

Winston took several deep breaths, the phone crackling. "Mari's had a vision. An astral fiend is breaching through a rip between dimensions. She saw people running, screaming from it. They were at the Promenade."

He'd already said that. Why'd it sound familiar? I hurried across the room, to a table set by the door. I had a pile of mail there, unsorted from the past two days of forwarding from the old address. I knocked it all aside, searching for the flier I needed. There. Pink paper, black graphics and lettering. "Blues Nights, Tuesdays at the Promenade, 7 to 11."

I checked my watch. Almost ten. There'd be hordes of people still there.

But it was raining. So, maybe not too many.

Was I really arguing attendance probabilities now? "Okay, hang on, I'm headed there! Keep me up to speed if Mari sees anything else!"

There was a new sound in the background. A rumbling. "We're headed to Procyon now. Watch yourself."

He hung up.

I was already sprinting down the front steps, hurtling

through the front door. My car was four spots down, pointed the wrong way from the Promenade.

I got in, gunned the engine, and flipped a U-turn in the middle of the light evening traffic. Headlights blinded me. Horns honked in outrage.

Never mind that. I hit a speed dial on my contacts.

"Ramos."

"Hey! Get down to the Promenade right now, with the biggest gun you can find!"

"Mercury? You'd better be drunk-dialing."

"Shut up and listen! There's a monster going to pop into our dimension in the middle of Blues Night, and I need a bunch of people cleared out so my fight with it doesn't become front page news!"

"*Madre dios.* You're serious."

"You think? Hurry up!" I hung up and drove.

There wasn't an empty parking space in sight at the Promenade, so I rolled up behind three cars and sprinted away. The rational, organized part of my brain chided me for leaving the door open and blocking the exit of potential victims. Whatever traffic infraction I was about to get would be expensive. Did Procyon's accounts handle incidentals like that? At least I had the presence of mind to grab the keys from the ignition.

The Promenade was a raised walkway of concrete pilings and wood planks, curving near the harbor. Trees crowned it every hundred feet, with benches interspersed. It had finishing raining, leaving thick, humid air and a sheen of moisture atop everything. I could hear soulful blues the instant I arrived, the songs growing louder with every step. I took the nearest stairs two at a time, catapulting myself to the top.

It was a party.

Had to be six dozen people, at least, within three hundred yards of my position. They were laughing, talking, eating, drinking—everything but freaking out because of monster attack. Which was good. But as I stood there, hand on my side, I couldn't help wondering of all this was caused by Mari experiencing bad case of indigestion.

I dialed Winston. "You got anything specific, or am I just going to stand here and listen to the jam? Because it sounds great."

"Standby." Fingers pounded furiously on a distant keyboard. "I've got drones coming up on your position. Tachyon emissions are through the roof. Whatever you're going to do, do it soon."

"Whatever I'm …? Come on, Winston!" I growled into the phone. "I'm here to slice and dice, not formulate an exit strategy."

Thankfully, Ramos took my frantic call seriously, because he pulled up in a black Dodge Charger with emergency lights flashing on top. Two squad cars joined him. Good, I guess, even if I had no idea what he was up to.

"Okay, folks!" He and a half dozen officers spread among the thin crowd. "We've got a notice of potential electrocution hazard due to faulty wiring! I need everyone to clear the premises, just for a half hour or so, please. Move in an orderly fashion toward the stairs."

I hung back as the police did their thing. A few people grumbled, but not too loudly. The music was farther up the Promenade, around a corner and out of sight. Ramos and his people shepherded these listeners, who I realized were stragglers from the main herd, toward the sounds.

That's when the first sparks of purple lightning appeared.

"Mercury." Ramos grabbed my shoulder. "What's going on? I'm going to take a lot of grief for provoking an inspection at this time of night."

Still staring at the sparks, I slowly removed Ramos's hand. "Not. Now."

He turned and gazed into the forming rip. Whatever he muttered was long and Spanish. Ramos made the sign of the cross.

I deployed the pulsar stave. "Get your people clear."

"If you need backup—"

"Go!"

Ramos barked orders, hustling his people off the Promenade.

The rip exploded, and boy, was I ready.

This fiend came barreling out like he was strapped to the front of a semi coming down the interstate. No sloth, all speed.

I didn't bother with grace or anything other than brute force. I met the fiend head-on, stave flashing, dodging the tentacles with a reckless abandon fueled by fury. This thing thought it could break the rules of engagement. Show up whenever it wanted? Put the people of San Camillo in danger?

Nope.

One, two tentacles went spinning off. The screams were piercing. I hoped the blaring sounds of the band, amplified by far-off speakers, were enough to cover the sound. They weren't, however, disguising what was going on from the cops.

So, there I was, taking on the astral fiend in view of the San Camillo Police Department.

Granted, it wasn't full view. Ramos had killed the lights, owing partly, I assume, to his need to support the electrical malfunction cover story. It also gave me the advantage of keeping my face obscured. Which was great, because I didn't walk around with a mask in my back pocket. Still, the flashes from the pulsar stave and the pale violet glow from the astral fiend's tentacles were sure to give them something interesting for their reports.

I ducked as one of the tentacles lashed out. It slapped against a tree, splintering the slender trunk. Yow. That could have been my neck. The strike was close enough it'd left a slimy streak across my hair. It was going to be time for a long shower when this was finished.

I rushed in close, avoiding the flailing arms, but man, this one was fast. A blow caught me in the midsection, sending me tumbling toward the Promenade's waterside railing. My arm hooked the metal; the rest of me dangled over the bay, shoes scrabbling for purchase on the boards.

Another tentacle slammed on the railing, and another, pounding with relentless force. Thank goodness for whatever engineer recommended the rails be made out of thick piping, because while they bent with each hit, they didn't give way.

I shoved off from the nearest post, shooting along my side underneath the fiend's bulbous body. It whirled itself in a slithering mass, elevated a couple feet off the walkway. Slavering teeth dripped ooze.

I broke the pulsar stave apart and stabbed with both ends.

One jab left a deep, burnt hole in the monster's hide. The other hit only clear air, because the fiend rolled away—in midair—before thumping back down. Great. I had an acrobat on my hands. "Nobody likes a show-off!"

The fiend screeched at me, garish eyes reflecting the stave's energy and the crackling sparks from the rip.

The rip? "Winston! Winston, do we have an Icon?"

"Negative! Mari saw it only through a haze, as a possibility, but the tachyon emissions are nowhere near what you encountered at the warehouse."

"Wonderful." I slid out of the way of an attack and fended off what could have been a quick beheading by smashing the stave back together. Yellow-white light swarmed from both ends to the center. The fiend's incoming tentacle liberated that pent-up power into a momentary, but brilliant, flare.

It was enough to leave globs of light in my vision. The fiend hated it more. He contracted his tentacles, shielding those hideous, compound eyes. Not able to see? "Sucks to be you."

The downside, however, was that the fiend barreled past me, right under the rip, and toward the bend in the walkway.

The Blues Fest revelers were around that corner, drinking and dancing, oblivious to the creature heading their way. I threw myself atop the monster, using the stave like a hook from—well, if you read *Dune*, you'd know I'd make a heck of a sandworm rider. It slapped at me, while hurtling away from both my incessant jabs and from the rip's vortex. Times like that, I thought it'd be nice if there were two of me instead of one, or even someone from Procyon for backup. But there was only one pulsar stave, and one operative.

Right then's when Ramos shouted loud and clear, "Fire!"

Bullets cracked through the night air. I wanted to curl my fist and whoop—until I realized I'd wind up just as punctured as the fiend, sitting as I was astride its bumpy hide like it was the world's most hideous rodeo bronc. "Hey! Stop! Cease shooting or whatever!"

Ever try yelling over the top of a monster's inhuman squeals and seven semi-auto pistols banging away? Doesn't work. I thought about asking Ramos for his bullhorn. Ha, ha. No.

Instead I planted my feet down the left side of the fiend, putting its body between myself and dozens of bullets. No idea if they were killing the thing. It sure wasn't getting less frisky, but it had ended its headlong rush. I leaned as hard as I could on the stave, levering against its hide. My body rolled sideways, until I was parallel to the walkway, and the spatter of bullets against the fiend's torso let me know I wasn't going to die of a police shooting.

The fiend veered right, bashing through a tree, up over a now-twisted railing, and slammed down onto the asphalt street. It swiped a car aside on either side. Poor Fiats. They would have survived better in a head-on collision with a bulldozer. Would insurance chalk that up to an act of God? Ramos might agree.

Speaking of Ramos, he and his officers backed up to the perceived safety of their squad cars. Pretty sure they emptied all their magazines at the fiend. Fat lot of a good it did. The thing used its remaining tentacles as passable shields, albeit bullet-riddled, slime oozing ones. Ramos's attack slowed it, yeah, but it was still alive, and dangerous.

Not for long.

I cranked up the juice on the stave and stabbed it deep down into the fiend's hide, far as it would go, until my hands were grasped around the center bar and wrist-deep in charred flesh.

The astral fiend bellowed.

"Dude!"

Wait, what? Fiends don't speak.

Check that. It wasn't the fiend. My opponent was slumped into a deflated, steaming heap on the street, sublimating as fast as an ice cube on summer pavement. And it wasn't Ramos. Whatever words were spilling out of his mouth were indecipherable at this distance.

I turned around.

A gaggle of six teens, a couple boys and four girls, gawked

at me from a distance. My view of them was broken by three trees and all their leafy camouflage. Every single one had phones aimed my way. Fear jolted me, worse than when I'd had to roll sideways to avoid a fusillade of bullets.

"What is that thing? It's so nasty!" Kid, if your eyes bulged any bigger, they'd pop out of your skull.

One of the girls squealed, hands pressed to her mouth.

Thankfully Ramos was in full-on crowd-control mode. He was on those kids faster than I'd ran after the astral fiend. "Clear out! Nothing to see here. Officer, take their statements. And check whatever they've got in their bottles, because from where I stand it doesn't look like cream soda. The paper bags are a giveaway, boys and girls."

The teens were suddenly reduced to scratching their heads and staring at their shoes. Two of Ramos's officers corralled them and herded them back toward the music scene, notepads and flashlights at the ready. The others circled the fiend's smoldering remnants, which were congealing in a sodden lump that smelled worse than any garbage accidentally left out during a rainstorm.

"Thanks," I said to Ramos.

"*De nada.* You might consider keeping your showdowns a little less public in the future." He shone a flashlight at the mess. "Was this supposed to be here?"

"Sort of." I glanced back. The rip was gone. I hadn't even noticed it falter, and fade. No warning. As if the whole confrontation had been a bad dream. Except Mari had been the one with the nightmare, and the astral fiend's rotting corpse was the proof. "This wasn't Forecast in the usual way, and I don't …"

Sudden fear seized me. I ran for my car.

"Hey!" Ramos was right behind me. "What are you doing?

Give me a statement! Something I can use for the press, because this isn't going to vanish like that thing's body!"

"The hospital!" That's all I had time to say before I peeled out of the street.

Last time I'd fought the monster, two had shown up, and one had gone after Wilhelmina. I'd told Ramos they didn't coordinate attacks. As far as I knew, that was true.

But these last few appearances had been abnormal.
If they kept up the pattern, she could already be dead.

CHAPTER ELEVEN

I lost track of how many cars I swerved around. Same went for the traffic lights I ran. Pretty sure it was three. I finally paid attention after a city bus decided it was going to try to sideswipe me.

About then is when I knew I definitely did *not* have the right of way.

I abandoned my car with its right wheels on the curb. If I could have flown up to the hospital floor where Wilhelmina was resting, I would have.

Nurses barked orders at me as I barged past the desk. Whatever. The cops were instructed to let me by, right?

I banged the hospital room door open. "You're in grave danger." Sounded very dramatic.

The fifty-something balding white guy stared at me. "Who are you?"

Awkward. Same room? Yep. But no homeless elderly black lady. This dude could have been my accountant. Heat rushed to my face. "Ah, okay. My mistake."

"I'm in danger?" Sweat beaded the poor guy's forehead. "The doc said the surgery went good. Were there complications?

I knew it. He was too friendly. Nurse! NURSE!"

And that was my cue to leave.

My phone harassed me all the way back to my car. Traffic cops must have been busy, because I should have had fifty tickets and probably a warrant. "Ramos?"

"Mercury! I've been trying to reach you since you blew out of here!"

"Hey, I had to make sure Wilhelmina was okay. It occurred to me another fiend could have tried an attack on her while we were mopping up the Promenade mess."

"So, you went to the hospital."

"Ah, yeah."

"Genius. They released her yesterday."

"Okay, well, you telling me yesterday would have been better than me charging in there and making an idiot of myself!"

"Of all the bone-headed moves." Ramos sighed. "Don't get me wrong. I would have paid to see you burst in there."

"If you request hospital security footage, I'm sure you can get a replay of my greatest hits." I rolled my eyes. "If she's not here, where is she?"

"Court Street bridge, if I had to guess. I've got uniforms watching her, periodically. You have to understand she's not top on the department's priority list. And speaking of department, my captain's throwing a tantrum. Check YouTube. And Instagram. And those other -grams my daughter uses."

I winced. "Bad?"

"Not as bad as it could be. Footage is grainy. Somebody wants to know if it's test footage for a new Star Wars movie. Apparently, your staff weapon reminds them of a laser sword."

"Lightsaber." I rubbed my forehead. "It's called a lightsaber."

"I thought you called it a pulsar stave."

"*The* pulsar stave. A lightsaber is—never mind. Can you meet me at Court Street bridge?"

"Why, because I have mounds of free time on my hands? No major crime scene to clean up? Go home, stay low, and wait for this to blow over. Better yet, tell your Procyon squad this is getting out of hand and I'm running out of patience."

Loredana would *love* that. "Which one's more important?"

"Take your pick. Hint: it's the second one." He hung up.

Can't blame him. I had no idea how he was going to spin the scene we'd caused. What did he and his officers shoot at, if not a monster? Threatening suspect with a gun? Probably he'd put out an APB for a few days then it'd go away once the next homicide popped up.

Me? I screeched away from the curb with Court Street in mind.

Ramos wasn't kidding. Do you know how many views there were on that video? I'm not going to say, because it's embarrassingly good.

He was right, though, about not being able to see the astral fiend. Blurry at best. The fight wasn't near as entertaining as the colorful commentary from the kids, most of which was Rated R. I skipped to the end, with the gunfire. Winced again. Yeah, you could tell they were cops.

Winston called me en route. "I trust you fared well."

"Yeah, sorry, things got messy. Bad messy."

"So I saw."

He had to be joking. "Oh? I didn't think there were any closed-circuit cameras in the Promenade area."

"I'm talking about social forms of media, chap."

"I don't want to talk about it."

"Fine, then, but know this: the rip closed, the fiend is gone, and we're scrambling to figure out why the arrival was missed. Our dear Ms. Lark is displeased."

"There's a shocker. Call you back later."

"Be careful. We're all on alert status here."

"Ten-four, good buddy."

I avoided any patrols on the way Court Street neighborhood, and also did not drive like a maniac. That helped. But I could have done without going anywhere near Court. It's … unpleasant. Cracked asphalt, crumbling buildings, crowds of young men hanging around who should not be out after dark. Not for their safety, I mean, but for the safety of others.

I sneered as I parked the car. Made a show of engaging the lock and the alarm. Let them decide I was an easy mark, please. This was not a night anyone wanted to screw with me.

Wilhelmina was easier to find than I'd first imagined. There were twenty people in clusters either around tents or conversing at barrels. Only three of them, though, looked like they were on guard duty. Two were younger, maybe late teens or early twenties, and the third had a scraggly beard peppered with gray. Their heights, though, were uniform—six and a half feet. While they didn't appear fit, they weren't scrawny, either.

Wilhelmina waved from behind them.

She sat in a lawn chair, with a slumping blue and orange tent as her companion. She was knitting, one of her needles crooked and repaired with duct tape. San Camillo Bay sprawled out before here, the golden light of the city to the north giving its surface the appearance of Christmas. Liquid, rippling Christmas. Buoys and sailboats added red and green blinking ornaments.

Christmas sucks.

Don't get me wrong. Winston and Mari invited me over last year for eggnog, board games, the whole shebang. But there's no family tradition. No dinners with far-flung relatives reunited. I'd rather ignore it.

"It's nice to see you again, young man." Wilhelmina smiled at me, needles flying. Whoever was on her Christmas list was getting a scarf as long as my leg, with competing blue and yellow stripes. "Don't get many visitors to my house, save for the police."

"I can't see why." I jerked a thumb toward the street. "Great view, nice and airy, lots of criminal delinquents and gangbangers. Property values must be through the roof."

She chuckled. "I find your humor refreshing, though I can see why some might want to knock you on your head. What's on your mind?"

"Well, I came looking to defend you from the—rogue elements." I wiggled my fingers in a crude approximation of tentacles. "You know, of the large, gross, and frightening kind."

"Been a quiet couple of days. Though I am touched. These fellas have been keeping me company." She nodded at her bodyguards, who seemed intent on swapping stories nearby. "Is that all that's on your mind? You seem troubled."

"I'm troubled because you're not. A monster tried to kill you and you're here knitting away. I half expect Martha Stewart to wander out of the shadows with decorating tips."

"Can't say I've seen her around. Listen, child, you keep on doing what you do, and I'll do what I do."

"What I do?"

"Of course. Takes a decent sort of man to respond to the call when the pulsar stave is extended to his reach."

I blinked. "I … That's a funny set of words."

"Now, don't you play coy." She wagged a needle. "Bad enough you didn't listen when I made my call."

My heart about stopped. Forget astral fiends, and potential gangbangers. "Your call. To my phone."

"It sure wasn't shouted from the rooftops, honey."

"You … Wait. That's impossible."

"How so?"

"You're … Well, you're homeless."

"That a fact?" Wilhelmina took in her surroundings. "I got a place to stay. Got friends to keep an eye on me and what's mine. People I can trust. I do for them and they do for me. Sounds like home. Tell me, what's yours like? Who has your back?"

I leaned against a bridge support. "You called me from a phone."

"It's called a TracFone, child, don't tell me you're not up on the latest in fancy gadgets. Me, I'd prefer a handheld telephone with a dial." She laughed.

I shook my head, hard enough I thought it would rattle loose the conflicting thoughts. "This isn't right. You talked about Procyon. Said I should look for the truth."

"And?"

"Procyon Foundation is a charitable organization."

"Yes, yes, it is. A genuine 501 c3 with an Historic Vault and a whole lotta secrets dating back to, oh, long before either of us were born." She tapped her needle against my side. It made a muffled *clink* where it hit the pulsar stave.

"Stop it!" I snapped. "You don't know anything."

"Come on now, child. I know how you earn your keep for Procyon. I know what you were out chasing tonight, and why you came to check on little old me. You weren't going to call 9-1-1." She leaned forward, the playfulness gone from her expression. "You were going to butcher the beast, like a warrior should."

I took a step back. My heart refused to slow. Who was this lady?

"The question remains, dearie, what are you going to do with what you've learned?" Wilhelmina went back to knitting. "Mm-hmm. There's a lot of things you need to discuss with your superiors. You got to press them for answers."

"That presumes I've got questions."

"Oh? These faulty fiend appearances aren't cause enough for alarm?"

"We're handling it."

She snorted. "If that's handling it, I'd hate to see dropping the ball. There's things moving too fast for Procyon to deal with—assuming, of course, you even want them to touch it. Ask them about File 6-1848. Ask them about the pulsar stave. And for Pete's sake, ask them about the Icon."

"I know about all this." I ticked them off on my hands, one by one, frightened to say them aloud outside the safe, secret confines of Procyon HQ but equally infuriated at this crazy old hag who, somehow, had an inside line on her operations. I wanted to call Loredana, but how would she deal with it? Curiosity drove me. "The first recorded rip and astral fiend attack took place in June 1848. The pulsar stave is the operative's weapon, passed down through Procyon, for the protection of humanity and the calling of the Icon. And the Icon is the key to forever banishing the astral fiends from our world."

"Recited well, like a good little schoolboy. But do you know what each of those pieces mean? Do you know why things are the way they are? Do you know the reasons for which you do what you do?"

"So nobody dies, and so lots of astral fiends do," I snapped. "This is ridiculous. I'm not going to answer a bunch of questions from you. How'd you get that info out of Procyon? Nobody knows it. Where'd you get a cell phone?"

"None of your business, child. Leave those worries to me. As for where I got my information, well, there's nothing like being part of the family—until nobody wants you around for the holidays. I'd suggest you run along and ask your handlers what's what. Especially that Icon."

"You're as obsessed with the Icon as everybody else there! It's just a goal for them." I threw up my hands and stalked around her chair. Those thugs of hers stopped their conversation. Didn't make any moves toward me, but they opted to glare instead. "I don't even know what I'm doing half the time, waiting for the stupid thing to show up! And what if it does? What do I do then?"

My throat was raspy, and my heart thudding. Wilhelmina examined her knitting project. She whistled a tune. "Truth's a bear to handle, isn't it? File 6-1848. Start looking. Before you do that, mind, you'll have to find your way home."

Great. The local brat pack circled my car like you'd see hyenas trotting around a wounded zebra. They were a mixed bag of pale, tattooed white kids and scraggly black teens, none of whom appeared to have taken a shower in days. Their clothes were a collage of bright colors and eighty-seven versions of grays and blacks.

"Hey, man!" The tallest, beefiest of the white guys rapped his knuckles on the hood of my car. He had arms so covered in tattoos his skin looked like an afterthought, plus Van Dyke shaved with military precision, and buzz cut hair colored blazing orange. "You want this back, you gotta pay the finder's fee! Lucky you, we found it."

That got a chorus of cackles from the other six. Just six? I sneered at them as I walked back to my car. The pulsar stave was colder than an icicle, pressed against my side. Its power lanced through my limbs, but I didn't bother taking it out. No need.

"Tell you what." I seized the leader by the throat and slammed him against the driver's side door so hard his spine left a dent. Perfect. Body work around here isn't cheap. "Let's skip the fee and play another game—the one where your buddies pick your teeth up off the pavement one by one."

I lifted him until his feet dangled off the ground, swinging at my knees. My arm felt like it was on fire, searing with heat from the inside out. It was as potent as when I faced an astral fiend. None of his pals felt brave enough to challenge my slow choking of their boss, because halfway through his sputtering of saliva they bolted.

"Party's over." I flung him into a pile of wet cardboard ten feet away. He scrambled to his feet and crawled off, shouting at the retreating forms of his close-knit gang.

I came to Court Street to save an innocent life. Instead I got a puzzle's worth of questions, and property damage. That night sucked.

CHAPTER
TWELVE

Wilhelmina was right. I hated that. I preferred being the one who was right.

Sleep was hard to come by. Nightmares swirled in my head, preventing me from grabbing more than a couple hours at a stretch. When I finally gave up and staggered into my new loft's kitchenette for a cup of coffee at 5:30, all I had to show for last night's foul-up was a tremendous headache and more questions.

Lovely.

I didn't really know what the Icon was. No one told me. Yes, it was important, and yes, we'd come so close to retrieving it on numerous occasions, but that was it. What kind of object was it? Maybe a powerful relic like the pulsar stave? I always pictured it as a miniature star, like the real thing dropped down from the cosmos and packaged in the palm of my hand. In those dreams, I held it close, like a proud dad holds his baby son, and used intense beams of light to blast every last astral fiend into tattered black smoke.

Didn't mean I had answers.

My phone buzzed, again. Loredana's fifth call of the very

early morning. Did she ever sleep? Did she do anything but enforce Procyon's will? Winston and Mari had a life outside those white tower walls. So did I, after a manner of speaking.

I ignored it. Bet Loredana was loving the attention my rapidly-filling voicemail doled out. I wasn't in any mood to talk to her. I sipped coffee, the cup filled with equal parts cream and sugar. Within a couple of minutes, I was way more awake. Still had the headache, but that'd be gone soon enough.

I sacked out on the couch, staring out the window at the creeping pastels of early morning—the opposite building turning from midnight blue to periwinkle, gaining streaks of pink and orange, until its true coloration of pale brick emerged. One window glowed orange. Who was awake with me at this hour? A father shaving before heading to the office? A mother taking a shower after a long night as an ER nurse? Either or both would take time to kiss their kids good morning.

Really? "Wow." I rolled my eyes at my sentimentality. The occupant could just as easily be a drug dealer coming off a night of executing a hit on a rival. But lately, I'd seen too many reminders of my orphan status. Poor old me. I scowled. Grow up.

The phone buzzed again. "No, Loredana, I'm not answering," I muttered. "So. Go. Away."

Someone pounded on my door.

Coffee sloshed over the rim, scalding my leg. I hopped up, wiping frantically at the brown stain on a perfectly good pair of jeans. At least it wasn't the white T-shirt. I'd just bought a new package. "All right, hang on, I'm coming!"

I checked my watch on the way to the door. 6:45. I didn't care if Ramos had a warrant and an entire squad of officer. He was going to get a massive fit from me.

Loredana was on the other side of the door.

"If you insist on being difficult, you'll find I can be equally, if not more, stubborn in pursuit of a goal." She walked in like she was late for a board meeting, except she didn't get the staff e-mail about the dress code. Her hair was a fiery storm, fighting against the single tie she'd used to make a ponytail. No makeup. Wearing Capri pants and sneakers, and a T-shirt. I had to blink twice and literally pinch myself to make sure I was, in fact, awake. The T-shirt was faded brown, with an odd blue box sketched on the front. A half second later I realized I was staring at an old-school British phone booth.

"Well?" She had her hands on her hips. Funny, isn't it? When you've got the major hots for a woman, your brain keeps telling you she's lovely even when the likelihood of your imminent demise increases faster than the odds of losing at a casino.

I started a couple of sentences, but all I could blurt out was, "You're a Whovian?"

She scowled. "Of course."

"Oh."

"Did you expect me to subscribe to the same mindless Star Wars fandom as yourself?"

"Hey, now, let's not get personal."

"You're right. I'd much rather discuss how you involved the San Camillo Police Department in gun battle against an astral fiend!" Her right eyebrow twitched. That was new. And ominous. "Then you disappear instead of showing up for debriefing."

Best to go for nonchalance. "It was worth it to see you in your top-secret wardrobe. Coffee?"

"Yes, please." Her tone softened, and then, "Are you a complete idiot? Where were you?"

I poured her a mug. Made sure it was the one with Darth

Vader's face on it before I handed it over. "Okay, fine, since we're in the all-cards-on-the-table mode. I went out to find my mystery caller."

"The one Winston tracked down?"

"Bingo."

"Who is she?"

"A seventy-something lady who lives on the streets. Calls herself Wilhelmina."

If Loredana recognized the name, she didn't let on. I couldn't tell what she was thinking, as she sipped the steaming drink. "Wilhelmina. She is the one who promised to give you the truth. Did she keep the promise?"

"All she did was give me nagging questions. Questions I normally wouldn't care about, but after last night ... Come on, Loredana, you have to admit things are getting really screwy really fast."

"The recent appearances have been unusual."

"See? Thank you! These last few incursions have broken the rules. How did Mari miss a Forecast? More importantly, how'd one get delayed until a few minutes before the rip opened—and what was a fiend doing popping up in a crowded public venue? They like to hide! They're not supposed to do that."

Loredana held up her hand. "Let's regroup around these questions. What did Wilhelmina tell you? How much does she know?"

"She knows I have the pulsar stave, and knows I use it against the astral fiends. She also knows about something called File 6-1848."

"I see." Loredana looked away.

Looked away? I made a face. Since when did she break eye contact during an interrogation? "Are you okay?"

"It's—fine. Let's continue. What else did she say?"

"No, I don't think so. What's in that file?"

"Irrelevant."

I shook my head. "Don't play, Loredana. Not after we've worked together this long. You know what's in that file—or at least, that it isn't important. I've always imagined the reason you don't fight astral fiends is because you could stand in front of them and give them one of your cute but scary scowls, prompting them to vaporize on the spot. But when I said the file's name, you got all sheepish."

Loredana smirked. "Your powers of observation are accurate, if not amusing. Very well. I don't know of that particular file, but the designation means it's restricted. It also means only the highest-ranking Procyon personnel know of its existence, let alone have access to it."

"Okay. I'm assuming the '1848' has to do with Procyon's founding year, right?"

"Founding year is a bit too precise a term. That is key to our existence, however." Loredana sipped her coffee, eyes narrowed. "Hence all the files associated with 1848 are treated with the utmost discretion."

I nodded, swirling the dregs of my cup.

"No," Loredana said.

"No, what? I didn't say anything."

"You're thinking it."

"Thinking what?"

"Don't play coy, Mercury. As you stated, we've worked together in close proximity for years." She stepped nearer. Loredana might not be wearing makeup, but there was something—else. Perfume? Nope. Probably shampoo. "You're thinking you need to get into the Historic Vault and read file 6-1848."

"Huh. How about that." I grinned. "You can read minds. So, when do we get in?"

"You heard the manager. Mr. Jackson will not let anyone access the Historic Vault until this leak is contained."

"Contained? Loredana, an old lady knitting by the side of the bay with a bunch of homeless guys and gangbangers blurted out Procyon's top-secret mission to me. I think we're beyond containing anything. Let me get in there."

She frowned, but she also didn't repeat her initial rejection, so I took that as a win.

"Look. Wilhelmina got me thinking about a bunch of stuff I'd been ignoring. Don't you want to know why it is we do what we do?"

"It's for the betterment of this world."

I rolled my eyes. "Yes, ma'am, but I mean the real *why*. You can't tell me how the pulsar stave works—what powers it, where it was made, who was the craftsman, and all that. It's never been relevant to our jobs before. With everything that's gone wrong in the past week, I'm thinking it just got very relevant."

"We should be asking this Wilhelmina how she knows what she claims to know, if any of it is in fact accurate."

"No argument there. The police are keeping tabs on her. Ramos isn't keen on the idea of anyone getting dead. Meantime, we've got to make a move."

Again, no outright rejection. Instead, she gazed into her mug, leaned against my apartment wall, and sighed. "What do you need?"

"Yes!" I clapped her on the shoulder. "That's the spirit!"

"Let's try that again," she said, dryly.

"Right. Ah, I need you to clear me with the clerk. Quietly."

"Behind the manager's back, so to speak?"

97

"Preferably."

Loredana punched a number on her phone. "You had better be right about this, Mercury. I would rather not be unemployed."

I snorted. "I always assumed we'd work for Procyon until we died. They don't seem to have a retirement package."

"That is what I was insinuating."

The idea of slipping into the restricted Historic Vault became a lot less exciting, right then.

Like most departments at Procyon, the Historic Vault was named with practicality in mind. Other than the name, it was anything but. The vault was in the basement of Tower Three, unmarked on any map and certainly not listed on plans. As far as San Camillo's planning commission knew, and the city building inspector had been allowed to see, the basement was reinforced against quakes. Like the other towers, it incorporated water-filled spaces to help with sway.

One of those spaces in Tower Three, however, wasn't filled with water, but irreplaceable records.

The young lady at the desk reminded me of a track and field gal I'd dated in college. Fit, trim, and capable of going toe to toe with me in a brawl. Granted, I had the pulsar stave's excess energy, so that gave me an edge, but it was obvious she'd been stationed down here as part of security's efforts to safeguard the vault. "You're not authorized to enter, at this time. The manager's instructions."

"Yeah, but you got the call, right?" I smiled. "Ms. Lark's made a special exception."

The woman frowned. "Is that because you're special?"

I spread my arms and shrugged.

She checked the computer screen on the edge of her desk. "I've got her message, so I'll grant you temporary access. Was the manager notified?"

"Absolutely." Not. I walked by her, and punched in my code. Massive steel doors reflected my smiling expression. Decent poker face. Maybe I should start playing.

The keypad flashed green. The doors cracked apart, and rumbled open along tracks set in the floor. First thing that hit me was the enticing musty smell of old paper. Man. I could have stood there in the threshold forever, gazing at the rows upon rows of files. The boxes got older and rattier toward the back. The smell intensified. Fortunately, everything was marked with precision. I followed the labels.

There. 6-1848. It was a leather-bound collection of yellowing papers, sealed inside a plastic container. I frowned. Where was the latch to open it? Maybe there was a lock around the back. I turned the box, one side at the time. Finally. The back edge of the lid had a metallic clasp holding the box shut. The puzzle part? What would open it. I didn't see a keyhole, or a thumbprint scanner. It wasn't big enough to be a retina reader, like the ones I'd seen on the top floors.

Hang on. The clasp had a shallow, circular indent. The metal was cold. Way too cold, even for this climate- controlled vault.

I hefted the pulsar stave. No mistaking the similarity—in temperature, in texture, even in patina. I'm no metallurgist but come on. They looked like the same kind of material.

I pressed it toward the indent.

The stave activated of its own accord. I didn't will it to do anything. Yellow sparks leapt the distance to the clasp and yanked the stave from my hand. It collided with the clasp, a sharp ring that sank deep into my ears. The box lid snapped back. The stave stayed lodged against the indent.

That was … interesting.

Each of the shelves had a box of gloves. I slipped a pair on, glancing back toward the entrance. Footsteps, yes, but nothing hurried. No alarms, either. Win. I opened the folder. Man. Each page was hand-written, in such a flowing cursive script I had to strain to decipher the words.

The reader of this volume must consider the times ahead. Whatever has transpired has been for a reason. We as a people are predestined to bring light into darkness. Where the pulsar stave rests, it draws the enemy to us, while simultaneously giving hope for a future free of temporal evil. But would the Lord guide us in our fight. When the first of the enemy appeared in our midst, we knew the Icon must be warned and sent away …

Wait a second. They *had* the Icon? I checked the date. June 1848. Are you kidding?

"Son, you must have a hearing problem."

A beefy hand slammed the lid shut. Jack Jackson shook his head. A pair of burly guys flanked him. Even if they didn't have white lettering that said, "Procyon Security" on their shirts, the black polos and black slacks would have been dead giveaways.

Loredana stood at distance, outside the vault doors. She could have been carved from stone—stone wearing a smart blouse and skirt. That was the Loredana I knew. She didn't look at me.

"You and I," Jackson said, "Are gonna have words."

Great.

CHAPTER THIRTEEN

The Bennetts were the last foster family I got stuck with. Nice enough couple, I guess, if "nice enough" meant an alcoholic father who cheated on his wife and a trio of surly kids age middle through high school who were adept at keeping their mischief secret from their parents. They didn't slap me around, and kept me fed, sheltered, and clothed. But I might as well have been a hotel guest for the lack of affection they doled out. Five seconds after I turned eighteen, I flipped them the bird and walked out.

Before that day, I was always butting heads with Daddy Bennett. He was no different than the other "parents" I'd accumulated in the decade and a half before. His rules were his rules; you argued, and you paid the price.

So, by the time I stood there in the Procyon manager's office and let Jack Jackson verbally tear me a new one, I'd run out of concern.

"What did I tell you, son? Off. Limits." He slapped his desk to punctuate those last two words. "What'd I say about the consequences?"

"There would be a heap of them," I muttered.

"Dang right! You're fussing around with things beyond your pay grade. Everyone here's got to fit into their role. Don't get me wrong, now, you're the finest operative we've had in, well, danged if I know how long. Your string of kills has exceeded any records I'm privy to."

"Probably because there's been an uptick in fiend incursions. Any guesses as to why that is?"

Jackson shrugged. "Winston tells me its cyclical."

"Apparently. Wouldn't it be nice to know for sure?" I sat on the edge of his desk. "That's all I was trying to do: Get some answers. If I had to dig around in Procyon's past, so be it. Don't you want to know why we're getting slammed all of a sudden?"

Jackson shook his head. "That's not my goal. See, everyone's got to have goals, Mercury. Mine's keeping Procyon outta hot water. Physical security and fiscal solvency. Those are key to our survival. Ms. Lark, tell me you're on the same page here."

Loredana stood at attention in the center of the room, several steps removed from our confrontation. I could argue all day long with an authority figure, didn't much matter who. She knew that. But I felt bad she was in the same hot water. Someone of her stature within Procyon was taking a great risk by making the call to get me into the Historic Vault. It hadn't paid off for her.

"I believe Mercury's concerns are warranted." Loredana spoke each word with deliberate inflection. She could have been cast in one of those PBS specials set in the Victorian era. What? My tastes are diverse. "While I am familiar with the cyclical nature, as you put it, of the astral fiend incursions, and have seen the data Winston furnished, there is more to this recent spate of attacks than I think Tracking and Forecasting have determined. The assault on Mercury's apartment—the dual appearance—the last-minute rip that opened in a public area—all three are peculiar in and of themselves. When aggregated, I fail to see how you and the board of directors are not more concerned."

Wow. I smothered a grin. Nice speech, but anybody who knew Loredana could tell she'd called Jackson an idiot.

Jackson was one of those in the know, it seemed, because red crept up his neck. "I'll take that into consideration, Ms. Lark, but I won't be bullied into lifting security protocols because y'all got a vague feeling about spooky things going on. If you're worried, get Winston and his boys tracking better. That's what they're paid for. I don't want anyone snooping into the vault again, 'til this mess is sorted out. Understood?"

We nodded in unison.

"Good. Speaking of mess, you made quite a splash on the YouTube last night."

The YouTube? "Ah, yeah, I don't think we're in danger there. Most of the comments were from guys labeling it 'fake news' and getting into flame wars against the few true believers. The ones who don't think I was auditioning for the next Star Wars blockbuster."

"Tougher to sell police intervention, isn't it?"

"Ramos has a good cover in place."

"Such as...?"

"I'm not in on the details." Mostly true, because I hadn't bothered to call him. "He'll sell it to the press as pursuit of a dangerous subject or something good."

"He'd better. Any luck finding that phone caller?"

I hesitated. "Why do you ask?"

"Why do I ... Son, she's the one got you running around like a half-baked spy!" Jackson poured a shot of whiskey. He offered me the bottle, but I shook my head. "This woman's out there in the wild, spouting off misinformation about our organization and you two don't seem a danged bit concerned about what she could do to us? I want her name, so we can ask her some questions."

"Right. Look, Jack, maybe I could try to contact her." I didn't really want my boss knowing I'd had an in-depth conversation with Wilhelmina, but then again, bringing her in might shield her from a second attack by astral fiends.

"You can do better than try," Jackson said. "I understand you've already made contact. She tell you anything interesting? She the one who pushed you in this direction?"

"I …" Wait. He knew? I glanced at Loredana. She was doing her best to examine the far wall, without meeting my inquiring stare.

"Her name is Wilhelmina," Loredana said. "Age indeterminate. She's a vagrant living on the waterfront. The police are aware of her and keeping track of her whereabouts in order to prevent a second attempt on her life."

Jackson grunted. "Attempt?"

"It seems she was attacked by an astral fiend at the same time Mercury was in an abandoned warehouse in the industrial district."

"Ah, right. The twofer." Jackson grinned. "Well, that's just dandy. Go on, then, get security to invite this dear old lady to our offices for a chat. We've got to find out what she knows."

"Hang on. You can't snatch a homeless lady off the street for questioning." I planted myself between Jackson and Loredana, with my back to her. What was she doing? I thought we were in this together. "We're not the police."

Jackson slapped my shoulder. "Son, we're not going to keep people from destroying Procyon by yapping about our secrets all over town if we leave it to the police and play nice. This is a war, if you haven't noticed. Besides, she needs protection, right? You two get out of here and make it happen."

I'd stormed to the door and flung it open when Jackson called out, "That reminds me—consequences. Gonna have to skip a paycheck this month, and your access privileges have been downgraded. Check in with Calvin about a new badge."

I sighed. "I thought for a minute you'd take the pulsar stave and smack me with it."

Jackson smirked. "Like I said, you're the best operative we have. That makes you my finest weapon—and with this lady causing trouble, I want all my weapons sharp. What I don't want is my weapon being used to pick a lock on a secure file's container, you read me?"

"Yes sir, roger and wilco." I waited a moment for Loredana, but she subtly shook her head. Fine. No denying I was angry with her. She walked away, toward Jackson's desk.

"Please close the door." Calvin was banging away on his keyboard, not even looking at me.

I slammed the door hard enough to rattle the hinges. That got Calvin to make a face, like he'd had something sour poured in his mug. It was steaming, so I assumed it wasn't whiskey. "The manager says you've got a present for me."

"Funny thing to call a demotion." He tossed me a security clearance card.

"Not a demotion. Consequences." The new card had a yellow stripe, instead of green. My same grinning face, but with the word "Probationary" stamped in red underneath.

"You're blocked from sensitive areas of Procyon, with the exception of the seventh floor of Tower Three, and the rooms vital to your operations status." Calvin could have been reading the financial news off the *Bayside Breeze* website. "You retain access to all buildings, and the gym."

"Wonderful."

"Your status is similar to that of non-sensitive Procyon employees. Don't try getting into places you shouldn't."

"Non-sensitive. Don't you mean insensitive?" I grinned.

"No, I mean non-sensitive." Calvin resumed typing. "The changes to your status have been logged with security. Try not to screw anything else up. I've lost an hour of productivity dealing with your mess."

"Should've gotten a non-sensitive janitor for that," I muttered as I left.

I needed to blow off steam. Badly.

Tower Two had a gym that took up most of the fourth floor. Sunlight poured in from all curves, and when I got there, a handful of employees were cycling away, earbuds in place, facing toward the shining sapphire of the bay. There were a ton of spaces dedicated to weights, treadmills, and all sorts of machines meant to contort the human body for maximum fitness.

My room was in the middle.

A large, windowless cylinder took up the center of the gym. I palmed the access panel. Motion-sensitive lights blinked on. Sparring pads were piled along one side. A few dummies and punching bags were also interspersed. But I had eyes only for the beast in the middle.

It was an animatronic device meant to mimic an astral fiend.

I stripped into a pair of shorts and a T-shirt, switching my dress shoes for sneakers, and set my phone on a micro fridge by the door. A few swipes and taps, and the training program started up.

The fake monster rumbled on gimbals hidden in the floor. It slapped a pair of heavy foam tentacles my way.

I ducked and slid underneath, the pulsar stave flaring to life. Those tentacles were fake, yeah, but they'd still leave a brutal bruise. I batted them aside, taking care to keep the stave's energy levels low. Learned that the hard way during my first few sessions. Procyon wasn't keen on rebuilding this thing.

I'd worked up a good sweat and was chugging from a bottle of ice-cold water when the door popped open. No chance of a random Procyon employee stumbling onto my fight room. Few others had access.

"We need to discuss what happened," Loredana said.

"Oh yeah?" I dodged a tentacle strike. "Which part? The one where our manager forbid me from doing my job, or the one where you stood there and let him?"

"Your job is *not* to sneak into the vault and rifle through restricted files."

"Funny, you were keen on helping me do just that."

"I was not keen. You made good points, but as soon as I understood how adamant the manager was that we not pursue that avenue, a course correction was necessary."

"Whatever, Loredana. I get it." I bashed three tentacles away, one after the other, and stabbed the stave deep into the ersatz monster's middle. The sparring program registered that as a win and shut down the animatronic arms. "You were looking out for your job."

Loredana folded her arms. "I was looking out for both our jobs. Getting yourself removed from field action will not help our cause."

"Yeah, well, I'm going to sit back and take a day off because Jackson's hiding something." I tapped the stave against the micro fridge. "And you know he is. He's willing to roll out and grab up Wilhelmina, bring her in for 'questioning.' How do we even do that? Procyon's public face is that of a non-profit developmental organization. Is there a line in the budget for black SUVs with tinted windows? Love to see him explain that to the IRS."

Loredana shook her head. "You're not listening, but I've come to expect nothing less, Mercury. Whatever his reasons, I'm sure he has the best for the organization in mind. Don't forget, he too has to answer to the board of directors. The manager never operates in a vacuum. The best we can do for now is be present when Wilhelmina is brought in. If you'd like, I can contact Lieutenant Ramos and advise him of the situation."

"Are you kidding? This is some serious extra-legal junk Procyon's about to step into. I don't want to be anywhere near it, and I sure don't want Ramos getting his shoes dirty." I scowled. "I need to find out what she's talking about."

I started for the door, but Loredana blocked my way. "What did you learn?"

"That you're a pain. Move, please."

"I mean, in the vault."

I scratched the back of my neck. "There wasn't time to read a bunch, not with Jackson and his goons breathing on me. Literally."

"Don't lie to me. You saw something. It was evident by the expression on your face." She smirked. "Or should I pull up the security footage from the vault's entrance?"

I grimaced. So much for my brief fantasy life as a world-renowned poker player. "The page I skimmed was hand-written by someone who knew a lot about how Procyon started. Whoever it was talked of danger, dark and light and all that jazz, but also said the Icon had to be both warned and sent away."

Loredana's eyes widened. "Sent away?"

"Yeah. As in, it sounds like someone already had it."

"I see."

"That's nice, because I don't. Why would Procyon's founders send the Icon away if it was needed to stop astral fiends from coming into our world?"

"Perhaps they were keeping it safe from an enemy who wanted to use it for nefarious purposes."

"Nefarious. Sounds like fun." I crumpled up the empty water bottle and chucked it into a recycling bin. "Look, Loredana, I'm all about fighting the good fight, but when I don't know the why, it makes it harder to reconcile."

"It's never been a problem for you."

"Different day." I reached for the door handle.

Loredana grabbed my wrist. Pretty iron grip, she had there. "Don't do anything foolish. If we are going to determine the truth, as Wilhelmina suggested, we will need to play strategically."

"Easy for you to say, when you can brown nose and then pretend you're my ally." I broke free.

She swept her foot under my ankles and knocked me to the floor with a blow to my chest.

My reflexes kept me from collapsing all the way. I rolled and dropped her with a side kick to her hips. Loredana crashed against the recycling bin, spilling its contents. She picked it up, and with a whirl, bashed it against my head.

Or would have, if I hadn't blocked the cheap shot with my forearm. I threw it across the room. It banged off the inert training monster. I grabbed Loredana's shoulder and shoved her against the wall, pulsar stave ready in the other hand.

She smiled. "Good. You still have fight left."

"Are you insane?" I backed away, appalled not only that she'd goaded me into a brawl but that it had worked. "Of course I've got fight. That's all you people want me for!"

"Use that. Channel it into solving this conundrum." Loredana fixed her hair and straightened her blouse. "I will assist where I can, but in my way, and I'll not have you question my methods."

"Keep Wilhelmina out of this, and maybe I'll trust those words."

"I can't promise she stays completely removed, but I will keep her from harm."

She walked out, as if we hadn't just tried to beat each other up. I wiped sweat from my forehead.

At this rate, I was looking forward to a few days off.

CHAPTER FOURTEEN

Two more days went by without any major or even minor crises. I tooled around San Camillo, buying replacements for my stuff that had been destroyed by the astral fiend. Except for the *Cowboy Bebop* poster. Turns out it was backordered, and it wasn't due in for a week and a half.

I also vented as much frustration as possible in my private gym at Procyon. Sure, it would have been easier to stay in my loft, but it was a tight fit. Besides, I didn't want to risk breaking anything else with the pulsar stave when the sparring dummies could absorb way more punishment.

Friday rolled around before I heard from Ramos.

"They're calling you Nightstick."

I snorted soda so bad it burned my throat. "Wow. That's a terrible thing to call your consultant, Lieutenant."

"I did not make it up. Get on YouTube."

Yeah, I'd been avoiding that. Last I checked after my fight with Loredana, there were two videos circulating the good old world wide web. I grabbed my laptop computer from the kitchen counter and browsed. "Uh-oh."

"That's about what I said, only with a handful of words

you'd have to translate." Ramos sighed into the phone. "Six, Mercury. Six independently posted videos, all of which are steadily gaining viewers."

"Going viral? Nice." Had to admit. Those kids who may or may not have been illicitly imbibing did a nice job. Very little shaky cam syndrome. You still couldn't make out the astral fiend, except for intermittent purple glows and slippery shadows, but there were a couple good shots of yours truly. Not my face, thankfully, but I had some slick moves.

"No, not nice. Not nice at all."

"Okay, I'll bite, Señor Cranky—what's the nightstick bit? Isn't that like a billy club or a baton? Cop tool."

"Exactly like that. Check the most recent post."

"Ah. Got it." I rolled my eyes. "Really? I'm not a superhero. That's just stupid."

"Your average Millennial doesn't know that."

"Hey, what'd I say about the M-word?"

"You are one."

"Only technically. I'm not running a job serving up lattes while I'm living in my mom's basement." Even without known parentage, the idea sounded terrible. Maybe because my list of foster moms didn't include any Parent of the Year award winners. "Whatever, Ramos. I'm not putting on a paintball helmet and smacking local thugs like that wannabe out in Drake City."

"Rumor has it he can fly."

"Sure."

"You're awfully quick to discount the miraculous for someone who slays monsters from hell."

"They're not from hell. It's another dimension."

"That all depends on your perspective. I called because you need to continue to lay low."

"Thanks for the advice." Something else bothered me, though. "Say, you seen Wilhelmina around?"

"Funny you should ask," he muttered. "She slipped the detail watching over her. One night she's in her regular encampment, the next morning, *poof.*"

I scowled. "That's what I was afraid of. Who grabbed her?"

"Grabbed? I'm guessing she finally got smart and left the drug neighborhood for safer environs. Why'd you assumed she was grabbed?"

"No reason."

"Mercury ..."

"Let's not worry about random things I may or may not have just said and get back to the part where I'm a popular download."

"Let's focus on how you're going to stay at your new loft on 25th Street, going only to and from Procyon and whatever errands you might have planned, because I've got enough on my plate what with Internal Affairs bothering me."

"Oh? IA didn't like your impromptu fireworks display? My ears are still ringing. I'm planning a donation to the American Tinnitus Association."

"The who?"

"*Archer* reference."

Another sigh.

"Hey, wait a minute," I said. "You found my apartment? I'm not in the phone book. And Google's never caught up to me, because I always rent."

"Please. You know how many years I was a detective working Homicide? I can find you."

Super. "I'd better check in with my bosses, see how they're handling my newfound social media celebrity status."

"Here's hoping they have a better sense of humor about it

than you do. Seriously, Mercury, do not leave town. And I do mean city limits, at least until this blows over."

"Yes, I get it, I'll be a good boy. Maybe I'll even eat my vegetables."

He hung up. I couldn't help smiling. Ramos took everything so seriously.

And speaking of serious, I texted Loredana. <Hey. What's the news on Wilhelmina?>

I closed down the laptop and dug out cold pizza from the fridge. Mushroom and black olive, from Carlito's. Nice and greasy two days later.

<Not a pleasant subject. Procyon has been unable to locate. Manager displeased. Offered me whiskey at 8:30.>

Guy was going to pickle his liver long before old age was ever an issue. <That sucks.> Sort of. I didn't want them locking Wilhelmina up, or even questioning her. This was my matter to handle. Of course, I'd been avoiding it for days. Why? Another good question, right there.

<Indeed. I have the next assignment. Sending details secure to your Procyon email address. Be careful.>

That was touching. <Worse than usual?>

<The vision is dim, as I understand. Distant from San Camillo.>

<I'll watch my back. Always do.>

<Will see you at the briefing.>

Hmm. Unclear vision. That was bad, yeah, but it didn't mean we had to scrub the assignment. It just meant Marigold couldn't give me details about the astral fiend I might face.

The "distant from San Camillo" part, though, could be a problem.

I plugged a flash drive into my laptop and let the encryption software log into my Procyon email. Supposed to be super secure. The stuff they sent to me wasn't what you wanted a hacker to get his hands on.

Loredana had attached a screenshot of a map to the email. Arbor Valley, out northeast of the city on the 311. Looked like Tracking determined the Icon was going to show up in an abandoned farm house, one of those big stone haciendas popular back in the Prohibition days.

A quick scan through the online property databases for the county confirmed it was purchased by an out of state owner years ago. The map image was blurry when magnified real close, but it was clear enough to show the road up the hill was overgrown and crumbling.

Bad news. It was eleven miles beyond the city limits.

Winston highlighted the data for me. "Case Four Oh Six Oh Nine Nine Twenty-One. Arbor Valley, is it? Quite lovely this time of year. You know, Mari and I have considered selling the condo and getting a house out there."

"That's great. Could we play house-hunting later? Like, after I slice and dice?"

"What say we postpone it after reeling in the Icon."

"Ah." I leaned against his monitors. "Better shot this time?"

Winston gently but firmly pushed me away. He brushed off the corner of the screen. "Ahem. Perhaps. Tachyon emissions are rated at nine point eight nine."

"Really?"

"Absolutely. The recalibrated scanners confirmed it. This is going to be one of the most potent collisions between our two dimensions in … well, I'd have to draw upon our archives to be certain, but decades before either of us were born."

Part of me wondered if we could find a definite answer in the Historic Vault, specifically File 6-1848. The other part wanted to blast down six levels and over into the adjoining basement to read that stupid file. "That'll be interesting."

"See what Mari has to say about it."

"Yep, time to sign off."

"I'll send a couple drones to shadow you, as per protocol."

"Yeah." I tapped the pulsar stave against the palm of my hand. "Look, uh, about that. Could you copy me with the data from the drones? Live, I mean."

Winston swayed his index finger to the soothing rhythm bleeding from his speakers. "Hmm. Why, yes, I could certainly provide that. Linked to your phone, I presume?"

"Yeah. That'd be helpful. In the fight." Also in giving me a close-up view of what's going on with the rip. "Whatever the rip is doing these days, you've said it yourself—it's stronger. Maybe there's something I can see when the tachyon levels spike, and we can match readings with personal observation."

"I do like the way you're thinking, my friend." Winston smiled. "Very well. Gary? Be a sport and task Drones Four and Five to follow Mister Hale on his nightly outing."

"Thanks, man." I rapped the table.

"Whatever you need, mate, I'll get it." Winston leaned in. "I've heard rumors. You got yourself in quite the mess with the manager. Lost a few benefits."

"Good thing I don't spend all my money at once."

"I meant security clearances."

"Well, not the important ones."

"Mercury, the point is, I can help with whatever it is you're considering. You need only say the word."

I offered my hand. "I figured. But it's nice to hear it. Go, team."

"Go team is right."

My brief time with Marigold was identical to the last. Any miraculous insight I was hoping for didn't happen. So, I signed the form, readied myself for the night's fight, and drove off to the edge of town. Loredana was nowhere to be found.

I scowled over the steering wheel at the dashboard lights. She was probably courting more donors. No, check that. She wanted to help, and her way of helping was sticking near to the manager and pretending everything was perfect.

That wouldn't do me any good.

Okay. Deep breaths. I was going to have to trust her. Maybe we could bring Winston in on this covert work of ours—and by extension, Marigold. Hey, having someone who could dream the arrival of alien monsters should be useful for other aspects, right?

It was 11:30 when my headlights illuminated the ruined hacienda. The only thing I could remember about its origins was a note in the county records speculating it was built in the mid-1700s. Greenery had overgrown everything, creeping through broken windows, concealing slumped walls. I entered through the massive vestibule, letting my phone light up a gaping space that reached up to a sinuous balcony.

"Drones will be in place in three minutes," Winston said through my earbuds. "Please be advised Drone Four picked up traffic in your area. Probably cars out for a late dinner."

"That Polish joint opened up a few miles from here." I followed the coordinates specified on my phone. "How's the rip looking?"

"Six minutes, forty-three seconds from formation."

Right. I found a comfy patch of moss creeping over a heap

of collapsed stone. Gave me a nice overlook with a wide-open hallway spreading into the dark. The ceiling was long gone. There was little light pollution up in these hills. The night air had a crisp quality to it.

"Ah, Mercury?"

I'd started in on a new Green Day track. "Winston, you know I like to chill during this last stretch."

"Far be it for me to break with tradition, but one of those vehicles turned off onto the property. Drone Five is tracking it up the drive and it's stopped behind your car."

"What?" That's bad. Last thing I needed, with the rip less than five minutes from releasing an astral fiend, was a couple of teens looking for a dark place to score. "Hang on. I'll check it out. Send the drones over the tachyon point."

"Aye, sir. IR confirms one individual."

Well, so much for the horny teens.

I snuck around the side of the house, back to the walls. Ivy brushed at my face. I kept the stave powered down but at the ready. Even without my will connected through our touch, it'll make a stout baton with which to beat someone down. Not that I'm planning said beatdown. Maybe I can warn them off.

Maybe I can call myself Nightstick, like on YouTube. I snorted. Nah. They'd want a selfie.

I hadn't got to the corner before I heard the shoes crunch on gravel. So much for a stealth approach. "Hey!" I shouted. "Better stay put and turn on a flashlight. You're trespassing."

The blue-white LED blasted me in the face. "Put your hands where I can see them."

"Put my … Ow!" I blinked away the bright patches. "Not a tourist?"

"Mercury?" The light flicked off. "We need to talk."

"Ramos." I groaned. "This is a really bad idea."

My phone buzzed in my hand.
Two minutes left.

# CHAPTER FIFTEEN

Ramos held a semi-automatic rifle at the ready. The flashlight was mounted below the barrel. So that's what blinded me. "I told you to stay within city limits!" he snapped. "Are you really that stupid?"

"I didn't have a choice." I rubbed at my eyes as I walked back into the house. Time was ticking away, and if the rip was going to open soon, I'd better put myself between it and Ramos. Speaking of him ... "You need to get out of here."

"As soon as you get in your car and I drag you downtown."

"For what?"

"Wilhelmina."

I was really hoping he hadn't found her body discarded somewhere. The image made me sick. "I haven't seen her in a while. We've been over this."

"Yes, we have, but I've got some questions about the people who have seen her. Specifically, the two silver sedans with tinted windows that were dropping people off all along Court Street. They were hitting up every dealer and prostitute they came across, doling out cash, asking about her."

"When?"

"Most of this evening. As soon as Patrol let me know, I swung by your apartment."

I gestured at his gun. "Did you bring that to my apartment?"

"I figured you'd be in some kind of mess. So, tell me, who's looking for Wilhelmina?

Winston's voice was tinny in my earbud. "Mercury, to whom are you speaking?"

I muted the pick-up. Ramos showed no signs of relenting. Fine. He was only worried about keeping people safe, Wilhelmina included. "I think Procyon is."

"Why?"

"Something about what she told me. She knows, Ramos. About what I do. For real. She's read in, just like you are, except nobody at Procyon has a clue who she is—or if they do, they're not telling."

Ramos appeared to mull that over. "The people out looking for her—they were led by a skinny black guy, well-dressed. Couldn't get an ID on him, but my detectives are on it. Are you sure it was Procyon? The cars were unmarked."

"If I were doing something shady from a legal standpoint, I wouldn't slap a logo on my ride."

"Fair point." Ramos grimaced. "All right, let's go."

"Okay, I so do not have time for this." I tapped my earbud. "Winston, how're we looking?"

"Tachyon emissions are through the roof."

"Yeah, I can tell that." The bar graph on my phone was spiking. I could feel the rip as it gathered energy, that sensation of a coming storm. Wind whipped around the house, making timbers groan and loose plaster flake off walls. The floor trembled.

Ramos had his weapon up, finger off the trigger. The light cut a brilliant beam through swirling dust. "Is it one of them?"

"Of course it is! What, you thought I was hanging out in an abandoned house and violating your demand to stay in town because I wanted some solo time with my playlist?" I willed the pulsar stave to live. It buzzed in my hands. The power jolted me, sharper and colder than usual. Whether it was my imagination or linked to the tremendous energy building around the nascent rip was for Winston and his crew to determine.

"Mercury, the tachyon leak is accelerating!" Winston said. "You have mere seconds. If there is someone else there, get them clear! You know the rules on civilian involvement."

"I'd love to get rid of this civilian, but since he's a police lieutenant, he doesn't have much incentive to listen to me!"

"Civilian?" Ramos scowled. "Who is that you're on the line with?"

"Your undertaker," I muttered. "Seriously, Ramos, unless you clear out in about thirty seconds, you're going to be seeing your department shrink real soon. Assuming you're alive."

"Mercury, put down your weapon and come with me. I'm taking you in."

I blew out a breath. "Fine, don't listen."

The rip exploded into view, without the buildup of purple sparks. Instead, huge bolts of violet shot out, busting holes in the walls, and knocking out the few remaining window panes. I shoved Ramos to the floor. The heat singed my back.

The astral fiends charged from the rip.

Yeah, that's right. *Fiends*. Plural. Not double vision. They were bigger than the one I'd faced at the Promenade, by about a third each, and there was no sluggishness like the one in the warehouse. We didn't have reports on whether they aged. Nobody'd ever let one live in our dimension long enough to find out. But if the one I'd faced was a young kid, these two were angry, hormone-fueled, greasy, zit-covered teens.

Their screeches rattled my teeth.

Ramos was on his knees, staring.

"If you're gonna stay, contribute!" I shouted as I ran toward them. Yes, towards. Sigh. Right about then I wanted to go the opposite direction, trust me.

But there was also a madness to the job. The same madness that made me grin while my brain's saying, "Okay, get out of there!"

They saw me and converged, tentacles cracking through the air, teeth flashing. I dove between them, sliding along their sides. Their rampage got them tangled up. Morons. It gave me the opening to slice through their hides with both halves of the stave. Jackpot.

Blue ooze sprayed. They caterwauled so badly it set my ears ringing, and I seriously considered donating to the ATA.

More surprising was the one inverting to counter attack. I landed, pivoted, and chopped off the incoming tentacle.

But the second one—kinda forgot about him.

His tentacle looped around my ankle. Bitter, painful cold sliced through my leg, clawing into my chest. The one in my apartment that had tried to drain my life felt like a tickle compared to his. This fiend, though, was more enraged than hungry, because it flung me across the room.

The sensation of flight was remarkable. I've had dreams, you know. Never able to get very far off the ground, and even when I do, I drift down, like a dropped feather. A curious, sedate part of my mind wondered if this is what Drake City's rumored superhero experienced.

Right before I slammed back-first into a wall.

That should have killed or at least crippled me. A bonus of wielding the pulsar stave was that all the energy bleed-off strengthened me. Hence the choke and throw of the thug hanging around my car. Instead of paralysis, I'd get a terrible backache and a matching bruise.

The fiends bellowed a challenge and swarmed toward me. Well, that sucked.

Gunfire crackled, like thunder up close and personal. Ramos yelled something, the words drowned under the three-round bursts he let loose. It must have perplexed the fiends, because they stopped in their tracks, flailing tentacles every which way. Definitely a different effect than when Ramos's cops had shot up the one by the Promenade. I'm no weapons expert, but that M4 was doing a lot better job holding them at bay than a 9 mm pistol.

Sadly, the advantage didn't last long.

The fiends collided and stretched out, like someone was pulling a giant rubber band, then launched themselves at Ramos.

He kept firing. Wasn't slowing them in this weird, conjoined attack mode.

But I had my feet back under me, and they were pounding across the floor, fast enough for me to mount a pile of rubble and throw myself atop the fiends. There was no way to stop both with the stave, not with it split apart, so I slammed it back together into its single, most formidable configuration and jacked up the energy. The white-yellow light soaked me with heat, helping to banish the last of the frostbite from the fiend's tentacle grip.

I stabbed it deep into Bachelor Number One, also known as the beast who tossed me.

My attack interrupted their momentum. They veered off course, my victim screaming, and his buddy realizing I was a more dangerous target than the prone but still-shooting

Ramos. We tumbled in a mess of blue ooze, two slimy fiends, and one battered human.

Bachelor Number One was done, limp as wet spaghetti.

Bachelor Number Two roared in what I was pretty sure was rage. Fear swept over me, because I'd never heard something so primal, something that promised me a long, painful death.

Ramos stopped firing. He swore, softly, and I could hear a clicking noise. Reloading, I hoped.

The surviving fiend didn't stab at me. Instead, he jabbed all his remaining tentacles—because I'd lopped off one or two; kinda lost count—into his dead buddy.

Bachelor Number One, instead of continuing his decomposition, glowed a dull blue, a hue that brightened and then faded to purple. Then, like water rolling across a countertop, he sublimated into the survivor's body, until there was nothing left but a sticky outline on the floor.

Bachelor Number Two rumbled, and he sounded oddly content. Like the world's biggest, happiest, and deadliest cat.

Then he doubled in size.

"Mercury!" Really? I don't know what was more surprising, than my earbud was still lodged in my ear, or that it still worked. "Good heavens! Have you seen the rate of particle decay? What's happening there? Drone Four shows the creatures—merged!"

"Yeah, that's what happening." I propped myself up on the stave. Bachelor Number Two swayed, like he was drunk. To be fair, so did I. Ow.

"Kill it!" Ramos shouted.

"Working on it." Doing this alone was much less of a pain.

The fiend lashed out with a tentacle—but not at me, or Ramos. I saw a burst of sparks overhead. Plastic pieces rained down.

"What the devil?" Winston snapped. "He destroyed Drone Four!"

Huh. Okay, that was new.

The fiend barreled away, gaining speed as it pulled itself along. It trailed purple lightning—because the sparks emanating from the still open, pulsing rip were tethered to it.

I staggered over to Ramos, but at a rapid stagger. My strength was rebuilding. Before we reached the front door, we were at a full-out sprint. You know, for a slightly-flabby guy in his mid-forties, Ramos could haul if he wanted. We were both sweating and stank like we'd walked out of the gym.

"Where is it going?"

"I don't know. This isn't normal."

Ramos glared at the fiend's backside. It had stopped outside the front steps, tentacles wavering. "Nothing about this is normal." His hand ducked into his collar, and pulled forth a gold cross, Jesus nailed to the front and everything. He kissed it.

Didn't blame him.

Suddenly, the fiend turned to face us, eerie and hazy purple. It seemed to be examining us, yet it made no move to attack.

"You give me covering fire." I flexed my grip on the pulsar stave, letting its power soak my cells.

"What are you going to do?"

"Charge. Like usual. I'm not used to having backup, so this will be a nice change."

Ramos sighted on the fiend. "Ready. Any tips?"

"Yeah. The eyeballs are squishier than the hide." I took a step forward.

The fiend whipped out a pair of tentacles, these longer and coated with double the normal jagged spikes and slashed my car in half.

Upholstery spilled out, followed by broken glass and tattered leather. The fiend picked up both halves, spun itself, and threw the two pieces of what used to be a perfectly nice ride forty feet—in opposite directions.

Ramos didn't wait for my signal. He opened fire.

The fiend winced, and screamed, but didn't seem nearly as bothered as it was during the initial fight. It turned away from us and leapt down the road. Instead of sticking a landing, it alighted on—well, the air, about four feet off the asphalt. Purple sparks burst from underneath, and it kept, I don't know, spark-hopping down the 311.

Or I should say up.

"It's not heading to the city." Ramos sounded relieved.

"No, but there's a really nice, new restaurant up the road that serves a mean pierogi, and unless you want to see the entire Polish-American population of San Camillo drained of their lives, we'd better get moving." I ran for his car. My mind focused on how to kill a spark-hopping super-fiend, because if I didn't, we could all die, and also, I'd have to start thinking about how to explain this to my insurance provider. And how much it would cost to tow the halves of my car. "Come on."

Ramos slipped into the driver's seat. He gunned the engine and stowed his rifle. "Seatbelt."

He said before he realized I wasn't next to him but crouched on the roof. I stabbed a hole through the roof with the pulsar stave.

"No thanks," I growled. "I'm getting off at the next stop."

CHAPTER SIXTEEN

Ramos floored it.

The Charger's tires spit dirt and gravel as it roared up the 311. Next thing I knew, he had the emergency lights blaring and the sirens going. That was fun. I about fell off the roof of the car.

"Hey!" I stomped over top his head. "Way to deafen a guy! He's not going to pull over for you!"

"It's for bystanders, idiot, not the monster!" Ramos shouted. "How is he doing that, anyway?"

The astral fiend continued its spark-hopping, for lack of a better term, never once veering off to swing in for an attack. I kept bracing myself—mentally, I mean, because physically I was expending most of my effort clinging to the top of Ramos's car.

But man, was it fun.

"The tachyon pulses are showing a very peculiar pattern," Winston said in my earbud. "If you follow their rate of progress, I shan't be surprised if they formed a structure not dissimilar to a rip, except stretched along the path the fiend is taking."

"That's amazing. Any thoughts on how to stop it?"

"Haven't the foggiest, my friend."

"Some help!"

"I have tasked Drone Five to continue on standby above your route, but I doubt she'll be able to lend anything more than the readings being transmitted to your phone. I would recommend engaging the creature as soon as is feasible."

I hung onto the stave and peered alongside Ramos's window for a peek at the speedometer. "We're doing eighty, and it's not slowing!"

"Good luck, then."

Great. So much for tactical support from home base. We were gonna stick with my original plan: catch up and stab.

Eighty turned out to be adequate for my purposes. Either we approached the astral fiend's top speed, or it was losing steam. I wasn't going to overanalyze. Downside? It finally decided we were a threat again.

It pulled the inversion trick, but I was ready when it abruptly reversed its body, even as it hurtled from invisible stepping stone to stepping stone. Two tentacles shot out, reaching three car lengths. I broke the pulsar stave apart and pushed off the Charger's roof. One tentacle battered the hood, then the spot I'd vacated, slapping around the half of the stave still embedded. I slashed the offending appendage clean off, then landed back on the roof.

The creature shrieked, and increased the ferocity of its attack, but it didn't slow its progress. Whatever was drawing it away from us was doing a great job.

I dueled with the other appendages as they took turns trying to cut me to bits. Most blows I had to parry, not even thinking about cutting them, because if I took a second to formulate an attack, one or the other would latch on and I'd be a cold popsicle of a corpse.

More gunfire, this time not as loud. Thank goodness, because that ringing in my ears was steadily fading. Ramos had his window rolled down and was letting the astral fiend try 9 mm rounds from his Glock on for size.

The fiend whipped a tentacle around, bashing into the driver's side door. The Charger shimmied and swerved. I let the stave reconnect and held on because I didn't want to get impaled on one of the many trees that made up black and green blurs along the side of the road.

"You're losing time." Winston's patience grated on the my very raw, exposed nerves. "The restaurant is seven miles from the hacienda. At your current rate of speed, you'll reach it in less than three minutes."

"Thanks, Bill Nye!"

"Mercury, what in the world does the Science Guy have to do with this?"

"Because—math! Shut up and give me good news!" I beat back an intruding tentacle, then split it down the middle like a carved watermelon. Blue ooze splattered all over my shirt and pants.

"The pulses supporting the astral fiend are peaking. It's going to stop its infernal leaping—"

Purple flashes exploded into a ring of light that grabbed the fiend and flung it down the road.

"My gracious!" Winston whistled. "That is quite the phenomenon. Good thing we're recording."

"Ramos!" I stomped on the rumpled roof. "Go, go!"

"*¡Ya basta!*" Despite his snippy response, Ramos goosed the Charger for more speed. If I hadn't been busy doing my best to not get splattered on the pavement, I would have been more appreciative of the way that hemi roared up the highway.

Lights twinkled between trees, over a set of hills off to the left. They didn't look that far off. Headlights? No, they were stationary. The restaurant. Wait, headlights *were* coming our way.

The fiend's new purple portal mode of transport was taking it into the opposite lane.

I yanked the stave free and slid down onto the hood.

Ramos honked. The Charger swerved. "Get out of my sight!"

"Can't jump off from way back there!" I batted a tentacle away. Fangs tore open my shirt and cut into my shoulder. Icy cold and searing heat ripped across my skin. "Catch up already!"

I didn't need to gripe. We were only feet from the fiend's body, hence its sudden and furious counterassault. Gotta give Ramos credit: even with a half dozen slime-streaked and fang-laden tentacles threatening to rip his car apart like mine had so unceremoniously been, he kept his ride straight. Straight enough to cut into the opposite lane and get me alongside the fiend.

All the launch point I needed.

I threw myself across the gap, colliding with the monster's clammy hide. The Charger roared even more, slamming the front right corner into the body mere feet below me. Between my frenzied stabbing, and the car's sheer muscle, we forced the fiend into the correct lane.

Two cars hurtled by, wind from their passage whipping my shirt, headlights brightening us into daytime. Their horns reminded us we were in violation of proper driving etiquette.

Yeah. I noticed.

Of more pressing concern—and I do mean literally pressing—was the fact that I was anchored to the fiend's hide like the finest sandworm rider once again. Maud'dib would be proud. And thanks, Frank Herbert. But that meant Bachelor Number Two was dragging me along through his purple-portal slides. My body did not like it. Every time we slipped through one of those sparking rings, I felt like I was shredded, then awoken from a really bad dream. At some muddled point I realized I was screaming, and so was the fiend.

If this ride was going to tear us apart, I might as well make it worth the while.

I hauled off, found the deepest cut I'd already made, and plunged the pulsar stave so deep my arm was buried up to the shoulder in oozing, shuddering fiend innards.

His howl rattled every cell in my body and was matched only by my insane response. We popped through five more of those shredding portals before an explosion of light dropped us into darkness.

The fiend rolled over and over across a very hard surface. I wound up underneath a bunch of times, until we slammed into an unyielding barrier. My head rang like a massive bell at San Camillo's biggest church. I was only barely aware of the astral fiend flailing beside me, and of car tires squealing on pavement.

The shouting woke me all the way up.

We were outside Kaszanka, the Polish restaurant. The giant red and white shield with a crowned eagle was the biggest clue. The place looked like a stucco chalet, an upside-down one, though. I dragged myself up the stone wall surrounding a patio, legs and arms trembling. Toppled chairs and tipped tables littered a wooden deck. Men and women, old and young, dressed to the nines and in casual clothes, screamed as the fiend's tentacles snaked after them.

What? How was he still hungry? After all this, his hide streaked with his slimy blue blood, the fiend's teeth gnashed, and his fangs splintered wood. He found a Hispanic woman, wrapped a tentacle around her, then scooped an older white-haired guy upside down. Their screams subsided as their skin faded, taking on a blue tinge.

"Everyone get clear!" Ramos. How the guy could maintain his cool I have no idea, but there he was, shepherding civilians away from the horror, his M4 rifle trained on the fiend. I assumed he wasn't willing to risk them to take a shot.

Not a concern for me.

I gripped the stave halves and willed them to rejoin. Its power flowed through my limbs, but it wasn't much, and not nearly fast enough. Didn't matter. I had one job.

"Hey!" The fiend turned toward me. Didn't drop its meal, though. "Hungry? Come get some!"

Four tentacles slung for me.

"Shoot those!" I hollered at Ramos and leapt as far as the stave would propel me. Turned out to be ten, twelve feet. I grinned.

Ramos's shots ripped up the incoming tentacles. Meanwhile, I was over them, spinning sideways, and with two swipes, I cut the victims free. They hit the deck pretty hard, but hey, they weren't being drained to death.

I landed on the astral fiend's crude imitation of a face, feet planted on those hideous, bulging eyes. He might not be the brightest creature, but I could feel his malice, his intelligence. Just like staring down an irate bully.

"Show's over." I stabbed deep into the face.

Bolts of yellow-white and purple intermingled. Then the fiend—popped. Like a soap bubble. Blue ooze spattered everywhere in a twenty-foot radius. Even Ramos's poor car got slathered.

I landed on a pile of chairs, gasping.

"Mercury." Ramos knelt beside me, his face dark with ooze. His eyes were wide. "Are you hurt?"

"Oh, probably." I winced. "I mean, yes. Gah."

"Hang on. Ambulances are on their way."

"Yeah, and that means a pile of cops, doesn't it? I gotta get back to the rip."

"We can't abandon the crime scene."

"Crime scene? Are you kidding? Wake up, Ramos. I'm not filing a report with your department on this. Get me back to the rip, and you can turn right around for this place, but I can't miss an Icon."

Ramos stared for a moment. "All right. Let's hurry."

Best idea of the night.

Winston hollered in my ear the entire way. "The tachyon emissions are overloading the sensors on Drone Five! You have to get there!"

"Already inside!" True, I was limping like I'd hiked the Sierra Nevadas, but I was there. And man, the rip was whirling like a miniature hurricane, still large enough to swallow Ramos's car. It flashed, turning white at the center, and then bulged out into a sphere. The rim was transparent, sparking with violet energy.

"Get into position! I think this is it!" Winston yelled.

The Icon. Finally. After three years of this mess, I was gonna end it. I stepped near, ignoring Ramos's shouts of alarm, and offered the pulsar stave.

"Please," I murmured. "End it."

The yearning surprised me. Tears welled. What was wrong with me?

Energy waves lapped at my arms, my body, enveloping

me in the warmest, yet most terrifying sensation. Everything slowed to a halt.

A silhouette appeared and solidified.

The rip burst with a magnificent *boom*, one that toppled more walls of the house, filling the air with dust. I collapsed to my knees, clinging to the crumpled floor, and refused to let the aftermath blow me away.

When it subsided, all I could hear was breathing. Two people breathing.

Boots filled my line of sight. The person knelt. A hand reached out.

I looked up.

A man, maybe a few years younger than me, smiled. He had hazel eyes, a black moustache with matching goatee, and was shaved so bald his head reflected the pale moonlight. White, yeah, but with some mingled ethnicity I couldn't place. "Let me help you, Mercury," he said. "I am the Icon."

CHAPTER
SEVENTEEN

had to admit, a helping hand was awfully inviting. But I was more interested in the triple-bladed ax he carried in the other palm.

It had a short handle, made of a gleaming brass metal imprinted with swirling lines that reminded me of the villa's rampant ivy. Each blade was set equidistant around the handle, thick and curved like a chef's knives on steroids.

Ramos noticed, too. He targeted the newcomer. "Drop the weapon! Show me your hands."

"I am on your side, sir." The young guy's voice had an undefinable accent. Not British like Loredana, or harsh and clipped as someone from the Mid-Atlantic states, but not from the West Coast. "I am merely offering a fellow warrior assistance."

"Uh, thanks." I decided the best way to work past my pain was to get upright, so I let him help me to my feet. "Hey, Ramos, let's not shoot him full of holes until he answers my questions."

"If you say so." Ramos didn't back down from his aiming stance. "Are you planning to start with, 'Why did he pop out of the same hole in the sky as the monster that tried to kill a restaurant full of people?'"

He sounded like he'd been hanging around me too long. "I thought about it. Speaking of the almost-eaten, shouldn't you head back there? Crime scene and all..."

"Only if you can handle this situation."

Situation? The new guy had slipped the ax into a leather holster he wore on the belt of his outfit, which I realized was a curious combination of padded vest, linen long-sleeved shirt, and slate gray baggy pants bloused into thick canvas boots. They all looked vaguely... Weird. Plus, he was smiling at me, looking happy for a dude who'd stepped out of the rip. "Yeah, we're good. Thanks, and nice work."

"I'll swing back for you when I'm done, seeing as how you're without transportation." Ramos hustled back to his Charger. He peeled out of the parking lot, siren wailing.

I winced. Right. My car. The back half was crumpled in the woods behind the house. Couldn't see the front, but it was somewhere on the other side of the 311. Great.

"So, listen," I said to the new guy. "Where's the Icon?"

"I told you. I am he."

"No, the Icon is supposed to help me lock the astral fiends out of this world for good."

"So I shall. That is why I am overjoyed to find you here awaiting my arrival." He put a hand on my shoulder and dragged me in, as if we were going to hug.

"Whoa, easy, buddy." I broke free and tapped his hand with the pulsar stave's now inert form. "We're not at the hugging stage."

"Ahem."

Winston's clearing of his throat made me jump. You'd think I'd remember he was there, but fact is, wearing the earbud throughout this whole thing I lost track of its presence. "Ah, Winston? Did you get the final readouts of the rip?"

"Drone Five is recording, yes." Winston sounded like he was Googling each word he wanted use before speaking. "Would you care to tell me why there is another man standing there with you who isn't Lieutenant Ramos?"

"This guy." I blew out a breath. "He says he's the Icon."

"That's not possible."

"Yeah, I thought that, but he came out of the rip, with his ax, and when that rip blew it—"

"What ax?"

"He's armed."

"I see."

I looked the guy head to toe. "Really wish you could."

"Hang on." Winston broke off. I heard insistent whispers away from the earbud.

"Mercury, if I may," the man said. "It is important we consolidate our forces. The time has come to shut down the link between this world and that of the astral fiends."

"That's great. And how do I do that?"

"We have two of the three necessary elements—your weapon, and mine."

I rolled the pulsar stave in my hands. "Okay."

"You seem perplexed."

"That's putting it mildly."

"Do you mean to say you were never taught our destiny?"

"Um, no. Not in specifics. Because I don't ..." I lost the thought as another entered my head. File 6-1848. Its reference to the Icon. *Must be warned and sent away.* The lock was keyed to the pulsar stave. Wilhelmina warned me to find the truth.

Was this what she meant? The Icon was a person, not a

thing? It fit with my brief vision of a silhouette, if so.

"You do know, Mercury."

"What I know is I'm creeped out how you've appeared from a dimension that's brought our world nothing but danger, and you spout off my name like it's been dropped from our inbox. How do you know who I am? Who are you?"

"Forgive me. My name is Teget. As to how I know your name, it is because I was told of it for years as I trained. You are the one to save both peoples—the peoples of Earth, and the peoples of my world."

I nodded, like I had a clue what he was talking about. For all I knew he was an astral fiend in disguise. "Sure. Yeah, so, let's go back to Procyon and get this sorted out. I'll get us a ride."

"Of course. I would be honored to meet your fellow warriors."

"They're not exactly that, but I think they'll be of help." I hoped.

"Mercury?" Loredana's voice filtered through the earbud. Guess Winston got moved from his chair. "Bring this man in. We have to contain this until we figure out what in the world's going on."

"I think you're right. Need me to prep him?"

"If you could insure his quiet cooperation, I'd appreciate it."

Quiet cooperation. I sighed. Hated that. She did have a point. Yet, I couldn't shake the nagging sensation I'd seen this guy somewhere before. Not around town. Maybe someone who looked like him?

A car engine rumbled into the driveway. "That's our ride," I said to Teget. "After you."

"Thank you." He walked ahead of me.

I brought the pulsar stave to the back of his neck and willed a sharp, strong pulse.

Next best thing to a Taser.

Teget crumpled, twitching, eyes wide. He eventually went still.

Ramos shone a flashlight on him, then in my eyes. "Did you knock him out?"

"Absolutely. Help me get him into your car." I removed the guy's ax. Felt like cold metal, to me. There was a funky indentation on the end of the handle.

Huh. That gave me an idea.

We stood outside the recovery room on Tower Three's seventh floor like the weirdest family ever, expectant for a peek at a brand-new baby boy. Of course, our guest on the other side of the reinforced glass wasn't a kid. He was a full-grown young man, albeit one who'd gotten dumped out of the rip on the heels of two very angry astral fiends. Teget lay on a couch-slash-bed in the plain room, adjacent to Procyon's infirmary. He could have been having a nice after dinner nap, except he had an audience—me, Ramos, Loredana, Jackson, Winston, and Marigold.

"How long are you planning on keeping this guy here?" Ramos asked.

"We ain't keeping anyone, Lieutenant." Jackson rubbed at his jawline. "Fella in there is our guest. All's we have is some questions for him."

"Good to hear. Because I'm not a fan of illegal incarceration."

"That's a stretch. Do our laws apply to him? He's not from around these parts, and I'm not talking someone with diplomatic immunity."

"This has to be some mistake." Loredana was pale. Her heels *pock-pock*ed on the tile. "He could not be from the Interstice."

"The what?" Ramos frowned.

"It's the name Procyon uses for the place the astral fiends live in," I explained. "We don't know much. It's dark, hence their love of all environments gloomy. All that's proven so far, is that fiends come out. No one else."

"Certainly not humans," Winston said softly. "My word. All this time."

"He is human," I asked. "Right?"

"Lab results are pending," Loredana murmured. "We'll know definitively within the half hour. Initial signs indicate he's as human as you and I."

"Whoever he is, he needs to be taken in for questioning." Ramos tapped the glass. "This young man showed up at the height of an attack on San Camillo residents. In a strange default, that makes him an accessory after the fact."

"Surely not." Winston rolled his eyes.

"My only other option is to contact my pastor and start calling for prayers," Ramos muttered. "This is something otherworldly. Have you people considered the spiritual implications?"

"That ain't part of your jurisdiction, Lieutenant." Jackson clapped him on the shoulder. "Why don't you leave the determination to the experts."

"Experts. Right." Ramos pointed at me. "Keep me in the loop. This guy gets back on the streets, I want to know which one, so I can have a unit detailing his movements."

I nodded.

As soon as he was gone, I glanced at Marigold. "You've

been quiet. What's up?"

She pursed her lips and closed her eyes. "I don't know what to make of this. I never saw it in my dreams, or in waking visions. I could Forecast the Icon's appearance. But the Icon being a person?"

"Maybe it isn't really a person." Winston put an arm around his wife's shoulders. I hadn't realized she was trembling. "Maybe it's that weapon of his. I have my department analyzing it. Mercury took it down to them."

"Yeah. About that." I reached under my shirt. There was a folder tucked into my waistband. Everyone stared at me as I waved it like a flag—not one of surrender, I hoped. "Surprise."

"What in Sam Hill?" Jackson muttered.

"This is File 6-1848. It describes in detail the first ever encounter with astral fiends, on a bleak hillside outside the booming but small port of San Camillo. One of the monks at Domingo monastery wrote it. Seems like a nice guy. Sloppy penmanship." I slapped it against Jackson's chest. "Know what it says? Here's the Wikipedia article version: The Icon is a person. The first people to fight the astral fiend back lost ten good men, until the Icon popped out of a rip and saved the day."

Jackson stared at the folder, red rising up his neck. "You broke in there."

I sighed. "Wasn't that difficult, when you spin a story about what we found at the abandoned hacienda tonight. Unlocking the box was easy. I skipped the pulsar stave, though, and used Teget's ax handle."

"His ax opened the seal on the file's container? Impossible." Loredana leaned against the wall.

"That's what I thought, too." I let Jackson take the folder. "Funny how a lot of things I thought were true turned out to be baloney. All this time we're supposed to be chasing down some thing, a kind of relic, to beat the astral fiends back into the hellscape that spawned them, and instead this dude shows up! Want to tell us why that is?"

"This is exactly why I didn't want you in that vault!" Jackson snarled. "If this information was supposed to be general knowledge, the board of directors would have had me post a memo. But they didn't, did they? They stuck it in a box that only one of our operatives could open. Our operatives, or the Icon itself."

"Himself." I banged on the window. "Hey! Wake up!"

"Mercury, please." Loredana put her hand on the crook of my arm.

"Don't. Don't try to defend any of this. I want to know what's going on! Hey!" I banged again.

Teget rose and crossed to the window. He was bleary-eyed but didn't appear worse for wear. "I am frankly surprised at this treatment."

"Me, too. Sorry I zapped you."

"A necessary precaution. Had it been you coming to my world, I may have done the same."

I turned to Jackson. "Let him out."

"Don't be stupid. We don't know a thing about him, 'cept he claims to be the Icon. I got a cousin in Amarillo who claims to be the love child of Elvis, but that don't make it true, either."

"Winston, come on." I waved a hand. "You got all the readings on Teget's arrival."

"There's no doubt he's from another world, and his ax came with him. How both it and the pulsar stave unlocked the file, however ..." Winston shook his head. "I don't know what to make of it."

"Whatever we make, will affect our next steps," Marigold

said. "None of us should act with rashness, or in anger."

I blew out a breath. She had a way of turning down the temperature in an argument. Jackson rubbed the back of his neck, looking sheepish. My reflection in the window wasn't much different.

A lab assistant in white frock and black slacks hurried up. He was a slim Indian guy, bearing a tablet. "The DNA results, Ms. Lark."

"Thank you." She accepted the devices and swiped down the page. Her expression froze. "Did you read this?"

"No, Ma'am. We compiled the results and had the program run comparisons. I haven't seen—"

"Leave. Now."

Jackson stared over her shoulder. "Good God."

"What? What's wrong?" I reached for the tablet.

Loredana shook her head. "I'm sorry. Once the DNA report was done, I instructed the lab to run a scan through our databases, a cursory comparison to see whether or not Teget had a familiar genome. Perhaps we could then ascertain whether or not his story is true—whether he's from the Interstice, or a fraud."

"Then give us the results, by heavens, and let us be done with it!" Winston stood by my side. Marigold held my hand; I squeezed it in response.

Loredana turned the tablet screen to face us. Her eyes brimmed with tears. I thought my heart was going to stop. "His DNA is a match to yours, Mercury. And I don't mean simple ethnic similarities. You share direct parentage. That man—he is your brother. Full-blooded sibling."

Blood rushed to my head. It roared so furiously I almost missed Jackson's next words. They weren't congratulations.

"Get security to my location now," he snapped into his

phone. "We got ourselves an intruder."

CHAPTER EIGHTEEN

Loredana took a cautious step toward me. "Mercury, is the pulsar stave in the lab, as well?"

"Sure. I left it with Teget's ax, so Winston's people could run their tests." I glanced at him. "Right?"

"Absolutely. Yes." Winston frowned. "I'm sorry, Ms. Lark, but this cannot be a correct result. Someone must have made an error. This cannot be Mercury's brother."

"Winston," Jackson said, "You'd best shut your trap."

"Why? A man shows up through the rip and happens to be a relative?" Winston snorted. "Please. We all know Mercury's DNA doesn't manifest any differences that—"

Marigold let go of my hand, and pressed close to her husband. "This isn't a wise course. Reconsider."

"Hang on. I'd like to hear it. And why do we need security all of a sudden?"

"Precautions, son." Jackson sounded like he was speaking at a funeral.

"Precautions against Teget?" Loredana said. "He's quite contained."

"No, not him." Jackson stared at me. *Me*, like I hadn't just risked my life on their crazy assignment.

I couldn't help but laugh. "You're nuts, okay? That's not my brother! The guy came from the same place as astral fiends! We can't be related."

"The DNA results are clear." The way Loredana said it, however, was with as incredulous a tone as I had. "You are siblings."

"How do we know he didn't come from here, and go into the Interstice?"

"That's not how that works," Winston said. "We've only ever observed things come out of the rips."

"Yeah? When was the last time a person came out?"

Winston was suddenly very interested in his shoes, and in whistling a complex symphony. Jackson was still glaring at me, as if I had a bomb strapped to my chest. Loredana was still confused—never seen her at a loss for words or action. Only Marigold made direct eye contact. "It was a long time ago."

"Marigold, perhaps this isn't the best time," Winston said.

"He is right, you know. The truth is ever present. We chose to ignore it, because we fear what it means." Marigold smiled. "Mercury, to answer you directly, the last time a person came out of a rip was when your family appeared."

"My family?"

"A man, a woman, and a child—a toddler. They brought us hope. But that hope was lost when the man and woman died. For a time, Procyon had no vision, no guidance, and no option but to continue the bleak war against the astral fiends. Then we found you, Mercury. You came home to us."

"I ... No. My mom abandoned me at a restaurant. I've been in foster homes and bouncing between apartments. There isn't a hope." I looked at Winston. "She's losing it, man."

He scratched the back of his neck. "Sorry, old chap, but it

is all spelled out in the dossier."

"What? What dossier?" I backed away, towards the window.

"Mother and Father would not have come to this world if they did not have a good reason," Teget said. "You were to be raised among Earth's people, to defend them, and eventually, to seal the route of evil."

"Shut up!" I snapped. "You're crazy, okay? You're not my brother. I don't care about what the stupid test says." I shook my head. "This is insane."

"Son, I know it's a lot to wrap your head around, but you got to understand, it was for the best of all involved," Jackson said. "Procyon's always known you were special. Just never expected none of your kin to come looking for you."

"You knew?" I glared at him. "This whole time, you knew about my parents?"

"We did not want you burdened," Marigold said.

"I didn't ask you!" The bits and pieces of my life that didn't make sense came smashing down together, piling on the heap of weirdness that had accumulated over the past week. Why hadn't I listened to Wilhelmina, as crazy as she sounded? "You've lied to me this whole time? You're the only people I ever trusted! You told me I was brought on board because I have gifts, because I have the skills. That had never happened to me before! Everyone else took me in because they could make a buck off the state! And now you're telling me I'm not … I'm not even human?"

"Yes, of course you're human," Winston said. "But you're different. Gifted. That's why we think you've been able to use the pulsar stave to such great effect, greater than any operative of the past century and a half. You were born to it, my friend!"

I shoved him. "Don't tell me that!"

"Hey now, no need for roughhousing." Jackson caught my arms from behind, held me like a guy who knew how to make a tackle.

"Let go, and I won't break anything," I growled.

"You'd best reconsider."

Four security guys came around the bend, in their all-black outfits. They were armed. Shotguns.

"This isn't necessary." Loredana stepped between me and the guards. "Sir, if I may, let me have the lab run further tests to determine—"

"Don't bother, Loredana. Matter's been solved. We've got these boys, and they're going to play key roles in our necessary next steps."

"But ..." Loredana frowned. "What you're saying ... He's not from the Interstice, is he? No one resides there."

"You know that ain't true, darling."

She looked at me, and then him, eyes widened. "Mercury can't be from another world. He's one of us. He's only ever done everything Procyon has required."

"And that's why he'll move along quietly, so we can have uninterrupted time with his baby brother." Jackson released me. "Take him, boys."

Take him?

The first guard—I think his name was Murray—reached for my upper left arm. I struck his grasp aside and planted my palm on his chest. In most fights that wouldn't have done much besides make him mad.

Since I still had a bundle of the pulsar stave's energy leached throughout my body, the blow slammed him against the nearest wall.

Two of the other security boys jumped me at the same time, laying in punches. One of them hooked his leg around my right ankle and twisted. I hit the floor.

Guard Number Three aimed the shotgun.

I felt a little better he wasn't going to kill me. Procyon security favored beanbag rounds, enough to crack ribs and knock the wind from lungs. Still, I didn't really want to get punched in the guts like I was getting kicked by a horse.

"Leave him be!" Loredana snapped. "This is ridiculous."

"Stay out of the way, Ms. Lark," Jackson said.

Her interjection was enough a distraction for the guards to take their eyes off me, for one second. I braced myself against the two holding me and pushed off the floor. My kick dislodged the shotgun from Number Three's grip.

I spun all the way around, slipping free of the other two security guards. I shoved one of them toward Number Three and blocked a punch from the other guy. I dodged his next blow, then struck him on the soft, squishy part of the throat. He gagged, reaching instinctively to protect the weak point.

That left the opening for me to double him over with a punch deep to his gut.

"Get down!" Murray was crouched by the wall and pulled the trigger.

The bang and flash were surprising enough. I contorted into the same kind of spin I'd use to evade an astral fiend, but without the stave's continuous flow, it wasn't nearly as quick or precise. The beanbag round grazed my left side. I slapped onto the tile floor. My elbow got treated to a jolt of pain that ended in my jaw.

A second round hit me on the thigh. Now *that* hurt.

"That's enough, y'all." Jackson stood between the guards. Winston and Marigold clung to each other, his face contorted in horror, hers placid and—I hoped—tinged with sorrow.

And Loredana was …

"Gun!" Murray shifted his aim.

What? Of course they all had guns. That idiot.

Oh. Loredana had a silver-plated revolver pressed to the side of Jackson's head.

"Sir, if I may, I'd like to schedule a meeting about Procyon's management." Her tone was ice cold, and solid steel. "If now is not a convenient time, I suggest clearing your schedule in the next thirty seconds."

Jackson held his hands easily at this side. His mouth quirked into a wry smile. "Darling, this is a quick way to the unemployment line, at least, unless we'd be better off calling Lieutenant Ramos back."

"That won't be necessary. Let Mercury leave."

"Not going to happen."

"I'd like to chime in here." I got to my feet, wincing at the throbbing pain in my leg.

"Shut up," Jackson snapped. "Ms. Lark, put your gun down."

"This is madness!" Winston said.

"Thanks for the observation, Threepio." I started down the hall.

"Stop him!" Jackson ordered.

Murray's aim shifted, but I wagged a finger. "Nope. You gonna risk the boss getting his brains splattered on this tile? Janitors will hate your guts."

He grimaced but didn't take his sights off me. Didn't pull the trigger, and neither did the other guards. I glanced at the other three. "You guys wanna take bets as to whether Loredana will shoot?"

Nobody stopped me.

I spared a last glance at Loredana. "Teget."

"Nothing will happen to him. I promise." She nodded at

him.

Teget, for his part, was watching us like a bird of prey unsure of who was breakfast and who was a threat. "Listen to the lady, Mercury. This is not the time to fight. You must leave us."

"Oh, I should? My supposed interdimensional brother and the only person standing up for me? How about you shut up, too, and let me think."

"You prat!" Loredana snapped. "Go!"

I sprinted down the hall, hating myself with every step.

There was an immediate ruckus, followed by a single gunshot, and Marigold's scream. My shoes squeaked as I skidded on tile. Loredana shot him?

"Stop him!" Jackson's bellow echoed down the corridor.

Nope. I wasn't going back. Not yet.

I got down to the lab on the sixth floor as alarms started blaring. Red lights flashed in strips along the ceiling and floor. Great. Not too obvious.

"What's going on?" The Indian guy frowned at me. "Is this a drill?"

"Doubt it. Probably serious." I breezed past him to the table at the center of the room, in the midst of all kinds of microscopes, test equipment, and centrifuges. The place had more computer monitors than a gaming center. Everything hummed, and between the lighting and the décor, I could have been in the newest J.J. Abrams sci-fi movie. Minus lens flare.

"Well, I need to clear your presence." His phone was singing. Seriously? Kelli Clarkson? "Oh."

"What is it?" I picked up the pulsar stave and hid it in its holster. The ax was still secure in the sling Teget carried.

"Security notice. 'The following personnel is considered dangerous and …" He blanched. "Oh. Ah, Mr. Hale?"

I strapped on the ax holster and headed for the door. "Yeah, I know, I shouldn't be here."

"No, it's, ah, your image they're sending to everyone." He showed me his phone. I grinned back at myself from that glowing rectangle. "I should call security."

"Be here in a jiffy, so I'll get lost." I patted the ax. "Thanks for the souvenir."

"Mr. Hale, please wait." The poor guy was frantically tapping on his phone. "I need to talk to you about that item. The strange hatchet. Its properties are very similar to the pulsar stave's. You have to understand—it's likely they were made in the same way."

I paused with my hand on the doorframe. "But Procyon's had the stave all this time. The ax came through the rip a few hours ago."

"We haven't had the time to conduct a molecular scan, but its energy signatures show the same potential. Please, don't take them. Let us have another chance to examine them further."

It was tempting. I had so many questions by then, especially since both the stave and the ax opened that box containing File 6-1848. I should go back for Teget—and Loredana. But with those red lights flashing, and security combing the building—

No.

The lab guy was stalling.

I broke into a run, heading for the stairs. If they locked the doors—

Yep. Locked. I stood back a comfortable distance, and willed power into the pulsar stave. I slammed it against the door.

The handle and the lock helpfully sloughed off like melting

snow from a sun-kissed roof.

I tore down the emergency stairwell, bursting through the door onto the first floor. A couple fast turns led to the lobby.

Three security guys were waiting.

"There! Take him!"

No other warning. I wasn't expecting Miranda rights, but something like "Put Your Hands Up" or "Drop the Energy Weapon!" would have been nice. Instead they all opened fire.

Beanbag rounds slapped the walls. I dashed back up the stairs. Second, third, fourth floors. My muscles and lungs were burning by the time I hit the main corridor running.

The glass walkway stretched out from Tower Three to Tower One. The bay was a glistening vista to one side, and San Camillo a jeweled landscape to the other.

I had a crazy idea.

The pulsar stave had done some major damage over the years. Lab guy had said this new ax was made in a similar fashion. And both ends opened that lock.

I drew the ax and held the end of its handle to the tip of the stave.

Yellow-white sparks leapt between the two. Something pulled them together, like the attraction from two magnets when the poles aligned. They clanked so loudly I was startled. Try as I might, I couldn't wrench them apart.

That hunch left me with a two-foot triple-bladed ax.

I swung it against the glass walls of the walkway.

Shards exploded into the night, letting cool sea air rush in. The burst of energy accompanying my strike rippled along the windows, breaking pane after pane. Yikes. That was overkill.

Shouts echoed behind me. Footsteps pounded up the steps.

"This is crazy," I muttered.

Then again, so was the whole night.

I jumped out the window, diving toward the wall of Tower One. Halfway down, I sliced the ax blades against the white concrete between rows of windows reflecting San Camillo's nightscape. They cut through the surface, spraying fragments in my face, the flecks stinging my skin. I kept falling, my body dragging against the wall.

If this idea failed, I'd splat pretty badly on the lawn.

Thankfully, the blade slowed my descent. Yellow-white sparks writhed up and down the combined weapon, and onto my arms. The old familiar combat boost reached my spine. My thoughts were clearer than they'd been in days.

I hit the ground running.

No idea how long I kept going. All I know is I didn't stop until I was blocks clear of Procyon, and I yanked the two weapon halves apart. Suddenly I was winded, enough so that I staggered against a building, gasping for air. I sank onto my backside.

I was out. But Teget was still a guest. Or patient. Or prisoner. Whatever. I couldn't leave him there. Brother or not.

Loredana was on the inside. Would Jackson take out his anger on her? She was highly placed in Procyon. Surely the board of directors wouldn't allow it. But she probably would be followed no matter where she went.

Wilhelmina. She was the key to this mess. I had to track her down.

Ramos might know.

My thoughts muddied. I really wanted to catch some sleep. But home was too far away, and I didn't have a car. Plus, if Procyon was looking for me, they'd check public transit. Had to walk.

Soon.

But first, I dozed off.

CHAPTER NINETEEN

Morning arrived way too early.

Every inch of my body hurt. Bad enough I didn't want to leave the semi-warm spot of concrete where I'd curled up by a stairwell.

"Dude's got an ax."

The voice jolted me fully awake, clearing away the haze. I blinked. It was a really bright day. I knew how vampires must feel.

"Don't touch it!"

"Whatever, man, he's wasted." Two scraggly guys, in their late teens or early twenties, loomed over me. Their clothes were a mix of Army surplus and thrifty hipster. The stench of pot hung heavy. Any closer and I might have gotten high. "That thing's, like, silver or something. We could take it to the pawn shop."

"I guess."

"How about this." I swung the ax out, to within a few inches of their faces. No, they didn't go cross-eyed. That's in cartoons. But they did put their hands up. "You let me rest up, and I don't split you like a Thanksgiving turkey. This thing's pretty sharp."

"Yeah, yeah, okay." The more cautious of the two backpedaled to the curb, slapping his buddy on the arm as he went. "We're good. It's cool. I didn't take none of your stuff."

"Thanks for that. I hate cleaning up severed limbs."

They took off running.

I sighed and sagged against the brick wall of an apartment building. Playing crazy worked well. Of course, after last night, my brain couldn't quite convince me I wasn't losing it.

I checked my phone, because why not? There were missed calls galore—most from Loredana, some from Ramos, even one from Winston. My finger hovered over his call, then Loredana's, before hitting the redial on Ramos's number. I didn't have anything to say to Winston. Whatever he said was going to be part of the lie. Loredana? Sure, she helped me escape, and seemed genuinely upset, but she was inside Procyon. That equaled a big old hazard.

Sadly, Ramos was my only option.

"Mercury?" He hissed my name into the received. "Thank God."

"You know, I'm not feeling real happy with him after the night I've had."

"Shut up and listen. We've only got a short time before you have to ditch your phone."

"Ditch it? Why?"

"Do you think after what you pulled Procyon won't be triangulating this call every second you're wasting? They've brought the police in on this. Jack Jackson is pressing charges for assault, destruction of property, and theft."

I blinked. Morning traffic wasn't heavy on this street, but I'd been staring at the cars rolling by, and the pedestrians heading to work. One or two noticed me, but that was only to give brief examination before returning attention to their phones. "Oh."

"Oh? Don't … Just stop talking." Which made me smile for the first time in a while, because Ramos was firing off words like rounds from his M4. "SCPD's dragging the streets for you. So far, I've steered them in the wrong direction, but I can't keep the patrols away from you."

"Wait, are you in charge of the manhunt for me?"

"Yes."

I rolled my eyes. "Well, that figures. How'd you roll that bad set of dice?"

"By being present at an attack at Kaszanka in which two people were hospitalized," he muttered. "There's no hiding it now, Mercury. Check the news—but not on your phone. The place is crawling with bloggers and reporters. We're dealing with at least ten eyewitnesses. This is worse than the YouTube video. The newest recording shows a great deal more."

"Enough to convince people it's not CGI?"

"We'll see, but my captain's furious. She wants answers. I'm stalling. You've got to do something about this."

"Me? I'm not a cop!"

"These devils are your responsibility!"

"Okay. Fine." I rubbed the bridge of my nose. That massive headache coming on. Car-sized. "I'll be at the library when it opens. Nine."

"Right. Keep your head low."

"Oh, hey, about Wilhelmina …"

"Nothing new on her." Ramos broke off. When he came back, his sign-off was hurried. "Library. 9 a.m. Don't go to your place. Godspeed."

He hung up.

I gritted my teeth and flung the phone as hard as I could. It bounced off a passing city bus's roof, ripped through the top of a tree, and smashed against the buildings on the other side of the street.

Great. Police manhunt. I tucked the ax behind me as far as I could, and draped part of my shirt over it. I needed a jacket. No way I was going to make it across town looking like this.

My watch told me it was 6:30. No wonder I felt wiped. Took me a minute more to get my bearings as I walked the street. Ramsey Hill neighborhood. Struggling middle class. Mostly residential, though I passed a couple shops at the corner of Twenty-Third and Thorn. The library was at least a mile from here, west, deeper downtown. Which was okay by me. More people meant it'd be easier to lose myself in a crowd, and as far as I was concerned, the farther from the waterfront, the better.

I grabbed a donut and orange juice from one of the stores. Probably wasn't a great idea, considering the place had a security camera, but I was hungry. It also gave me a chance to grab concealment for my weapons—a beige windbreaker with a gaudy orange, yellow, and red "San Camillo by the Sea!" logo the size of a pizza box on the back. Thanks, Chamber of Commerce.

At least no one would see my semi-medieval hardware. Carrying the two weapons, one on either side of my body, felt strange enough. One moment I be freezing even in direct sunlight, the other I'd sweat so bad I had to knuckle through the urge to toss the jacket. Then it'd be a combination of the two sensations. Thankfully the morning was cool, with a light mist burning off the bay.

Thinking about the weapons filled me with a sickening worry. What if Tracking and Forecasting picked up another incursion? Who was going to stop an astral fiend? Forget one.

There'd been two last night. Of course, there'd also been a guy claiming to be my brother.

The headache throbbed. Teget. The ax. Astral fiends gone wilder. Procyon's hiding of my background, of the truth about the Icon. Secret files. Wilhelmina.

My friends.

This was getting me nowhere. If I kept wandering around like a mopey teenager with angsty songs by Brand New and Dashboard Confessional leaking out of his earbuds, Procyon would sweep me up faster than trash in Rosa Roja Park. My awareness had been shot to pieces.

A silver sedan slowing in the opposite lane helped put it back together.

Nothing fancy about it. Lots of people drove Chevy sedans. But most lacked two beefy guys in sunglasses and black polo shirts.

I ducked into an alleyway and ran.

Yes, I know, alleys are classic places for traps. Fully aware of that. Had a bad run-in with a fiend between two run-down tenements a couple years back that put alleys top on my list of unpleasant places. But when you wall jump up onto a fire escape, your reflexes and speed heightened by the pulsar stave's power, you ignore that sense of dread.

My fingers closed around the railing of a fire escape. I swung onto the wrought iron surface with a *bang* I guessed was as loud as a howitzer and started climbing. I didn't slow or look back until I got to the roof and laid down.

The car had stopped by the alley entrance. Two guys, neither one I recognized. If they were armed, it was concealed carry. So far, they hadn't figured out I'd gone vertical instead of horizontal.

I hustled to the rooftop access door and made my way

downstairs like I lived in the place. A pleasant old black gentleman held the front door for me as I waltzed out onto the sidewalk. Made it across the street and onto the next block before those goons emerged from their search.

By then I really was sweating. Enough of this walking. I was never gonna make it to the library by 9 a.m. if I stayed on foot.

I waited at the nearest stop for the Orange bus that'd take me west, to downtown. There were a handful of people there, including two huge black guys in baggy sportswear. Both of them had athletic club membership cards dangling from lanyards around their necks. Since everyone else was shorter than me by half a foot, I stepped behind them.

Without my phone to pass the time, I picked up a discarded copy of the *Bayside Breeze,* their eight-page paper version. So much for camouflage. Everyone else was reading their phones, doing the whole hunched-over-and-scrolling thing. The paper was crumpled, so I spread it out.

Customers Claim Monster Attacked.

Oops.

The article was cursory, with that rushed feeling you got from something slapped together the night before just so the editor had a leg up on the competitor and prevented the paper from looking like a bunch of idiots when the competition scooped them. The photo was blurry, smeared with purple splotches, but I could spot an astral fiend upside down in a typhoon. It was a better image than the grainy video from the Promenade appearance.

The eyewitness accounts were the worst part. "Giant space octopus." "Cthulhu himself." "I thought I'd drank too much."

No interviews with the two victims. They were in the hospital, and police were questioning them. Great. Perfect.

This would be a bad enough mess if I hadn't made myself an enemy of Procyon.

I mashed up the paper right when the silver sedan passed. Thankfully those two big guys who were headed to the gym and debating which one could get the hot chick on the exercise cycle to smile first in his direction stayed right where they were, an impenetrable shield of muscle and testosterone.

I exhaled as the car disappeared. You know what? The library could wait. I had somewhere else to go. And if it turned out to be a bad idea, well, I'd have to exert myself to screw up worse than I already had.

The Court Street bridge wasn't any prettier in daylight. Fewer people were about, but those that were clung to the shadows.

Wilhelmina's tent was right where I'd last seen her. Even the lawn chair was parked out front. No Wilhelmina, though, and no volunteer bodyguards.

A couple of guys beelined for me the instant I walked onto the street. I recognized them as tattooed compatriots of the dude I'd tossed around after the Promenade fiasco. "Hey, fellas. You seen Wilhelmina lately? Asking for a friend."

"Yo, man, you better gets gone." The pasty, pink haired with the piercings sneered a good sneer, but he also stood ten feet back. His buddy, slightly tanned and bulging with muscle, let me see the pistol tucked in his waistband. "We got orders to take you out if you ever show up again."

"That's cute." I pointed at Bulky's semi-hidden firearm. "Is that a NERF gun or are you happy to see me?"

He drew it and aimed.

I'd already whipped out the pulsar stave and swung it. The energy flare from its business end swept across the gun's barrel, leaving behind dripping, molten metal. The guy screamed—surprisingly high-pitched—and dropped it.

I gave them three full seconds of me standing there, the pulsar stave deployed and crackling, the ax gleaming at my hip. "Here's how it is. You guys see everything, judging by how fast you jumped on me, since I've only been off the bus a minute and a half. So tell me where Wilhelmina went, and I promise to only leave bruises, not burns."

They stared at me, brains having apparently frozen. So much for threats as a decent form of coercion.

"My, my." The mellow voice laughed long and richly from behind me. "Child, you've given up on the precept of subtlety, haven't you?"

Wilhelmina was on the doorstep of the dingy tenement a few buildings over. None of her guards were visible. But she leaned on a dented cane, a knitted bag hanging from one shoulder. A talented crafter—Wilhelmina herself, I assumed—had emblazoned a brown and white striped kitten with huge green eyes on the side of that bag.

"Oh, hey." I pointed the stave her direction. "You busy? Because I've got a lot of questions, and I'd rather you not become the next person who ticks me off with threats and lies."

"I promised you the truth," she said. "Let these boys get back to their street games and come on with me. Won't take long."

The two guys were already sprinting away, swearing a blue streak at each other. I'd love to be in the same room when they explained to their gang boss how I melted their gun.

"You want to do this outside? Because I've got a few silver sedans trolling the streets of San Camillo that make me think we'd better take our conversation elsewhere. Like the East Coast, or Russia."

She laughed. "Such a bright disposition. No, no, this is not the place for the things we have to say to each other." She dug a flip phone from her pocket, a cheap plastic model you could buy from any big box store and load up with prepaid minutes. "Jamie? Come 'round front and pick us up, all right? That's fine."

I was still puzzling over which of her bodyguards was Jamie when an '80s vintage Ford Bronco rumbled around the corner. It sparkled, right down to the bumpers. I don't think there was a single scratch on the windshield. Jamie, it turns out, was a black guy with a light complexion, no hair, and two gold earrings. He was as big as an astral fiend. Okay, maybe not literally, but when Wilhelmina climbed onto the red leather seats, she seemed to shrink.

"I thought you were homeless," I blurted as I got into the back door.

Wilhelmina smirked. "And you also thought Procyon always had your back. How's that working out for you?"

CHAPTER TWENTY

J amie drove us east, the opposite direction from the library, which put a wrinkle in my plan to meet up with Ramos. Well, hopefully he'd give me a ride back, because the idea of bus-hopping from one end of San Camillo to the other while both Procyon and SCPD were keen to lock me up did not appeal.

I was starting to wonder if Wilhelmina's homeless status was a front, and perhaps we'd wind up at a two-story McMansion in Wells Heights in the far suburbs, when Jamie braked by a rusting chain link fence. Ah. One of the city's skate parks. Built in the '70s, as far as possible from the concrete stairwells and street corners where the boarders loved to show off their tricks. The plan to draw them away from the complaining business executives failed, and all San Camillo had to show for it was hundreds of thousands of dollars spent on crumbling ramps, tubes, and bowls in what was otherwise a bustling commercial complex on Dean Road.

"That'll do nicely." Wilhelmina patted Jamie on the cheek. "Be a lamb and circle back in twenty minutes."

"Twenty minutes?" I followed her from the truck. "That's

all the time you need to explain Procyon's big secrets?"

"If I need more than ten, I'll be severely disappointed in you." She pulled back a gash in the fence with the curved handle of her cane. "Come on, now, don't dawdle."

We walked deeper into the park, following the L-shaped property behind a strip mall containing a tattoo parlor, nail shop, gaming supply store, and Western Union office, winding around the curved obstacles. There were maybe three square feet of concrete not covered in graffiti sprayed in every shade of the rainbow.

"Love what they've done with the place." My shoes crunched broken glass. There was more of it than grass on Procyon's immaculate lawn.

"Shame people let the things built for the community go to pot." Wilhelmina shook her head. "'Course, never was a good idea. They should have left the young folks like you to their enjoyments. It's never a bad thing to let people pursue their passions. Too often we let the dark things in life pull us away from the light."

"That sounds great, Mrs. Miyagi, but I'm interested in stopping monsters, so if you have answers—"

She cracked that cane across my shins so fast I'd have testified in court I never saw it move, other than a flicker of silver out of the corner of my eye. I gritted my teeth. What was I going to do? Pretty sure beating up an old woman was frowned upon by both law enforcement and society at large—the latter including Jamie, the taciturn but gigantic chauffeur.

"Push, push, push," Wilhelmina murmured. "I can see why Procyon values you. Never still. Never thoughtful. Well, now you're going to do both—sit and think. I'll do the talking, child, and there's more where that come from if you give me lip." She tapped her cane on a low-slung rise of concrete.

I sat, and for the first time that morning, let the dawning sun warm my shoulders. This wasn't how I wanted to spend my day. It could have been hours filled with training, reorganizing the new apartment—oh, right. And car shopping.

Wilhelmina stooped. "Tell me about the Interstice."

I was way past being surprised that she knew about the things Procyon labored to keep secret from the world at large. It barely mattered, what with astral fiends showing up in the newspaper and on YouTube. "It's the dimension the astral fiends call home. A land of darkness. Big on purple lightning. Perpetual gloom."

She took a shard of concrete and drew a circle on the nearest ramp. "How do the fiends get here?"

"Through the rip." I rolled my eyes, as soon as she turned her back to draw a short line bisected by an X. She etched a smaller circle on the other end of the rip.

"You put those eyes back in place before I make 'em stick that way." Her voice was mellow and sing-song, but you bet it made me sit up straighter. "The rip. Forecasting calls them out, Tracking maps them, and you run to them."

"Yeah. An astral fiend comes out, I kill it, and I try to stabilize the rip with the pulsar stave if Tracking's got enough of a tachyon read to indicate a possible Icon appearance." I sighed. "That's what was normal for the last few years of my life, until last week. Then I get an uninvited visitor to my apartment, miss a fiend attack, get them showing up in public, and—bonus!—two at once."

Wilhelmina nodded. "Then there's your Icon."

"Yeah." I ran a hand across my hair. "Teget."

"Teget?"

"His name. He says he's the Icon, not an artifact meant to save us."

She pursed her lips. "He ain't wrong. Teget. Good name. Comes from Latin, you know. Translating to English muddies it, but you'd be safe with 'shield' or 'covering.' Appropriate for a protector."

"Yeah, except he's got to be lying, because people don't come out of the Interstice. Only astral fiends."

"Really. You know this for a fact? Your two and a half decades, plus a few years, gives you the wisdom to put certainty behind that blanket assertion?" Wilhelmina snorted. "There's a reason I keep calling you 'child,' Mr. Hale."

"Then educate me. If this guy didn't come from the Interstice, he's either a nutcase or he ..." I lost the rest of the sentence as my mouth caught up with my brain.

"Mm-hmm. You see it now, when you sit still long enough." She drew a line up from the center circle and added a triangle to its other end.

"Another dimension?" My voice cracked. "Beyond the Interstice?"

"Beyond, next to, neighboring, those kind of descriptions ain't relevant." Wilhelmina tapped the triangle, leaving a white mark at its center. "Point is, you can't get here from there. Your friend would have had to transit into the Interstice, then make his way to the rip when it opened in this vicinity."

"Teget isn't my friend."

"He's kin, ain't he?"

I slapped the concrete. "How do you know all this? Who are you?"

Wilhelmina smiled, but for the first time since I'd met her, she exuded exhaustion. She sat down beside me. "Child, it doesn't matter who I *am*. What's important is who I was. You see, I was *you*."

I stared at her, and she continued, "Twenty years. Two

hundred nine incursions. Oh, it was a glorious time to serve. To feel that power rushing through your body, letting you leap like the greatest gymnast, to fight like the most skilled warrior of old, to leave those filthy fiends smoldering in their own juices, to know—to *believe*—you'd made a difference in a way no one else could. Meant a lot, too, being a woman of a particular color who everyone else said ain't worth a care."

"Twenty years." I couldn't picture Wilhelmina turning somersaults as she severed tentacles and dispatched astral fiends with my weapon. "Wait. If you used to do this, how did you stop them?"

She brushed aside my jacket. The pulsar stave glinted. "May I?"

Part of me screamed that it was a really bad idea. The other shrugged. "Okay, but it's a stick of metal to anyone else but me."

She slid the stave from its sheath and proved me wrong.

Wilhelmina took the weapon through a series of graceful stretches and lunges, before it activated, yellow-white light washing across her face. Her stiff movements smoothed out. She separated the stave, its crackling forces buzzing in the morning air. The longer her exercises lasted, the more the years melted away from her 70-plus frame.

Finally, she swept the halves across each other and sliced the top corner off the ramp she'd sketched on. The strike left a blackened, flat cut. The missing chunk rolled to a stop at my feet.

"Yow," I muttered.

Wilhelmina reconnected the stave's halves and held it close to her chest. She closed her eyes, tears glistening at the corners. "My God, but I never thought I'd feel that again. Mercury, you have no idea the gift you've got access to."

"So you were trained to use the stave? You were chosen?"

"Chosen is a poor word. Procyon didn't choose me. I inherited this, as you did."

I couldn't help a chuckle. "Doubt we're related."

"Not by any near branch of a family tree, but you go back far enough, there's genetic markers scattered throughout humanity that allow access to the weapons against the astral fiends."

"The weapons."

"The pulsar stave." She gave it back to me. "The ax at your waist. And the night's blade."

"All knights carried blades."

"Night as in darkness." Wilhelmina hobbled back to her drawing. She almost fell before she reached it, but I was there in an instant, hand holding her arm, cane at the ready. She smiled at patted my cheek. "Just a mite wobbly. Let me do this on my own. The stave gave me enough to remember the way I was."

She leaned on the damaged skate ramp. "Millennia ago, the rip wasn't a periodically appearing gateway. It was an open road, the broad one, and that was bad, to put it mildly. Astral fiends poured onto the Earth, killing at will, ravaging the land. Humanity couldn't stop them. All we could do was get ourselves drowned in the flood of evil."

"Then they came." She tapped the triangle again. "No name for their kind, but they were people—human, like us, but different. Full of love and hate and all the things that make us who we are as a flawed species, yet somehow less damaged. And they fought. Lordy, how they fought. They pushed back the threat and stopped the astral fiends from having free access to Earth. But their win was a loss for a handful. You see, to seal the way between here and the Interstice, the three weapons—

stave, ax, and blade—had to be separated."

I looked down at the two silvery objects affixed to my belt. "All three were one?"

She nodded. "Terrible power to be wielded together. When they closed that huge rip between worlds, they had to break apart and to remain that way, to keep things shut, someone had to stay with each piece."

Wilhelmina folded her hands. "A brave few from that defending realm were trapped here. Over time, they lived and married, had children with and among us, until their bloodline was subsumed by humanity's. It's been diluted over the centuries, but enough remains in our genetic code to trigger the weapons, to let us continue the fight."

"But if the way was sealed, why did the fiends come back?" My eyes widened. "The file. 1848."

"That was the year." Wilhelmina scowled. "Some fool brought the blade and the stave together and did her best to reopen the way. Thought it would cleanse our world of rampant woes, so to start things over. A different take on the big Flood, mind. That's when the first Icon showed up, with the ax, and defeated her. That Icon took the ax back with him. And why Procyon was born—to find the descendants of the old protectors, to give them the stave with which to protect the world from these rips. They're the damage left over from that battle."

"Man." My head was spinning. Figuratively, of course, but if I gave it enough time, I'm sure it might whirl around for real. "Where's the blade?"

"No one knows. Lost in the fight. The worry is, it's somewhere on Earth, not dropped into the Interstice like many hoped."

"What do you think?"

"Don't matter none what I think, Mercury." She pressed her hand to my chest. "What do you know?"

"I know the astral fiend incursions are stepping up, both in frequency and intensity. They're hiding less. They're targeting me, and innocents. I know Procyon hid everything you just told me, like they were afraid of it."

"In a way, they are afraid. Things have been so quiet, so predictable, for so many years. Can you blame them for wanting that to continue? Ever since that day one hundred seventy years ago, Procyon's been holding its breath for Armageddon, fighting a secret, whispered war, but at the same time not wanting to acknowledge how serious it is." Wilhelmina shook her head. "That's part of why they kicked me to the curb. I asked too many questions. Took too many risks."

"What was the other part?"

"My body couldn't take it. Using the stave, it wears you down, until the day comes when you rush into battle and it isn't the fiend that tries to kill you, but your own weapon, the very thing that's been your steadfast ally for years. I'm not bitter, mind, but ..."

"You miss it."

"Won't you, when your time is up?"

I considered that, as I stared first at the Interstice drawing, and then up at the skyline. The city stretched on and on, seemingly forever from down here. "Okay."

"That's it? I drop the weight of the world on your shoulders and all I get is okay?"

"Look, I don't want to do any of this. I like my life—yeah, even the part where I fight monsters. It's comfortable, in a weird way. Conspiracies? End of the world doomsaying? Couldn't care less. But here's the deal: Teget could be my family." I looked at my hands. They were normal hands, I guess. "Loredana said Teget's DNA and mine were close enough that we're supposed to be brothers."

"Not just distant relatives? She actually said brothers?"

"Yeah. And one of the others, from Forecasting told me about people who came through the rip years ago—not centuries, but decades. They left me here." The realization hit me worse than a fiend's tentacle.

"Child." She hugged me. I tried hard not to collapse, but this was too much. My heart was sick. "You're not like me, not someone carrying the keys of a long-gone people that lets us fight evil. You're far more than that."

She beamed, regaining the radiance the stave had given. "You're from beyond the Interstice. They sent you here so you could save the world."

CHAPTER
TWENTY-ONE

San Camillo Municipal Library sat at the intersection of DeLeon and Sixth, a shining piece of blown glass art dropped among its straight-edged, fresh from the store skyscraper brethren. A great swoop of stained glass reached twelve stories for the sky, framed in bronze metal, severing the curved halves of the eight-story building. It looked like a rainbow breaking apart a sculpture whose edges were worn away by the sea. Everything else nearby was functional, squares and rectangles galore, except for the old Mission Santa Clarita, its terracotta roofs surrounded by white adobe walls and stately fig trees.

Jamie parked the Bronco between a pair of hybrid autos that looked small enough to each fit in the trunk. He turned and stared at me.

"Okay. Thanks for the ride." I gestured to the door handle. "Let myself out, I guess?"

"I'll be in touch," Wilhelmina said.

"I don't have a phone. Kinda had to ditch it to evade pursuit." The memory of my one and only smartphone smashing against a middle-income rowhome made me wince.

I felt something vibrate in my pocket. Phantom notification.

"Jamie will keep watch for you. He'll let me know when it's a good time." Wilhelmina took my hand in both of hers. "Remember: you've a vital task ahead of you. Keep the stave and the ax safe. Free Teget. Find the blade."

"Don't forget stop the apocalypse."

"There's no need to be flip."

"Oh, I think I've earned it. Besides, if I'm not from around these parts, as the ranchers say out past the valley, I think I get to flout the rules."

"There's nothing shameful about your heritage. You're from a long line of venerable warriors who once saved this world, and now they're gonna do it again."

I glanced around at the people walking to and from the library, at the vendor selling hot dogs to a family of five, at the women in business suits and skirts debating something on their phones. "I don't know anything about that. However venerable you say they were, they still left me here. My list of allies is short."

"You'll find them. You're never alone."

I closed the door, then thought twice. I leaned in her window. "The blade. You think it's here?"

"The ax was beyond the Interstice, and the pulsar stave's been in Procyon's possession. The rips are bound to come faster and with worse effect the more of the weapons wind up in the same realm. If someone is pushing to open the way for the astral fiends, it makes sense they're trying to use the blade, if it's even here." She patted my cheek and smiled. "Don't worry. We'll sniff around, but you best do some searching, too. Now run along."

The Bronco eased away from the curb and disappeared in traffic. I watched it go.

"Well," I muttered, "Better not stand around here waiting to get pinched by the cops."

The circulation desk was dead center of the main lobby, on a carpeted floor with the compass rose set in the middle. A tall, slim guy in his forties with a salt and pepper beard was helping an older woman with her monstrous smartphone, while a shorter, cheery woman with long brown hair and a dazzling smile welcomed an expectant mother carrying a bag of children's books. Signs overhead directed me to the media center, where four dozen people were hunkered over computers inside smoky glass walls. Row upon row of book spines gazed down on them from the upper floors of the west wing. Long racks of newspapers were interspersed among reading tables. A couple TV screens ran the day's news.

There was Kaszanka. I hunkered at one of the tables, folding a newspaper so I could look like I was reading while watching the screens. Lots of police and ambulance lights. Interviews with eyewitnesses. Then that grainy attack video.

"Can you believe this?" An old guy with buzz cut white hair frowned. "Looks fake."

"At least it isn't CNN," the black man next to him said, without looking up from his paper.

"What, is Fox any better?"

"Fake is fake."

They went on grumbling, but I was paying more attention to my surroundings. No sign of Ramos. It occurred to me I didn't set up any other parameters for our meeting, besides the 9 a.m. time. My watch said 8:58.

The TV news switched, and suddenly my argumentative neighbors locked their jaws. This dateline was from Drake

City, East Coast time. A building was engulfed in flames. I tried not to think about how many funerals would take place in the next few days. Then the camera whipped sideways, catching a dark streak. It zipped in and out of the windows, pausing only for a second to allow a glimpse of a flying man.

"Airfoil."

Ramos's voice made me reach for the pulsar stave. He eased into a chair next to me and set a plastic shopping bag between us. Ramos kept his gaze on the TV. "A man flies around, saving people, and it's on the morning news."

"Probably CGI." I said it, but I couldn't get rid of a strange, excited rumble in the pit of my stomach. "Also, stupid name."

"No worse than Nightstick."

I snorted.

We watched the TV in silence. So did the other people at the table.

"My grandfather fought in World War II," Ramos said. "Got shrapnel to the knee saving a man from a German stick grenade. He was shipped stateside and assigned to a motor pool with a research team. A year later, he watched from afar as a man-made sun threw a mushroom cloud into the sky. He was so horrified that when his term of enlistment was up, he moved his family to San Camillo. He'd tell us that story often, right up until he was wasting away from cancer."

I nodded. Don't know what answer he wanted, but it seemed appropriate.

"This is on par with the first nuke. It changed everything. So will what's happening in Drake City, and here."

"You're telling me."

"Did you find her?"

"I'd rather talk about it somewhere more private."

"That's what I thought. Go to the northwest stairwell. Stop

177

on the black tiles at the third-floor landing, in the corner by the Shakespeare bust. Wait for me." He pressed the plastic bag into my hand.

I followed his instructions. Will Shakespeare's blank-eyed stare unnerved me so bad that after two minutes, I was digging into the plastic bag.

"You're kidding me." I held up a pair of silver-rimmed sunglasses with red-orange mirrored lenses.

Ramos hustled up the stairs. "They're for confusing facial recognition if you get caught on city cameras. It won't completely defeat it, but it will buy you time, and throw the system into doubt."

"Okay. And … Wow. A flip phone."

"Fresh from the drugstore. Thirty bucks. There's a card for minutes and text."

"Gee, thanks. I'll place my first call to 2005."

"You can be ungrateful later, when I'm gone." He crossed his arms. "So?"

"Wilhelmina had a lot to say, much of it stuff you don't need to worry about. Bottom line: I've got my weapon and Teget's, but there's a third one I've got to find in order to stabilize the wobbly barrier between our dimensions. If not, whoever's messing around with the astral fiends lately could use the blade—the third weapon—to open that door for good."

"There'd be no stopping them."

I shook my head.

"This is what I was trying to talk about," Ramos said. "Things that change at such an accelerated pace, people become afraid."

"You say that, and you don't seem the slightest bit worried about a monster onslaught."

"I'm worried. But I'm doing my best to not be afraid. I've

been promised that I don't have to." Ramos pointed at the phone. "I put my number in the contacts. It's already activated. You should hide out, now that you've heard from Wilhelmina. Stay at my house."

"Are you kidding? I'm on the run from police and my boss, so I don't have time for a slumber party in the middle of a new quest." I made a face. "Why are we in this stairwell, anyway?"

"Security camera's down. It won't be reinstalled until the weekend. No one's watching our conversation."

"You're sticking your neck out an awful lot for me." The thought of Ramos getting disciplined, or even losing his badge, made my guts churn.

"It's the least I can do to help defend my city from those devils," Ramos said. "You're only one man."

"About that." I scratched the back of my head. "Procyon ran DNA tests. They say Teget is my brother. As in, from the same mother. And father."

Ramos refrained from comment.

"Marigold made some vague statement about a couple coming through the rip, from the Interstice. Wilhelmina confirmed people live beyond that space. So, I guess I'm from way out of town. I'm not human like you are."

"Maybe. Yet, you're risking your life to keep regular old humans safe."

"Force of habit. And also, paycheck."

Ramos chuckled. "Right. Call me when you need a hand."

"Like when I break into Procyon to free my interdimensional brother?"

"Anything you need. I'll do my best."

"I don't want you breaking the law."

"Let me decide what I should risk. My conscience will only allow me to ignore so much, and where it's confused, my faith will guide me the rest of the way."

I shrugged. "Whatever, Ramos."

"You're welcome. Keep to the side streets."

Easy for him to say. He was the one leading the manhunt. Hopefully that meant he'd keep his officers *away* from the side streets.

I headed downstairs, mind churning with possibilities. I couldn't go home. Probably a bad idea to attempt a headlong rush at Procyon without scouting out their heightened security. Of course, it helped that I knew what protocols they'd take after what was being treated as a break-in: security personnel in the parking lot checking IDs; lockdown of Tower Three; Winston's drones flying surveillance at a hundred yards around the property, in addition to over the towers. Everything going into and out of their property was gonna get the stink-eye.

Which meant I'd have to be extremely clever to get inside without everyone saying, "Hey, isn't that the Mercury guy who used to work here? The one who stole the trans-dimensional weapons?"

I grimaced at my distorted reflection in the gaudy sunglasses Ramos gave me. No matter what he said about facial recognition, I doubted I could Clark Kent my way through the situation. Still, I didn't want to take the risk, so I put them on. The lenses made everything look like it'd been dunked in orange juice.

Next step: transportation. My bus and trolley pass was one of those yearly deals that let you ride unlimited on San Camillo Bay Transit Authority's routes. There was a monthly fee, yeah, but when you compared it with parking expenses, it was decent value. If it weren't for having to periodically leave the city to chase down astral fiends I probably wouldn't have bothered with a car. But it also had a handy app for tracking usage online. Which meant that last bus ride I took showed up in my account.

I'd seen Winston use his computer network wizardry. Had he hacked into my accounts? Tracked my phone? No idea. But if anyone could, it'd be him, so no point taking chances. I dropped it in a trash can.

Hmm. Better cancel the card later so some homeless dude doesn't binge-ride on my dime.

I walked back down to Court Street.

I needed a car. Preferably one that didn't scream fugitive. As much as I appreciated the rides from Wilhelmina's mute giant, Jamie, their shiny Bronco wasn't exactly subtle.

But I'd seen some guys who knew how to get around quietly.

Finding the same gang I'd run into on Promenade last night and this morning was easy. I must have freaked them out both times because they were still on guard, only this time, the four guys hanging out on the doorstep of the sagging rowhome didn't rush me. They waited.

I made things easier by walking right to their sidewalk. "Hey, fellas. Got a favor to ask."

The guy with bruises on his neck fingered his injury as I reached their stoop. "You got a funny way of asking to die, man."

"Not interested in dying."

"I seen you on the news. In some kinda trouble, right? Cops wanna know where you are." He grinned. A gold tooth? Really? "Might be worth our while."

"Let's see." I ticked off on two fingers. "I threw you away from my car with one hand, and then I melted your boy's gun.

Which of those would you like to repeat?"

The grin faded to a smirk. "You got brass. Okay. What can we do for you?"

"I need a car. Preferably one I don't have to go through the loan process for."

"Oh, yeah? What, you got a stack of bills you gonna give me in exchange?"

That triggered his men laughing. I chuckled too, but mostly at the desperation I must be feeling to ask drug dealers to borrow one of their cars. There were three of them, lined up at the curb: a sporty Subaru sedan; a gray SUV; and a Dodge Avenger. Hmm. Which one did I like the least? "Tell you what, let's make a different deal?"

He spread his arms, lifting part of his shirt so I could see the gun in his waistband. The other three guys were armed, too. Melting one weapon had been a neat trick; four at once might be more difficult.

I drew the pulsar stave, engaged it, and drove the energized staff deep into the engine block of the Avenger.

All four shouted and rushed down the steps, reaching for their guns. I kept the stave sputtering sparks from a glowing red and yellow hole in the Avenger's hood and whipped the ax from my belt. I reflexively willed it into action like I would the stave, and it responded, with a slower run-up but man— it buzzed with such strength my hand trembled. My posture improved. Every muscle felt like it was made of steel.

"Give me the keys to the Subaru, and I'll leave you a not-dead ride," I snapped. "Pull a trigger, and I'll melt off way more important things than your gun barrels."

I could *hear* the ax humming, in sync with the stave. Maybe those guys could too, because nobody shot. Each of the three gave the boss sideways glances, as they fidgeted where they stood in a phalanx around my position.

"Your choice." I separated the stave, leaving one half embedded in the car's hood, and tossed the other half end over end. "Keys."

# CHAPTER
TWENTY-TWO

The Subaru helped me accomplish two goals.

One, it provided a decent platform from which I could observe Procyon's heightened security. Knowing their protocols and observing them firsthand were different.

Two, it helped salve my itch to drive. Yeah, I know, it'd been less than 24 hours since the double-XL astral fiend had chopped mine in two.

I took a long, looping route into the heart of the city, then back down to Bay so I could cruise along with the coastal traffic right past Procyon's property. A quick pass hinted they had indeed ramped things up. There was a silver SUV with tinted windows was parked just inside the driveway, beyond the granite stone bearing the foundation's logo—a four-pointed star outlined in black, with twin parallelograms flanking the right tip.

A hop around the nearest block gave me room to reverse direction and slip into a parking spot between two similar-sized cars on the opposite side of Bay. The harder I looked, the more I saw: two security guys walking a leisurely track by the sidewalk from the parking lot up to Tower One; a second

SUV on the waterfront side of the property, near the footpath along the harbor; and … Yep, four drones spread out to the points of the compass high above the compound.

Hmm. Any direct approach would get me snagged by the guys on foot, or at least pinpointed by Winston's drones. They had simple cameras, IR scanners, the works. What about those modifications Loredana had forced him to make?

Her name resurrected the sharp memory of her holding Jack Jackson at gunpoint while I rabbited. I shouldn't have left her behind. But I didn't really know whose side she was on. She gave me the window to escape and retrieve both weapons. Sure, a few of the calls on my phone—at least, before I'd smashed it—were from her. There was no way of knowing whether she'd had a change of heart and wanted to report me. Plus, she was highly placed in Procyon. If I were her, would I risk that power to help an operative who'd blown it?

I drummed my fingers on the steering wheel. I should contact her. It was too risky to call, text, email, or even throw a folded-up paper airplane across the highway. What would I say, anyway? "Miss you lots?" Blargh.

Down the street, a couple of kids walked into Blaze Comics. The store had a sign in the window for a sale on graphic novels and geek gear of all kinds. Hmm. I still had cash in my wallet.

Mindful of what the security goons were up to, I followed the kids into the store. The place had one wall of comic books, row upon row of brilliant, noisy covers full of promised adventure. The other wall had action figures, hats, bags, T-shirts, plush figurines, and a billion other pieces of merchandise nobody really needed but man, were they fun to get. Like badges to a secret society, letting you walk down the street and get a few knowing winks from the scattered geek brothers and sisters.

I found a T.A.R.D.I.S. ornament easily enough.

As soon as I paid the guy, I grabbed a pen from his counter, flipped the ornament over, and scribbled "Star Wars Forever" on the base. Then I tapped one of the kids on the shoulder. "Got a job for you."

The three boys—one black, one white, and one Latino—eyed me with mutual suspicion. One had his cell phone out. Probably ready to dial 9-1-1 in case I offered them candy or a puppy.

"You see that truck across the road?" I pointed at the Procyon security SUV.

"Yeah." The black kid folded his arms. "So?"

"I'll give you guys ten bucks to give this to the guys in it." I waved the ornament in front of them.

The white kid fidgeted with his phone. "Why wouldn't we just take the money and the box?"

Tough crowd. "Because if you do it right, there's ten more bucks waiting with the store clerk when you come back in here. Twenty total."

The black kid shook his head. "Ten bucks *each*."

Sixty? We were seriously scraping the bottom of my non-electronic funds. Be cool. "Five each to take it over, then five each when you get back. Thirty."

The Latino kid whispered something to the white boy. "And you buy us each a comic we want," the white kid added.

I scowled. "*One* comic. To share"

"Deal." The black kid held out his hand.

"Fine." I went to shake it.

"The money, man."

Sheesh. I dug out enough ones and fives to make it worth their while. "Wait ten minutes, got it? Or no second half."

"Yeah, whatever."

They took my cash and the ornament. I bought them their stupid comic. Got a $20 bill changed from the clerk, gave him the instructions, which earned me a shrug and mumbled, "'Kay."

Once I was back in the car, it seemed to take forever for the little brats to finish up in the store. Even thought my watch was lying. Had it really been ten minutes? Felt like an hour.

Finally they scooted across the road—at a crosswalk up the block, thankfully. I couldn't see much of their interaction with the security guys, but it only lasted a few seconds.

The reaction was worth it. Once the kids were gone, two men got out of the car. One was jabbering away on his radio. The other scanned the street, both sides.

I slid down in the driver's seat.

After a spell of concerted but ineffectual searching, the guy holding the T.A.R.D.I.S. started walking toward Tower Three. Someone came out of the lobby and met him halfway.

Loredana.

There was no mistaking her, even from this distance. Her red hair blazed like a lighthouse's beacon. Whatever she said to the guard was lost to me, but he straightened up like a drill sergeant was berating him for scuffed boots.

That's when I noticed the drones shifting position.

One of them was coming right for me. Really? Maybe I was imagining …

No. Hang on. I interrupted my own thoughts about the drones. Loredana again. She'd had Winston recalibrate them for greater sensitivity in detecting tachyon emissions, like from the rip.

But the pulsar stave also leaked tachyons.

I started the car and whipped out into traffic. Didn't bother looking at Procyon, Loredana, or security, just got out of there.

I made several random turns, twisting a nonsensical route across the lower hills of San Camillo, until I was headed back up DeLeon.

Nothing in the rearview mirror. I loosened my grip on the wheel.

So. One successful surveillance, at the cost of almost getting myself nabbed.

"Way to go, idiot," I muttered to myself.

I needed a place to hang out, until I figured my next moves —namely, where this blade was, and how to get Teget out of custody. Some place quiet, and open, but not swarming with people.

Rosa Roja was perfect.

It wasn't Central Park, but close. Twelve blocks long, four across, it took up a decent rectangle of city real estate in the northwest neighborhoods. You could follow the historic walking trail of old Spanish missions right to its front gates. A pair of pitted, weathered griffins glared down from stone pillars flanking a paved path beneath the verdant forest.

The two-dozen species of flowering and leafy trees didn't make the park special. The row upon row of namesake rose bushes helped, but what really marked Rosa Roja as unique were the ruins. A fire in early San Camillo destroyed two-thirds of the old downtown, I mean burned it right to its foundations. Those foundations and some crumbling walls were now overgrown by vegetation, with an artificial pond reflecting the sun's rays down what was once an extension of DeLeon. The ruins gave the place a melancholy feel, as if specters of the old settlers could drift up from the ground and start walking beside the scattered pedestrians.

They also provided hidden corners and nooks in which couples could make out, or drug dealers could push their wares. Or, say, an operative with a secret monster-slaying organization could practice with his new toy.

After a few minutes wandering the park, spent looking for the best such secluded spot, I was satisfied Winston's drones hadn't followed me. Don't ask me why not. Maybe those recalibrations weren't good enough. Maybe the tachyons emitted by the pulsar stave weren't traceable over greater distances. I was happy with the sky being drone-free.

The best spot turned out to be the crumpled corner of two walls, ten feet tall at the highest point. A bastion of cork oaks shielded the nook from passersby, as did the hedges and shorter trees arrayed along the winding pathways. I joined the pulsar stave with the ax, watching as sparks like miniature lightning crawled up and down its length.

Talk about a rush. I swept the joint weapon through a series of warm-up exercises, recalling not just my regular practices but also the moves Wilhelmina exhibited. The sheer power flowing from them was unlike anything I'd ever felt using just the pulsar stave. I could have run out to Arbor Valley and back again, twice. Take your favorite cup of coffee, the one that gets you humming in the morning, drink about six of those, and you'd be good to go.

That exhilaration, though, was accompanied by sadness. The weight of the weapon pressed hard—not literal weight, but the responsibility kind. This wasn't about me cutting off tentacles and banishing individual monsters anymore. This was a full-on quest, one of good versus evil, and my employers were in the mix. It was a matter of separating friend from enemy, right from wrong.

Said the guy who bullied drug dealers into lending him a

car by causing several grand in property damage.

I whipped the ax-stave in a blinding arc, one so bright it made me glad for the goofy sunglasses Ramos lent me. A chunk of stone blew out, shards flying everywhere. I stared through a long, foot-wide slice in the dilapidated wall. Yikes. Good thing nobody was walking anywhere nearby.

I held the ax end close to my face. Did Teget use this thing like I used the stave? Was his life one of sitting around, interspersed with moments of raging adrenaline while he fought astral fiends?

More importantly, was the guy really my brother?

The DNA test was one thing. The physical resemblance was another.

I had a lot of questions for him, which weren't going to get answered out here. I needed to get into Procyon. Which meant I needed one of two things—a disguise, or help.

Probably both.

I could see my reflection doubled in the ax's blades. I slipped off the sunglasses, because the things looked stupid, like I was a celebrity making a half-hearted attempt to avoid the paparazzi.

Instead my reflection dragged me in.

I felt myself falling down a tunnel, sides made of pure light. Only time I'd ever tripped out like that was when I'd gone under for some major tooth work as a kid. Brightness grew.

Then I got dumped into hell.

Red skies, black clouds, searing lightning, the stench of death. Stick your head in a Dumpster full of a month's garbage and some dead cats. I would have thrown up, but I think I was having a vision. Can you puke in a vision?

A great, violet-trimmed arch spread across a hilly landscape. The inside pulsed with latent energy. Astral fiends poured out, some small with stunted tentacles, others huge and brimming with fangs. They swamped across the hills, among buildings in flames. Soldiers mowed them down as they came, but it was useless, because for every fiend that was blown apart in a blue mist, five took its place. The monsters overran the troops, bleeding them dry of their energy, leaving behind cold, mummified husks.

A person stood on a nearby building, wreathed in shadow. Whoever it was held aloft the ax-stave, the same joint weapon I'd just practiced with, except it was longer. A sword was attached to the other end of the stave, its blade straight one edge and curved on the other, the latter portion sweeping down close to the hilt.

Power radiated from this weapon in waves, pulsing. Astral fiends raised their tentacles, drawn towards it.

The blade pulled me in, too.

I rushed headlong, screaming, until the nightmare scenario vanished.

I was in a dark room. Metal shelves. Humming machinery. Cold. Air conditioning? There was a pedestal in the middle, made of faded, weather-beaten stone.

The blade rested on top, by itself.

There was lettering on the door ...

I landed on my hands and knees, shivering. The bright, happy sun of Rosa Roja park filtering through oak leaves was grotesque and foreign, until I remembered who I was and where I'd been.

Then I puked.

I wiped my mouth with the back of my hand, fingers trembling. Had I really seen the blade Wilhelmina mentioned? If so, not very helpful. Air-conditioned room, in some place, with some label I couldn't read.

Worst. Vision. Ever.

But it was undeniable. If this is what Marigold went through each time a rip was Forecasted, I didn't envy her. "The blade's near," I muttered at the grass. "It has to be."

Too bad I couldn't just Google it.

The heavy tread of boots told me to get up off my knees and quick contemplating. Nobody wore boots in downtown San Camillo in the spring. Especially not on the park's paths. That was sneakers and sandals territory.

I glimpsed men in black polo shirts and slacks coming up the path.

You could tell Procyon wasn't used to undercover work. Of course, with the police on their side, why bother?

I hurried in a roundabout route to my borrowed car, only to find three of them coming at me on a perpendicular. They slowed fifty feet away.

"Hey, boys." I saluted with the ax-stave. "Nice day."

They had Tasers and zero interest in small talk, I guess, because they came running.

I ran, too, and let's just say that caffeine-jolted feeling from the weapon translated into more than just fighting, because the next thing I knew I was bent double over the Subaru's hood, exhausted and sweating. Couldn't catch my breath.

No sign of my pursuers behind me. Only a path of broken limbs and ripped leaves.

Well, that was—awesome.

Less pondering, more escaping.

I dove into the Subaru and floored it.

CHAPTER
TWENTY-THREE

The silver sedan pulled out into traffic three cars back. They sure weren't wasting any time.

Problem was, neither of us could plow through the streets. They didn't want to get themselves pulled over for speeding, and I didn't want to draw attention in the same manner.

Speaking of the cops, where the heck were they? I'd seen periodic patrols, but nothing I'd expect for a department that was supposed to be sniffing for me. Ramos must have been doing a bang-up job keeping them aimed in the wrong direction. Of course, somebody higher up might have decided a supposed thief posed way less a threat than the combined murderers, rapists, and shooters who made the headlines every day in this city.

I led the chase car west, scooting through yellow lights, but he stayed close. I wondered at his plan. Not like he could run me off the road.

I was still mulling that over when a silver SUV pulled away from a parking spot in front of a U-Hall truck. It braked hard.

So did I. Personal safety aside, I didn't want to add to the drug dealer's anger by wrecking his car. I really did intend to return it.

The SUV's rash action brought traffic to a standstill, at least in our lane. Horns erupted in angry chorus around us. I added mine, not wanting anyone else to get the impression I didn't think this was just another commute's irritation.

That ploy worked right up until I spotted four guys sprinting from the silver car behind me.

Two more got out of the SUV in front. Tasers again. I wondered how they were gonna explain this bit of vigilantism to the police. It occurred to me I might disappear, leaving the cops no one to investigate. Besides, these security guys wore no badges and their vehicles had no markings that would link them to Procyon to curious bystanders.

The cars in the opposite lane finally got moving. Two slid by, the drivers gawking at me. My fingers tightened on the wheel. If I got lucky …

The third car didn't budge. More horns. I could see a teenage girl in the driver's seat, face locked in zombie-gaze fashion at her phone.

I changed gears and backed up.

The guys running from behind shouted. They scattered onto the sidewalk and into the street as I missed them by inches. I braked way too close to the car behind me, which also went into reverse in order to avoid a mashed bumper. I heard *his* rear fender hit the car behind *him*. More shouts, this time from open car windows. I felt really bad for about two seconds.

Then I put the Subaru into second gear and raced around the SUV.

That little car could slalom with the best downhill skier, let me tell you. I caught a glimpse of the teenager shrieking—and the security guys glowering—before I was back in the correct lane. Had a nice straightaway caused by the backup in my wake, enough so I put some serious speed between me and the mess. Only once my heart had stopped racing did I decide the car should do likewise.

I made a bunch of right-left-right turns, taking me to the northwest side of the city. Downtown's skyscrapers gave way to multi-story townhouses and storefronts, which in turn petered out, replaced by wall-to-wall suburbia. Wells Heights was home to all the snobby rich people you could stomach, the kind of people who glare at you when you're shouting at a baseball game on the bar's TV while they're trying to have dinner with their equally snobby neighbors. Or so I'd heard.

Right then, I'd never been happier to be amongst the rich and constipated, because whatever idiot designed their neighborhood decided there shouldn't be a straight road or right angle in the place. Useful for confusing, say, a driver trying to follow you.

I tooled around the place until I felt as lost as those goons hopefully were. Wells Heights had a mini-mall centered around a Whole Foods grocery store. I slipped into the parking lot, and found the biggest, most ostentatious SUVs between which I could squeeze the Subaru.

Five minutes went by before I could bring myself to get out of the car. There was a warm wind blowing up from the coast. San Camillo was a cluster of silver blocks and brown lumps down by the sparkling blue bay. I took it back. Whoever designed the neighborhood did a great job of providing an expansive vantage point from which one could see, well, everything. No sign of silver vehicles.

I sat on the hood. Taking a breather felt great, especially after that vision had wrung me out. I reached under my coat for the pulsar stave but hesitated. Not sure I wanted to repeat what had happened in the park.

Instead I concentrated on my memory of the vision. A closet. Wasn't much to it, except it seemed clean. The wording on the door bothered me. It didn't make sense. Who puts lettering on the inside of a door? The only people who would see it would be someone standing ...

Okay, forget the logic. I had to try to read it.

Nobody bothered me, but I must have looked like a lunatic sitting there, legs draped over the side of the hood, fingers pressed to my temples. Maybe if I put out a hand somebody'd leave me loose change. Since I didn't dare use my debit or credit cards, I actually wouldn't say no to extra cash.

Enough of that. The door.

What did it say?

Black marks became scratches. Scratches became scribbles. Scribbles became words. But the words didn't make a bit of sense.

I quick scrambled into the driver's seat. There had to be a pen, or a pencil. I popped open the glove box, and immediately wished I hadn't. A half-empty bag of potato chips hit the floor, spilling its contents. Papers of all kinds, some crumpled, some pristine, avalanched after. Thankfully there weren't any weapons, or paraphernalia. Last thing I needed was to get brought up on possession charges.

There were three pens among the debris. I tried the first two before uncapping the filthiest one I'd ever touched. Pretty sure yellow wasn't the original color. I wrote down what I could remember.

One to sever. Two to unbalance. Three to liberate.

Okay. So, that was cryptic. I thought about Wilhelmina's history lesson. She said all three weapons could unite and close the path to the Interstice for good. But that didn't sound like liberation. It sounded like imprisonment.

Still no clue as to where the blade was, though. Kinda wish I'd envisioned in what building the closet sat. Maybe the link between the weapons only took me to the precise space the blade inhabited, and since someone was smart enough to lock it in a windowless room, I was up a creek. Maybe Marigold could give me some pointers, if I ever got to go back to Procyon as an operative instead of a fugitive.

I flung the pen into the back seat and slapped my hand on the dashboard. "Or maybe they should have covered all these stupid secrets in Orientation!"

Neither the chips nor the Subaru were impressed by my tantrum. Whatever. There was only one way to find this stupid blade.

I was going to have to try another vision.

Five attempts.

That's how many I made before I stopped getting sick to my stomach.

After the seventh time of gazing like a doofus into the ax's edge, I knew two things: the blade was still stashed in a closet, and I couldn't tell if I was getting closer to its hiding place. No new details appeared, except that each time I tried the vision-thing, the surroundings got sharper.

Downside? Whoever had the blade was smart enough to keep absolutely nothing on the closet shelves that could identify the place. Nothing except that aggravating saying on the wrong side of the door.

Perfect. Now what?

I'd managed to kill most of the day. Not a word from Ramos, but then again, he hadn't said anything about him calling me. This was supposed to be a lifeline phone, something I could use if I were in a tight spot.

Well, I don't think being confused was the kind of tight spot he had in mind.

And of course, Wilhelmina hadn't left a number of her own. I drove out on the 311, eyes on the rear view mirror. Were any of those headlights hers? Or Procyon's? No idea. By then, I didn't care.

I needed answers.

That's why I figured my bottom of the ninth, score tied, bases loaded at bat would be to revisit the old hacienda. The double astral fiends appeared there. So had Teget. Everything that broke, broke at the abandoned farm house.

My car was gone. A furrow in the grass and several trees denuded of branches marked where the halves had been tossed. A light rain washed away engine fluids, spreading the slick across the yard as it steadied. Otherwise, I was standing in front of the same creepy, dark house I'd been to the other night. Last night. I shook my head as I headed into the room where the rip had appeared. I was banking on the tachyon emissions still being strong. Winston thought they faded at a slower pace when the initial breach was stronger. Some kind of correlation he didn't understand.

Yeah, well, he could get in line.

I stood at the point where the dust had been blasted clean from the floor. This was it. I joined the stave and the ax. The cold, slick surface of both made me shiver. Did I really want to go for an eighth try? It felt pointless.

A car's engine rumbled out on the road. Headlights washed across the building, highlighting deep shadows. I expected a squad of Procyon security guys, but it was only one car, by the sounds of it. I stuck to the walls and edged forward for a better look.

Jack Jackson shone his cell phone's light into my borrowed Subaru, raindrops flickering through the beam. He must have seen the pile of junk on the passenger side floor, because he frowned and leaned in for a closer look. That gave me my opening to harness the ax-stave's energy and leap the intervening space. I landed right behind him and touched the stave's tip to the back of his neck. "No sudden moves. Never beheaded a person before, and I don't want to clean up the mess, not after the day I've had."

Jackson chuckled. "Son, you near had me wet my shorts." He turned—slowly—with his hands loose at his side, and grinned great big. He didn't need that cell phone light; I was sure his teeth could have lit up the Subaru's interior. "I'm glad I found you. I want you to come back in."

"So I get charged with trespassing on top of theft and assault? Nope." I disconnected the weapons and tucked them away. This wasn't an astral fiend. It was the guy who signed my paychecks and liked to dump Maker's Mark in people's coffee.

"They *do* join." Jackson shook his head. "By golly, if I'd known that … Mercury, this is a whole new ball of wax. I'll be the first to admit, we botched things badly. Should we have told you the true nature of your work? Absolutely. Was there a good time to do it? Nah."

"I'm more concerned with learning the true nature of *me*, let alone my work."

"You're not from around these parts."

"So I've heard."

"Don't pout. I've admitted we done wrong. Point is, we all know the score now, so why not put the whole team back in the game? These attacks are increasing in frequency and unpredictability."

A sickening feeling settled in my gut. "There haven't been more since I left, have there?"

"Not that we know of. That's why I need you back." He put a hand on my shoulder. I must have let my guard down because I didn't immediately cut it off. "We'll figure out how to stop this craziness together."

I wiped water from my face. "Teget. He shouldn't be locked up."

Jackson sighed. "Yeah, I know. He's been fine. We ran a few tests, but none without asking him first. He's been wondering about you, mind. Confirms what the DNA tests told us—he's your brother. Says there's a third weapon that needs finding, one he's afraid is already in the wrong hands."

It was about then I realized there was someone in the driver's seat of Jackson's sedan. Someone tall, dark, and slim. "You brought Calvin?"

He snorted. "The dope thought I'd be in mortal danger from you. I told him to tag along if he needed to feel better, but there wasn't a chance you'd hurt me."

I smirked. "Maybe a small chance. Okay, so you call off the manhunt. Then what?"

"Then, son, we dig deep. We get into File 6-1848 and anything else in the Historic Vault that helps us stop whatever's going down. The board of directors has tasked me with keeping a lid on this thing. I've got your back. Let's get talking with Winston and Marigold, see if we can't pinpoint the disturbance."

My heart swelled. I knew it. They wouldn't turn their backs on me. Not my team. Not this foundation, to whom I'd given the past years and all of my life. "We can start by figuring out why my parents left me in this dimension."

"Sooner the better. Calvin!" Jackson beckoned. He didn't seem bothered by the rain in the slightest. In fact, I half expected Calvin to bring a six-pack, so we could celebrate. Or a bottle of whiskey.

Calvin had a gun.

I couldn't tell what kind, except it was small, and black, with a ridiculously long barrel. Scratch that. It was a suppressor.

Jackson had time to scowl and reach out for his assistant before Calvin shot him in the forehead.

Blood spattered on me, sticky and hot on my face. I froze, unsure of what I'd seen, of whether or not this was another vision. Jackson's body getting soaked on the muddy terrain looked real enough.

Calvin didn't shoot me. Instead, he tossed the gun at me.

My reflexes activated, snapping me back to the present. I caught the gun.

"Thank you for that. Your fingerprints on the gun help sell the story." Calvin's dry monotone was gone, replaced by a smooth, lilting baritone. "We're going to be careful about what's to come next."

"Are you insane? You killed him!" I pointed the gun at him, realizing belatedly that it was exactly what he wanted.

"Of course I did. The idiot couldn't be on your side. Not when there's so much at stake." Calvin leaned into the sedan and honked the horn.

Men in black fatigues swarmed us—four from across the highway, two from the woods on either side. They were wrapped in body armor, heads helmeted and faces obscured by goggles and masks. Eight blazing white flashlight beams cut through the gloom, forcing me to shield my eyes, but not before my brain registered semi-automatic rifles behind those lights.

"Drop the gun! Do it now!" Sounded like Murray the

security goon. Since when did these guys have S.W.A.T. gear in the budget?

"He shot Mr. Jackson!" Calvin hunkered against the car. "Take him!"

Turns out those guns were automatics.

# CHAPTER TWENTY-FOUR

I did what the man asked and dropped the gun.

That didn't stop all eight of them from shooting at me. But I was already moving.

I leapt back and to the left with same speed I'd managed fleeing them at Rosa Roja Park, when I'd slammed into the Subaru. This time I went headfirst over a broken wall, slamming my shoulder onto the ground. Pain stabbed through, however, I counted it a plus versus what I'd feel from hundreds of bullets.

I cowered there under the barrage of gunfire, unable to think or move with the weapons' roar echoing around me. The sound was a physical force, a giant hand holding me in place. Thoughts barraged me at the same time:

Calvin shot Jackson.

He framed me for the Procyon manager's murder.

A hit squad was trying to kill me. Self-defense? How was that going to play with the police?

Speaking of, I was regretting Ramos's interference on my behalf. A jail cell seemed a whole lot safer than being out in the rain, huddled from my current—former?—co-workers trying to kill me.

The ludicrousness struck me like a lightning bolt. Last night I killed two slavering monsters from a parallel dimension. Tonight, I was hiding from eight men with guns. Seriously? This was *nothing*.

I drew both weapons from under my coat. Fine. They wanted to kill me? They were gonna have to work for it.

I waited until a lull in the gunfire and sprinted deeper into the house during that moment of silence. Said moment wasn't long. Flashlight beams illuminated my body and the bullets flew again. But I was behind another wall, flinching as shards of adobe and wood sprayed around me.

The guns went silent, yet again. I strained against the downpour for sounds of their movement—boots tapping on stone, squelching in mud.

Three groups, like they'd come in. Four through the front, two each around the sides. Trying to surround me.

I willed the stave to life. Ditto for the ax. I kept them separate because, well, if I got sandwiched between a couple of these guys, I wanted to be able to smack two at a time.

As furious and sick and scared as I was, I also vowed to take a look at Procyon's handbook, which I was pretty sure did not recommend keeping armored death squads on the payroll. They had to be something Calvin cooked up.

The fact that there were eight of them was a bad sign.

Metal clanked across the floor. A canister? Tear gas. It spun a couple feet away, smoke already billowing from both ends. How did these morons think they were gonna see? Rain would keep the stuff from my face, no matter how bad it stung, and their visibility would be toast.

Oh. They probably had night vision goggles.

I got on one knee and swept the canister away in a slapshot

that would have made any hockey player on the San Camillo Rays proud. The four men coming from the front of the house shouted, their flashlights thrown into disarray.

That was my cue.

I sped into their midst and used the stave's energy to slice one gun in half, an H&K MP5. So, not a rifle. I stand corrected. There was a split second in which the security guy stared at the two pieces of firearm clutched in each hand before I walloped him across the helmet.

The next guy swung his gun toward me, but I slipped out of his way. The muzzle flash half-blinded me, so I could only see out of one eye. Fun. I planted the dull end of the ax in his midsection and pushed hard, like I was giving a kid on a playground swing the best shove ever.

Poor sap flew twenty feet across the room, raindrops shimmering as his flashlight beam swung wildly.

The other two guys thought better of shooting that near to each other. One used his submachine gun as a billy club and bashed me on the arm. Wasn't time for standing around and assessing damage, so when the next blow came, I blocked it with the stave. The second remaining dude did the same thing at the same time, but a quick swipe with the ax, its blades trailing white lighting through the black night, sent him staggering backward. His arms pinwheeled, the gun spinning into the rain, its halves glowing red like campfire coals where the ax had done its work.

See? It was better to keep the weapons separate.

The first guard threw a couple punches my way but come on—fighting him was like dodging a turtle. Astral fiends send tentacles slashing at me from all angles at incredible speeds. I couldn't help feeling sorry for him. Had I ever had lunch with him in Procyon's cafeteria? That was what crossed my mind as

I planted the ax hilt in his gut, and my fist in his mask.

Light blazed around me. Right. The other two duos must have circled back. Better not stand around. I brought the weapons together, let their surge of power build, and leapt straight up.

You know, I'd never tried that before—not indoors, I mean. The plan was to execute an acrobatic landing among the rafters. Instead I shot through the rotting roof with the speed and force of a less lethal missile.

Wood and terracotta tile exploded around me. I tumbled across the undulating surface, scrabbling for a handhold. The stave jabbed between beams as my legs dangled off the edge of a huge gap.

Okay, so that was a mistake. I'd escaped their clutches but also the cover of being mixed among my opponents. They figured it out faster than I did.

Bullets ripped through the roof. Something hot and painful, as bad as a fiend's fang, slit my right shoulder, and another sliced across the right leg. They buzzed so close it was like hundreds of enraged bees made of metal were trying to kill me. Not too far from the truth.

Anger refused to ebb. I wasn't going to roll over and let Calvin's stooges get away with this. Someone had to know what really happened here.

So, I let go of the roof.

I plummeted into the dark space, flashlights sweeping the air in a vain attempt to center on me. By the way they were aimed, I gathered most of the men were in a ragged circle around my hiding place on the roof. All the better to make it easier for me stomp all of them at once.

I flipped in midair, my shoulder and arm seizing with pain, but I could've cared less. The power from the combined weapons made everything slow, and I could see way better than when this fight started. It was as if I had my own pair of night vision goggles implanted in my eyeballs. Every raindrop traveled so slowly I could have picked them out of the air and stuck them in my pockets.

Things got crazy when I hit the floor, stave-first.

A white and yellow blast of lightning rolled off me in a tidal wave of extra-dimensional energy, sweeping the floor clean of water, dirt, trash, and more importantly, the kill squad. They tumbled like leaves knocked off trees, heads over feet. Weapons that weren't held in place by straps went missing in the darkness.

Good a time as any for a phone call. I hit the redial.

"Mercury?"

"Ramos! They're trying to kill me! Calvin blew Jackson's head of! They've got a whole squad of guys with automatic weapons!" I ran for the front door.

"What? Where are you?"

"The hacienda where the two fiends—"

Something metal hit the floor to my left. The detached, curious part of my brain couldn't figure out what good a miniature green pineapple would be in a fight, until the grenade exploded.

The concussive force blew me sideways off my escape route. I didn't remember anything for the next five seconds or so, until I woke up in the grass and mud outside. Rain pelted my face. Everything hurt. There was a me-sized hole in a ragged section of wall. I was surrounded by adobe fragments and a couple shattered wood beams. The ax-stave lay four feet away.

Sounds were muddier than I was. I rolled over. If I screamed from the pain, I couldn't hear it. Had to get the weapon. Had to get out of here. The phone? Lost.

Feet entered my line of sight. Nice loafers. Not boots. A hand picked up the ax-stave. Everything snapped into focus.

"It's too bad I'm not one of the kind who can make use of this." Calvin turned the weapon over in his hands. The sparks were gone. It could have been a thick piece of rebar. Nothing but a hunk of metal. "Amazing device, isn't it? Procyon has never been able to date the pulsar stave. Winston's run innumerable tests using the latest methods, building upon the research of the last century and a half. All we know is it's powerful, and it draws that power from the Interstice. Roughly."

"Give that to me, murderer." That's what I tried to say. Whether or not Calvin understood was unclear. I got onto my knees. Even that slow, pained move was enough for the nausea and dizziness to knock me back over.

He planted the ax end against my chest. "Nice thing about this bit your buddy Teget brought us? It has sharp edges, so I don't need to access any esoteric energies to kill you."

"Moron." I coughed and wiped my mouth. Blood. That was bad. "Do that and no one can use it for you."

"Nice try. Oh, I'm the good guy, so I'll make a sneaky deal with the bad guy and pretend to be on his side." Calvin shook his head. "I'm not an idiot, Mercury, or a moron, as you so creatively put it. Besides …" He smiled. "Why do I need you at all?"

The realization hit me worse than the vertigo. Why hadn't that grenade blast killed me? Or the trip through the wall? The stave's energy gave me enhanced strength; maybe both weapons upped my game even more. "You have someone to use it for you."

"Now you show intelligence. Of course there's someone else. How do you think the increased rips and more powerful fiends have come about?"

"Don't do it."

He rolled his eyes. "We already have done it. It's a matter of time before we make it permanent. Then the astral fiends will scrape the scabs off this wounded planet, and let it bleed, so it will heal itself."

"Scabs? You mean people. Men. Women. Children."

"Scum. Every last bit." Calvin leaned on the ax. The blade tips cut into my chest. "And I have to say, congratulations on getting me to wax poetic about the evil scheme. Not that I minded. It's nice to have someone besides fellow conspirators with whom I can share the joy. But you screwed up, Mercury, and now we've got all three pieces. So much for the handpicked traveler from beyond the Interstice. You're as bad as the old lady, except where we've failed to end her interference, we won't make the same mistake with you."

I didn't want to die. Who does? The though had crossed my mind a thousand times before, especially when an astral fiend got its life-sucking tentacles around me. But as Calvin withdrew the ax-stave, and brought it up for a downward blow that would crush my skull, I was struck by the possibility that This Was It. What did I have to show for it? What was it like when the lights went you? Too many questions, not enough time for answers.

I was envious of Ramos's crucifix.

A car horn blared, like a foghorn. A foghorn attached to a big white blur with a roaring engine. There was a second sound—a boom like thunder.

Headlights made Calvin shield his eyes, ax-stave still clutched in one hand. Before he could react to the giant Ford Bronco barreling down on us, the truck braked hard, splattering more mud on his nice shirt.

The passenger door opened smack against his chest, better

than any battering ram.

Wilhelmina hopped out of the seat, sans cane. She helped me to my feet, hands warm and dry. "Child, you look terrible, but you ain't dead."

"Feels like it." I cringed with every move.

"Jamie? Be a lamb." She handed me off to him.

Jamie scooped me up. I felt like I was flying. My head swam. Everything turned sideways. "Stave," I croaked.

"Yes, yes, I'm aware of the problem." Wilhelmina picked up the ax-stave. It sprang to life under her touch, sparks and light appearing with an eagerness I hoped was imagined. "Can't have this fool walking off with it."

"Stand down!"

Seriously? Three of the security guys, their body armor scratched, their masks askew, stepped out of the broken wall with a sprightliness I envied. I'd hit them *hard*, and here they came, like they were fresh for another fight.

Wilhelmina shook her head. "Don't be stupid, boys. Let's make a trade." She swept the stave and the ax apart and poised the stave's cracking beam of energy—the same part I used to sever fiend tentacles—over Calvin's throat. He moaned, eyes fluttering, but didn't seem ready to get up after having a steel door bash his chest. "You'll toss your guns out in the mud and I won't bleed your boss like a slaughtered pig."

They hesitated, but only for a few seconds. Then they threw their guns outside.

Jamie eased me into the long back seat of the Bronco, taking care to fasten my seatbelt. He gathered up the guns, slinging two over his shoulder, and taking the third MP5 for his personal new toy.

"Good idea." Wilhelmina winked. "You kids have a good evening. Do give San Camillo's finest my best, you hear."

She kicked Calvin in the ribs so hard he rolled over twice.

The guards hurried out the instant Wilhelmina got back in the Bronco. I heard sirens whining in the distance. "Jamie, dear, let's put the pedal to the floor, shall we?" she asked.

Jamie's head bobbed.

The truck raced off into the night, and with every curve it took, my perception whirled faster than, well, I did in a fiend brawl.

Wilhelmina's face appeared, fuzzy and upside down. "Stay with us, child. You've got to heal. We'll find you the place and time. Here." She pressed the stave into my hands.

Warmth spread over me like a blanket, and I blacked out.

CHAPTER TWENTY-FIVE

The next thing I remembered was the cool feeling on my forehead. Blue skies, lapping waves, calling gulls. Palm trees swayed in the breeze. Sun beat down on my skin.

"You're awake." Loredana lounged in the chair next to me. She wore a navy-blue swimsuit and tipped back a pair of sunglasses until I could see her eyes. Talk about a heavenly vision. "Here I thought you would be content napping the day away."

I wanted to tell her how happy I was to see her, but the words wouldn't form, no matter how much I worked my jaw.

"Would you care for a swim?" She stood and tossed the sunglasses on her beach chair. She walked backwards toward the jewel-like sea, finger crooked, inviting me to get up off my butt. Pronto.

I found I couldn't move, either. That sucked.

Loredana sighed. "Blast it all. Get. UP!"

Her voice took on a man's timbre, and I shook all over.

I was in bed. No sand. No sea. No Loredana, either.

Plenty of sun, though. The room was awash with it, casting everything in a golden glow. The bed sagged in the middle, and beyond the wood frame I saw a portrait of Christ on the wall. He gazed up, hands extended, fingers aglow. Sported a mean halo, too.

The guy seated below and to his right was not an apostle, and definitely not the only woman I wanted to see. Ramos sat in a thick, olive-green chair with more bald spots than, well, a guy going bald. Give me a break. I'd taken a beating.

Ramos looked up from a weathered, leather-bound Bible. "Welcome back."

"Didn't know I went anywhere." My body protested even the simple act of propping myself up on my elbows. "Ow."

"Easy." Ramos flipped to the next page. "You had a concussion, some broken ribs, and probably internal bleeding."

"So why am I in some grandma's bedroom?"

He glared at me.

Good job, Mercury. "Let me guess. This is your grandma's bedroom."

"My *abuela* passed ten years ago. We bought her house. Olivia and I thought we could use the bigger space when our third child came along, because it turned out we were having twins. This is the guest room."

The only other decorations in the room were a broad painting of a monastery, one I assumed sat on the hills around San Camillo a century ago. "Your *abuela*'s work?"

"One of her better ones. Most were plain ugly." Ramos set the Bible aside. "How do you feel?"

"Lousy. I'd be better in a hospital."

"That's doubtful, considering you'd be under police guard. The department's combing the street for you right now."

"So, you took me home?"

213

"Not exactly. Your new friends parked beside my car and waited until I came outside."

I rubbed my face. "Great plan. What, did they sit in front of the police station?"

Ramos smirked. "You tell Wilhelmina that. No, they found my address online and were playing a round of Phase 10 in that Bronco when I got back from the hacienda."

"Speaking of …"

"Jackson is dead. Calvin's pressing charges. We found the gun. CSIs are lifting prints. I assume by your expression, they're yours."

"Yeah. I stepped right into that bear trap." I shook my head. Everything rattled. Someone had packed loose rocks alongside my brains. "What about the soldiers?"

"What soldiers?"

"Calvin's black ops kill squad, decked out in enough gear to make your S.W.A.T. team salivate."

"Oh, we found plenty of brass they hadn't policed, and what appears to be evidence of a couple explosions, but no people. Calvin denies knowing anything about that aspect. He even got all choked up when he described when you shot Jackson in the face."

"Come on. You know I didn't kill the guy. He was welcoming me back into the fold and promising me cooperation in my quest when Calvin murdered him."

"I figured that from your panicked phone call. It's going to be harder to prove." Ramos leaned forward, fingers intertwined. "You're staying here until we determine our next move."

"We? Our? I'm not getting you in trouble."

"This again? We're dealing with evil, Mercury. I'm not going to let you stand against it alone. Even with that crazy old lady and her ... Who is Jamie, anyway?"

"Beats me. A chauffeur who can drive like Steve McQueen?" I chewed my lip. "They still here?"

"In the living room, reading. I brought a couple pizzas from Carlito's."

As generous as the old grump had been to me, it wasn't until he said "pizzas from Carlito's" that tears gathered in the corners of my eyes. "Hey, that's great." I cleared my throat. "You didn't have to. Okay. Thanks."

"You're welcome."

"Hang on. Did you say lunch?"

"Yes. It's two o'clock."

Wow. I was out for a *long* spell. "Did, uh, Loredana stop by?"

"I sent her a text, from a new phone with a pre-paid card." Ramos frowned. "She said something about you contacting her at a phone booth or with a phone booth or some nonsense, so she knew you were okay."

I smiled. "Yeah. Glad she did."

"She'll be here soon."

A cane thumped the door. Wilhelmina stood there with two slices of pepperoni stacked on a plate. "Bout time you woke up! How's the body healing?"

"Ramos makes it sound like I was a goner, but I think I'm okay. Got a headache, and I'm sore, but I don't feel as thrashed as last night."

"That's 'cause the pulsar stave has worked its wonders on your slightly-different body." Wilhelmina made a show of wafting the aroma from her plate. "Hungry?"

"Yes, ma'am."

Ramos got between us. "No. Not in this room. Or any other room but the one reserved for dining. Come on."

He helped me out of bed. I was wobbly for the first few steps and managed to swipe a pepperoni off the top slice without falling down. "Perfect. How'd you know?"

Wilhelmina made a face. "What other kind of pizza is acceptable?"

I hugged her.

The house was sparsely decorated with bright, bold colors. A family portrait hung in a broad hallway off of which most rooms opened—Ramos standing next to his wife, Olivia, a short, pretty lady with long black hair and a mischievous grin. Two boys, one probably in his late teens and the other a middle schooler, sat to the left, and two identical girls of indeterminate elementary age sat to the right.

I would have missed Ramos's reaction as we walked by if I hadn't been examining the photo. If his chest swelled any more he'd have broken through the walls.

Jamie was perched in a spindly, antique rocking chair crafted of a gorgeous mahogany. Don't know how he wasn't breaking it, but he was swiping through something on his phone that engrossed his attention in a big way. He glanced at me, pantomimed shooting as a way of greeting, then went back to reading.

"Don't want to interrupt his Clash of Clans round," I muttered.

"Jamie? He doesn't waste his time on that nonsense," Wilhelmina said. "This afternoon it's *The Economist* online."

I rubbed my forehead. "Why is it you're homeless, again?"

"Because life ain't always neat. It isn't tidy. Sometimes you run out of money, you get shut out of work, and when you pass seventy, who's going to bring in an old black woman with no marketable skills when there's plenty of young folks?" Wilhelmina patted my cheek. "Don't you worry about me none. I won't starve, and I won't go through the rest of my life without friends. Could I have found a way off Court Street? Probably. Probably still could. There's people out there, though, who have no options, and get no love. Better I stay near them, to show them that just because they don't have a roof over their heads doesn't mean they have to give up."

I stared after her. "Wow. Okay, I thought you were just going to say it was all part of your secret identity."

"I still say she should be in a shelter." Ramos grabbed a pitcher of water from the refrigerator. He poured five glasses.

"You should have seen her in action."

"Seen what?"

"Never mind." A car door closed outside. I hadn't heard anyone pull up, but a peek out a nearby window showed me it was a silver sedan. "Guys? That had better be Loredana."

Jamie dropped his phone. He was on his feet, sweeping between the doorway and Wilhelmina, the confiscated MP5 aimed at the peephole. Wilhelmina had the ax—wait, where'd she get it from? Her cane lay discarded on the floor. Maybe Jamie had stashed the ax behind his chair.

I powered the pulsar stave and held it at the ready. Energy surged through my body. Man. I imagined I could feel it erasing my bruises.

"Hey, hold on!" Ramos put up his hands. "I called Loredana, remember? She said she'd be here, and she's right on time. Everyone breathe, please, because if you damage this house you'll have worse than astral fiends and Procyon to face. My wife will be displeased."

He opened the door.

Loredana stood framed like a portrait, in that gray suit jacket and matching slacks. She was dressed for work, ready for action. I wondered where the silver revolver was stashed.

She had on sunglasses and carried a reinforced briefcase.

She set the case inside the door and closed it behind her. Bright blue eyes peered over the top of the sunglasses. One eyebrow arched. "Lieutenant, when you said we were to meet, I had no idea I was considered enough a threat to warrant an ambush. I'm flattered."

"You're okay." I put the stave away and tried not to grin like a big idiot. Guess what? Failed. I grabbed Loredana by the shoulders. "It's, ah, good to see you. In one piece, that is."

I was waiting for that smirk, the one that told me our partnership was intact and everything was going to be like it always had been. Instead, Loredana took off her sunglasses and hugged me. It was a long embrace, one of old friends, of two people who shared secret lives they spent most of their time pretending were normal. "I'm glad you're still with us," she whispered.

She broke the hug and fixed a loose strand of hair that had fallen across her face. Her cheeks were tinged pink. "Yes, things have gotten considerably more complicated, I see."

"Yeah, that's putting it mildly." I gestured behind me. "The guy with the gun is Jamie. Looks scary, says nothing, drives like Steve McQueen."

"How do you do." Loredana extended her hand.

"Nice to meet you." Jamie's voice was smooth, soft, like melted chocolate poured over a sundae. He shouldered the gun and shook her hand.

"And I'm Wilhelmina." She smiled and patted Loredana's arm. "You're the young lady with Procyon, aren't you? My condolences."

"Thank you. The death of Mr. Jackson has us all in a state of disarray and mourning."

"Not that, girl. I meant condolences, because the Procyon

you knew is dying. We have to conduct radical surgery if it's going to survive."

Kinda cold to say it that way, but Loredana nodded. "I concur. That's why I'm here. Teget is under heavy guard. He's been sedated, but the drugs Procyon staff used are not having the effect they hoped. I'm concerned he'll suffer lasting damage."

"They're adjusting for a normal guy," I said. "But Teget's like me."

"A stranger to our world."

"Yeah." Didn't want to think about that right now, but if it bothered Loredana at all her hug sure didn't show it at all. "This stranger's figuring out how to break into his workplace and bust his brother from another world out, while avoiding interdimensional apocalypse."

"For the record," Ramos said. "I think we should all slow down and discuss legal alternatives before contemplating a robbery. Mercury, you'd better sit and eat something before you get paler."

Eat? Wow. I'd completely forgotten the pizza.

Five minutes later I'd packed away two slices and downed a glass of water. Our conclave was weird. Jamie picked every slice of pepperoni off his plate, and stacked them neatly on the placemat, while balancing the submachine gun on his lap. Ramos scowled. He chucked the pepperoni stack onto my plate and rubbed furiously at the orange grease spot with a damp rag.

Loredana patted her lips with a napkin. "Ah, Carlito's."

"Amen, sister." Wilhelmina sighed.

"So, what's in the box?" I jerked a thumb back to the door.

"A gift. Something Winston has spent the past year or so developing, a hobby during his spare time." Loredana crossed the room and retrieved the suitcase. We all moved plates and pizza boxes from the dining room table, so she could set it on the edge. She popped the latches. A strong plastic stench escaped. "Keep in mind, it is a prototype."

She pulled out a jumpsuit. It was a navy blue so dark as to almost be black, with parallelograms of lighter gray shades arranged in wild patterns along the outside of the arms, on the rib cages, and the inside of the legs. Lines traced contours up and down the body, extending outward from an octagon on the test.

"This will help you get in and out of Procyon, unseen," Loredana said. "I understand it's your size."

I stood, taking care to wipe my hands on a napkin before I touched the clothing. It was lightweight, yet strong. I yanked on a sleeve with all my strength. Not a seam popped.

"Wait a second," I blurted. "Do I get a superhero suit?"

Loredana smirked. "I do believe that's what I said."

CHAPTER
TWENTY-SIX

I tried that sucker on immediately.

It was form-fitting, making me wonder how close attention Winston had paid to my personnel statistics. As tight as it was, the suit let me move with every bit of range I was used to. "How does it work?"

"There was no instruction manual," Loredana said wryly. "I doubt Procyon is aware I took it. Winston had it locked away in storage, tucked behind several of his more harebrained projects. The bulk of Procyon staff familiar with our true mission are working today. This made—discretely removing the case less than simple."

"It's Sunday," Ramos said. "Don't these people have other priorities?"

"Defense against astral fiends is our priority."

I checked all over the suit for a switch, a button, anything that would help with the supposed camouflage. Nothing. I reached behind my neck. "Is this a hood?"

"No. A mask. Primarily for avoiding facial recognition."

It fastened neatly over my head and face. I could see out fine, but when I checked a mirror, there was no slit for the eyes evident. Must be hidden among the material for the mask, a transparent panel maybe. Jagged angles down my cheeks and slashes over the top fit the overall pattern of the suit.

"Reminds me of dazzle," Ramos said.

"You better not be talking about jewelry."

"World War I designs, used by the Allies to confuse U-boat captains. They painted cargo vessels and warships with wild stripes, zig-zags, and colors in the hope the submarines would be unable to tell whether their targets were coming or going." Ramos shrugged. "Maybe that's what your designer was going for."

"Not a bad idea." Hang on. There was a raised surface to the right glove, between the thumb and forefinger. I squeezed.

I vanished from my reflection in a smear of color. Ramos's family appeared, intact but distorted, across my chest.

"Don't that beat all," Wilhelmina murmured.

Ramos poked my chest.

"Yeah, still here." I waved. "How's it look?"

"Like someone Photoshopped my hallway onto your suit, somewhat badly." Ramos turned, and glanced sidelong at me. "How about that. When you're not in my direct line of sight, you're much more concealed."

I walked past them, into the living room. The suit's patterns adjusted to the change in décor. "This is awesome."

"If you say so." Ramos sighed. "But it's going to take more than fancy colors to beat whatever sensors your foundation has set up. I'm guessing they're a lot better than cameras."

"Infrared, as I mentioned, but the suit takes that into consideration by masking body heat." Loredana pinched the fabric—on my arm, I should mention. "The meta-materials used in its construction also emit a low-level frequency that can interfere with video surveillance."

I frowned. "What you mean, can?"

"I mean precisely that. Can. As in, formal testing was never completed because Winston was tasked with greater priorities—namely, tracking the increased occurrence and magnitude of astral fiend incursions."

"You're telling me we don't know all this suit can do, or if it's even—wait for it—suitable for me to use."

Ramos groaned. Jamie rolled his eyes.

"I'll continue this conversation while pretending that inane comment never occurred." Loredana couldn't hide the smile, but went on, "It is our best chance."

"Our? No way. I'll go in solo. Calvin shot Jackson in the face, Loredana. I'd be horrified if something happened to you."

Well, that particular cat was out of the bag. Loredana folded her arms. "Let me make this plain: I will tolerate no one's corruption of Procyon's mission. No one's. If Calvin indeed murdered the manager, it is my duty to see him brought to justice, as it is my duty to help uncover the truth about whoever is using Procyon for foul purposes."

"About that. Wilhelmina is of the opinion there's a third weapon, one that when combined with the pulsar stave and Teget's ax will seal the rips into our world forever. Or open them permanently. Whichever."

"I see." Loredana looked from Wilhelmina to Jamie then back to me. "You trust her information?"

"Darn well better, young lady." Wilhelmina powered the ax, then picked up the pulsar stave and did likewise.

Loredana gawked. "Good heavens."

I chuckled. "Exactly. Hey Ramos, if we're going to plan our illegal activities, you might want to steer clear. And, um, are we putting your family out?"

"They're at a friend's. I'm supposed to be there too." He

checked his watch. "We're having dinner with them, so it'll be 9 at the latest before we're back. Also, I didn't hear a word you said after you woke up."

I shook my head as he left. "Can't figure that guy out."

"What's to figure?" Wilhelmina asked. "He's determined to keep you safe and protect the people of his city. Ain't no higher calling—and believe you me, that's what he considers this. Not just a paycheck for your Lieutenant."

"Yeah. I get it." I wished it was more than self-preservation driving me, too, but one step at a time.

First, we needed to plan our assault.

Nighttime. Obviously. Those were the best hours of the day during which we could conduct our raid. Loredana would be the distraction. I mean, seriously, how could you not be distracted by her?

Anyway, she had enough foresight to bring along a tablet full of Procyon's security plans, so we knew where guarded corridors were.

"If we avoid these patrolled points, access should be easier," she said.

"I can work with that. It's about the same as I observed when I was spying on the property. What I don't like is the idea of you going back in." I frowned. "How are you not under suspicion?"

"I don't follow."

"Come on, Loredana. You threatened Jackson with a gun!"

"Ah. That." She went pink in the face again and examined the surface of her tablet with incredible scrutiny. "Mr. Jackson absolved me of that particular sin. He knew I was under stress and too close to the situation. He was, however, concerned you wouldn't come back to Procyon if I were no longer associated with the foundation, and still needed my help with the more mundane aspects such as fund-raising. I am writing a substantial grant for housing renovation along Court Street."

Fighting monsters and evading a hit squad made me forget about the public face of our foundation. "Jackson's dead. What about Calvin?"

"Until the events of last night, I assumed him to be an arrogant but capable assistant to the manager. Now ..." She shrugged. "He may well view me as an asset rather than a threat. As far as he is aware, I've not made any attempts to contact you, and I threatened his superior, the very same man he killed. I will offer my services to him."

"Is he the manager now?"

"The board has not appointed a replacement. In the interim, Mr. Jackson's responsibilities are divvied among the various departments."

"This is all very interesting, but lest you children forget, we've a man to rescue." Wilhelmina had replaced Jamie in the rocking chair. She knit swiftly on a red and orange beanie with a matching pom-pom. "What do you want us to do?"

I pointed at Jamie. "He's the getaway driver. You okay with that, McQueen?"

He nodded.

"My man." I ran a hand through my hair. "Okay, Wilhelmina, I'm gonna leave the ax with you, outside, so these guys don't get their mitts on it."

"Y'all don't realize Teget's the one who needs it more than I do. Do you want him stuck inside with no way to defend himself?"

"She has a point," Loredana said. "As much as I hate the idea of bringing both weapons back inside Procyon, now that we know someone has the blade and is using it for nefarious purposes, Teget will need protection if you two have to fight your way out."

"Okay, fine. I'll take both." I grit my teeth. "Not the best idea. Don't like it. But sure, we'll try it that way."

Fast-forward to 10 o'clock that night.

Jamie parked a block away from the compound, where he and Wilhelmina would remain as backup. I know. I laughed at the idea, too, until I remembered that Jamie was still armed.

One thing troubled me, in particular. "What about the tachyons? I thought Winston's drones could track me via the pulsar stave's emissions. Hence me leaving you the T.A.R.D.I.S. and running away."

Loredana removed the ornament from her pocket. "That was quite clever. Your concerns are well-founded; however, the suit interferes with all manner of particle and radiation readings. So says Winston's specifications."

"The ones you didn't read."

We walked on in silence.

"Wait." I blocked her way. "Do you actually not know?"

She looped around me, as if I didn't present enough of an obstacle. "I drew logical conclusions."

"Well, that's super, Mrs. Spock."

"Mercury, this is our single option. Unless you prefer an all-out tactical strike by an armed assault team, which I sorely lack, and I am certain Calvin does not wish to share."

"Fine. I'll take your word for it."

Still wasn't feeling great about my chances of not getting spotted twenty minutes after she went inside, and I was crouched behind shrubbery along the bayside walkway. That was the agreement: Loredana would proceed to her office, as if she had important business to accomplish. Even at late hours on a weekend, nobody would think it was strange for her to randomly show up.

I crept along the path, stepping as lightly as I could. Winston hadn't cut corners on the suit when it came to the basics—the tread of the thin boots made the barest sounds on the pavement.

The suit came equipped with a built-in earbud, through which Loredana left an open line on a phone. Not hers. It could have been monitored. She'd gotten a cheap TracFone like Ramos had given me. I couldn't say a word to her, unless I wanted to blow her cover. But I could listen in as she talked to Calvin:

Loredana: "Thank you for seeing me."

Calvin: "Of course. This is a troubling time for us all at Procyon. I'm glad you've shown the confidence in my position."

Loredana: "It is terrible what happened to the manager. If I'd realized how unhinged Mr. Hale had become, how blinded by his power ..."

I grinned. She was laying it on thick, but the way she choked out those last few words? I bought it. Maybe she added tears to the act.

Two guards ahead, near the entrance to Tower Three. I slunk along hedgerow to the end, less than 30 feet away. No alerts. No sign the cameras had picked me up. Loredana would have signaled me. My heart battered my rib cage. *Easy. Slow your breathing, like this was another training exercise. Don't freak out. You've got the stave and the ax strapped to your thighs. The drones overhead are ignoring your presence.*

Do. Not. Freak. Out.

I stepped out from concealment and walked across the path, through the shadow between two lamps.

Those guys yakked about the Rays game as if a costumed

intruder wasn't within tackling distance. One offered the other a cigarette, right next to the sign proclaiming Procyon a no-smoking facility.

Calvin: "We're in crisis mode, Ms. Lark. I'd like to know I can trust you."

Loredana: "Have no doubt. I am on Procyon's side. Whatever it takes to bring Mr. Hale in, I want to be a part of the effort."

Calvin: "That's what I like to hear. Do you have any thoughts on the matter? He seems to have stymied us for a moment, seeing as how he's in possession of the two weapons."

Loredana: "Let me speak with Teget. I believe I can persuade him to provide insight. If you allow me to conduct the questioning correctly—not in the amateur fashion which has already been attempted—the methods should draw Mr. Hale's attention."

I was ten feet from the side door, a quarter of the way around Tower Three from the main entrance. It was a maintenance entrance, which opened to only the most vital personnel. My card, sadly, had been downgraded.

I unhooked the pulsar stave. Guess what? New key.

The stave sparked too loudly, hissing as it cut the electronic panel. I knew which wires to cross, courtesy Loredana's tablet of awesome intel, to open the door and avoid an alarm.

"Security, this is Patrol Three. We've got something. Investigating."

Perfect. They heard me.

Footsteps left the walkway, instantly muffled in the grass. Fortunately, the guards' guns clattered against their armored vests. Unfortunately, it was MP5s again. No beanbag rounds from a shotgun for me.

I backflipped onto the wall above the doorway, hand

standing on the short, concrete awning that provided limited shelter if you'd forgotten your card and were stuck in the rain. Hey, it happens.

The guards were right below me. I held my breath. My arms trembled.

"It's damaged."

"No kidding. Hang on." Guard One leaned in for a closer look.

Calvin: "Let's arrange that. What did you have in mind, Ms. Lark?"

Loredana: "The goal is not to get information from Teget. What we need is to draw Mr. Hale out. I can communicate with him. Surely you've monitored my phone closely enough to realize I called him after he escaped Procyon."

Calvin: "Yes, we'd noticed. We'd also noticed you hadn't made any more attempts."

Loredana: "I suspect I'll be more convincing if I send a video of his long-lost brother being tortured."

Calvin: (long pause) "I can see we'll work together well. Follow me."

And that was my cue.

I flipped down, landing between the men. Guard Two spun, gun aimed at me, but I'd never seen anyone look so puzzled. "Harry?"

Harry—Guard One—mirrored his companion. "Ernesto, man, put your gun down! You trying to shoot me? Wait ..."

"What is that thing?" Ernesto's finger tightened on the trigger.

I must have looked like a concrete statue standing erected between them, still camouflaged from my handstand on the wall.

I separated the stave, and in that instant of powering up,

must have shattered the suit's reflection, because they both swore. Two simultaneous swipes broke their guns. Follow-up blows put them on the ground.

"Sorry, guys," I muttered. "Procyon's got a great HSA to pay for the hospital bills."

I clocked Ernesto across the forehead, and smacked Harry likewise before he could get off the ground.

Now for the hard part.

CHAPTER
TWENTY-SEVEN

Those guys weren't going to stay unconscious for long. At least, I hoped not. Traumatic brain injury wasn't in my normal arsenal. I'd much rather be stabbing fiends than beating humans.

Theoretically, they should be on my side.

Tower Three's lobby was deserted. Normal business hours were long over. That was the good news. Bad news? Cameras everywhere.

I stuck to the shadows as I slunk toward the emergency stairwell. Seemed like years ago that I made my very hasty, yet aborted, escape down those same steps. Wonder if they repaired the door handle I damaged?

The list of property damage I'd caused that week was growing longer.

I stood still long enough to let my senses adjust to the half-lit lobby. The black dome of a small security camera was ten feet away, glaring right at me. No alarms sounded, thought. No indication anyone saw me. Good deal.

I took the stairs straight up to the Sixth Floor.

The hallway was silent. Loredana's pilfered security layout

showed four guards traipsing this level, making a complete circuit every five minutes. I checked my watch. Should be one coming by in the next 90 seconds.

Someone clomped along the tile. Man. He was either dragging his feet or it was one of the big guys in security. I waited until the footsteps passed the door, and started the other direction, before I cracked the door. Slowly.

Yep. One of the huge guys. G-something. Gerald? Grant? Garvey. That was his last name. Saw him lifting weights in the gym when I'd hit my private training space. He could bench a lot.

Great.

Okay, I had less than five minutes before the next guard came along. And Loredana was on her way to see Teget with Calvin salivating, no doubt.

I pushed the door open. Better to not knock this guy out in the middle of the hall. Where was I gonna stash him? It'd be best to stick with stealth.

Halfway to the darker wall, my boots squeaked.

No lie.

Garvey froze. Me too. He was a half foot taller than me, rippling with muscle, so his black polo shirt looked painted on. When he turned around, he wore a frown of puzzlement, somewhat masked by a thick beard that framed his face all the way up to a buzz cut so sharp he could have chopped a few astral fiends on his own.

Whether the lighting was just right, or Garvey had poor vision, I don't know, but he eventually turned back the other way and continued his rounds. I waited until he disappeared around the curve in the hall.

Really wished Procyon would have gone with carpet like they did upstairs.

I eased along the wall until I reached the recovery room. The window was dark, the space inside a void except for a tiny red light on the ceiling. Another security camera. I stared long enough for the shape inside to coalesce.

Teget. He lay on the bed-slash-couch, except he didn't appear to be pleasantly napping. Nope, they'd strapped him down and hooked an IV to his arm. Loredana had said something about sedatives during her talk with Calvin.

Lights flared to life in the infirmary. The door into the recovery room opened.

"Wake him up." Calvin flicked the light switch, bathing the room in a warm glow. Teget looked even worse—pasty, limp, with bags under his eyes. Man. I'd only been gone from there 24 hours.

"I'll need to taper off his sedatives." Loredana sat on the edge of the bed. Her words were muffled by the tempered glass, but I could hear well enough, especially with my head pressed to the wall. I ducked beneath the window and crouch-walked to the infirmary door.

"I didn't say I cared how you woke the man. I said get him up." Calvin moved Loredana's hand away from the IV. Then he slapped Teget's cheek a couple times. "Hey! Rise and shine, stranger."

You know, whether or not Teget was my brother, I felt compelled to give Calvin some slaps back. Better save it until I was in the room, rather than breaking down the glass like I wanted to do. Instead, I snuck into the infirmary, worming my way through the office and around the cabinets, exam tables, and desks. They'd left the door to the recovery room open.

"I'd recommend against that," Loredana said. "If we need this fellow to respond to our questions, brute strength may not force his cooperation."

"Funny, considering you'd told me torture was the way to go."

"Coercion need not involve fisticuffs."

Teget moaned. Loredana fiddled with the IV, then stood back from the bed. "Sir, we need you to answer a few questions.

"There would have been better ways to wake me." Teget squinted. He tugged at the straps. "Ah. I see my accommodations have not improved."

"How did you get to our world?" Calvin asked.

"I followed the tears between dimensions. The astral fiends feed on your realm. I came here to put an end to their frenzy."

"Your weapon, that ax. Is that what you used?"

Teget shook his head. "How I arrived here is of no relevance. What matters is the reunification of the three weapons, the sealing of the tears, and the removal of the blade from your possession."

Calvin snorted. "What makes you think I have it?"

"You, or someone in your employ. The astral fiends would not be drawn to your world were it not for the blade. It beckons to them, a great light on a dark horizon."

"Does the pulsar stave act in similar fashion?" Loredana asked.

"Your questions amuse me. Let me free, and I will end the terror that wounds your world and mine."

"You assume we want to close the way to the Interstice." Calvin dug a knife from his pocket. "Let's try a new question: Why are you really here?"

"I have told you all I can. Do not let the darkness encroach on your soul."

"Bad answer." Calvin lowered the knife to Teget's abdomen.

"How about you don't." I closed the recovery room door behind me.

Calvin spun, and threw the knife. Not a bad shot. It flashed end over end. Decent aim. Promising trajectory.

I slashed it midair with the pulsar stave, leaving a molten lump on the tile.

"A specter?" Teget mused.

"Don't I wish." I closed the room's blinds, then flipped back the mask. "Hey, Calvin. Nice to see you again. You gonna downgrade my clearance one more time? Or maybe we should skip to the part where I free my brother and restrain myself from lopping your head off like a dead branch."

"You're a first-class idiot bringing that thing back in here." Calvin's hand drifted inside his suit jacket.

"Hands in the open." I joined the stave with the ax and swung the crackling energy discharge under his chin. "Or you lose more than your fancy tie."

A klaxon sounded. Red lights flashed along the hallway. "All personnel, proceed to the exits. An intruder is on the premises." The grating, electronic voice repeated in a loop.

I winced. "Okay, new plan." I slit the bonds holding Teget to the bed. "He's leaving with me."

"Thank you, Mercury." Teget let me help him off the bed. His muscles trembled in my grip. I glared at Calvin.

"You two won't make it off the floor," he snarled. "Ms. Lark, summon—"

"I won't be summoning a thing at this juncture." She produced her revolver from, well, nowhere I'd seen. If she had a holster, it was better camouflaged than I was.

"This is getting to be a bad habit of yours, Ms. Lark. Jackson might have been the forgiving sort, but I'm not, so if you're going to point that thing at me, you'd better pull the trigger."

"Sorry, Calvin, but homicide's not on our agenda." I

grabbed his arm and shoved him face-first against the wall. A quick touch with the pulsar stave to the back of his neck, and the secretary with delusions of grandeur was drooling onto Teget's pillow.

"We could have strapped him down, if you hadn't severed the restraints," Loredana said.

"Yeah, well, we'll have to lock him in here." I checked the door. Hmm. Didn't seem to have a lock. But we couldn't leave Calvin able to traipse around calling for security.

"There is an alternative," Teget said.

"I'm game for anything."

"He could guarantee our safe passage from the building."

Kinda what I'd been thinking. I put my hands on my hips. "That's great. Would have been a better brainstorm before I'd Tasered him senseless, but …"

By the time security reached us, we three had Calvin trussed up like a Thanksgiving turkey and were halfway down Tower Three.

The guards let us pass but judging by their glowering expressions and the incessant squawking on their radios, someone wasn't happy about the situation. Between the stave, Teget's ax, and Loredana's gun, we had enough weaponry on our side—most of it threatening Calvin's well-being—to keep the security guys from doing anything other than shadow us.

We reached the lobby without incident, which was good, because as many guns as were pointed at us, I was sure we were all going to get shot.

Of course, Calvin couldn't keep his trap shut, as groggy as he was from the zap.

"You won't get away with this," he said. "The powers that

you're messing with—"

"Dire consequences, end of the world, we get it." I gave him a firm jolt with the stave, right between the shoulder blades. "Tell you what: you quit from going all Scooby-Doo villain on us, and I won't knock you out cold again. Unless you want to leave a matching drool stain on the pillow upstairs, which doesn't seem like your style."

"You should be more concerned about the police response."

In spite of, or maybe because of the situation, I chuckled. "Right. Your boys are gonna phone 9-1-1 and tell them what, exactly? 'Help! I've been kidnapped by an interdimensional traveler and his brother! They're stealing tachyon-enhanced mythical weaponry we keep around for chopping tentacles off life-force-draining monsters.' Let me know how that works out."

Calvin didn't have a snippy comeback for the one. The lack of sirens and people issuing demands through bullhorns told me I was right on the money.

"Front doors ahead." Loredana's announcement seemed silly, considering we could see the entrance from where we exited the emergency stairs.

"That's nice, but I'm not done here yet." I steered Calvin and our crew toward the elevators.

"Those are shut down," Calvin blurted.

"Well, good thing I've got a temporary manager-type who can get them turned back on."

"I do not understand," Teget said. "If our goal is to escape, returning to the upper floors will not confuse the men watching us."

"Who said we're going up?"

Calvin fumbled his card but got his act together, so we could take a quick ride to the basement. More specifically, to the Historic Vault.

"Load up everything that looks interesting." I found a messenger bag sitting on a shelf and handed it to Loredana.

She looked at me for a moment, unmoving, and if she was going to argue the point, she must have fought against the impulse. She carefully tucked file folder after file folder into the bag.

"Teget, you'll have to use the end of your ax on that lock. Get the file out of the clear case. Carefully. It's old."

He retrieved File 6-1848.

We headed back upstairs, Loredana with the messenger bag bulging, me and Teget with our squirmy, surly prisoner. A couple handfuls of security guys waited in the corners of the lobby, weapons trained on us. A quiet, doubting part of me wondered if Calvin would order a massacre at the expense of his own life.

What a pain. I'd rather be home watching TV.

Breathing the cool night air took the edge off some of the tension. We made it outside. Problem? There were five SUVs in an arc facing the entrance to Tower Three. Three teams of four guys each—all of them in the same tactical gear I'd seen out at the ruined hacienda—waited, heavily armed, using the trucks as their barricades.

"Loredana," I said, "You might want to take a second look at Procyon's books. Something tells me there's a lot of money getting diverted from the Seventh Floor's budget, unless the board of directors found a small army under their collective pillows."

"A sound suggestion." She had her gun trained on Calvin, but her eyes flicked around the cordon from potential target to potential target. I'd pay money to see her pop them off one at a time.

Of course, I'd have better luck taking them out. "Okay, kids! Here's the deal. We leave with your new boss, and if we stay unhurt and unfollowed, he doesn't wind up like your old boss."

"Oh, Mercury." The sing-song reply carried from behind one of the SUVs, dreamlike and full of peace. "You're not a killer of men. You're a slayer of nightmares."

Marigold and Winston stepped into view. Marigold carried the blade.

"No," Teget whispered.

I felt the same way, if his heart had fallen straight through his shoes. There was no mistaking the weapon in Marigold's right hand. Same straight edge on one side, same curved edge on the other. Though I had to admit, outside of a hazy, ax-induced vision, it looked far more intimidating. For one thing, the blade itself was four feet long, and a half foot at its widest. I became aware of a steady hum, just out of hearing range, more like a vibration than a sound.

The blade was bleeding power.

"Do you hear its song?" Marigold held the blade against the side of her face and closed her eyes. "I do. I've heard it all my life. So did my mother, and my grandmother, and her mother, all the way back to the start. We've waited such a long time for this moment. Mother saw it, and shared her visions, until we were united in our goal."

"Wait. Your mom? Your grandmom and …?" My eyes widened. "Multiple generations. You had people there? In 1848?"

"For seven generations we waited, watching listening, dreaming. Yearning for the time when the blade would reappear. And it did. Mother found it." Marigold ran a finger along the dull edge. "And do you know what she saw? Her reflection. Her face, and her mother's, and her mother's, all the way back to the first woman of our bloodline who used the blade and the stave to open the gate for the cleansing of our world."

"The Icon defeated her." I glanced at Teget, who seemed as in shock as all of us. Loredana's arms trembled.

"Not this Icon, but yes, one of those who held the ax."

"Also, I don't like the sound of that word. Cleansing."

"Come off it, Mercury," Winston said. "You've seen what we've done with civilization, haven't you? Rampant corruption, rotting drugs, disintegrating families, the dissolution of cultures as they mingle without restraint. Humanity is polluted and weak. Earth needs a fresh start."

"Okay." I couldn't think of anything more elaborate. Sweat slicked my palms. "I bet we can come to a truce, right?"

"You broke into our facility. Our home."

"Yeah, right, Winston. You guys lied to me the whole time—and not just about my zip code, either. I come back for my brother, and find you, Marigold, and Calvin planning the end of the world. Not what I signed up for. The blade isn't yours. None of these weapons are."

"They're not yours, either, technically." Winston pointed at me with the tablet. "There's your theft of Procyon materials—namely my prototype suit, let alone whatever Ms. Lark has in the bag."

"Sorry, Winston. All I have on underneath is boxers, so I'm hanging onto these threads for decency's sake, if nothing else." This was getting me nowhere. Time for fresh tactics. "Mari, let's put the giant sword down. Please."

"Don't be so naïve. I can't let go. Neither can you give up the pulsar stave, or Teget can relinquish the ax." She smiled at him. "I'm so glad you're awake for this. It was unsporting, somehow, to drug you and take the ax. That isn't befitting a warrior."

"Filthy enchantress." Teget whipped the ax in front of him, Calvin all but forgotten. White sparks sputtered along its length. "Bring the blade forth and I shall show you what it means to be a warrior."

"I wouldn't do that." Winston had a smug grin. He waved a tablet at us. "The drones are monitoring this very change. Care to know why?"

"Not really, but I'm pretty sure you're going to monologue this out," I muttered.

"Tachyon emissions are spiking. The drones are quite well-recalibrated—thanks much for that order, Loredana— and they're giving me a readout in exquisite detail. Having the three weapons in such proximity to each other shows me exactly what I wanted to see."

"And what is that?" Loredana asked.

"The answer to the question we've worked our whole lives at Procyon to answer." Winston grasped Marigold's hand. "How to stabilize a pathway between our world and the Interstice."

That sounded like a terrible idea.

Marigold kissed Winston's hand, then his lips. She stepped onto the broad circle of parking lot around which we were arrayed. The blade glowed purple around its edges. The metal surface faded to black, so black I thought I'd fall into its endlessness. And then the wind started swirling. Purple lightning skittered across the parking lot.

Great. Just great.

CHAPTER TWENTY-EIGHT

willed power to the pulsar stave and deployed it in halves. White and yellow energy blazed along its etchings. Felt good to be heading into the fray, although I didn't like the audience. The monsters would be here soon. "So," I said to Teget, "We should probably have a long talk over pizza, about things like your home and where I'm from and what my parents were like."

"Our parents were legends among our people." Teget's ax blazed in resonance with the humming and sparking around this eerie scene. He grinned. "And I see you have trained as a warrior in accordance with their wishes. Yes, we have much to discuss."

"Awesome." I wiped sweat from my brow. "Assuming we don't die."

"Agreed. Mercury?"

"Yeah?"

"What is this thing, pizza?"

Talk about a deprived childhood.

"You're all dead," Calvin said with a sneer. "When they

pick up your pieces from the asphalt—"

Loredana whipped him across the shoulders. "Kindly shut up."

"Why? You don't got the nerve."

Loredana fired.

Calvin yelled and staggered away. I thought for one panicked moment I was going to see blood pouring down his shirt, but nope. Loredana must have fired the gun right next to his ear.

Shouts erupted from the guards.

Loredana hooked her arm around Calvin's and dragged him back to her, face to face. "A demonstration of my willingness to do what is necessary," she said. "Lest you mistake caution for lack of confidence."

The rip erupted through space-time, spinning like a crazy mini-tornado dropped on its side. Funny thing? It wasn't as ragged as usual. The edges were clear as jewels, sharp and distinct.

Consequence of the three weapons acting in concert? Winston seemed to think so.

"Do you feel it?" Marigold cried. "Do you see? It's the place of our dreams mingling with the land of the awake."

"You're making less and less sense," I muttered, but I gripped my weapon even tighter. "Loredana, get out of here."

"I won't leave you alone to face this."

"Thanks, but Teget's here. Quality family time." I forced a grin.

She smiled back. "If this is where your family must be, then it's where I'll stand."

Man. Talk about making a guy's heart explode. I could have launched myself at Procyon's entire goon squad.

Then the astral fiend came through.

Yikes.

It bellowed into the night, breath climbing for the sky in a billowing plume. Foul spittle sprayed everywhere. This beast was gigantic. Easily twice the size of the one I'd defeated on the 311, probably forty feet across. Tentacles smashed a pair of the Procyon SUVs, crumpling their roofs as if they were sheets of paper. Windows blew out, raining glass. Fangs ripped troughs in the parking lot.

Loredana lowered her gun. "My God."

Calvin beat a retreat into the waiting arms of his forces. It was more a gambol than a run, what with his arms still lashed tight. "Shoot them! Shoot them!"

"Take out those guns!" I hollered at Teget and threw myself at the astral fiend.

A tentacle intercepted me in midair. The thing was as big around as a tree trunk. I stabbed both halves and used them as leverage to flip around. A second tentacle lashed out, cutting across my shoulder—the already wounded one. Blood sprayed down my arm. I shouted, but the pain faded fast.

As if that weren't lousy enough, bullets filled the air. Some struck the fiend, others chipped pavement. The fiend writhed under the fire but seemed more interested in removing my body parts than it did with fending off the tiny stings. If the gunfire was leaving marks, I missed them.

The tentacle flailed around, with me attached to it. Finally, the fiend must have decided I was a limp and potentially tasty meal, because it whipped me toward a maw crammed with teeth, each one as long as my forearm. The mouth could have swallowed the Subaru.

I yanked the staves free and landed on what should have been its head.

Teget let loose a long, reverberating howl. The fiend

swiveled in his direction, in time to lose the tentacle nearest to him. Blue slime smeared all over an SUV. The resultant scream made me want to lose whatever meal I'd had last. Instead I jabbed both halves of the stave deep into the nearest eye lumps.

More screaming. If the fiend could have released the souls of every person it had killed, they must have all come rushing out, by the sounds of it.

Those screams morphed into squealing brakes. The white Bronco barreled through shrubbery, high beams blinding everyone within a hundred feet. It slammed against the nearest SUV—one of the ones pre-smashed by the fiend—and shoved it out of the way to the tune of squealing metal.

The fiend's attention was pulled a dozen ways at once, and what had been a concentrated battle against the two wielders of the weapons—namely me and Teget—became a frantic free-for-all. It scooped up two guys in Kevlar, silencing first their weapons, and then their shouts. Their faces went blue-tinged, then white, before shriveling into a frost-fringed, mummified state. I couldn't breathe. Never seen a fiend work so quickly.

"Clear the area! Move, move!" Calvin waved his arms, as if flagging down the last bus out of Baghdad. His buddies must have cut him free.

Wait, where was Loredana? Panic jolted me, even as I dodged the tentacles pelting the fiend's own hide. With good reason. I'd put out four of its eyes.

One of the guards fell, clutching at his Kevlar-armored torso. Loredana leaned over the hood of a truck, arms propped up, revolver smoking. Her hair was tousled, and her jacket discarded. The black shirt underneath had a long tear across her abdomen. There might have been a smear of blood on her face, and a bruise along her chin, but nothing about her expression betrayed panic.

The rest of the guards fled to the towers, and deeper into the parking lot. A couple SUVs revved their engines, as if to join the flight, but Jamie emptied a magazine of his MP5 into the engine blocks of both. Their occupants opted to move on foot. Jamie opened the Bronco door and slapped in a new magazine before shooting at the fiend.

I joined Teget on the ground, where he'd just severed a fiend tentacle wrapped around one of the guards. The poor guy was freeze-dried. I pushed from my mind any thoughts of loved ones or family. "This thing's not going down easy."

"The beasts often reach this size deeper in what you call the Interstice." Teget wiped blue slime from his face and gestured far off with his ax. "Her control of the incursion site is more troubling."

Marigold? Right. She stood alongside the rip, the blade extended toward the sky. Winston was back by one of the trucks, intent on his tablet. His quartet of drones circles high above, artificial moths to this dimensional flame Purple lightning danced between her and the portal, lancing out across the parking lot. Marigold was shouting something, the words lost in a growing rush of wind. The rip's center wasn't a dark haze anymore. It was clear, like a window, with a crystalline sheen that rippled with the gusts. Beyond that sheen, a forbidding, stormy landscape roiled.

The Interstice.

I'd never seen it so real. That couldn't be good.

"Mercury!" Wilhelmina limped between us. "You planning to stand about gawking, or are we going to end this?"

"Yes, ma'am." I handed her one of the stave halves. "Have fun."

"Fun isn't the word for it, child." She dropped her cane, posture straightening as the stave's power coursed over her arms. "It's duty."

Wilhelmina charged through a flurry of fiend tentacles, shearing one off in mid-run, headed straight for Marigold.

"She knows our ways." Teget bashed aside an incoming appendage, sparring with it as if it were a gigantic sword.

"Take this thing out and we can focus on that later." I ducked a blow, then slit a tentacle ten feet along its length before slicing both pieces off.

The fiend wasn't impressed by all this. In fact, he picked up a pair of SUVs and brought them down as his weapons. I rolled aside, the impact tremor rattling my bones. Teget was sprawled on the pavement, eyes wide, either stunned that an astral fiend could learn to use a weapon or wondering what the heck an SUV was.

Unfortunately, no matter how much damage we inflicted, the fiend didn't seem to be tiring. It had wrecked all the vehicles within reach—well, except the Bronco—and chased off the Procyon guards. Those guys weren't even shooting. Purple lighting played through the rip, across Marigold's blade, and onto the fiend's hide. Soon the blue ooze quit dripping from its wounds. My stomach turned as I watch a short, severed tentacle regrow its lost length.

If this thing regenerated while we were fighting, the show was going to end prematurely.

Teget and I kept up our assault, aided by a steady stream of fire from Jamie. How many magazines had he swiped from the Procyon goons? Enough to let him concentrate on one portion of the fiend's hide. Ooze splattered across the Bronco as he finally punched through.

"There!" I shouted. "There's our opening!"

"I see it." Teget bashed a tentacle to the ground, pinning it in place with the ax, and let me cut it off with the stave.

The fiend noticed this new wound, too, because it inverted itself in a mad rush of tentacles. They slapped me and Teget, tossing us into an SUV. The wind rushed from my lungs, leaving me gasping. Teget bled from a cut on his forehead. Red blood.

So, not an alien. Good to know.

Jamie cried out. He was wrapped up in a tentacle, the gun crushed and useless at his side. His dark brown skin faded rapidly through blues to white, shriveling as I fought gut-wrenching vertigo.

I threw myself atop the tentacle, hacking away until Jamie and I dropped to the ground with the offending appendage. I slit it away from Jamie's body, ignoring the slime and the stench. His huge, muscular frame was withered as badly as any corpse. I sagged against the stave. His eyes stared up at the night sky.

"Come. He did his part." Teget's hand rested lightly on my shoulder.

Shoes clicked on the asphalt. Loredana put a hand to her mouth and knelt beside me. The messenger bag full of Procyon files was looped from her shoulder to waist, the strap cinched tight. "I'm sorry."

"Didn't even know him." Did that matter? He was a person, a living, breathing man with a soul, and then he was gone, food for an astral fiend. I gripped the stave. No one else was gonna be food today.

Metal clanged against metal. Wilhelmina was toe to toe with Marigold, swinging the stave for all she was worth. Whatever training Marigold had received was adequate to take on a former Procyon operative, because she gave no ground. The two circled, trading blows, parrying thrusts, their weapons throwing off showers of sparks like some twisted version of a rock concert.

"She won't last long on her own." Loredana rushed off, taking a long loop around the fiend. "Cover me!"

"Hey, wait!" She was already gone, leaving me to launch a new attack against my monster opponent. "Teget ..."

"I have the wound in sight. You defend her." He clapped my shoulder. "Fear not."

"Working on it," I muttered.

Teget fought off the fiend's tentacles, single-handed, taking stabs at the wound Jamie's gunfire had opened. Each successful strike antagonized the creature until it was a shrieking, flailing mass. I slid under one tentacle, sliced a second out of my way and stepped through the pieces. A third slammed right in front of me, so fast I didn't register its presence until I tripped and tumbled. My recovery was quick, thanks to sparring practice, and I immediately thought of Loredana sweeping my legs from underneath me when we, uh, quarreled.

But I wasn't fast enough.

The fiend scooped Loredana up in midstride. She yelled, fear evident on her face, and I realized I'd never seen her afraid. Meanwhile the wind tugged me off balance, its speed and force building so much I had to anchor myself to the fiend with the sharp end of the stave's energy. "Loredana!"

She was still able to push that fear aside in favor of action, evidently, because she used up the last three bullets in her gun, putting them square in the fiend's sort-of-face. At least one eye exploded. The fiend wriggled, twisting side to side. It flapped Loredana around. Her eyes rolled up into the back of her head.

I scrambled up the fiend's hide, using the stave as a climbing pickaxe, ignoring the fetid breath, the intense cold clawing at my body, the blue slime coating my arms. A few more quick steps, and I leapt off its head. A swift stroke cut the tentacle off three feet from Loredana's body.

Together we fell down the monster's opposite side, tumbling and sliding until we landed in an ooze-slicked pile. Man, I smelled bad. Forget about that. I turned Loredana over. She was gasping, quick, tiny breaths. She was staring beyond me. Any longer in the fiend's grasp and she'd have been dead. Thankfully color was seeping back into her face.

I placed my hand on the side of her cheek. Had to shout over the roaring wind to be heard. "Hey. Hey! Are you okay?"

She nodded and grabbed my wrist.

Marigold screamed.

I glanced across the urban battlefield. Wilhelmina knocked the blade from Marigold's grip. It spun across the parking lot. "No! I'm almost there!" Marigold yelled. "You've unbalanced it!"

The rip bent sidelong, twisted, and sucked Wilhelmina off her feet.

A couple SUVs followed, tires thudding. Even the fiend couldn't escape the pull, as howling winds dragged it home. I tried using my half of the stave as an anchor but no dice. Just dug a trough along the ground.

Marigold leapt for the blade. She scooped it up, but her shoes scraped along the paving. No luck getting a grip.

"Mari!" Winston pulled his wife behind a truck, with the blade tucked under one arm. The vehicle tipped over, and bashed into the astral fiend's side, stalling its progress.

Teget tumbled end over end, grasping for the ax. We saw each other in the split second before he, too, vanished through the rip.

Loredana told me something, but I couldn't hear anything but the storm's fury. I couldn't hold onto her any longer. Heck, I couldn't hold *me* in place, either.

She slipped from my arm and spiraled into the abyss.

I shouted in fear and anger until my throat was raw.

The fiend was seemingly stuck, halfway inside the rip. Whatever the gateway was doing to its body wasn't pleasant, because it moaned in such a piteous fashion I kinda felt bad for it. Would've felt worse if I hadn't just lost my allies in this fight.

I had to kill the thing.

The wind yanked me off the ground. I stopped fighting, stopped resisting, let it pull me along into the whirlwind. As I twisted through the air, I lined myself with the fiend's gaping wound as a target.

This was gonna suck.

The stave plunged into the wound first, its energies setting the fiend ablaze. I followed, holding my breath, refusing to look as the wind used me as a human, energized bullet.

Together the stave and I punched through to the other side.

The fiend exploded with a final bellow and a tremendous thunder. The resulting purple flash of light left me seeing nothing but smeared colors.

My body felt—awful. Like it was being torn apart and duct taped back together in the wrong order. Somebody wasn't following the instructions for this puzzle.

At least it was quiet.

Then sounds burst around me. I crashed through a pile of dirt. Stones battered me. Gonna have some nice bruises for the collection.

I opened my eyes again. It was still dark. And violet. The landscape before me was a jagged, gloomy nightmare.

"Welcome to the Interstice, Mercury," I muttered.

CHAPTER TWENTY-NINE

A t least it wasn't raining.

The air was so dry I started to sniff. Allergies? Took an awful lack of humidity for that to affect me.

Right then, it was the least of my worries. I staggered out of the sand dune, swiping it from the suit. The ground nearby was firm, riven with cracks, and devoid of vegetation. Scratch that: a couple spiky weeds protruded, each one with more spines on it than an astral fiend's tentacles.

Took a moment for my eyes to adjust fully to the darkness. Mountains spread in every direction, separated by long, broad valleys. If there had ever been rivers in the Interstice, they were long gone. Lots of boulders around, too. The sky was laden with thick clouds, writhing black and violet. Lightning skittered here and there. Occasionally a huge bolt scorched the ground, at the limits of the horizon. The thunder's rumble made my insides reverberate.

The immediate surroundings were full of stuff from my world. Two Procyon SUVs were on their sides, windows smashed, hoods and roofs crumpled. Long scratches marred the paint.

More important, though, were the people.

Loredana was easy to spot—out in the open, red hair a beacon in the monochromatic gloom. She'd pushed herself onto her elbow and was staring into the distance. She was frozen like a gorgeous statue. The messenger bag, smeared with dirt, was still strapped to her body.

"Hey." I shook her shoulder. "Loredana."

She blinked several times, as if she could force what she was seeing into a corner of her mind where she could analyze, compartmentalize, and report upon. Her expression solidified. "I'm not hurt, aside from bruises."

"No broken bones?"

"You will have to take my word and refrain from close inspection." That smirk. It reassured me more than any doctor's exam. "Have you found anyone else?"

"Not yet. Just made the trip myself." I stood and turned in a circle. "So, this is it."

"Yes." Loredana brushed sand from her skirt and made a face. "Quite coarse."

"Yeah. Gets everywhere, doesn't it? But this place looks a mess."

Something clanked against an SUV. I pulled Loredana behind me and willed the stave—the half I still had, anyway—to life.

Imagine my shock when a bolt of energy exploded three feet from either end, crackling, swirling, like Thor himself had handed me extra lightning. The power surging through me was, well, electrifying. You're welcome. My arm shook so badly I had to steady it with the other hand until the tremors stopped.

"It seems the pulsar stave is pleased to be in this realm," Loredana said.

"Um, yes, please." I leveled the weapon and grinned, ready for whatever was around the bend.

The SUV door opened. The ax emerged, followed by Teget. Blood flowed freely from the cut on his face. "You both survived," he wheezed. "The miracles continue."

"Take it easy, man." Loredana and I helped him climb out. His steps were shaky, and he nearly tripped on a rock, but we gave him some space. He breathed deeply, hands on his knees. "You good?"

"Good is a relative term. My injuries, I believe, are minor. I can be fully refreshed at home." He tapped the ax against the stave. "Of course, a more rapid healing in the interim will be most acceptable."

"You got your own, don't you?"

"The ax does not carry such power. Only the stave."

I shrugged. "Have at it. I'm going digging for Wilhelmina."

I gave him the stave and trudged between the trucks, leaving the "if she is still alive" unspoken. There were no blood streaks, though I did find a couple desiccated bodies. They were part of Calvin's armored crew.

Loredana lifted the face mask off one. "I don't recognize him."

"Me neither." Didn't want to pay close attention. The guy reminded me too much of Jamie. I glanced around while she inspected the body. No sign of astral fiends, either. Which was great, because I had no clue how to keep an eye out for one that hadn't freshly popped out of a rip. Kinda missed Winston, the traitorous monster-loving backstabber.

"His facial features—those that can be ascertained—do not remind me of anyone on Procyon's security staff. Also …" Loredana prodded deep in the corpse's mouth.

"Okay, you'd better wash your hands, though you're

probably gonna have to use a sand scrub."

"This man has a gold tooth. No one on staff at Procyon has such dental work."

"And what, you have all the personnel files memorized?"

"Not memorized." Loredana took the man's MP5, checked the magazine, and held it ready. She shifted the messenger bag full of files around her back, freeing up her range of movement. "Perused."

"That's great." Really hope she wasn't perusing mine. Privacy's privacy.

"We should not stay in the open," Teget said. "The beasts will be upon us soon. Our energy and our fear attracts them."

"I'm plenty energetic, but who said I was afraid?" Truthfully, I was anxious. But not full-on panicky.

Teget's expression was grim. "To set foot in this place and have no fear is the mark of a fool."

Amen to that.

Someone coughed, a wretched sound. Like a smoker who'd finally had one too many packs a day. "Under here."

The second SUV. Teget and I scrambled around it. Wilhelmina was hunkered under the arch formed by the mashed hood and battered windshield frame. The truck's impact had torn a furrow through the dirt, burying part of it. Sand and rocks filled the gaps.

"I'm fine, just fine." She had some bruises on her arms, and blood on her blouse, but no other marks. "Can't say I'll be walking well, though."

"Stay put. We'll get you out."

"No rush, child. The stave's knitting this old body together." The glow from the weapon illuminated every wrinkle around her smile.

Seeing that expression made me feel much better, because

it would have been terrible if she'd survived a showdown with the blade and an astral fiend attack only to get mashed by a truck.

A long, low howl sounded in the distance.

Speaking of fiends …

"It would behoove us to be swift." Sparks blazed from Teget's ax.

I carefully extended a glowing slash of energy from the stave. "Right there with you."

"I'll stand guard," Loredana said.

While it felt good to have a colleague armed with an automatic weapon at my back, I couldn't help remembering how many guns and how many bullets it had taken to open that single wound in the giant-sized monster. I cut faster.

Teget and I sawed at the truck's frame until we'd removed metal and plastic to allow Wilhelmina's escape. She crawled out on her hands and knees, the stave cutting a trough. "Well done, boys."

"Thanks." I helped her to her feet, though her grip seemed stronger than I'd ever recognized.

"Where's Jamie?"

Right. I didn't know how to put it.

"He fought bravely," Teget said.

That summed it up nicely. Wilhelmina got it. She clutched my hand even tighter, and tears welled up. She took a breath, and it steadied her arm from shaking. "That's all right. He was a strong man. A good man. Took him off of the streets and gave him a greater purpose. I'm just sorry he had to leave us when he did."

"If it is any consolation, he died defending us all," Loredana said.

"It is, indeed."

For a while the only sound was the distant thunder and the whisper of dirt tossed by the wind. Finally, I cleared my throat. "So, Teget, now would be a good time to tell us if there's somewhere safe in this joint, because I don't like the idea of wandering around on the astral fiends' home turf."

"Yes. Home is near." Teget closed his eyes. He held the ax perpendicular to his arm. Its typical powered-up sparks faltered, replaced by a subdued glow. "This way."

We set off down a steep embankment, alternating between a winding path and sliding on the loose gravel. The valley floor below was cracked like a long-dried out river bed. Some more of those spiky weeds clung to the shadows, as if they were in hiding. I couldn't blame them.

More bellows, and shrieks. They sounded closer. Of course, they also sounded like they came from all sides, so I couldn't pinpoint where the fiends were concealed.

"Hurry." Teget broke into a jog, without looking at the bewildering, craggy terrain on display to all sides. Me? I felt like I should be uploading every picture to Facebook—if I still had a phone. Or signal. Or, you know, social media presence of any kind.

"Do we have a location in mind?" Loredana asked. "I'm not one for rushing blindly into the unknown. This is where Mercury excels."

"Har-har." Granted, she was right. "Seriously, though, Teget, how about some directions?"

"The way home shifts with the tides surrounding the Interstice," he said. "I can sense where the entry is strongest, aided by the ax's power, but it is fleeting. If we do not open the way when it is at its peak, we will be forced to spend a length of time here before another opportunity presents itself."

"What kind of length?"

"Days. Weeks. Longer. It varies."

"Fantastic," I muttered.

"Less jabber, more movement." Wilhelmina kept up our pace. She still had the other half of the stave; while I knew the two pieces reconnected would make a better weapon for me if things went sour, I also knew she'd revert to her frailer self without its energy. Plus, it was nice to see her carrying the thing like I assumed she'd used to. The memory of her practicing with it in the old skate park and then dueling Marigold filled me with chills. The good kind.

A rockslide far off to the left broke through my reverie. Teget slammed on the brakes and held his hand out for all of us to do likewise. Without thinking, we formed a semi-circle, me at the center, Loredana with her MP5 on the left, Wilhelmina at my right shoulder, Teget beyond her.

There was a black smudge, a fleeting shadow. Then nothing. Any sounds of movement were lost beneath thunder. The rockslide turned into a trickle of pebbles.

"Fiend?" I asked.

Teget nodded.

We resumed our trek, at a speedier pace. Wilhelmina's breathing became labored. However much assistance the stave gave her, it must have reached the limits of her body and age. But she trucked along, never complaining.

Soon other sounds became apparent, when the lightning and thunder gave up for a while—more breathing. Except these were ragged, slavering gasps, coupled with a strange thumping, crackling noise. Something about it was familiar.

Oh, no.

I glanced behind us. Yeah. Three astral fiends, not big ones, but still deadly. They were dragging themselves across the terrain, slinging from crag to crag with long, spindly tentacles.

They moved *fast.*

"Your portal better be close," I snapped at Teget, "Because we've got angry locals on our six."

"It is near."

"You already said that! I need precision."

"That rock."

Oh. Well, that'd work.

A lumpen, pasty-gray boulder was propped against the base of a towering spire of basalt. The boulder had split into a shape that reminded me of a wide-open mouth. At first, I thought Teget was wrong, or imagining things, because I didn't see a solid gateway, or anything resembling a rip about to open. The more I stared, though, the more the air seemed to shimmer, like over hot asphalt on a blistering summer day in downtown San Camillo.

Thinking about the city brought on a bout of melancholy. Who knew? I missed the place. Would rather be there than here.

Of course, I'd also rather stay not dead.

"You must hold them at bay until I can open the path!" Teget planted himself in the middle of the atmospheric warping. Bolts of energy shot from the ax, one at a time at first, then a half dozen, then more and more until he looked like he was standing in the middle of one of those static electricity generator-things. Van der Graaff?

"Okay, then." I turned and faced our on rushing attackers. The pent-up energy of the stave begged to be release. I could have been holding a car in my bare hands, trying to keep it from driving off. "Wilhelmina, now would be a great time for suggestions."

"Didn't think you needed help from an old lady, child." She held the stave in a pose I'd never tried—right arm straight out, left arm back, as pointed as any Hogwarts wizard's wand.

"Oh, in this case, I'll bow to experience." I mimicked her pose. "What do you think, Loredana?"

"I think you could do with fewer words." She opened fire.

The MP5's barrage echoed off the rock walls, and I'm pretty sure I'd never seen a more surprised trio of astral fiends before. Guess their buddies who died on my world didn't text back with warnings about Earth's automatic weapons. Their formation burst apart, each one taking a different route at varying speeds.

Wilhelmina shot one with the stave, a gnarled, pulsating burst of white-yellow light that left a bubbling, smoking burn on its hide and cauterized the tip of a flailing tentacle.

These things could shoot?

I fired mine, too.

Talk about kick. I wasn't exactly proficient in the firearms department, but I'd handled one a time or two. Ramos made sure of that. The pulsar stave's recoil—proper term? Whatever—was enough to send my shot wildly off center. A rocky overhang exploded in shards that pelted my intended target, irking him sufficiently. He screamed.

I grinned and fired again.

Bullets and streaks of the pulsar stave's energy filled the air, slowing the fiends' approach but not stopping them. They were fifty feet away, getting closer despite the onslaught.

Behind us, a dazzling white light dawned like the sun on a perfect morning.

"Come!" Teget shouted. "The way will not remain!"

The white light washed out all colors around us. The fiends halted less than 30 feet away, writhing, screaming, and generally behaving like they'd gotten the worst sunburn in the history of beachgoers.

Oddly enough, there was no wind. No hurricane force tearing us away. Only the gentlest breeze.

It was only then I looked behind me.

Teget was so brilliantly backlit I couldn't make out his face, or details—only a silhouette. That silhouette beckoned us.

"Go!" I pulled Loredana away from the fiends. Wilhelmina was already fading into the light, her outline an afterimage, like I'd imagined it.

The fiends slapped at the ground, apparently trying to overcome their pain. Fissures opened in their hides. Tentacles withered, but still they snapped their jaws and slashed with fangs. They could sense meals slipping away.

Loredana hesitated in the midst of the portal. "Are you sure?"

"No. Absolutely not." But I squeezed her hand in mine.

She smiled, even as her face disintegrated into flecks of light, as if that's what she'd been built of the entire time.

My hand did the same thing. And I know I sure wasn't made of light.

Teget's silhouette twisted the ax in a swift, violent motion.

Light collapsed around us. Sound amplified, until I was holding my ears against a piercing squeal.

Then I was deaf. And blind.

Until I heard water trickling.

Pale blue-green skies. A small but sharp white sun. Dark-green leaves on pasty-gray trees speckled with brown. And the smell. Like walking into the freshest flower shop that ever existed.

Loredana was there. So were Wilhelmina and Teget.

I couldn't breathe. If I did, I was sure the illusion would shatter, and this peaceful forest would be replaced by the dark horror we'd escaped. Something about the forest, the stream gurgling at my feet, the sights and sounds and smells, called to me. Reminded me. "Teget, where are we?"

He put his hand on my shoulder and smiled. "Home."

CHAPTER THIRTY

My heart thudded. Every muscle trembled with the adrenaline of the near-escape from the astral fiends, and the pulsar stave's influx of power. With the danger past, and the sudden change in environment, my body was saying, "Um, what happened?"

Fair question.

Teget led us along the stream. Sunshine dappled by leafy shadows marked a lightly worn path. I stumbled a couple of times over gnarled tree roots and moss-slicked stones jutting through the patchy, pale-green grass. Teget, though, didn't lose his footing. He navigated the trail without looking down, intent on whatever was ahead.

It was a city.

I should specify: It wasn't San Camillo. No gleaming skyscrapers, no church spires, no apartment blocks, all crawling up a hill. The city sprawled along a flat plain. The buildings at the edge were short, single-story dwellings. Taller structures with slanted sides topped by domes filled in behind them. At the center, a series of massive stepped edifices loomed over the rest of the town like they owned it. Probably they did.

And they were all so—old. I can't explain it. Think of a National Geographic spread, in which they reconstruct what an ancient Mayan complex or a Greek citadel looked like in its glory days. Step into it. A dark-blue ivy with a greenish tinge draped walls. Pungent moss filled cracks. Everything felt like it had been there forever, yet from the looks of it some contractors could have built the smaller homes less than a century ago.

Never seen the place, outside of say, the Lord of the Rings, Peter Jackson style. Yet, every step I took forward, my pulse steadied, my breathing slowed. The racing, raging need to be *ready* just … went away.

I could relax.

"This is Meda." Teget said it *mee-dah*. "Avenue of the West. We are not far from my house. You may stay there while we recover and consider our next steps."

"Yeah. Next steps." I gazed at the copper flashing of the roofs, as the sun glinted off razor-straight edges. A flock of birds flew overhead—long-necked birds. With teeth? Wait. They didn't have nearly enough feathers.

"Glory." Wilhelmina had her hands pressed to her mouth. "I've never seen anything so beautiful in all my life."

"For all you have done to keep the *ch'irak'i* from overrunning your world, you have earned time spent among us."

Ch'irak'i. Astral fiends, I assumed. But Teget wasn't slowing his pace for a local linguistics lesson. He waved at someone in the distance. "We can discuss this later. Now is the time for you to meet our kin."

"Whose kin?" I stepped ahead of Wilhelmina. "Ours, as in yours and mine?"

"Exactly so."

That stopped me cold. Teget and Wilhelmina continued on, toward a group of maybe twenty people spilling out of side streets. They were dressed in a combination of working clothes similar to Teget's gear and flowing robes that seemed too ornate for something like planting crops or chopping trees. A babble of voices greeted him, and they gathered around for hugs and handshakes. That babble was a mix of English, Spanish, and other tongues I couldn't identify.

Loredana's shadow lined up with mine. She didn't seem in shock, and definitely wasn't gawking like a dope same as yours truly. She took in everything with a mixture of calculation and appreciation, or so it seemed.

"You're not freaked out," I said.

"No, I am not. Your observations remain astute."

"Funny lady. What I mean is, this is bizarre. We skipped into the Interstice, then took another portal—one that doesn't look like any rip *I've* encountered—that dumped us into an ancient city. One that Teget says is his home, and mine, since the DNA tests established us as brothers." I paused, waiting for a reaction. All I got was a raised eyebrow. "That's it?"

"What is it?"

I raised my eyebrow, an intentional exaggeration, and just in case she hadn't gotten the point, poked at my forehead. "This, Loredana. This place is weird. And yet you're standing here like we're strolling down DeLeon for the Bay Arts Fest. Hello! Dimension full of people!"

"Yes, it is a dimension full of people, not unlike our own."

"Yeah! Duh! So why aren't you …" It struck me harder than a fiend's tentacle. "This isn't a surprise to you at all."

"The specifics are intriguing, I have to admit, but no, I'm not astonished. Teget must have come from somewhere. You came from somewhere."

"Okay, that's not what I mean. You've made a trip like this before. To another world." I frowned. "But the Interstice scared you."

Loredana rubbed her arm. Her hand trembled. "I … Yes."

I shook my head, trying to bash the puzzle pieces together.

"Mercury, it's best if we're truly honest with each other. Yes, I have seen other worlds beyond the Interstice. The existence of this world—though its form is remarkable—was not unforeseen. But I never stepped inside the Interstice before today. There are ways to bypass it and gain access to dimensions separate from Earth."

I blinked.

"Is there something you're having trouble comprehending?"

"No. Yes." I walked off.

"What's troubling you?"

"Specifically? It would have been nice to know what we were walking into."

"This was not a planned excursion. Nor is this the time for us to come to conflict."

"Yeah? When should we save that for? Maybe a barbecue?" I pointed to the forest. "Back there, past the Interstice, Marigold and Calvin have Procyon and the blade. We're over here with the other two weapons. She's going to try again to open a rip. You saw how she was able to do it."

"I understand that. Is that your concern, then?"

"No. It's not."

"Then what?" Loredana touched my arm.

I brushed her off. "I don't want to go anywhere. This place—"

What was I going to say? Even when I walked up DeLeon, or into Carlito's, I didn't feel like I did right then. The scents in the air, the tread of the stone underfoot, it was a hundred times more familiar.

Maybe Teget was right. Maybe this was home.

"There they are." Teget had his posse or whoever they were filling the street. "This is a joyous occasion. Come, the house is in the next quadrant."

The people made way for our group, though there were only three of us. "What about Wilhelmina?"

"She has gone to see a healer. The interaction between the pulsar stave and its true birthplace did much to give her power, but I am afraid the strain on her physically has been extreme. Permanent adjustment is required. Do not fear. She will be well cared for."

I glanced at some of the faces watching us. They were a mingle of ethnicities, I guess, though the majority had Middle Eastern or Greek complexions with hints of Asian heritage. Like Teget. And me.

Loredana stood out like a ruby in someone's gravel driveway. Murmurs spread among the crowd. If she was bothered by their staring, she didn't show. I was just happy no one confiscated her gun.

We reached a long canal, our party following the road up over a stone bridge. From its center, I could see the canal stretched out to the north and south, until it bent at angles behind more buildings. A boat trundled beneath us, steam billowing from a fluted bronze stack.

A house sat beyond the bridge.

It was a single story, made of white blocks with sandstone-colored columns at each corner. Hexagonal in shape. Copper dome. Ivy framed a wooden doorway. Brass hinges squealed when Teget twisted the handle.

A short vestibule opened into a broad space, a smaller hexagon. Doors and open arches led into six compartments of varying size. Rugs covered tile floors. Plants hung around globes of light, which pulsed brightly as we walked in.

"I don't believe it," I murmured.

"You see? Father and Mother would have held you over there." Teget pointed to a long, low divan curved like a letter C. "Mother called it the child's chair. Grandfather says it was her favorite part of the house."

"Grandfather says." I looked at him, straight in the face, anything to break the spell this building had on me. "You don't remember what Mom—what your mother said?"

"They died when I was only a few months old." Teget's expression darkened. "I have no memories of them, or of you. All I knew is what our family taught me: that our parents sacrificed themselves to save two worlds and left you on Earth. It was left to me to safeguard the ax, to inherit the only one of the three weapons remaining among our people."

"Our parents left the pulsar stave and me on Earth. In the same place as the blade. How could that possibly be a good thing?"

"I do not know. This is what I have been told, for years. My whole life was spent training for this moment. It is why I was the Icon, so that I could join you, and together, we could mend the gap between your world and the Interstice. We must fulfill their purposes, Mercury."

"I didn't want a purpose." I sank onto the divan. Felt the soft cushion beneath my fingers. Music swelled in my head. A song. Lilting notes, words in a language I didn't understand. I closed my eyes. A pretty face, brown hair, dark eyes. Warm hands that held me close. "I wanted a family."

"You have both now." Teget beckoned someone from the doorway.

The man who entered was tall, with stooped shoulders

and thinning gray hair shot through with black. He wore a long, pale blue coat, and pants the same color. He watched me like a potential new owner sizing up a puppy, curious, I guess whether I'd try to run or hide.

He also had the other half of the pulsar stave in his hand.

I glared at him. "You'd better explain why you've got something that belongs to me, and what happened to the friend I gave it to."

The older guy grinned. "That is the spark I expected from Sabik. It is not surprising to hear his fire issuing from your mouth."

"Sabik."

"Your father, Mercury. And my son." He held out the pulsar stave to me.

I stood, legs wobbly. Had to be hearing things. I took the stave half and reattached it. How I found the harness on my belt without dropping the thing, I have no idea. "You're my grandfather."

"I am Naos. Call me that, if you will. It has been such a long time, titles are of little use." He hugged me.

It should have been great. Should have left me a sobbing mess. Except, the first thing that flashed through my mind was a little version of me, bawling in the middle of a pizza shop in San Camillo. Bawling until the owner took me aside. He found me a seat, got me a pitcher of soda, and brought a whole, steaming pie of pepperoni. I must have eaten it for hours, until the police came, and then a soft-spoken woman from children's services. Days after that were a blur and turned into years of surly fake parents and trips between the orphanage and bad homes. For a moment, though, that restaurant was a refuge, a haven, better than the harbor for a sailboat when storms rolled in.

Carlito's.

I accepted the hug. Gave him one back as best I could. Sure, there were tears, and I coughed in a manly fashion to draw attention away from those that showed up. Pretty sure it didn't work.

"I have waited a long time to see you again." There were tears in Naos' eyes, too.

"Yeah, I don't really remember you, sad to say." I shrugged. "Sorry."

"There is no need to apologize. Teget told me what you have done on your world. You alone have stood against the darkness that threatens to overtake your world."

Sounded good when he put it that way. "About that. I've got a lot of questions."

"Understandably so. Together we shall find the answers." Naos embraced Teget next. "It is good to see you alive and well."

"Thank you, Grandfather. I did not know it would take me as long as it did to make my journey and return. There were complications."

"There always are. Yet, you brought your brother home." Naos nodded at me. "Your friend is well. She is resting. The healing has restored her body to what it was before she came here, however, I am afraid she has taxed herself through repeated use of the pulsar stave."

"She said something about it taking a toll," I muttered. "Didn't know what to think of it. Don't know what to think of this, either."

"You must be exhausted by your journey, as is your other friend."

Other friend? Oh. Kinda forgot about Loredana. First time for everything, I know. She stood in a corner, away from us three guys. Her MP5 was demurely tucked behind the messenger bag, and her hands were clasped together. No one else had followed us into the house. People clustered outside. Snippets of conversation filtered through the door.

"Sorry." I cleared my throat. "This is Loredana Lark, with Procyon Foundation. She's, ah … That is, she's my … Or she's …"

"I'm Mercury's supervisor." Loredana strode to Naos and offered her hand. "As well as keeper, one could say."

"Delightful." Naos kissed her knuckles. She didn't flinch. "A warrior with inner strength to match her beauty."

Yeah. That was the perfect way to summarize Loredana. I grinned.

"Like your mother, I see."

Oh. Okay. That was awkward. Loredana winked sidelong at me.

I made a face. "Time to change the subject."

"Very well. You should accompany me to the temple at the center of our city. Your friend can remain here."

"No." I placed my hand on Loredana's back. "Wherever I go, she goes. We're a team."

"Indeed." Naos nodded. "But we do not let people from beyond the Interstice delve into our guarded secrets, Mercury."

"Yeah, well, I bet your long-lost grandson doesn't pop up from another dimension every day, either, so today's just full of surprises." I gestured to the door. "Lead the way, Grandpa."

Teget looked appalled, like I'd stepped on that same puppy I'd figured Naos was sizing up. He actually clenched his fists, which made me snicker. If he wanted to throw down, I was game. We were overdue a brotherly tussle.

Naos contemplated my oh-so-polite request in complete silence, then burst out laughing. It was a boisterous, happy sound. My heart ached at the thought of how often it must have filled this house when our family was all gathered.

This house, in a dimension parallel to Earth and across the Interstice, in a land with weird-colored skies and a sun that was too small. I shook my head.

"The words of your father, and the indomitable spirit of your mother." Naos chuckled. "I acquiesce. Come. You said you have questions for me? I pray, then, the answers will put your mind at ease."

Actually, as we left the house, I guessed that I really didn't want to know.

CHAPTER
THIRTY-ONE

The temple was seven stories tall. Not a gigantic building, by any stretch. There were plenty of places in San Camillo that dwarfed it. Keeping with that National Geographic theme, however, it was a step pyramid that seemed untouched by centuries. Sure, the edges of stone were eroded and the steps we took up the side to a yawning archway on the third level were pitted, but otherwise it could have been an apartment complex built by local contractors.

Intricate carvings covered the walls. If you stared at them long enough, they moved. No joke. I glanced at my side. Yeah, they were pretty close to the ones on the pulsar stave, and Teget's ax. A quick Google search could have probably given me some Earth-like comparisons, but first off, I no longer had a phone, and second, I wasn't likely to get signal here anytime soon.

Four guys stood under the archway, a pair flanking each side of a massive wooden door. These fellas could have joined Calvin's hit squad, no problem—tall, thickset, muscled, wearing padded vests of similar make as Teget's. Each one had a large bladed weapon sheathed on his hip, and a rifle propped at his shoulder. Correction. A musket, not a rifle. These weren't any flintlocks I remembered from cool pictures of the American Revolution spotted during the rare moments I was paying attention in Social Studies. Nope. The guns had huge gears the size of my hand that were linked to the trigger mechanism. Brass fittings held the weapon together. Goofy as they looked, I still wouldn't have wanted to be on the receiving end of a musket ball in that caliber.

Naos nodded to the guards, two of whom opened the doors without ceremony or comment. The hall inside was cool, damp stone, lit by shimmering yellow—stones? Yeah, stones, not lightbulbs or torches.

They illuminated dozens of paintings.

Not Michelangelo quality, I should point out, but fancy enough to get their point across and make my jaw drop.

"We do not have a good record of how long we have lived on this world," Naos said. "What is known is the first of our people arrived here through the same manner you traversed our worlds. From the beginning, it was viewed as a deliverance from evil. This land was established as a refuge from evil, a way for people to escape growing hatred, to preserve knowledge that was scoured from every corner of the world when it was drowned in sorrow."

I rubbed my hand across the textured paints. People in ancient dress stepped through a glowing purple line streaked with white. They left a swirling, cloudy mess and emerged to pale-green sky over lush fields. I shivered at the drawing. Tentacles writhed among those dark clouds, and pinpricks of red dots—astral fiend eyes—pursued the people on their trek.

"It took many millennia, but we established a civilization here. Our cities thrived. The gift of knowledge guided our hands in the creation of powerful technologies. They were meant to protect us from the evil lurking beyond our boundaries, in the depths of what you call the Interstice. But like most technology, it could be misused."

The next panels showed an epic war, and by epic, I don't mean great. Cities burned. Bodies lay strewn about, crushed and stabbed and burnt.

"The schism that rent our people was brutal, so much so whole volumes of our history were erased. By grace alone were we able to turn the tide, to reclaim what was gifted to us. We rebuilt, with greater care and humility, establishing Meda as a gathering place for those who would safeguard the technologies."

"Point of clarification." No, I did not raise my hand, but I felt like I should. "When you say technologies, you mean the pulsar stave, the ax, and the blade."

"Those, among others."

We entered a yawning room with a high ceiling that must have reached to the other four floors above us. Steps led up the sides, to balconies and catwalks surrounding the space. Archways were cut into the walls. There were no guards I could see. No people, either. Tiny channels crisscrossed the stone throughout the room, draining away from a square pool. A marble platform stood a couple feet above the water, with an onyx pedestal four feet tall at its center.

Flashback. I'd seen something like that, in the blade visions doled out by Teget's ax when I was trying to track it down. Granted, that pedestal wasn't made of shiny black stone, but the shape was the same.

"This is the Atrium. It is the heart of Meda and, in many ways, the heart of our people." Naos's expression was solemn. "This is why you are tasked with wielding the pulsar stave, Mercury, and why your brother holds the ax. This is what you protect."

"You should have mentioned this in my job description," I muttered to Loredana.

She gazed about the chamber, drinking in the starry patterns etched on the ceiling, the mysterious carvings on the walls, and the water trickling through miniature canals at our feet. "If I had any inkling this place existed, it would've been the very first thing covered in our initial briefing."

Score one for protocol. "Naos, where are these things kept? When Teget and I aren't using them for trans-dimensional travel and stabbing monsters."

He led our party onto the fifth level and gestured inside a short corridor lined with what looked like quartz blocks. Three onyx pedestals stood empty. I say empty because they were carved with gaps in their middles meant to accommodate objects. Long, skinny ones.

"The stave and its siblings have been removed from here for many years," Naos said. "Only the ax returns when its need for rest arises."

"Our weapons need rest?"

Teget brought the ax forward and plugged it into the middle pedestal. A hum emanated from the weapon. Stones underfoot rattled, then the vibration subsided, but I swore I could still feel it in my teeth, like the aftereffects of a bad trip to the dentist. "It is a necessary step. Without it, the weapons would eventually be drained."

"Nothing in Winston's research suggested such a possibility," Loredana said.

"Let's mark Winston's advice in the 'Not Trustworthy' column for now," I said. "But you've got a point. I had no idea the pulsar stave ran on, well, a battery."

"That is a crude summary, but accurate," Teget said. "It

is possible the pulsar stave draws its power in a fashion that allows it to last longer. We simply do not know. Such details are the kind lost during our civil war."

"Still." I removed the stave from its harness. "Might be nice for it to take a break."

"For the weapon to be restored to its full potential, yes." Naos pointed to the right-hand pedestal.

I inserted the stave. A jolt of energy flashed its length, and a hum of a higher pitch joined the ax's keening, which curiously returned as soon as the stave started its recharge. They faded in unison.

"Fascinating," Loredana whispered.

"Come, please." Naos led us from the chamber. "You are beginning to understand the importance of this place."

"Hang on." I got ahead of Teget and Loredana in our entourage. "You said your—our ancestors came here."

"From Earth, yes."

"Thousands of years ago."

He nodded.

"That's insane. How'd Bronze Age or worse off cultures manage to step across dimensions? Or survive a trip through the astral fiends' home turf?"

"We were guided. Luminous beings showed us the way. They were messengers—or so the legends go."

"Messengers. Luminous beings." I rubbed my forehead. "Like angels?"

I didn't expect anything but a blank look from him. After all, how current could a guy on a different world be about our religions? But Naos smiled. "We have no evidence to that supposition; however, faith does not always require the same evidence as the human mind finds rational."

I rolled my eyes. "Of course. Angels. Why not? That's not

crazy at all."

"As 'crazy' as your journey to date? Did Teget not lead you through a dimension full of our deadliest nightmares to a planet separated from yours by space and time? One would think your mind would be open to the greater possibilities of the universe, Mercury."

The tone of voice matched the words perfectly. Forget him thinking I sounded like my lost Dad. Naos could've been *me*.

We passed another chamber, this one home to a lumpen, misshapen rock. It looked like a huge piece of lava, cooled and dropped whole into a room lined with scale-like tiles. There was a round indentation at the center, big enough to contain a fist. "Another weapon? That one get checked out with an extended due date?"

"During our war, not only did our people very nearly exterminate ourselves, but we fragmented over our ideas about how the artifacts now contained in the Atrium should be used. Some felt they were too dangerous for anything other than permanent isolation. Most recognized their capacity to be used in defense of the innocent and defeat of evil, yet new precautions were necessary. A small group stole several, in the heat of our worst battle, before fleeing Meda. We know not what has happened, only that we must remain vigilant."

My stomach turned at the idea of items like the pulsar stave and the ax running lose on Earth—or anywhere else. Of course, that fit the blade to a T.

The next room was sealed by a metal door, etched with a single carving that looked like a set of interlocked triangles. The one beyond was open, so I assumed something was missing. Sort of. The room was all gray stone, top and bottom, lit by a single yellow jewel in the floor. A sandstone statue of a man, to correct proportion, stood there like a utilitarian version of the famous David sculpture. Only problem? His hands were broken. They lay at his feet, surrounded by shards. Nothing else was disturbed.

"Someone snatched up whatever was on that guy's wrists, I take it."

Nobody found the quip amusing. Naos seemed especially grim. "Yes. When we determine a lost item's location, we must reach a decision as to whether they can be retrieved. In this case, action was taken before we could take steps to neutralize a threat."

Loredana had a weird, sickly expression on her face. "You okay?" I whispered, as Naos and Teget walked on.

"Quite." She adjusted the bag, and her gun. "I was thinking about Jack Jackson's comment regarding consequences. Some actions carry greater ones than others."

I glanced at Broken Man's busted wrists. "And this one triggered something important?"

"It did indeed. One Procyon contained." She frowned. "We'll discuss it later."

I blew out a breath and followed the gang.

One of the last rooms around the fourth-floor walkway was sealed behind the strangest door I'd ever seen. It was framed in metal, yet looked like it was built of a thick, cracked crystal. I tapped on it. Red light flashed across the surface.

Naos slapped my hand away.

"Hey!"

"Your father's headstrong nature will not serve you here," he said. "This is by far the one chamber with which we must take the utmost care."

There were hundreds of metal shapes suspended in a shimmering sphere of liquid. Water? Or dissolved crystal? No idea. Some were triangles, others were circles, still more were rectangles. Most looked brand new, but a bunch were beaten, worn down, so much so that strange lines poked out. I squinted. "That's weird."

"Yes," Loredana said. "The patterns resemble circuitry."

The language etched above the archway was indecipherable to me. "Naos, let's check out that room."

"No." He blocked our path. His voice was exactly what I imagined a stern grandfather's should be—firm, allowing no argument. "It is far too dangerous a space in which to meddle with the contents. Hence the warning. I do not dare expose you to what was our greatest failure. Too many went wayward on your world. It is best silence prevail."

He led us on, though not before muttering "medallions" under his breath. I really didn't want to know what was wrong with that brand of jewelry.

We ascended to the sixth floor, following a narrow, twisting staircase. It opened outside the temple. From there we took the last steps onto the summit. Meda spread out to all points of the compass, built on an octagonal pattern. The canal we'd taken the bridge over? One of dozens branching out of the city to the north and south, where they formed a much larger channel that stretched far into the horizon. Rectangular fields filled the landscape south and southeast. The forest we'd exited was a huge carpet covering everything in sight to the west. Huge, craggy mountains of sandy pink rock capped with gleaming white snows loomed to the north, rising above long, rolling hills.

There were roads, too. Long, broad paths of stone led to the east and the south, with a narrower one to the north. Sunset turned the sky brilliant oranges above the western forest.

"Mercury, are you okay?" Loredana asked.

I was standing on the edge of the roof, arms spread at my

side. I could feel the breeze between my fingers, my hair, across the stealth suit. "I've been here before, right? Not Meda. I mean the temple."

Naos smiled. "Not inside the Atrium. But to this roof? Yes. While your parents sparred with the pulsar stave, I brought you topside. You liked to say you were ready to fly into the clouds, beyond the sky, to the next world. It brought me joy, and also sadness, because I knew it was true."

"Why?"

"Your parents trained hard, Mercury, when we learned the blade was still on Earth. They recognized a threat to that world, and though this is our home, we could not turn our backs on the innocent lives at stake. If evil was allowed to open a permanent path between your world and the Interstice, it would only be a matter of time before the same fate was visited upon us. Our council left the choice to them. They knew the dangers, and they chose to take you with them."

"I was left here," Teget said softly, "As the inheritor of their mission. For many years, we thought there would be nothing to inherit."

"Doesn't make sense." My throat tightened. "How could they put a kid at risk? How could they leave his baby brother alone?"

"Teget had family. As for you, Mercury, your parents knew they needed a contingency. The pulsar stave had shown its affinity for you even at birth. If anything happened to them …" Naos' voice shook. "You were their hope."

Loredana took my hand. There was no offer of comfort, or hugs, or any of that stuff. Just the promise of being there. "Procyon knew two people from outside our dimension were killed and their orphan was left on Earth. We didn't understand the significance, until our foundation discovered Mercury and hired him for the work. Yes, the pulsar stave was his. That was clear from the moment Procyon first let him use it. But his role remains vital."

"That doesn't matter." I cleared my throat. "What was her name?"

"Who?" Teget said.

I half-smiled. "Our mom."

He returned the gesture. "Cyllene."

"Sabik and Cyllene. Okay. That's a lot to take in. Doesn't mean I'm not sore they left me, but knowing they died, knowing it was for a good reason ..." I lost the rest of my words.

"Procyon's dossier on you can shed some more light," Loredana said. "I can walk you through it. You'll see why it's so important for us to finish what we started. To go back."

"Go back?"

"To stop Marigold. She has the blade, and if she retains it, the consequences will be dire."

"Like I said, that doesn't matter. She'll be preoccupied there for a while." It was cold, but I didn't care. After a lifetime of being alone, here I was standing atop a temple my warrior parents trained in, with my brother and grandfather standing before me. "We have the pulsar stave and the ax. She can't stabilize the portal without them."

"What are you suggesting?" Loredana let go of my hand. "A stalemate?"

"A truce." I gazed out over the city. My city. "Forget San Camillo. I'm home."

CHAPTER THIRTY-TWO

And since I was home, my family threw me a welcome-back party. I suspected it was also somewhat a "Hooray, Teget didn't die on his recent mission!" celebration, too, but that didn't bug me.

There had to be a hundred people flocking around the house, spilling onto the bridge and adjacent homes. Some of those latter folks must have been dragooned into supporting the festivities, because food poured out of their kitchens like water from a tap—savory meats, sharp cheeses, succulent fruits. I didn't recognize much, though the flavors were familiar, and I was pretty sure I ate apple slices. Of course, I was also pretty sure there was something that tasted like chicken and looked like chicken. Maybe it was one of those fanged flying critters we saw earlier in the day.

Anyway, the whole block was full of talking and joking and singing and laughter. At the center? Me. A bunch of kids crowded at my feet. They were cousins. No matter how much food I chowed, no matter how much of their fresh cider I guzzled, I couldn't quite convince myself they were real. Eleven kids, all grade school age, and they were all related to me.

You'd think they'd be all about hearing of my battles with monsters. Nope. Apparently Teget had the corner on that market, because he was in the midst of three young men and five women, all about his age, sweeping through the motions with an imaginary ax.

I shook my head. If he wanted to be the action hero, more power to him. The kids around me were way more interested in something mundane—from my perspective.

"How fast could the auto-motives go?"

"Automobiles. Cars, kid. A hundred miles an hour, easy."

That got me some oohs and aahs, except from one skeptic, a short, thin boy with long black hair. "That is not possible. Our wagons cannot go faster than forty."

"Your wagons must be pulled by some swift horses."

"They use steam engines." The kid wrinkled his nose. "What is a horse?"

Naos joined us. "Perhaps you could give Mercury some space to relax, children. You have been questioning him with a relentlessness even our council would appreciate of its temple guards. Off with you, now. Find your kin outside."

They ambled away, one mass of arms and legs, voices raised in debate. Like watching an astral fiend arguing with itself. I chuckled and had some more cider.

"You seem to have found a quiet corner."

"Don't get me wrong. This is all great." I waved at an older woman who sat on a spindly chair. "My great-aunt? My cousins? My brother's friends? Up until a couple weeks ago the only people close enough for me to consider family were the guy who tracked monsters for me and the girl who interpreted dreams. Turns out I had misplaced trust."

"It must be like awakening from a nightmare to a dream."

"Sort of. There were just—too many people. For a little

while." Didn't like to admit it, but I'd become accustomed to quiet. All these faces clustered nearby, their words overlapping, grated on my senses. Part of me wanted to have my earbuds plugged in and tunes flowing through my head while waiting to skewer an astral fiend. "I'll be good to hang out in a bit."

"Take your time. We are overjoyed to have you back among us in this time of celebration."

"So, this wasn't all for me?"

"It was for the reunification of a storied family. You, your brother, and I are heirs to a great promise. I do not mean it as a boast. It is fact: our bloodline is meant to protect this world, and the wonders therein."

I swirled cider in the mug. The music outside accelerated. Judging by the clapping and stomping, a whole lot of people were dancing. I was ready to join them, now that the onslaught of elementary school interrogation had ended. "Do you really think angels brought our people here?"

"I believe it is possible. Is that not enough?"

"I prefer certainty to hope."

"Hope is all we have, sometimes, and it must suffice when all else fails. I do not mean wishful thinking—I mean trust in an unbreakable promise." He leaned nearer. "I know who cares for my soul when death arrives. So does Teget. Consider that, when you wonder about mysteries we cannot comprehend."

I don't think his words helped me clear up my muddied thoughts, but they were worth a good ponder. At least, they were until I joined the crowd outside. Teget accompanied me, arm around my shoulders and head tossed back with uproarious laughter. Did I miss a joke, or was he that happy? Didn't matter.

We danced and spun to the clapping of my newfound kin, in the city built by our ancient ancestors.

⌗ ⌗ ⌗

One thing: the party was missing elements. Wilhelmina was off recovering, I supposed. When I asked Teget, he shrugged and replied, "She wanted to explore Meda in silence. I cannot blame her. This is a place of legends more than a house of refuge."

Made sense.

What worried me more was Loredana's whereabouts. She was nowhere outside the house, or on the streets within a block. I checked. Good thing was, other people noticed where she'd run off to. She was the only redhead in town, so that made it easier to track her. After getting caught in a dozen more conversations over the next half hour, an elderly couple finally pointed me toward the local library.

Like most buildings, it had slanted walls and a small dome for a roof. The locals called it a "bibliontum," which was close enough to what I knew. Fact is, the place was packed wall to wall and floor to ceiling with books—giant leather-bound volumes, thick paperback types, and everything in between.

The place was deserted. Shocker. The whole neighborhood was partying at my house. I grinned, thinking about how that compared with Friday's pizza nights.

Loredana wasn't in the mood.

"I thought you'd be busy enjoying your newfound social life." She didn't look up when I entered the main room. She had the contents of the messenger bag sprawled across a huge reading table. Never seen so much Procyon letterhead in my entire life. Old, yellowing documents protected in plastic sheets were scattered among the official memos. Loredana leaned on the table, with the glow from of those yellow crystals as her only source of illumination.

"Light reading?" I shoved a folder aside and sat on the edge opposite her.

"Everything we took from the Historic Vault. Some of it may interest you, if you can find time in your busy schedule of stuffing your face." She slapped a folder against my chest.

"Speaking of which, you should eat something, too. It's been—well, I kinda lost track of time." The title of the folder gave me pause: **Mercury Hale, Personnel Dossier.**

"That's the problem. You've lost not only your sense of time, but of priority."

"Pretty sure getting the grand tour of my people's storehouse of magic weapons should have topped the list. That and getting to know who I really am."

"Your answers are in your hand."

She wasn't kidding. There were photos of me from the start—age 3, then up through middle school, that really bad hair phase in high school, community college, and various odd jobs I held before Procyon scooped me up. Had to hand it to them. Their surveillance teams were top notch. Way better than the mercenaries Calvin hired to kill me. You know, subtle.

"According to those records, your parents arrived in the midst of an astral fiend outbreak that was unprecedented."

"Like the uptick I've experienced."

"No. Worse." Loredana's expression seemed haunted, especially with the dim light casting shadows across her face. "There had been a lull for a few decades, with incursions of far less frequency than even you'd experience. Then, five fiends appeared through one rip at the same time, followed by another four."

My hand instinctively went for the place on my suit where the pulsar stave should hang. Check that. It was being recharged in the temple. But man. Nine fiends in one night?

Two was bad enough, and that giant one was no picnic either. Kinda wished there were more lights on in the library. I read on, dreading the end result of the report but already sensing what was coming. "Is that how they died?"

"Yes. Sabik and Cyllene fought bravely, but in the end the injuries they sustained were too much. Even our operative was overwhelmed."

Of course. There would have been an operative present. I flipped to a page, and there was a photo of a very attractive, 40-something Wilhelmina. Only, that wasn't her name. **Sherry Jean Crown. Dismissed: 1994.**

"She didn't tell you?"

"No. She knew of what happened, but never said anything about the details. I knew she was a Procyon operative."

"She was one of our greatest, according to what I read. Quite remarkable."

I ran a hand through my hair. Wilhelmina had been there. She'd fought side by side with my parents, in the battle that had killed them both. But … Wait a minute. I flipped back, skimming details. Something didn't square with what Naos had told me. "My parents trained using the pulsar stave. So, they would have brought it with them to Earth."

She nodded, watching me as if I was going to metamorphize or explode.

"Okay, but Procyon's report says Wilhelmina turned in the pulsar stave to the foundation when she was let go."

Loredana nodded again.

"You gonna tell me how there could be *two* pulsar staves?"

"There aren't. That is, not at the present." She moved closer, paged through the files in my hand. "Here. 'Operative recovered a weapon identical to the pulsar stave. Both weapons were analyzed at the Procyon lab. Upon completion of initial examination, weapons were placed in close proximity to each other. Resultant conflagration nearly destroyed the lab facilities. One weapon was left behind in the merger.'"

"Merger."

"It's a dry explanation that says two pulsar staves became one. I don't know how."

I considered that. "Grandfather—I mean, Naos—he said Mom and Dad sparred with the pulsar stave. I assumed he meant they each had a half. They didn't, did they? They only had one weapon."

"Two." Loredana indicated I should continue reading.

My eyes widened. "The ax. Of course. That's how Wilhelmina knew what it was like, and how it worked. She'd seen it in action. Obviously, she didn't turn it in to Procyon."

"No. The operative's report states she threw it into the diminishing rip before it vanished, after the fiends were dispatched." Loredana frowned. "Which explains both why she was sacked, and why the ax was new to us when the lab got hold of it."

I went back to perusing Wilhelmina's file. The attack took place in a civilian neighborhood, one that was being built at the time. Malhorn and Campos. There was some property damage.

I felt sick.

"Her home was destroyed," Loredana whispered. "Her husband and daughter, killed."

"Procyon just covered it up?"

"Gas leak. You understand how these things are handled."

"Yeah. Shades of my apartment." I closed the file. "Then they cut her loose. Flash forward two decades, she's living on the streets of San Camillo, minding her business, watching for astral fiends and Procyon's goons, until a fiend attacks her from out of nowhere."

"Hardly. Marigold must have found the file and ascertained her identity."

I kicked the table. Great. Just great. "You know, I was really enjoying the party."

"Terribly sorry to have spoiled your evening. By all means, go back to indulging." Loredana swept the file away.

"Hey, I came looking for you."

"You certainly did. How long had I been gone, prior to that?"

"What am I, your chaperone? I figured a woman walking around a town filled with musketeers would be okay since she had a submachine gun."

"That isn't what I meant. You—" She waved a hand dismissively. "Never mind."

"You've been weird ever since the tour, when you went on your rant."

"It was not a rant. It was a reminder of what things you should hold important."

"No need. This place is important."

"What of the city we left?"

"I'm not worried about that. I'm worried about you." There it was. Out of the bag. I'd imagined she'd put a hand to her mouth, maybe be flattered at what that sentiment implied.

Didn't expect a roll of the eyes. That was my gig. "Touching, really. My problem, Mercury, is you seem quite content to sit here and fatten yourself while others of us are preparing to deal with the larger problems facing our world."

"Your world, maybe. Not mine."

She gestured angrily at the door. "Didn't you hear what Naos said? If the way between worlds is stabilized, astral fiends will run rampant!"

"Yeah, and, news flash! Marigold can't do that when we've got two of the three weapons here!"

"A fine point, Mercury, except for one flaw: what will happen if she figures out a way to come to Meda? To bring astral fiends with her? Where will you hide then?"

Talk about a verbal kick in the gut. "I am not hiding."

"Of course you are." She scowled. "What a fool I've been. Nothing's changed. You're still the scared little boy crying in a pizza shop, waiting for mummy to return when everyone else knows she's dead."

"I wouldn't have been standing there if Procyon had taken me in!" I snapped. "Instead I get spied on, roped into a supposed chance hire, then used to fight the same monsters that killed my parents! Meanwhile nobody tells me the truth. Nobody! Not even you."

"I didn't know! They kept as many secrets from me as they did from you. I knew pieces, yes, but not everything. Certainly, I would have told you."

"Yeah, right. I bet you would have. You would have broken all protocols surrounding Mercury Hale's personnel dossier." We were toe to toe, fists clenched. My arms were shaking. Loredana's cheeks were flushed red, and I was really glad the MP5 was sitting in a chair on the other side of the table. That triggered the memory of her holding a revolver to both Jack Jackson's and Calvin's heads. "So what are we gonna do now, Loredana? Because I've found my family, and I'm not inclined to go back to a world that doesn't want me and a foundation that'll use me until I'm spent, then toss me out with the garbage like Wilhelmina."

No idea who moved first. I think it was simultaneous. But we kissed. One second, yelling. The next second, colliding fires.

After the shouting, it was utterly silent in the library. Her arms were around my neck. Mine were on her back. We pressed together like we could have merged into one weapon, driven by blazing heat.

The evening breeze carried music through an open window.

We broke apart. Good thing too. We were both gasping for air, as if we'd surfaced from San Camillo bay.

Loredana shoved the files pell-mell into the messenger bag. I stood there, a statue. Felt like the carved guy in the temple, the one with the broken hands.

"Do what you will, Mercury." Her voice was soft, and quaking. "I will find my own way back, to face what you won't." She brushed past me in a rush for the door.

"Loredana, wait."

Gone.

CHAPTER THIRTY-THREE

Loredana pulled a disappearing act on me again. This time, though, I wasn't in the mood to chase her down, because whatever I was going to say was going to be borderline rude, hold the borderline.

Whatever. Didn't help that she had a point. If Marigold was successful, San Camillo was going to face an invasion the likes of which hadn't been visited upon Earth in a really long time. But my point was just as valid. With two of the three weapons here, what could she do.

Okay. She had managed to not only create a more stable rift but also summon the biggest astral fiend I'd ever seen. That meant major damage, and lots of life lost. San Camillo PD would be up a creek.

That reminded me of Ramos. I wondered how he and his crew had responded to everything that had gone down at Procyon that night? Between the gunfire, the smashed vehicles, and the dead mercenaries, there was a lot that needed sweeping under the rug. Too much to be explained away by a gas main leak, to borrow from Procyon's favorite.

Jamie was dead, too.

I gritted my teeth. Don't think about that. All that stuff? Part of another world. I wasn't from there. It was an adopted home that, frankly, didn't care about me. See Procyon's lies as Exhibit Number One. I felt bad about Jamie's death, and it stank Ramos would have to deal with the fallout from that last fight, but it wasn't my problem. I was here now. There were relatives who I hadn't seen in more than 20 years, and people who could be my friends.

I didn't need Earth.

The party was winding down by the time I got back, with adults chasing children off to bed. Teget sat in a chair by the front door of the house, waving good-bye to some of his young friends. "There you are. Did you find your companion?"

"Yeah, I did." My lips were still burning from the kiss. It was even odds which surprised me more, that or the fight. I know which I liked better.

Teget's smile faded. "You seem perturbed."

I dropped into a chair next to him. "That's putting it mildly. She and I have different ideas about my role. You know, here versus there."

"Ah." Teget thumped my arm with his fist. "Such is the hazard. Women are a mystery even to the greatest minds, which we are not."

"You guys have the same problem?"

"Certainly. Where would be the allure to either if men or women fully comprehended each other? It is the stuff of adventure. I am certain we are equally baffling to them."

"No joke," I muttered. "I don't know, Teget. This is where I want to stay. Is it really so bad if I never go back?"

"This is home, Mercury. This is where you belong." He shrugged. "Mother and Father did their best, but in the end, Earth proved too dangerous. It took them from us. What allegiance do we owe that world when our family is finally reunited?"

"The blade's still there."

"It is. When the time is right, when Grandfather believes you have trained well enough, we shall return and seize it. With the three weapons reunited, we will close off the portal to the astral fiends for good. Then we can seal the weapons away permanently in the temple."

I gazed at the shadowy pyramid looming against the night sky. Yellow lights flickered as guards passed in front of them. "Do you go there often?"

"The temple? I do, yes. For mediation, and prayer."

"You sound like Ramos."

"I will not pretend to understand what you have endured all these years separated from us, but I took solace during your absence through the presence of the Truth. If your colleague Ramos has indeed found the same Truth, he speaks with wisdom."

"Let's not drag me into a religion debate." I ran a hand across my hair. "It's the last thing I need to worry about right now."

Teget leaned back in his chair. "Perhaps it should be the first. Spend time at the temple, if you must, but do not be deceived—the answers you seek will not come from anywhere else than above. The Truth has a plan."

"Funny how you think a word can be a person."

Teget laughed. "Not *a* word."

"Okay, don't start again." I got up. "I'm going for a walk. I'll let you know if I meet God."

Teget tipped a glass of sweet-smelling cider. "If you do, give my regards."

⌗ ⌗ ⌗

Perfect. If I'd wanted a lesson like that, I would have hitched a ride to church with Ramos. Come to think of it, he'd never offered. Did that mean he was hoarding God?

Funny how little I thought of Him when dealing with all this dimension stuff. Winston had always couched the interactions in terms of science—albeit, a fuzzy version of science I didn't understand. Tachyon particles involved time travel, essentially. And then there were Marigold's dreams. Winston never bothered trying to explain those away.

What about my vision of the blade, courtesy of the ax? How would that hold up under a mission debriefing?

I shook my head, angry at the complexity of questions this mess brought up. Things were simpler when I could hang out in my apartment, enjoy a movie, and wait for the call that would send me out into the night with one purpose—destroy astral fiends. I liked keeping it simple. Sue me.

The guards didn't ask me for ID or frisk me as I stormed up the temple steps. Guess being Naos' grandson had perks. I ignored the Atrium, bypassed the side rooms, and headed straight for the roof.

The view sucked my breath away.

The city's roads sparkled with amber jewelry. Torches burned at the entrances, reflecting like fireflies off the canals. Far to the east, clunky wagons bled steam into the night as they descended a long, low hill. There were settlements out there, it seemed, and this steampunk caravan was bringing who-knew-what to Meda.

More impressive was the night sky. I'd never seen so many stars. Even driving around the hills outside San Camillo, up and down Arbor Valley, they were blotted out by light pollution from the city and its suburbs. Here, though, the sheer weight of the stellar spectacle made me stand up straighter, as if they'd crush me if I didn't push back. It was the most beautiful sight I'd ever encountered.

Only the shadow sitting on the edge of the roof ruined the moment.

"Now I know how the three bears felt." I joined Wilhelmina at her perch. "But you're kinda old to be Goldilocks."

She slapped my leg. "You hush. I'm enjoying the moment."

I let silence envelope us. That lasted about 15 seconds. "The stars look odd."

"Mm-hmm. They're in different positions."

"Makes sense. We're on a different planet, right? They don't look the same as from Earth."

"Doesn't make them any less gorgeous."

"Yep." I drummed my fingers on my knees. "So, Sherry Jean, let's talk."

She sighed heavily. "Lordy. That is all you ever do."

"Not all. There's pizza-eating, and monster-slaying."

"I stand corrected. What's on that busy mind of yours?"

"My parents, as always."

Wilhelmina nodded. I couldn't see her face well, but there was a tinge of regret when she said, "I'm sorry, child. There were so many fiends. When your parents showed up, I figured them angels from on high. But angels don't die. They don't bleed out while you're holding onto their limp bodies."

I shivered. I couldn't handle the mental image. Still, I had to know. "You fought beside them."

"Bravest folk I ever saw. Your Daddy? He laughed when an astral fiend almost took his head off! Laughed, then slit tentacles like he was trimming a tree. And your Mama—never saw someone move with such grace. Elegant as a dance, and deadly as a mob hitman."

Tears burned my eyes. I blinked furiously. "Yeah. I'm sure

they were great. But they're dead."

"And you're blaming Earth."

"Can't I?"

"Ain't no one to blame for their deaths except Marigold and her kin, the ones been using the blade to try drawing astral fiends out of the Interstice. Evil isn't some intangible force, Mercury. It's people. They do the wrong thing enough times it becomes the right thing, even when others see it as something horrific. You'd better believe in her mind, she's doing this for a glorious goal."

"I heard Winston's speech. Cleansing the Earth, blah-blah. How come whenever the bad guys talk about 'cleansing' something, they never translate it as, 'Lots of innocent people will die'?"

"Because they don't see anyone as innocent. Which is true, from a theological standpoint."

"Yeah, not here for that. You been texting Teget?"

"Not with the lousy signal I'm sure you've already fussed about."

I smirked. "Well-played."

"Don't change the subject on me. When your parents died, no one knew what was going to happen next. I sure didn't. I was standing there with the goo from dead fiends and the blood of two warriors slathered all over me. Suddenly I had an abundance of weapons."

"You threw the ax back into the Interstice."

"We didn't know much—or rather, I didn't. What we did know was that all three weapons could be used to either stabilize or destroy the rips for good. But no one knew where the blade was. Plenty of folks inside Procyon thought it a bad enough risk to have the pulsar stave in our dimension. I had people shouting in my ear to bring the ax in for analysis, but all I could think about was fiends destroying everything in their path. So, I chucked it."

"And the staves joined."

Wilhelmina made a face. "Didn't see that one coming."

I nodded, not wanting to ask the next question, but even as I struggled with the words, she nudged me. "Out with it, child."

"I wasn't the only one who lost everything that night, was I?"

She stiffened. "That's in the report, too, is it?"

"Yeah."

Wilhelmina wept.

I couldn't do anything but put an arm around her. The shaking subsided after a lot shorter time than I would have taken. She sniffed. "Bruce. His name was Bruce. On the city's Public Works payroll. And my baby girl—Annalise. She wanted to be an archaeologist, go 'round the Southwest digging for lost settlements. The fiends drained them cold, and I couldn't stop them."

"Procyon should have helped you, after."

"How?"

"I don't know. Just—somehow."

"It was my call. I walked away. Spent years killing myself, letting drink and the elements do their job, screaming at the sky over the bay, waiting for God to end it. But He wouldn't. I hated Him for it, until I realized why He was keeping me around." Wilhelmina looked at me. "I didn't know what to do with you. That's why I left you at that restaurant. Procyon wanted me to bring you in, or to drop you back through the Interstice. Your Mama, bless her, told me where they'd left you waiting. Poor child, alone in the dark in a motel room. I couldn't be your family, and neither could they. So when I heard Procyon was watching you, years later, waiting to see if you'd be dragged into their fold, I knew I had to be ready."

"Ready for what?"

"For the end. For this." She waved out at the city. "Mercury, we were meant to come here, but we weren't meant to stay."

"Why? You said it yourself. There's nothing for us there. You could belong with these people, and … Well, I could always use a new grandmother." I grinned. "Especially the blade-dueling type."

"That's sweet, but you know you're faking your way through. Think about Ramos."

"What about him? He's a good guy and all, but—"

"But nothing. Ramos is strong. He's committed himself to ridding the Earth of the same darkness you fight, except he ain't got the gifts. No pulsar stave. No Medan strength. No warrior training. He has a piece of pressed metal for a badge, a gun, and the authority of the San Camillo Police Department. How's that gonna help him against otherworldly threats?" She prodded my chest. "His heart. His faith. Ramos believes there's better than the darkness, that there's light worth pursuing. He knows he's powerless, yet he still shows up to help you. He faced down the very creatures of humanity's nightmares, with the same determination as he would a murderer or a rapist. That man brought you under his roof when the world was against you. Know why? Because you're a son to him. He won't admit it, and you sure won't. Why would he care about some orphaned smart-mouth? He can see, Mercury. The Lord's opened his eyes to what's really going on, the truth that most people hide from."

Her tirade left me speechless. Shocking, I know. When I finally recovered my senses, my throat had gone dry. I rubbed sweat-slicked hands against the suit. "Truth. You and Teget are reading from the same playbook."

Wilhelmina chuckled. "Don't know what all they got on this world that passes for the Good Book, if that's what you mean. There's truth and there's *Truth*, child. I'm familiar enough with both. So's Ramos."

"You're telling me I should go back."

"I'm telling you *we* should go back, because while staying here is nice, it ain't what we were meant to do. Fighting that destiny means we live unfulfilled lives."

I considered that. And them—Ramos, Loredana, Jamie, heck, even Winston and Marigold. My parents. People who had died and people who'd dedicated their whole lives to either protecting innocents from monsters, or in the case of my former co-workers, done their best to infect Earth. All those places I'd hung out, all the people I'd seen yakking and laughing in restaurants and parks ... Was I really going to lounge here and let them face obliteration?

Please.

I blew out a breath. "You know what? You're right."

Wilhelmina snorted. "'Course I am."

I stood, then helped her to her feet. "Let's go get my brother. Time for us to get tickets for our ax-trip back through hell."

CHAPTER
THIRTY-FOUR

Teget was puzzled by my insistence that we return to Earth. Frankly, so was I. "What of your training?"

"Look, I don't really have time to do the whole Luke-in-the-swamp thing, so you'll have to find someone else you can be Yoda to, okay?"

That analogy didn't help his confusion. "I do not know these people, unless you are referring to the saint."

"I ... No. Let's skip to the part where you tell me how to get back."

Teget glanced at Wilhelmina.

"Eyes over here." I poked him on the shoulder. "Yes, we talked about it, and yes, she made good points, but this is my call."

"Very well." Teget rubbed at his eyes. First time I'd seen him tired. "We should inform grandfather."

"We can do that after you show me how to get back into the Interstice." Truthfully, I wasn't interested in turning the one remaining relative with authority into a scowling, disapproving parent.

"Your companion still has not returned."

I winced. Loredana. "I'll, ah, go look for her."

Wilhelmina slapped my arm. "I wondered why she wasn't side by side with you up on that temple roof. What'd you do?"

"Nothing! I … She was …" I ground my teeth. "Can we skip over this part, too? Come on."

Wilhelmina rolled her eyes, and shared a look with Teget, who kept his own expression inscrutable. Gotta love it when friends are thinking you're the biggest idiot in the world—or in this case, two worlds—and keep their traps shut instead of laying it all out. "Follow me," Teget said.

He took us right back to the temple, which made me think I should have set up a cot or something in the Atrium to save travel time. Teget had us wait at the edge of the pool as he went upstairs for the ax. I stared at my wiggling reflection. Looked confident, bold. Which was not how I was feeling. If it was possible to have third, fourth, and fifth thoughts after your second ones, I'd lined them all up after each other.

"Ain't that a sight," Wilhelmina said.

The ax was glowing. Not full on like those light sticks you could snap in half and shake up, but there was a sheen about it I hadn't seen. Teget trotted back downstairs, ignoring the glow creeping up his arm. He led us to the pedestal in the center. We had to traverse stepping stones across the pool. The platform shifted under our weight.

"What is this thing?" I tapped my foot against its glossy marble surface. "Are we floating?"

"This thing, as you put it, will show us where and when the next rip into your world from the Interstice will open." Teget inserted the ax handle into the pedestal. He twisted it 90 degrees counterclockwise. "It is possible you will experience discomfort."

The platform shuddered. Metal clanked beneath us. The

whole assembly rose slowly from the pond, water streaming from its sides.

Wilhelmina stood near the center, as close to Teget as possible without interfering with his work. I got down on my hands and knees, curious about the construction. Yep, we were floating, eight feet off the roiling surface of the pool and rising. A handful of green jewels, each one the size of an apple and pale green, pulsed and crackled. No machinery or engines I could see. Okay then.

The platform lifted up, higher, until I became concerned by the possibility of getting smashed against the inside of the roof. Thankfully Teget was on his game. The ceiling cracked open, splitting into eight sections, letting the night sky flood the Atrium with starlight.

We rose past the roof, settling twenty feet above it. The lands around us were even more breathtaking from this height.

But nothing happened, other than a soft breeze whistling over the stone.

I cleared my throat. "So, do we need to insert a coin for the next twenty minutes?"

Teget glared at me. As intimidating as the expression was coming from this warrior, it also warmed my heart because, hey, brothers occasionally want to smack each other, right? The old softie.

Light flooded from the ax, coating the pedestal, the platform, and all three of us. It felt like I'd been dumped out of a hot tub into an ice-cold bath. Wilhelmina yelped. My teeth chattered. The sky and city washed away in a pure, clear glow. Stars faded out, and the glow did, too, until we were gazing upon a muted, shadowy version of the regular world. Well, as regular as Meda could be, existing in a dimension separate from Earth's.

We got a light show of an entirely different kind.

Purple.

Yeah, streaks of lightning shot across the sky, slamming into portals all over the place. It was hard to judge which ones were where, and how close. Soon the air was spinning with dozens, hundreds. My brain couldn't process fast enough. Words and thoughts and emotions spiraled out of control. Wilhelmina clutched my arm, mumbling quickly and quietly. Possibly prayer. I was ready to join her, because after everything we'd been through, I didn't want to die from brain melt.

Finally, the insane imagery coalesced into a single portal—a rip. I'd recognize the black tear, the purple energy crackling at its edges, anywhere. A miniature sun rose into position above it, tipping onto the left quarter. Then everything spun out of control again, hurtling us along a jagged footpath through a smeared landscape of blackened peaks and crags. Once more, we wound up standing in front of the rip.

The vision or sneak-preview or whatever it was offered a tantalizing image through that rip—San Camillo's skyline, under a golden late afternoon sky, the buildings gilded by the rays. I could imagine I smelled the sea spray.

Then it all blinked out with the suddenness of snapping awake.

Stars returned. The glow vanished. I dropped to my knees, stomach heaving. I managed to not throw up this time. Hooray for small things.

Wilhelmina remained standing, but she leaned heavily, hand on my back. "My God."

"Precisely." Teget's voice was shaky, and his face was dripping with sweat, but as he turned the ax clockwise, he didn't appear otherwise worse for wear.

"That was it?" I wiped at the edge of my mouth. Muscles

trembled as I got back to my feet. Vomit or not, I was regretting all the food I'd gulped. "Easy."

Teget rolled his eyes. I grinned at him, and yeah, got a smirk in response.

"I'm assuming that wonder we saw will get us back to the Interstice," Wilhelmina said, "'Cause I don't want to try it a second time."

"Fear not. The path is now clear. The next portal leading from the Interstice to Earth will open mid-morning, tomorrow. We should prepare ourselves."

I'm guessing he meant by getting weapons, which was fine by me, because I'd missed the familiar weight of the pulsar stave by my side. Kinda had double meaning when he said it, however, because Naos was waiting when the platform gently landed in the pool.

"If I had known what you two were doing, I would have told the guards to bar your admittance." He folded his arms.

And right there was the intro to the scolding I was hoping to avoid. I tried my grin, seeing as how well it'd worked on Teget, but Naos didn't crack. An earthquake wouldn't have moved him. He'd have stood there, scowling at the giant stone blocks that had the audacity to crush him. "Look, there's no easy way to put it. I have to go back. If Marigold's gonna try to bring more astral fiends into San Camillo, someone's got to stop her."

"Surely your adopted people have their own warriors."

"The police can't handle it. They need someone like me. And I'm saying that with all the humility I can muster."

"What of your people here?"

"You guys have been doing fine without me for decades." I hesitated. "I love this place. I really do. But staying here, training myself for a war I'm never gonna fight, for enemies that are too busy sucking the life out of another dimension to bother with Meda, that isn't right, no matter how much time it buys."

"Let me appeal to your sense of self-preservation, then," Naos said. "You could die, just as your parents did. Their sacrifice was noble, yet, what good will it do anyone if you leave here and face a threat that killed them? One man cannot stop evil of this magnitude."

"I've been handling things pretty well on my own." Not that I wanted to continue being the lone gunslinger.

"You won't be solo, child," Wilhelmina said. "There's two parts to the pulsar stave, aren't there? Let's use them."

"Sounds good to me."

"Grandfather." Teget cleared his throat in a manner that sounded like a distorted recording of me. "Would it not be prudent to afford Mercury support on his quest? Surely the Icons together can better face the darkness."

Naos stared. "Are you mad? You would return?"

"I have made a life of venturing into the Interstice and surviving against our enemies."

"Yes, to find your brother. To bring him and the pulsar stave back."

"And that goal has been met. It is time to embrace another."

"Hey." I waved my hand between them. "Naos, this isn't how you made it sound before. Teget's right. New circumstances, new mission. Whatever my parents did, it was a stopgap measure. Threw off the bad guys' plans for twenty years. We can argue back and forth about whether saving Earth or keeping Meda safe should take priority. Doesn't matter, because somebody somewhere is gonna die. I'm not going to wait around here to see where it happens first." I took a breath. "Besides, there's people back there counting on me."

Naos didn't budge. "Well said. I cannot forbid you, and I suspect were I to convene the council and push for their intervention, even they could not prevail against the sons of Sabik and Cyllene."

"Probably true."

"Then you three are prepared for what you shall face."

"Absolutely." I hoped.

Naos sighed. "Fine. You shall retrieve the pulsar stave. But consider this: should you defeat your enemies and take steps to seal the way between your world and the Interstice, Earth and Meda will be as far apart as the east is from the west. Be certain you know on which side of those closed doors you will spend the rest of your days."

He left in a whirl of robes. The guards positioned at the doorway straightened their posture as he stormed away.

"Do not be discouraged," Teget said. "He is simply stubborn and cannot fathom why you do not see his path as the correct one."

"Well, that figures," I muttered. "We're definitely related."

Ironically, it was Naos who located Loredana. He sent one of my tiny cousins running to me the with location.

"Thanks, kid." I tousled his hair. That's what you do with little kids, right? It was kinda greasy, though.

"Are you really leaving?" He put his hands on his hips. "You just got here."

"I did, but I've got important stuff to do far away."

"Like Teget does?"

"Yep." I checked my watch. It was late, and I really wanted to get some sleep, as much fun as it was taking the grand tour of every back street in the city.

He smiled. "That makes you the Icon, too!"

The kid sprinted away, bounding with each step. I couldn't help but smile, too. I was gonna miss that.

Loredana had found an alcove off a marketplace, tucked behind a pottery kiln. Moping? Brooding? Nope. Field-stripping the MP5. She was cleaning it with a piece of black fabric. The bottom edge of her shirt? Must have torn where it had ripped.

"Hey," I said.

"Hello."

"Surprised you're not asleep."

"There was work to be done. I thought the same of you."

I shrugged. "Been busy with the schedule. You know, stuffing my face."

That earned me the faintest smirk. I'd take it.

"The rest of us had a chat with Naos. We're going back."

She stopped in the middle of wiping the barrel. "What changed your mind?"

"Lots of things. Things other people said."

"If this is your manner of apology, it leaves much to be desired."

"How about we both agree we were both hotheaded and leave it at that? Because I got a feeling neither of us is willing to be that humble."

"True." She clicked the gun back together in way less time than it would have taken me, especially since I had no idea where the pieces went. "Is there anything else we need to discuss?"

Ahem. "That sounds like a trap."

"You could have said no."

"Still, though. Trap."

She stood and slung the reassembled weapon over

her shoulder. "I trust we are all sufficiently armed for this endeavor."

Yeah, I had the pulsar stave affixed to my suit again. "I'll share with Wilhelmina. Teget's worried the strain might be too much for her."

"And you?"

"I think she'll be okay. It's her call."

"No, I mean, how will the strain affect you? The strain of leaving Meda."

I scratched the back of my neck. "There's things I have to do. And as much as I hid it from myself, San Camillo is home, too. The best way to protect both places is to stop Marigold on Earth."

"If the rips are stopped, you can't come back."

Way to sugarcoat it. "I know."

Loredana nodded. "Then let's get some rest."

Everyone lodged at the old family home for what precious little remained of the night. Daytime came way too soon.

We ate eggs Teget cooked up over a blistering stove. Not bad for a bachelor warrior. Nobody had anything inspiring to say. Can you blame them? We all got maybe five hours of sleep.

Naos joined us for the trek to the woods. Teget paced off the spot where we'd exited the Interstice. The air was already writhing with twisted light.

"Take care of yourself, and your people," Naos said. "We have entrusted you with a great responsibility. Remember that. And never forget, no matter the distance that separates us, I will always love and be proud of you."

"Thanks. I'll miss you, too." I hugged him. It was too much for my prickly exterior to handle, and the façade crumbled.

"Love you, too, Grandpa."

We parted with much clearing of throats and wiping of eyes. Teget held the ax ready. Inter-dimensional energies brightened the spherical area. Wilhelmina hummed a song to herself. I separated the pulsar stave and handed her a half. "Don't lose it."

She smacked me with it.

I held out a hand to Loredana and raised an eyebrow. Subtle, right?

She matched my grip and nodded.

"Okay, Teget," I said. "All aboard."

White light burned away my grandfather and my real home, until his waving silhouette was an afterimage.

CHAPTER THIRTY-FIVE

Returning to the Interstice sucked.

I could feel the darkness, the anger, the sheer disease of that realm, settling into every pore and coating every surface. Like bathing in sewage, or what I imagined that to be like, because, you know, haven't actually done that.

After a day or so in a heavenly realm, surrounded by newfound family and generally getting some decent rest and relaxation, the last thing I wanted to do was set foot in that arid, death-ridden landscape. I'll tell you what, though, as soon as we cleared the portal, I was on full Red Alert.

We followed Teget as quickly as we could across the harsh terrain, ignoring the thunder blasting in the sky and the lightning leaping between clouds. I wanted to make sure we were on time to catch the rip back to Earth, but my watch wasn't cooperating. It started forward, spun a couple hours ahead in a matter of seconds, then wound 45 minutes back past what time I thought it was, before settling back into a steady rhythm.

"Hurry." Teget said that like we hadn't jogged the entire way so far. Granted, the guy wasn't even winded, while I was regretting lack of sleep and a very full stomach. Loredana's barb about stuffing myself sounded more like reasonable advice.

He was the first to crest the hillside. I knew we were in trouble when he dropped to his knees and concealed himself behind a cluster of person-sized rocks.

"Get down." My warning got Loredana and Wilhelmina to follow suit. I crouched beside Loredana, peering over our hiding place.

Two astral fiends waited a hundred yards away.

They were big suckers. I'd say easily the equivalent of the combined brute who slashed my car in half, but not giant-sized like the 40-footer in Procyon's parking lot. Twenty-five? Whatever. They were *big*.

Loredana propped the MP5 on the rock. "What's our play?"

"If by that you mean strategy, we wait until the portal has formed and pursue them," Teget said.

"I'm with him," I said. "If we attack now, we get surprise on our side, but I've never known a rip to form and *not* bring an astral fiend through."

"You're insinuating that if we do not let the fiends transit, we won't make it back," Loredana said.

"Bingo."

Teget nodded. "I concur."

"I'm glad we're all on the same page," Wilhelmina cut in, "But that's quite the sprint from here to there, and over wide-open ground. Ain't much chance they're gonna let us ride their coattails unnoticed."

I grinned, remembering the wacky way in which I'd run from Procyon's forces back at Rosa Roja Park. "Thought about that. Teget, have you ever used the ax to accelerate yourself?"

He looked at me like I'd just asked him if one and one were indeed two. "Certainly. It is taught in the second year of training."

"Well, I missed that regimen. How about it, Wilhelmina?"

She scrunched her nose, as if she smelled something foul. "Done it before, but that was a long time ago, child."

"Then brush up in the next however many seconds, because it's our best bet."

Loredana raised an eyebrow. "Forgive me for interrupting this strategy session, but my weapon doesn't impart the same abilities."

"I'll hold onto you, like when the Flash carries people."

She skewered me with a wordless, cool gaze. Not being figurative, either. I swear I could *feel* the puncture wounds.

"Okay, fine, you can hang onto me," I said. "Just don't let go."

"Mercury!" Teget hissed.

The rip tore apart the air in front of the astral fiends, crackling with purple lightning. The monsters ceased biting and snarling at each other, waiting instead as if trapped in a trance. The rip widened, from a pitch-black jagged line into an undulating wedge.

The first one stretched out its tentacles and let itself be dragged in.

"Go!" Teget vaulted over the rocks.

Wilhelmina took off after him, their forms blurring as the ax and the pulsar stave flashed with blazing energy. Their tracks kicked up dust.

Loredana slung one arm around my shoulders and neck, leaving her free to aim with the other if she needed it. I grinned at her. "Kiss for luck?"

She sighed. "Just run."

"Suit yourself." I siphoned off as much energy as I dared from half of the stave and imagined that escape again, hoping—praying this wasn't a stupid idea.

Took that first step, and everything went crazy.

It felt like I was running in the hardest PE class sprint from middle school, but man, everything around me smeared—mountains, sky, dirt, and rocks, all wiped like smudged paint. Loredana pressed her head to my neck and squeezed her eyes shut.

Eat your heart out, Barry Allen.

We were at the rocks and then we were at our destination, in what seemed like one second somehow dragged out into eternity. Timed it pretty well, too, because the second fiend had just squirmed its backside through the rip. Which was my reminder that I needed to stop!

I let my concentration falter, on purpose, and the insane speed fell away. The landscape surrounding us snapped back into crystal-clear reality. I skidded so hard there had to be a couple pounds of sand flying through the rip. Teget and Wilhelmina were already there, looking dazed, and bracing themselves against the wind pulling at us. Didn't want to be yanked off their footing, I'd assumed.

Loredana let go. She brushed sand off her slacks. "That was painless."

"See? Nothing too it." As I tried not to vomit. Again. Not to self: dimensional shifts and hyper-acceleration are bad for digestion.

Teget dove into the rip without preamble.

"I'm going to guess that's our cue." I gestured. "Ladies next."

Wilhelmina hopped in, followed by Loredana. Which gave me a moment by myself, the only human in this twisted, nightmare joint. I looked around as the winds whipped with newborn ferocity, turning the sands into a biting, blinding storm.

So, you remain.

I spun around, pulsar stave at the ready. Who …?

Your brother was never brave enough to admit I was anything more than a bad dream, or the screaming terror imagined by anxiety. You, though, are curious. Curious about this place. About me.

"Okay, I don't know who's talking, but pretty sure we haven't met!" I hollered over the rising wind. Probably not my best plan.

Sand coalesced in a flash of lighting. A shadow, its edges black and swirling, walked toward me, down the same slope I'd just run. Didn't look very impressive, or so the rational part of my brain told me.

That part was overwhelmed by terror. Sheer, unadulterated, screaming horror. It made me gag, drove me to my knees.

Yes. You see? We have met. When you were at your lowest, when you heard whispers of doubt, when you considered yourself with the ultimate contempt, I was there, feeding thoughts into that pathetic excuse for a mind. You need direction, Mercury Hale. You need a master. I am he. Do not forget it. That is why you wait for me now, so you can be shown your true potential.

It extended a hand. Thick, slopping ichor dripped from claws.

The power surrounding it was undeniable. The things I could do by sharing it! He would teach me, and I'd be able to fix all the awful things in life. In the world. By controlling it.

No.

Run!

The twin urges came so clear, so fast, that I broke free of the terrifying vision and hurled myself through the portal.

My insides twisted every which way, and I saw two places at once—the swirling maelstrom of a stormy Interstice, and a quiet intersection in downtown San Camillo, overlapping, mingling in grotesque combinations.

Light flashed.

I landed, but the surface was not as hard as I thought asphalt would feel. Fourteenth and DeLeon. I recognized the buildings. Funny. They looked shorter than I remembered.

"Mercury!"

Overlapping sounds hit me all at once. My name, sung by a lovely voice with an English accent. Gunfire. Hideous screams. The sizzle and crackle of something like electricity.

Huh.

I was on the backside of the second fiend to make it through the rip. Unfortunately, he realized my presence the instant I did his, and proceeded to slap at me like an irate camper going for a record number of mosquito kills.

I tumbled off the side, using the pulsar stave to slow my fall. By that, I mean I carved a long, jagged cut with the energy end, the yellow-white sputtering in the best bit of reassurance that things were back to normal. The fiend shrieked. Music to my ears, baby.

Now this, I could handle. No Interstice, no terrifying shadow vision, no mystical home realm. Me versus the monsters.

Correction. Me and my crew.

Teget and Wilhelmina had the first astral fiend in its final throes. The thing had lost six tentacles, the stumps smoking. It was slashing at them, albeit limply. Wilhelmina jumped over razor-sharp spines that bashed through the windshield of a pickup truck and opened a gaping wound on the monster's face. Blue ooze was slathered across the intersection and parked cars. Plus, there were cars abandoned in the middle of the street.

Wait, there were? Yeah, and people, too. Dozens of bystanders fled down all four streets. Loredana, thankfully, herded the screamingest of them away from the battle zone. Those who didn't listen were treated to her firing the MP5 into the air, loud bursts that must have set some eardrums ringing.

Back to the second fiend. I slid underneath, stabbing into its unprotected underside. The smell and weight were suffocating, but I drew all the power I could from the stave, until the weapon threatened to yank free of my grip.

"Mercury!" Wilhelmina hurled the second half across the pavement, spinning it like a baton.

I snatched it up, reunited the halves, and drove an eye-watering flare of the stave's energy deep into the monster's core.

It wailed. Tentacles smashed windows along a row of storefronts. They crushed outdoor seating at a restaurant—abandoned, mercifully. Sparks skittered across the fiend's body. It flopped atop me, giving me about three seconds to roll out from underneath. The creature slumped and started melting away.

"Nice one!" I sped to Wilhelmina's side, in time to parry a blow from a tentacle. I quickly separated the stave and gave half back to her, but another tentacle swept in from my right, slashing across my leg. I hit the ground face-first. Wilhelmina toppled over a bike rack.

Dizzy, I saw spines come down at my face.

The attacking appendage exploded in foul bits of shredded hide, splattering blue ooze everywhere. Loredana crouched behind a mailbox, emptying an entire magazine from the MP5 at the fiend. Don't know how many bullets that was but let's say a lot. They turned the tentacle into a pitted, torn stump.

Teget let out a brutal cry as he battered the fiend's eyes with his ax. It screamed in response, trying to rid itself of the deadly human pest. No luck. Teget swung the blade overhead until it was so bright staring at it hurt worse than looking at the afternoon sun, then drove it through the monster's ruined face.

It died with a huge, shaking groan.

The sounds of weapons fire, crackling energy, and monster howls were gone. All that was left were the screaming people. And sirens. That figured.

"Nice shooting." I coughed as Loredana helped me to my feet.

She wrinkled her nose. "You look atrocious. And smell awful."

"Double-a adjectives. Must be a special day." I lifted Wilhelmina. "You did pretty well, too, old lady."

She walloped me with the pulsar stave. "Someday, boy, I'll show you how it's done, operative to operative."

"That sounds like a fun but painful sparring session."

Teget slid down the fiend's rapidly disintegrating corpse. He was grinning like his football team just won the Super Bowl. "Well met, all of you! By the heavens, had I all of you as brothers—and sisters—in arms, we could sweep the Interstice free of astral fiends!"

I don't know. We were a bruised and battered bunch. Everyone needed a shower, and a trip to the laundromat. Interestingly, the suit I wore had taken only a couple minor tears throughout the two battles and intervening interdimensional traveling. *Not too shabby, Winston, even if you are my archenemy.*

SCPD squad cars cordoned the four-way intersection. Fire

and EMS arrived, too, with emergency responders rounding up as many people who were still ambulatory and, well, present. Everyone was shouting, especially the police, who were pointing their guns at us. Wilhelmina gave me her half of the stave, then leaned on my arm like a frail old lady. Loredana ejected the magazine, and set the gun on the ground, before putting her hands over her head. Teget smiled, looking somewhat puzzled. I nudged him. "Put the ax down, okay? It's procedure. Also, you're not bulletproof."

"Surely, they will not slay the warriors who have saved them," he scoffed.

"Probably not. These guys are pros, but if there's one nervous rookie in the batch, I'd rather not take a bullet."

Teget complied, though he muttered about "silly customs."

Ramos pushed his way past his officers, M4 in hand, Kevlar vest strapped on. He gaped, then smiled a big huge, smile. He shouldered the gun and slapped me on the shoulder. "I thought you were dead. Then I heard about this mess and knew it had to be your doing."

I grinned. "Miss me?"

He seemed to become aware of the huge police presence and resumed his regular Ramos face—scowl and crinkled brow, plus a surly voice. "Not if this is what you've brought back. You four stay put. I'll get everything cleared up. Wait by my squad car. Officer!" He beckoned a young black cop over. "Get these people medical assistance. And keep the people with phones away from them, you got it? We don't need them showing up on Facebook in the next five seconds. Move it!"

The cop hustled our crew away, but Ramos didn't let go. "I am glad you're not dead."

"Yeah. Me too."

"What was it like?"

I chewed on that. "A little bit of heaven, and a lot of hell."

Ramos nodded. "I prayed for your return. Thank God you're safe."

"Thanks, Ramos." I had a newfound appreciation for the guy's gruff worrying. In the absence of Naos, it was kinda nice to have that level of backup. "We'd better get going before things get worse, because I doubt those two were it."

"How bad?"

"It could be very bad. Don't know yet. First thing's first— got to find out where Marigold's stashed the blade."

"You happen to have it marked on GPS?"

"Funny guy. No. I can find it." I pointed to the ax. "But I need that."

CHAPTER THIRTY-SIX

No dice.

I tried a handful of ax-visions, like before when I'd attempted to track down the blade, but I kept getting the same stupid pedestal in the same stupid, nondescript closet. When I tried to, I don't know, widen my viewpoint, it was like zooming out in Google maps only for the thing to glitch, or the Internet connection to drop.

A whole lot of shadows and nothing.

"Clear your mind of distraction," Teget said. "Shut out external stimuli."

"That'd be a whole lot easier to do if you'd zip it," I muttered.

We were in a waiting room at SCPD. It was the only quiet spot in the entire building, except for the drunk tank downstairs. Uniformed cops and plainclothes detectives hurried every direction, arguing over reports, issuing orders. Easy to see why. A couple TV screens down the hall were running continuous footage from the—well, the thing downtown. It was hysterical watching those men and women with fourteen layers of makeup trying to look serious while tossing around phrases like "unconfirmed reports of giant monster squids."

"They don't even look like squids," I said.

"Will you please focus?" Teget handed the ax back to me.

"Why don't you take a turn?" I paced to the other side of the room. There was a full coffee pot on the counter, next to the trash can that contained a crumpled cup. Tried that. Might as well be drinking motor oil. "Obviously I can't get the job done."

"This doubt is unseemly, brother. It was not present when you fought bravely in the streets a few hours ago."

He had a point. Since I saw that shadow guy, though, I couldn't rid myself of doubt. Every idea, every concept, was challenged. Unusual for me, since I'm usually so sure of myself. Shocking, I know.

"Teget, have you ever seen a person inside the Interstice?"

He sank back on the ugliest sofa I'd ever seen. We're talking, you could phone the 1970s and they would not take it back, thanks very much. Color drained from his face. He picked at his beard, suddenly reminiscent of a nervous kid in the principal's office instead of the warrior. "The Whisperer."

"That's a stupid name."

"I will not speak anything else to give credence to that foul tempter," he snapped. "You saw him, yet you returned?"

"Yeah."

"Flee from him, Mercury. Whatever he tells you is a lie. There is no truth to his words."

"That's a little redundant."

"Cease your mockery!" He stood so fast the sofa rocked on its legs. He slammed the ax onto the low table between us. Sparks jetted from the ax blades, scorching the ceiling tiles. Magazines scattered onto the floor.

We got more than a few looks from the cops walking by. I

was thankful I'd had the brains to keep half the mask in place. Though I had to snicker that with everything else going down, I was worried about a secret identity.

"Take it easy." I gestured at the windows. "Ramos isn't gonna be able to talk us out of having our weapons confiscated if you throw a tantrum and break their police station."

"I apologize. You must promise me." Teget pointed. "Do not attempt to engage him. When the time comes for us to seal the rip, no matter what you see, no matter what he says, turn from the Whisperer and do what needs to be done."

"Okay."

"Promise me, Mercury."

"I said okay! I'll do it. I won't listen."

That seemed to placate him. Good thing, too, because Ramos entered the room, followed by Loredana. She'd gotten a new outfit—clean T-shirt, light jacket, and blue jeans. Even washed and dried her hair. Me? I'd showered up and rubbed as much off the suit as I could. Wasn't about to change back into civvies.

"What're you two idiots doing?" Ramos said. "I've got officers out there telling me you're trying to set fire to the waiting room with a sparking ax."

"Minor disagreement, Lieutenant." Teget smiled.

"Yeah, not a big deal," I added. "Thanks for keeping things quiet."

"Quiet." Ramos sighed. "This is anything but. The captain's furious, because she's getting heat from the commissioner. We can't sweep this one under the rug, Mercury. Gas leak won't fly—there's no damage to anything on the street, and pipes are intact. Add to that the twenty YouTube videos and Facebook Live posts swimming around the Internet, and we're not going to be able to put a lid on it."

"Perhaps that is for the best," Loredana said. "Perhaps it is time people became more acquainted with the true threats to their existence, besides increasing property taxes."

"If that was a joke, I'm going to ignore it. Besides, I doubt your bosses will be so blasé about this public exposure."

"Thanks to you, Procyon's involvement is hidden."

"Thanks to me." Ramos shook his head. "We're ending this, tonight."

"That's the plan," I said. "Where's Wilhelmina?"

"In my office. I've got an EMT sitting with her. She's exhausted. You should have known better than to drag an old woman around on your maniac quest."

"*My* quest? She's the one going all Yoda on me. And you should have seen her battle alongside us." I grinned.

"Stop it, Mercury. This isn't a game. I've got bodies stacked up in the morgue from the fiasco Sunday night."

Sunday night. I glanced at the calendar. Yeah, it was late Wednesday. We'd been gone more than seventy-two hours. Our time at Meda seemed only like an overnighter. "Yeah, I get that, Ramos. I was there when Jamie died. And I had to leave my grandfather on my real home world, so don't talk to me about things that have been lost."

Ramos blinked. He started to say something, then must have thought better of it. "We can tackle that later. I'd recommend you leave Wilhelmina out of this."

"She will make the decision," Loredana said. "If having her along increases the chances of our success, I will not dissuade her."

"You're all insane," Ramos said. "*Dios me de contienda con quien me entienda.* Sort this out. Find that last weapon. Tell me where I need to roll S.W.A.T."

"Might want to consider the National Guard," I murmured

as he walked out the door.

"Don't think I haven't," Ramos said over his shoulder.

Loredana held her hands behind her back. "Perhaps we should refrain from antagonizing our one ally on the police force."

"Yeah, you're right. What'd he say?"

"*God grant me to argue with those who understand me.*"

Can't blame him for that.

"I take it no one has been able to ascertain the location of the blade," she said.

"Nope. My guess is Procyon, maybe down in the vaults, but it'd have to be a hidden compartment."

"There are several off-site storage facilities, however, most of them are out of state."

"That won't help." I rubbed my forehead and grimaced. "Anyone got the phone number of that flying guy in Drake City?"

"That's an urban myth. The attacks there were the work of terrorists."

"You say that, but we're slicing and dicing monsters, so …" I shrugged.

"I have a thought." Teget held the ax out to me. "Perhaps you need a partner as you attempt a vision."

"How's that work?"

"If we are connected through the stave, when you see its location, I may be able to discern how to get to that location."

That could work. At that point I was willing to try anything. "Go for it."

We held the ax handle together. I stared deep into my reflection, in all its masked glory.

I spiraled into the vision.

There was the same dark room. Knew it by heart, after

umpteen times searching for the blade. It was still cold. Nothing on the shelving I could recognize.

This time, though, the blade sat atop the pedestal.

I could feel Teget's presence, inside the vision. Couldn't see him, though. He was at the edge of my sight, and when I tried to turn sideways to look at him, no one was there.

The pedestal pulsed with barely contained power. Dust trickled free of its carvings. I got the distinct impression it was not happy being caged.

"I see the blade." Teget's voice was reassuringly clear, in this muddied environment. "Move beyond the room. I will remain."

I forced myself to leave the blade, which was about as easy as pulling apart two powerful magnets. How much effort did a guy have to exert in a vision?

The walls melted away. I was in a basement. Concrete floor, cinderblock walls, unfinished. There were windows up high. Wasn't very big. I could see cars parked outside. The door to the dark room was painted gray, and metal. Secured with an electronic lock.

Could be at Procyon, but the cars were too close and the room too small. Had to go further.

The edges of everything I could see started to wobble. The vision was coming to an end. Get the lead out!

I moved onward, through the ground, up through a sidewalk.

Cars on either side, most of them new. Pastel town-houses. Trees that could be clones.

No.

I came out of the vision gasping for air. Loredana's hand was on my back. "Steady," she said.

"Thanks. I'm good." I straightened up and braced myself

on the counter.

Teget was doubled over, clutching his knees. "Did you succeed?"

"Yeah. I know where the blade is."

"Procyon will be a difficult nut to crack," Loredana said.

I shook my head, glad to have found the answer but horrified at what it meant. "Nope. Wayfarer Drive, in North Beach. Marigold's got the thing in her basement."

Ramos had everyone within a block radius evacuated, on the pretense of—you guessed it—a natural gas leak. I wondered when the *Bayside Breeze* would get wise to the rampant utility failures and write an exposé.

Squad cars were positioned at either end of the street. S.W.A.T. teams lined up outside massive trucks across from Winston's and Marigold's townhouse.

"That's great, but what're the odds they're even in there?" I asked.

"We had confirmation they were up until an hour ago." Ramos listened to private communications in his earpiece. "No sign of them since. All we can do is prevent them from leaving."

"You sure brought a big enough army." I paced the length of Ramos' car—a different model Charger, since I assumed his was still in the shop from the damage it'd sustained. "Okay. I'll get in there and get the blade. No problem."

"I think you mean 'we' will retrieve the blade," Teget said. "It would not do us good to split our forces."

"Actually, it would, because on the off chance someone made a mistake and Marigold comes traipsing down Wayfarer like she's gone out for groceries, you've got to grab her."

Teget stared at me. "Very well. If you feel that is best."

"Yeah, I do." What I didn't say aloud was I had this nagging feeling that if I didn't go in there, solo, the people I cared about would die. Specifically, Teget, my one and only link to family that remained on this side of the Interstice. I had to take responsibility to end this nightmare, and not put him at risk. "Give me the ax. The combined weapon will be my best bet to stop her."

"Take care, Mercury."

I joined the weapons. Man. I could have jumped the length of the street, as powerful as I felt. The power had to be enough to defeat Marigold, because as far as I was concerned, part of the pulsar stave wasn't going to cut it, as evidenced by Wilhelmina's failure.

No one else can fail.

Yeah, I knew it.

Wilhelmina was there, with Loredana, farther down the block. I could see them watching from behind the barricade, as officers did their best to keep nosy pedestrians and insistent reporters far from the potential action. Loredana gave me a curt nod, a bob of red hair. I gave her a thumbs-up.

Wished I could have said more, but it was what it was.

I walked straight up to the front door. It was unlocked. Not a good sign. I glanced over my shoulder. Ramos was behind his car, M4 trained on the door, not me, I assumed.

In we go.

The Yen's home was deserted. Lights out. Not the bright, cool enclave of boisterous dinner guests I remembered from a week ago. I let the stave-ax illuminate the path.

The door to the basement was ajar. Golden light spilled from the gap.

"Mercury ..." A voice, soft and singsong, dragged out the

syllables of my name.

Really didn't want to go down there. But I didn't have much choice. Good time to mention I wasn't a fan of the Greek myth about those sirens.

The steps were wooden, and despite their new construction creaked under every footfall. My opponents stood in the shadows, the only light a dim purple haze emitting from the blade.

Marigold held the weapon lazily in her right hand, twisting the blade. Winston was a statue behind her, armed with his tablet.

"You guys waiting up for me?" I flexed my grip on the stave-ax.

"Why wouldn't we? Your desperate casting about for the blade was cute, but I knew what you'd be looking for." Her eyes were dead black in the darkness. "What have you come to see, besides the end of your world?"

"Didn't come to see anything, except you two hand over the blade."

Someone rushed out of the shadows to my right, and it was only years of sparring practice with the pulsar stave that prevented me from getting stabbed by a combat-grade knife. I dodged the incoming weapon and brought the ax up into the guy's gut. A quick twist, and I held the glowing, energized, and sharp end of the stave-ax under Calvin's throat.

"Drop it," I snarled.

The knife clattered on the concrete. Calvin sneered. "You're too late."

"Seem like I'm right on time for this party." It didn't calm my nerves when I noticed no one but me appeared anxious. And the fact they were waiting for me didn't bode well.

Suddenly, I froze up, worse than the rusted Tin Man. I

couldn't move—my arms, neck, and head were welded in place. "What?"

Calvin broke free of my grasp and kneed me in the abdomen.

I crumpled, gagging. Couldn't break my fall. Nothing would respond! My body was malfunctioning.

No. Not my body.

The suit.

Winston chuckled. "My dear boy, did you think I'd not find a way to use the technology I built to our advantage? The suit was wired to absorb and enhance the pulsar stave's energy. That wiring is linked to a central processing unit, which in turn is connected to an RFID signal. Thus I can download the performance specs after your mission—or that was the original purpose. It was a simple matter to write a new program allowing me to exert control over the suit."

Calvin kicked me in the ribs. "Stay down."

"I think—" I coughed. "You're enjoying this."

"The only joy is mine." Marigold wrenched the stave-ax free from my hands. She connected the blade to the free end, and all the lights went out.

Then the weapon burst with the color of Meda's sun, and the dazzling color of a prism.

Marigold cried out. I thought she'd injured herself, but she was smiling—and her eyes blazed the same rainbow-tinged white. "At last!" Her voice sounded like storm-tossed waves on the bay. "The way will be open!"

She slammed the pulsar blade into the floor.

Everything exploded.

CHAPTER
THIRTY-SEVEN

When I say everything, I mean everything.

The basement ceiling and walls of the Yen's townhouse shattered, hurtling up into the sky. The homes on either side lost half their structure, raining rubble onto the streets and adjacent roofs. I could hear shouts of alarm from the cops.

It was easy, because I landed on one of the squad cars.

My head swam with the pain, and there was a me-sized dent on the hood. That impact should have killed me, but the suit must have had enough residual energy from the pulsar stave to keep me shielded.

Hang on. It wasn't only the stave.

Yellow-white lines shimmered across the suit, tracking along the irregular patterns. The pain started to fade, slowly.

"Mercury!" Ramos loomed upside down. Or maybe I was upside down? "What happened! Get off there."

"I'd love to, but I'm stuck. Winston put a glitch in the suit. Can't move."

Teget joined him. "Where is the stave? And the ax?"

"She has them." Pain shot through me that had nothing to

do with bruised muscles or battered limbs. "They got the drop on me. Knew I was coming. I'm sorry."

"No." He gazed into the distance, I assumed at the wreckage of the house. "We must regain it."

"Gonna be tricky, since she's got all the weapons, and I can't move."

"Stay still." Loredana, too? I squirmed as best I could, so everyone I knew was not topsy-turvy. "What a fool I was. Of course Winston would have installed a failsafe in the suit, in the event it fell into the wrong hands."

"Don't feel bad. Our budding supervillain said he only got the lockdown working after our first showdown in the parking lot." I grimaced. Healing was going to feel better when everything was back in the right joints. "That said, I'd love to be able to move again."

"One moment." She dug around the base of my skull, plucking at the tough fabric. All of a sudden, I could lift my head. "Better?"

"Partially." I could see everything going on, instead of staring at the night sky.

That turned out to be a bad thing.

The biggest rip I'd ever seen had opened up where the Yen's first floor had been. It was fifty feet across, easy, and the same height and depth, because it was a giant sphere of roiling purple light with a pulsating black core. Bolts of energy struck the basement, slammed into the homes on either side, dug gouges in the street, and shot up into the air. A rushing wind blew out, not dragging things in, but slowly pushing them away. Parked cars skidded on their tires and tipped over, forming a new barricade against the police vehicles.

Ramos hollered into his radio, "Get everyone back! Maintain the perimeter! If anything is coming out of this storm,

I want it contained! And where's that air support?"

"Air support?" I muttered. "Did you actually call the National Guard?"

"Our airborne division. No one's taking me seriously at the state level." Ramos grimaced. "Not yet."

A keening whistle grew, emanating from the portal. Even the S.W.A.T. officers, those guys in black helmets and body armor, winced at the noise. I would have loved to have been able to cover my ears but Loredana was deep in surgery on the suit's controls, trying to get me unfrozen.

"You all had best get out of here." Wilhelmina joined us, staggering against the wind with each step. "Hello, Mercury."

"Hey. She did it. She opened the way."

"I know. It's all right." She patted my arm, like I'd spilled coffee her best knitting project and not let the enemy win. "You made the wrong call. It happens."

"I thought it was right! I didn't want anyone else getting killed. Should've been me, alone, going in. That was my plan."

"You didn't clear that plan with the rest of us," Loredana pointed out.

An arm loosened. I pushed back the bottom half of my mask, so I could speak more clearly. "It was … kinda what I kept telling myself, and …"

What an idiot I was. How much of that was my own thinking, and how much was influenced by the whispers that filtered through my head? Ever since meeting up with that guy in the Interstice, they'd plagued me. Even now, murmurs crept at the back of my mind. *All is lost. Run. Flee as far as you can. Better yet, return to Meda. Abandon Earth.*

I gritted my teeth. "He'd better shut up."

"If you're done talking to yourself, we'd better come up with a new plan." Wilhelmina pointed.

An astral fiend came through. He was of that second tier, 40 feet long, bristling with spines, fangs covering a yawning mouth. The beast crashed atop the prim trees lining the street, most of which had their leaves blasted clean off, and crushed them flat.

Another one followed. Same size. Then two more, of the 20-foot variety.

Then another.

"Shoot!" Ramos ordered.

Every conceivable weapon on that block opened up at the fiends. You couldn't hear anything other than a storm's fury of gunfire. Loredana shouted something at me, and my body could move again. I was so elated I kissed her.

She kissed right back, then brought me to my feet. She looked straight into my eyes. We stood there like the heroes in the middle of an epic battle, with devastation swarming us while everything in our small space was tranquil.

Then she said, "Go get them!"

The SCPD attack drove the fiends into a fury. They lashed out at everything in reach, slamming tentacles on cars, pulverizing walls, but they didn't move far out of the portal. They walled it off, with the automobile barrier between them and the arc of police officers shooting every bullet in their arsenal. I had to go *into* that mess. "Sure would be nice to not do this with our bare hands!" I yelled at Teget.

He smiled that mischievous, sly smile that must run in my otherworldly family, and produced two daggers from his vest. These suckers were as long as my arm. More like slender machetes. "There is no power to these," he said, "Only the strongest metal with which they were forged."

"Good enough for me." There was still plenty of energy from the pulsar-ax filtering through the suit. "Ready?"

"As always." He clanked his dagger against mine, like we were making a dinner party toast.

Hear, hear.

I looped an arm under his shoulders and hurtled with Teget at the nearest fiend, one of the biggest. It had already taken dozens of small wounds from the gunfire, more from the automatic rifles sported by the S.W.A.T. team than the small arms of the regular officers. The damage was bad enough the fiend was in a blind fury, and those cops were the target of his wrath. Didn't pay us the slightest attention until Teget and I landed on his head. I swung the dagger at a tentacle that came too near. Lopped it clean off.

Yeah. That dagger would do just fine.

The fiend shrieked, adding its piercing anger to the shrill notes of the storm. Those tentacles reversed course and did their best to clean us off the top—but, please. Teget and I weren't amateurs. I mean, technically he was, I think. Procyon paid me to do this.

Teget stayed atop the fiend, gouging its eyes, while I slid down its hide to the pavement. "Ramos!" I hollered and gestured with the dagger. "Get the other side!"

Ramos redirected his fire at that flank, and got a couple other officers to join in. The fiend rolled to protect that wounded area. In doing so he ignored the back end I faced, giving me the gap to scurry underneath and start stabbing.

Between Teget up top and me down below, we finished the fiend off before it could find me and plot a counterattack.

Its death threw the other fiends into a frenzy. They spread out into the street, chasing individual targets instead of acting as a unified force. Gave us our gap to get through.

Marigold was there, standing in the middle of the storm, with the portal churning overhead. She held the pulsar blade aloft, arms bathed in the multicolor energy streaming off the weapon. Winston was huddled behind the pedestal, that stupid tablet lifted to the heavens, no doubt giving him all kinds of data on what was spewing out of the interdimensional gateway. Who knew what the drones and Procyon's satellite were picking up.

Found Calvin. He'd been smashed against a wall by the metal door that used to bar the way to the pedestal, his eyes wide and unseeing. It was awful seeing someone dead like that, and I felt for the guy, until I relived Jack Jackson getting a bullet through the head.

"Give us the weapon," Teget said, "And we shall be merciful."

"No, you won't. You'll have to kill me. Because that is the only way you'll stop this wonderful beginning." With that, Marigold leapt at us.

To be fair, I'd never seen her do anything more than run the treadmill in Procyon's gym, so I wasn't expecting the full spiral accompanied by a whirling blade. I threw myself sideways, fast enough to avoid dying but not soon enough to get clear of the pulsar blade's searing energy. Teget must have gotten hit—he cried out, and landed in a crouch, blood streaming down his right shoulder.

I lunged for Mari, aiming for her wrist with the dagger, but she blocked the blow. I adjusted my shot, so it clanged off the metal parts of the weapon, rather than getting melted by the energy discharge. She swung the blade at my midsection. I flipped over her and brought the dagger crashing toward her spine. She spun and parried it, our weapons locked together.

"You can't defeat me with toys, Mercury." Her voice was distorted by the waves of energy pouring from the weapon. She wouldn't be nearly so intimidating if her eyes weren't still glowing like red-hot coals. "This is a divine implement. It's the key to bringing long-lost worlds home."

The shrieks of the astral fiends mingled with the constant gunfire and the shouts of the police. Three helicopters scooted overhead, so low the *whup-whup* of its rotors beat against my eardrums. Single shots cracked from its sides. Concrete chipped the floor.

Great. Now I was gonna get shot.

"This isn't yours," I growled. "It can't be left together. The fiends will destroy everything."

"That sounds lovely." She kicked me in the mid-section.

Normally it wouldn't be a problem, but I was still in pain from Calvin's cheap shots, and this was agonizing. I hit the ground, hard.

Teget roared a wordless cry, hurling himself into the brawl. He stabbed again and again, forcing Marigold toward the basement wall. His dagger was a blur of metal, and man, could he dodge her strikes, going so far as to bend backwards as the pulsar blade missed his face by inches.

A gunshot echoed, this one much closer. Teget staggered, blood splattered across the same wounded arm. Winston aimed a semi-auto handgun. He stared, mouth agape.

"You shot him!" I got to my feet.

"I … I'm terribly sorry, Mercury." He waved the gun about. "I know he's your brother, but … My wife! She's so close to achieving our goal! Together we'll …"

I walked straight up to him, ignoring his rant.

"I say. That's quite enough. Stay back." Please. The way Winston's arm was shaking he couldn't hit the broad side of, well, an astral fiend.

I batted aside the gun with the blade. Winston pulled the trigger. I was gonna be deaf in that ear for a while. "Shut up,"

I said, and punched him.

He hit the wall with a meaty slap, rebounded, and I brought the dagger's pommel down on the back of his head.

That left Marigold.

She had Teget backed into a corner, so I rushed her from behind. She used the ax end of the weapon to halt my attack, while fending her other opponent off. On and on, back and forth, the sounds of the war above us and even the roar of the portal fading until the only thing that mattered were our three weapons and our ragged breathing.

But as good as she was, as fervently as she believed in her cause and as powerful as the pulsar stave made her, Marigold wasn't a warrior. I was trained to fight, and Teget was, too.

She slipped up.

One missed block, one stab unchallenged. My blade was the one protruding from her chest.

She stared. The dazzling lights faded, and for a moment, our gazes locked. Those deep brown eyes saw me.

Teget wrestled the ax from her weapon. I took the blade.

"I'm sorry, Marigold," I murmured.

She screamed.

Full on banshee. The sound drove me to my knees. Pretty sure I screamed, too, but the sound vanished among her primal song. Teget was on the ground, hands clasped to his head.

Glowing purple fissures erupted across her skin, her clothing, rooting her to the basement floor, until they covered every inch of her body. They pulsed, causing her to ripple.

She exploded.

Not blood and guts, but blazing, swirling particles of light and dark. Millions of tiny buzzing motes shot into the center of the portal. The wind howling from its core came to a sudden halt.

I grabbed the pulsar stave before it could be dragged away.

The portal solidified. It didn't pulse, or wriggle. Nope. It could have had walls of solid steel. Instead of a morass of impenetrable energy, I stared up at a picture-perfect rendition of the Interstice.

"The way is open," Teget said, his voice hoarse.

And there was an army of astral fiends on the other side.

CHAPTER THIRTY-EIGHT

Teget jumped up from the basement, hollering at me to follow him. Duh. What'd he think I was going to do, sit here and take a selfie with Armageddon as the ultimate photo-bomb?

I hesitated. What had I said earlier about not wanting anyone else to die? Marigold and Calvin were gone. Didn't mean Winston had to pay the price, too. Sure, he'd committed who knew what crimes, but I wasn't his executioner.

You were Marigold's.

Whisperer or not, I was getting sick of that.

I scooped up Winston. He moaned something but stayed limp. I hurtled onto the street.

The battle had been rough. I was impressed SCPD had brought down a second astral fiend, its corpse melting across several squashed cars. A third one, the smallest of the bunch, was in the process of getting pelted by—grenades? That would explain the explosions I could hear now that my ears weren't ringing. Those trucks rumbling down the street were decidedly not police issue.

"Mercury!" Loredana and Wilhelmina took the knocked-out Winston from my arms. Ramos hurried over with EMTs. "Are you hurt?"

"Always." I had a nasty cut on one arm, and another on my leg. The bleeding had stopped. Mostly. "Check on Teget. Winston shot him."

"Don't reckon he's going to make the time for an exam." Wilhelmina pointed.

Yeah. My brother was cutting into one of the two remaining fiends. That small one? A final fusillade from grenade launchers held by soldiers in mottled khaki fatigues put it flat on the street.

Soldiers?

Yeah. Apparently, Ramos had taken my urging about bringing in the National Guard seriously. There were at least a hundred troops, up and down the street, on rooftops across from the battle site, all over the place. A bunch of Humvees and a couple of those eight-wheeled Strykers stood out like big ugly rocks among the battered civilian rides.

"Get this man treated." Ramos shoved Winston at a young, skinny officer. "Then cuff him. He's under arrest. Read him his Miranda rights when he wakes up."

"The portal," Wilhelmina said. "Good Lord. It's been locked into a gate."

"It has. I need to kill those last fiends and get the ax from him."

"Then I'm a'coming with you." Wilhelmina held out her hand.

"Can't make you."

"Shut your trap and give me something to fight with."

"Yes, Ma'am." I handed her the blade, and Wilhelmina immediately straightened, old age cast aside for the interdimensional power of her weapon.

"We'll cover you the best we can." Loredana had an M4 identical to Ramos'. "Do you need anything else?"

"Yeah." I grinned. "You across the table from me at Carlito's, for pizza and beer, when this is all over."

"I shall enter a reminder in my phone." Loredana smiled. "In case I forget."

"Way to wound a guy."

"Come on, then." Ramos put a new magazine into his gun. "We'll divert the National Guard to the portal and hold the incoming at bay."

"Hang on. You and Loredana can stay back. This isn't your fight any more."

"Of course it is. It's always been my fight."

"No way. You won't last five seconds against those two, especially if the Army is diverted."

"It doesn't matter."

"Yes, it does! You've given up enough for this battle, Gabriel. Don't make your kids orphans and your wife a widow. It's already enough a pile of works to get you seated at the best table in heaven."

"Is that what you think I'm doing?" Ramos took me by the collar. "That isn't how it works, son! If the time comes, and I fall, my place will be at His side, by his grace alone."

I stared at him as he took up his position behind a toppled Honda. The guy was insane. Right?

Didn't stop him from throwing his life into the mix with monsters.

I jumped as far and as I high as I could. Wilhelmina was right beside me, the blade swept back as if she'd spent every day of her entire life wielding it. The fiend saw us coming and reached into the air. A forest of tentacles filled our path.

Wilhelmina changed direction midair. She sliced down one

tentacle, cutting it clear to the stump where it connected to the fiend's body.

I lopped the tip off one offending appendage. Dodged a second. Got slapped hard by a third but managed a controlled landing where I hacked it off at the base.

Thankfully we didn't jump into a hail of gunfire and grenades. The National Guard had reinforced the police barricade and were lighting up the gateway to the Interstice with everything they had. Astral fiends piled up just beyond its threshold, their otherworldly wails resonating. Couldn't see how many were backed up or how far, but it sounded like an army's worth.

The first vision I'd had while holding the blade haunted me. If they got out into this world, it would be literal hell on earth.

I bent backwards, ducking spines as they whipped across the space where my upper torso had been a second before. A swift cut with the stave left the tentacle as smoking, seared mess.

Ramos put several shots at the fiend's face, causing it to shriek and shield its eyes. Wilhelmina took that cue to go at it from behind, opening a huge, long gash in its hide. Slime sprayed out like from a leaking garden hose.

I rolled atop the fiend and brought the stave down into the gap. Wilhelmina stabbed deep with the blade.

The fiend burst like a soap bubble, splattering its remains on both sides of the street.

That smelled terrible.

Teget had taken out his opponent, and for the first time since this mess erupted, I felt better. All five fiends that had initially come through were destroyed. Their remains were already dissipating. And the National Guard was helping the police hold an invading army from another world at bay.

"This cannot last." Teget limped to us. "The mere metal weapons of your world are not adequate to stem the tide."

"I know." I held out my hand. "This has to be shut down."

Teget hesitated. "Not yet. I will help you fight your way in, but I cannot remain behind."

"Are you serious? You can't just jog back to Meda. There's dozens of astral fiends clogging the only way into the Interstice! You waltz in there now, and you're dead!"

"Not if we clear him a path." Wilhelmina pointed with the blade. "The weapons can't all stay in one place, Mercury, not if we want to prevent this from happening again. Meda's the safest place around."

"She is correct," Teget said. "The ax and the blade, at the very least, must return to my world—if it is possible."

"What's that mean?"

"Sealing the gateway may destroy all three."

I glanced at him. "I'd be stuck here, and you'd be likewise in Meda."

He nodded.

Great. So much for family reunions. I twisted the pulsar stave in my hands. I didn't want to shut it down. Sue me for being selfish. Why wouldn't I want to return to my rightful home?

But I saw those police officers doing their best to hold the monsters back. The soldiers protecting not only San Camillo but the whole of their country from an inconceivable threat. Ramos knowing full well he could die and have to leave his family, yet still shooting bullets at creatures no person should ever have to see outside his nightmares. And Loredana, confronting what must have been the realization that Procyon, her home and her purpose, had caused something pretty close to the End Times.

I couldn't abandon them. Because even if this worked, and the way to the Interstice was forever sealed, there'd be other problems. The mundane ones that threatened people every day—well, mundane compared to astral fiends.

"Screw it," I said. "Let's drop kick them back through their dimension."

The three of us sprinted for the portal, taking care not to get our heads blown off by the combined fusillade put out by the Army and police. I heard my name. Your guess is as good as mine as to whether it was a warning from Loredana or Ramos, but it was answered by a whisper.

Yes, Mercury. You've brought your kin and your ally. What a pleasant gift. Are you ready to join me? Your place is ready.

Our trio launched through the gateway. It wasn't nearly as traumatic as the two previous transits into the Interstice. This was like stepping through someone's front door, except there was a slight pressure field we broke through, like a wall of cold air a foot thick.

Then we were inside.

My God. I don't mean that like it sounded. I mean, I really did say that to Him, because I figured only He could understand.

There were astral fiends everywhere. Not just the couple dozen we could see backed up, but hundreds, spreading across the desolate hills. The Interstice's skies were wracked by the worst storm I'd ever seen. Black and purple clouds battered rock spires so badly chunks were thrown down. Stone shards rained. Lightning slashed everywhere, transforming sand into glass and blowing craters.

And the storm started seeping into San Camillo's sky, infecting it with the malevolence that wouldn't be contained.

A helicopter was thrown aside like a toy discarded by a kid

throwing a tantrum. It crashed into the harbor.

We fought.

White-yellow energies and flashing metal cut down every bit of astral fiend that tried to make it past us. Tentacles lashed far beyond the gateway, encircling officers, snagging soldiers, draining them faster than what I thought possible. I hacked and cut and chopped until my arms were on fire, my motions a blur. How many were dying? How many would be drained of life if we failed?

We fought.

Teget was a madman, diving amongst the fiends, throwing up gouts of sand and rock with every landing and launch. He killed one, then two, then three, four, five, on and on until he was smeared dark blue from their innards.

We fought.

Wilhelmina could not be moved. She was a mountain among the waves, mowing down anything that tried to make it past her, freeing captured cops and troops. More than one fiend tried to take a bite out of her. She cut them *in half*.

We fought.

Our weapons glowed with the sun's intensity, as bright as stars. A triangle pulsed in the air between us, driving the fiends back, away from the gate and deeper into the Interstice. Wilhelmina's and Teget's eyes glowed with a yellow brilliance, a warmer version of the fearsome cold in Marigold's before she disappeared.

"*Mercury …*"

That voice. The Whisperer's. Yet … feminine.

The shadow walked through the battle, among the fiends. Same power. Same evil.

Except it had taken Marigold's shape.

How much was her? How much was the Whisperer? Did

it even matter? She was carved from obsidian, with amethyst eyes and veins of silver. *"Mercury …give us the weapons. Let us bring the worlds together. All this pain, this suffering, can end, when we snuff out the darkness of your world with the light of our own. Then you can truly go home.*

I met Teget's look from across the battlefield. As otherworldly as his eyes were, the sadness was apparent. I bet I had the same expression.

Marigold-Whisperer flicked her fingers, and astral fiends fled her approach. She raised her arms, and a wall of sand slammed into Wilhelmina, hurling her out of the gateway. Wilhelmina lay prone on Wayfarer Drive, among the battered defenders.

The blade rested in the threshold.

"Teget!" I ran for it.

We reached the blade at the same time, standing in that wall of frigid air. I clamped the blade to the top of the pulsar stave. The golden light among us reverberated with the sound of a beating wings, a million pressed into one rushing noise.

"I will never forget what you have done here today," he said. "Farewell."

"Not farewell. You stay alive. I'll find my way back to Meda, someday."

"If it is the will of the Truth."

We hugged. I didn't want to let go.

Yeah, I said I'd find my way back. But I knew I could lose my brother forever.

Teget slammed the ax to the other end of the pulsar blade. Light exploded from it, flaring out into San Camillo's streets and back through the Interstice. On one side, it bathed humans in what looked like the sunniest afternoon ever. On the other, it burned astral fiends and ignited the most blood-curdling shriek-fest, chilling my insides.

Marigold-Whisperer roared like a dragon straight out of the movies. And in that moment, I saw.

Majestic beings of light shot through the air, warring against twisted, bloody shadows. It was no contest. The light beings cut their enemies down, shredding them to wisps of smoke, forcing them through the gateway. There were thousands upon thousands, an endless wave of sound and energy, ringing like the loudest bell that reverberated through every fiber and bone.

I held on to the weapon, bridging the gap between dimensions, hollering for help. I didn't want to die. Not today.

But if I was going to, let it be for the right reasons.

Teget held to the weapon, too, crying out to the sky as the portal collapsed. Its sides rushed in, pummeling us with a blizzard of freezing air.

The weapon broke apart, leaving me the pulsar stave.

Teget took the blade and the ax, one in each hand, and whirled around.

But Marigold-Whisperer was tumbling end over end through the dirt, her/its body tearing itself apart. Light barraged it with an even greater intensity, until all I could see was a sun-blasted version of that dark domain.

The way shut.

No explosion. No shockwave. Just a *crack* of thunder, as if from invisible lightning. And I collapsed, on my hands and knees.

The pulsar stave rolled away, hitting a chunk of sidewalk with a *clink*. No energy. Dead hunk of metal.

Blood trickled from my mouth. My bones were on fire. Sounds faded away. I fell through a tunnel of darkness. Could I heal from this level of punishment?

Pain lanced through my chest and everything went away.

# CHAPTER
THIRTY-NINE

When I finally woke up, it was to the sound of Ramos snoring.

Morning sunlight poured between the blinds. Squinting helped resolve the bright blobs into San Camillo's downtown, a reflection bounced off adjacent office buildings. I was in a SC General Hospital room. Monitors beeped a steady rhythm. Had my own private IV and TV. And, apparently, a bodyguard.

Ramos was slumped in a chair. His feet were propped on the bench seat under the window, brown argyle socks exposed to the world. A pair of Oxfords were lined up neatly on the floor. He hadn't changed since the battle. The pale-green shirt was stained dark in several places, and he had a bandage on his forehead.

Had he been here all night? The thought made me feel a whole lot better than the prospect of being alone. I had to clear my throat, because it inexplicably tightened. "Hey. I thought it smelled funky in here."

Would've been funnier if my voice wasn't a raspy croak. Ramos snorted, and wiped the corner of his mouth. His eyes cracked open. "You're up. Good. The doctor was concerned you weren't going to come to. Want me to call him?"

"Nah. Give me a second." I tried to sit up. Ow. Felt like I'd been hit by a truck. Or an astral fiend.

"Take it easy." Ramos adjusted the bed's height and helped me scoot up. "Your injuries were pretty bad."

"How bad?"

"Everyone here was amazed you weren't dead. Though, you came close."

"I believe it. Everything feels fairly terrible. So." I folded my hands. "What's the verdict?"

"Verdict?"

"Come on. You're not just here because you were worried I was gonna kick the bucket. I assume I'm facing charges."

Ramos chuckled. "The only thing the DA has mentioned is destruction of public property. As if that weren't caused by rampaging monsters. No, Mercury, you're off the hook, so to speak. Though you've got a new set of worries."

"I figured, since I'm wearing scrubs and my boxer shorts instead of a fully-charged super suit." I sighed. "No more secret identity."

"That secret remains safely here. We've kept hospital personnel to a minimum. Those who have seen you are, as it turns out, amenable to remaining silent when offered a generous payoff by your employers."

"Oh. Well, that's good news."

"Bad news is, you're going to need a new ID. Loredana assures me they can wipe your records, what little exist."

"But there's no sign of the astral fiends. Right?"

"Not so far as Loredana can tell. It's barely been ten hours. However, if they show up again, the city has agreed to unofficially support your activities."

"Okay."

Ramos frowned. "Mercury, look at it this way. You're not considered a criminal. A lot of people know you saved our city—and a lot more than that. The National Guard's tipped off the feds. They'd like nothing more than to sweep in and make off with both the pulsar stave and you. Of course, they have to find you first."

"Guess I should thank the City of San Camillo for not allowing it."

Shoes clacked in the hallway beyond the door. Ramos smirked. "We don't have that kind of clout. Procyon, it seems, does."

Loredana entered the room, carrying a large handbag. She was, again, cleaned up like nothing had happened, though there was an exhaustion to her if you knew how to look—lines around the eyes, paleness to her complexion. Still, she walked in like she owned the place.

"Hey." I straightened up even more. My reward was a spike of pain through my ribs. "Ack. Okay, I should have stayed prone."

"You should be, so that you have time to heal." She sat on the edge of the bed, hands folded in her lap. "Good morning, Lieutenant."

"Ms. Lark. I was about to tell Mercury about your visit from Homeland Security."

Loredana's mouth quirked in a tight smile. "Indeed. I rather expected them to have tried to show up at the nurse's station. They would have, had Procyon not made several contacts within the federal government aware that it would be in the nation's best interest to exercise a light touch."

I stared. "You have that kind of pull?"

"I do not. But the board members who arrived earlier

this morning do. Procyon does not make its, shall we say, extracurricular activities common knowledge, but certain individuals are read-in when it comes to them. The board is willing to take whatever steps necessary to protect you and the pulsar stave, given your role in averting the invasion."

"Well." I shrugged. "Another day, another dollar, right?"

"Your humility knows no bounds."

"I am *amazingly* humble."

Ramos coughed. "Anyway, if you kids are okay here, I'd better report back in. This mess isn't going to clean itself up."

I grabbed his arm. "Hang on. Did anyone …?"

"Eight officers are in this same wing of SC General." Ramos' words were clipped. "Five died. So did ten National Guard soldiers, good men and women. They sustained heavy casualties. A lot of broken equipment, too."

I sank against the pillow, my bravado deflated. "That's on me."

"Is it? They knew their jobs, like you knew yours. They put their lives on the line for the people they swore to protect."

"Except I didn't swear to protect anyone, Gabriel. This is a job. A paycheck."

Ramos shook his head. "And did that matter when you were on the run from Procyon? When you came back from your real home? Loredana told me what happened on the other side of that dimension. In the end, you were ready to die so that your friends—and the people of San Camillo—could live. There's no greater love than that." He patted me on the shoulder and headed for the hall.

"Hey, Ramos?"

He stopped, hand on the frame.

"Thanks for everything."

"*La paz esté contigo*," he said.

Loredana watched him leave, then placed her hand on mine. I squeezed it. "I'm very glad you're well."

"Yeah, me too. I take it whatever I did worked."

"Initial investigation shows no evidence of tachyon emissions. Nor have we detected any further rips. Things are quiet."

"And by we, I'm assuming you don't mean Winston."

"Mr. Yen is in custody." Man. The way she said his name, like it was frozen in an iceberg, made me glad we were on the same side. "We've had other members of Tracking step up to deal with vacancies. There will be major reshuffling of staff. The board has taken the lead interviewing personnel, since even security is complicit in this scheme."

"It'll take some time to sort out who knew what about Marigold and Winston." I grimaced. "And Calvin."

"The police consider his death to have closed the matter. They arrested several of the security contractors Calvin hired, who were all too willing to turn evidence against their former employer if it meant reduced charges. Procyon has a lawyer on retainer for you, if the need should arise."

I nodded. "Sounds like everything's wrapped up in a neat bow."

"Almost." Loredana drew the pulsar stave from her purse. "Here."

The metal was cooler than usual, with none of the simmering energy I was used to. Why'd that bother me so much? Its power had been reduced to a mere trickle of its former glory. That meant I was free to live my life apart from its purpose. Right?

If that were the case, what the heck was I going to do?

"Your position has been frozen for the next 60 days," Loredana said. "Consider it a sabbatical."

I rubbed my forehead. "An unpaid sabbatical. Great. That'll help pay bills."

"Hopefully it won't last long. Unfortunately, the board is hesitant about maintaining the status quo. Keep in mind the last person who came in contact with one of the weapons used it and her resources for less that savory purposes."

"Except they're letting me keep mine."

"We will need to analyze the pulsar stave, to be certain it does not pose a threat. In the meantime, we shall assess your role at Procyon, to determine how you'll best fit in moving forward."

"Kinda hard to employ a monster slayer when all the monsters are locked away from our world, Loredana."

She smirked. "I'm sure you can find other ways to maintain your training until the time arises. I believe in preparation for every eventuality. As such, I think you'll find the new set of clothes I had delivered to your loft especially appropriate." She squeezed my hand. "Rest well. Call me when they release you, and I'll give you a lift."

"Sounds good. And don't forget …"

"I remember. Carlito's."

She left. The room was empty, but it didn't feel bad. I wasn't alone.

Jamie's funeral was on a sun-lit afternoon, a week later. It'd been a rough several days. The first few were filled with sleeping and eating. It was only after I didn't feel like complete garbage that I started my training routine again, or at least, the routine that didn't involve returning to Procyon's gym yet. My body was tired, beaten, but appreciated the return to regular exercise.

I hadn't been to a funeral in, well, ever. He was buried in a crowded section of the Lilac Ridge Cemetery, overlooking the city from the northern hills. A crumbling monastery peeked through the junipers on the rise above. It was a gorgeous afternoon, with a bay breeze wiping away the worst of the heat.

Wilhelmina and I brought the crowd to eight, including Ramos's pastor. I didn't pay much attention to the sermon, except when he preached about the Father awaiting Jamie's return up there. The peace of his eternal rest. Peace, like the *paz* Ramos had mentioned.

"He was a good boy." Wilhelmina had tears running down her face, but she held onto my arm and didn't shake. With her cane, and absent any enchanted weapons, she was just another homeless old lady—to other people. I knew better.

"No family?" The guys standing nearby were either scraggly or musclebound. None of them looked like relatives. For one thing, two of them were black. The rest were a mix of white and Latino.

"Not a one. That don't mean no one cared for him."

"Yeah. I get it."

We walked down the hill to my car. Yeah, I ponied up and bought one. A Subaru, same model as the one I borrowed from the drug dealers. Shiny blue, like a grinning beetle. "What's your plan? I bet Loredana could find some work for you at Procyon. Historical consultant, maybe?"

She socked my arm but was grinning. "No. Not yet. Loredana was kind enough to offer me tickets to Drake City. I've got relatives out there. My husband's family."

"You could have gone to see them all this time? Wilhelmina, they would have helped you out."

"Wasn't ready for that, child. After that fight, after your

parents died and my loves were lost, I'd convinced myself I wasn't worth it. Took finding you to remind me that I am loved, and I am valued—not only by people, mind."

This was getting pretty heavy. "Come on. I'll give you a ride to the bus station. But first we're going to dinner. Ramos invited me over."

"Oh? And you're taking me as your date?"

I blushed. "No, ah, I'm taking Loredana. But Ramos won't mind. Seriously."

"I'm joshing you." She patted my cheek. "I'll miss you, Mercury. Your parents would be proud. Know that. Just like Teget and Naos are proud."

I was trying not to think about them. Had Teget made it back through the Interstice to Meda? There was no way to know. I'm not one to rely on dreams or visions, because I've found you can't often trust the source. But I'd like to think if something had happened to my brother, I'd know it. I had confidence he'd survived.

Faith, if you want to call it that. I'd gone so far as to pray.

Wilhelmina and I hugged. "You take care of yourself. Text me photos—or send a postcard, if that's too high tech."

She chuckled and wiped away the tears. "I wish Jamie could be coming with me."

"He was a hero, Wilhelmina."

"I know it." She winked. "And call me Sherry. 'Bout time I took that back, too."

Two weeks later.

There's a pair of guys running down Tenth Street, bags of stolen jewelry under their arms. The store owner, a wiry Chinese man, is bleeding from a head wound. His wife shouts obscenities I can't translate, though I suspect Google could. The crooks will get away if someone doesn't stop them, because police response is spotty in this part of town. The woman's screaming at 9-1-1 in her cell phone.

I drop down onto the sidewalk between the pair.

It's a landing timed with perfection. Come on. We're not talking astral fiend tentacles here. The guy in back skids to a stop. His friend hasn't even noticed me.

"Um?" The guy aims his gun at my forehead.

That's all I get? I'm wearing the suit, my entire body shrouded in dark slate. Yellow lines appear on the arms, legs, and torso, like an incandescent bulb's filament. See, the pulsar stave wasn't full drained. Neither was the suit. Kudos to Winston, as deranged as he'd become, for engineering an awesome piece of tech.

I bat the gun aside with the stave and block the guy's wild punch. He gets a sharp blow to the stomach, one to the back, and a swift kick to the gut while he's down. Starts whining, like a sad little puppy.

The lead thief has finally noticed his buddy's behind him, forty feet later. He spins around, and shouts, "Andy! Yo, Andy! What're you—hey!"

"Andy's busy," I mutter, and fling half the stave at his forehead. It knocks him out cold.

Cool move. I saw it in a TV show once.

I gather the jewels and dump them at the woman's feet. She's rambling on and on. I help her press a cloth to her husband's head, until the bleeding stops. Turns out he can speak English. "Who are you?"

"New to the neighborhood." I wink, trying for the dashing look, then remember they can't see my eyes. Or any part of my face. Idiot. I lift the bottom of the mask and grin instead. Hand him a shiny black business card. It's got an email address linked to an account that can't be traced back to me, and one word etched in silver:

Mercury.

"No charge," I tell them. "But if you're inclined to donate, I accept PayPal."

It's a long haul back to the loft after I make sure the cops have the jewelry thieves in custody. Climbing up the fire escape quietly isn't the easiest task in the world, and I slump onto the couch. Fortunately, there's leftover Carlito's in the fridge. Amen.

My phone buzzes. I freeze, a cold slice laden with pepperoni halfway to my mouth.

Ramos. <Got a report of an armed robbery at 17th and Applehans. Suspects in the wind.>

Duty calls. Again?

I glare at the pizza. "I literally just sat down."

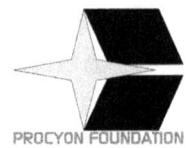

PROCYON FOUNDATION

Mercury's adventures continue in

Mercury for Hire